T0368395

MAE POLES

CURTIS MILLER

authorHOUSE'

AuthorHouse™
1663 Liberty Drive
Bloomington, IN 47403
www.authorhouse.com
Phone: 833-262-8899

Published by AuthorHouse 01/03/2025

ISBN: 979-8-8230-3777-8 (sc)
ISBN: 979-8-8230-3778-5 (hc)
ISBN: 979-8-8230-3776-1 (e)

Library of Congress Control Number: 2024923879

Print information available on the last page.

Contents

Chapter 1

We know what we are, but not what we may be. William Shakespeare said that. I would have to agree. I know who I am, but is that really my identity? Or maybe knowing who I am has nothing to do with my identity. Maybe it is just a label that society has given me. I am not a fan of labels, but who is? The fact of the matter is, I know what I am, but I am more than that. That's where this story begins.

The sun was shining through my blackout curtains. The rays of light danced on the floor, my desk, and unfortunately, my face. Though my eyes were not open, I could feel the warmth from its rays. I rolled over in my bed, hoping to steal a few more moments of peace before waking. Unfortunately, my effort was in vain. I laid there for about ten minutes or so but was unable to fall back asleep. I rolled over and looked at my alarm clock on my nightstand. It was just about seven in the morning. I knew that I didn't have to be up for at least another hour, but what was the point? I knew it didn't matter. No matter how much sleep I get I never wake up feeling well rested…that's my curse.

I decided that trying to sleep for another hour or so was a lost cause, and I violently shoved the covers off the bed. With a grunt, I rolled myself out of bed and placed both of my feet firmly on the floor. I reached over and with another grunt opened the curtains and let the sun pour into the pitch-black room. I sat there with my head in my hands, a ritual of mine as old as I could remember. If anything, I am a creature of habit. I sat there for a while as I did every morning. Letting the memories of the previous day gain some traction in my mind. Memories rushed in and out of my mind like a motorway and there was no stopping it.

1

I decided to take another look at the clock. The second that I did, it began to ring. I couldn't believe that it was already eight o'clock. Time seemed to sneak up on me like that every single morning. For me, the mornings were always the worst part of my day. They were confusing, and they were chaotic.

I chuckled to myself slightly. "At least I woke up alone this time." I grinned as I rubbed the sleep out of my eyes. I double-checked the bed and the room around me to make sure that what I said was true. You would think I wouldn't have to do that, but after some of the nights I've had, it had become a regular thing.

The sound of the buzzer on my alarm clock began to scream for attention. I reached over to hit the snooze. I must have misjudged the distance to the alarm clock because instead of hitting the snooze, I just knocked it off my nightstand. It rolled onto the floor like it had done many times before, landing softly onto the pile of clothes that lay beside my bed. I sighed as I reached down and picked it up and pressed the button gently. This time hitting my mark, the clock stopped blaring.

"Well, it's time I get going," I said to myself, again expecting someone to answer. After a few seconds, I realized I was still alone. I stood up and began walking to my bathroom to brush my teeth. When I turned on the bathroom light, I suddenly lost my ability to see. I waited a moment for my eyes to adjust and I was greeted by a familiar face. There he was, looking back at me in the mirror. The events of the past few weeks had taken a toll on me. Large bags hung under my eyes, and you could barely see anything other than red in them. I pulled on my eyelids to check out the damage and rubbed my hands down the side of my face. The stubble that had grown since the last time I shaved pricked at my fingertips. I hated the feeling of facial hair and reached behind me for the basket where I kept all my shaving stuff.

I ran the water as hot as it would go and splashed the water on my face. The burning sensation that the hot water provided seemed to wake me up. This was something I needed in the morning. Something to snap myself into the present. Something to remind me of where I was. I lathered up my face and started to perform the daily ritual known as shaving. There was a knock at the door, and without hesitation, I walked out into my living room and opened it.

"Hey there," a familiar face said as she walked into my apartment. She threw down her purse on my La-Z-Boy and walked toward my refrigerator, grabbed the carton of orange juice, and took a drink. She turned to look at me and blushed. "Are you going to put some pants on or are we going out like that?" she said, wiping the orange juice off her face.

I instantly realized that I was in my underwear and shrugged. "Give me a minute," I said as I walked back into my bedroom. "I didn't expect you. As usual you're way early."

She put the carton of orange juice away and walked into my room. She smacked me on the ass and sat on the bed. "Just get dressed and let's go shopping. I need something for tonight."

I sighed as I checked my closet for something that was relatively clean. After a few moments, I found something and threw it on. I walked into the bathroom to do my hair and make myself look somewhat presentable. I realized that I hadn't even finished shaving. I looked in the mirror at my face. Shaving cream was spread all over since I got sidetracked and tried to get dressed rather than finishing. I sighed, as I knew I would have to find another clean shirt once I was done.

Before I had a chance to even pick up the razor again, I realized that I wasn't alone in the bathroom. Mae had snuck up behind me and was making faces in the mirror. "Are you done yet?" she asked as she grabbed my cheeks and pushed them around. After she was done having her fun, she took the shaving cream and sprayed a bit onto her hands. She rubbed it all over my face, covering my nose, mouth, and eyes.

"Really?" I said through my shaving cream-covered lips. Licking off some of it to properly speak. The shaving cream's menthol burned a familiar burn as I grimaced at the taste. She laughed a bit more to herself at the sight of my face.

"Wow! Doesn't taste good, does it?" she said as she wiped off her hands on my shirt. She smiled and walked out of my bathroom, leaving me in peace. I could hear her opening the refrigerator again and taking another sip of orange juice. I hated it when she did that. I decided to just finish shaving and get started with my day.

"So where are we going again?" I asked as I walked into the living room, wiping off the shaving cream from my face with the shirt I had just been wearing. I threw it into the dirty laundry pile that had been collecting near my door and then walked into my room to grab another shirt.

"Like I said yesterday, we are going shopping for an outfit for my date tonight. It's like you don't even remember the conversation we had last night." She gave me a scowl and walked past me and slapped my stomach. The truth was, I remembered two things about the conversation from the night before. One of the things was that Mae called, and the other was that we were going somewhere in the morning. Other than that, my memory was a bit hazy.

"Well, you know how it is," I told her as I put on the second clean shirt of the morning. "I have a terrible memory."

She looked at me and walked over to my counter. She grabbed the empty bottle of whiskey and held it over her head. "Yeah, I'm sure it's just your memory that's the issue." She put the bottle down quite aggressively. "Didn't you just buy that?" she asked.

I looked at her and shrugged. "What are you, my girlfriend?" I joked, knowing the response I would get.

"Wow!" she yelled. "Unless you have one of these in those pants of yours, you haven't got a chance at dating this." She motioned down toward her body, showing it off like it was the prize at a game show. I smiled awkwardly as she did a little dance. Little did she know every time she pointed that out to me, I died a little on the inside.

"Come on, let's get some coffee and breakfast into your stomach and get some new clothes onto me." She walked toward the door and opened it. She motioned for me to leave.

"Let me get my stuff." I walked over to my computer desk and grabbed my keys and my wallet. I pulled my cell phone off the charger and noticed I had three missed messages from Mae and one from my mother. I made a mental note to call her back. I didn't bother looking any further and shoved the phone into my pocket. I walked out into the living room and then out the door. Mae shut the door behind me, and we walked out to my car. As I put the keys into my Chevy, she kept on walking toward my garage.

"Where are you going?" I asked. "Let's go." I said, motioning for her to get into my car.

She gave me a devilish little smile. "I was hoping we could take your bike," she said, biting her lower lip. "You know how I love riding on it." She folded her hands and pretended to beg. The truth was, I loved riding Mae around on my bike. I liked it far too much.

"Are you serious?" I asked as I sighed a heavy sigh. She slowly started backing up and pressed her body against the garage door.

"Please?" she said again, her words stabbing a dagger into my chest. I sighed and pulled the keys to my Suzuki off the carabiner of my key chain. I tossed it up and caught it in my hand.

"Fine," I said as I closed the door to my car and locked it. "You owe me," I said as I started walking toward my garage. I opened the garage door. There, sitting in the garage, was my bike, covered in dust.

"Wow, really?" she said as she walked over and brushed the dust off the seat. "You should really take this thing to go get cleaned." She got onto the bike and started bouncing up and down excitedly.

"I haven't driven it since the last time you made me drive it," I said, walking over to the bike and putting the key into the ignition. I turned the keys, praying that the bike would start. After a few groans, the bike's engine revved. I pulled the throttle a few times to make sure that it was not going to die. I could feel Mae grabbing my shoulders each time I revved the engine. She slapped me on the back.

"Let's go!" she yelled as she thrust her arms in the air. I put on my sunglasses and handed Mae the pair I had reserved for passengers. I drove the bike out of my garage and made the turn into the parking lot. I didn't even bother closing my garage because my bike was the only thing inside of it. I stopped at the sign outside my parking lot and turned onto the frontage road. Knowing I had about three miles to go until the next stop, I opened her up a bit. As I pulled on the throttle, I could feel Mae pressing her body against mine. As the engine of my bike began to pump faster and faster, so did my heart. As we drove down the road toward downtown, I could barely focus on the road. All I could focus on was her fingernails pressing into my skin, her chin on my shoulder, and her thighs pressed against my torso. This was the reason I didn't like to take my bike anywhere, and it was also the reason I didn't argue when she wanted to take it.

"Faster!" she screamed as we flew down the road. Knowing that we were already going about ninety miles per hour, I decided to slow down and prepare for the stoplight that I knew was up ahead. Mae was not happy. She slapped me on my back and pouted. To be honest, I could not actually see her pouting, but I knew she was doing it.

As we approached the stoplight, it turned yellow, and then red. I slowed the bike down to a stop. Reached my legs outwards and caught the bike before it tipped over.

"Way to be a baby," she said as she tried her best to put her curly raven black hair into a ponytail. She was obviously struggling as the light prepared to turn green. I turned back toward her.

"You better hurry up!" I yelled as the light turned and I pulled the throttle. The bike groaned as I accelerated and went from a standstill to a sprint almost instantly. Her fingers dug into my side as she struggled to hold on. I relished the pain as we continued down the road. I slowed down to cross the railroad tracks that signaled we were almost to our destination. As we approached it, I began dreading what was about to happen.

"Wow. I love riding your bike!" she said as I pulled into the parking space and turned off the ignition. She jumped off the bike and fixed her skirt. I caught a slight glimpse of her underwear before she had a chance to finish. I blushed and turned away toward the only store that sold women's clothing, and Mae followed. I had to stop myself from requesting whether we could just get breakfast first, but I knew that she would insist on getting her clothes first. I knew her well enough to not try to change her mind.

We walked down the sidewalk for a few moments in silence. In my opinion, silence is always the worst kind of conversation. Yes, I understand that it doesn't really count as conversing, but in a way it totally does. You can read someone you know well by their body language like a book. Mae's read that she was anxious and edgy for her date. It was understandable because she had been pursuing this particular girl for a few weeks. She had first mentioned her when she took a night course at the local community college. I remember the conversation like it was yesterday.

We were out having a cigarette at a mutual friend's party. Of course, Mae was there because she was my go-to invite. We were sharing a cigarette while sitting on the porch, and she mentioned a girl in her class. I had never seen her talk about a girl that way before. To be honest, it was a bit unsettling. Up until now all the women that she dated were just short-term flings. The fact that she was going on another first date with someone she had actually pursued scared me a bit.

"So, what do you think?" she asked as she pressed her painted lips against the Marlboro Light she had in her hands. Her lipstick left a mark on the filter as she passed me the cigarette. I put it to my lips and took a drag. I could taste her lips as I inhaled the smoke deep into my lungs and exhaled.

"I think you should go for it," I managed to say. As I handed her the cigarette back, I noticed my hands were shaking. The funny thing was it was hot that night. Hot enough to notice the sweat gathering just above her...never mind. Her low-cut top was not doing either of us a favor.

"You really think so?" she asked as she took another drag. She spoke as she exhaled. "You normally aren't on board when I want to date someone." Knowing she was right, I sighed. "Well, I just want you all to myself I guess," I said as I wrapped my arm around her and pulled her close. My skin had goosebumps where our bodies touched. Even through my sweat-covered shirt, her body drove me wild. I took the cigarette from her outstretched hand and took a few more drags. The moment I tasted the filter, I stood up and tossed it in the empty coffee can that sat by the steps into the house.

"Wow," she said as she watched me dispose of the cigarette. "It's not like I wanted another drag, but ok." She smiled and stood up as she opened the door and walked into the house to join the party. The music hit me in the face like a hammer. I watched her disappear into the crowd, and I just stood there for a few seconds. For some reason, I knew it that night, but I hoped it was not true. I said a little prayer hoping that she wouldn't disappear for good. I followed her inside.

We continued to walk down the sidewalk toward our destination. Mae was the one to break the silence first. "So, what do you think I should try on?" she asked as she caught up to me and locked her arm into mine. She must have sensed the tension between us, and this was her olive branch.

"I have no clue," I said, shrugging with my one free arm. "Maybe you should take one more look in your closet before you go spending a ton of money on clothes." I could feel her gaze on the side of my head. Man, if looks could kill, I am pretty sure I would not have survived that day.

"Because I want to wow this girl. I don't want to just look good; I want to look good." She elongated the words to express how she wanted to look.

"You look amazing right now. Why not wear that."

She looked down at the skirt she was wearing and grabbed the bottom of her flannel top.

"Are you serious?" she asked as she did a little spin. "Men really have no clue about fashion, do they?" she said as she continued walking and put her arm in mine once again as I sighed.

"All I know is that you look amazing right now, and I wouldn't change a single thing about you." She had struck a chord and she knew it. Normally, I didn't say things like that to her, but I felt obligated to defend myself.

She looked up at me and smiled. She has such an amazing smile. "I know what you mean," she said as she hugged my arm. "Thank you. It means a lot that you would say that." She continued to squeeze my arm until we arrived at the storefront. She let go and opened the door and gestured for me to enter. "Ladies first." She laughed as she did a slight curtsy. The hair stood up on the back of my neck as she muttered the words. I entered the store.

I watched her as she went from rack to rack in search of the perfect outfit. Every time she found something, she handed the hanger to me and moved onto the next rack. When she saw that I was struggling to carry the weight of her outfits, she decided it was time to head to the dressing room. The reason Mae liked going to this specific store was obvious. It used to be a wedding dress store, and each of the dressing rooms was very large. We walked into the dressing room, and I placed the clothes she wanted to try on into the room and sat on the small couch against the wall. She hummed a little tune as she tried on the first outfit. I had heard that tune before but could not remember where. After a few moments, she walked out in a tight black dress. It only was about mid-thigh. My heart jumped into my throat as I caught a glimpse of her.

"So how do I look?" she said as she did her best to mimic a fashion model on her own private runway. When she made it to where I was sitting, she did a little spin and walked back toward the dressing room door. She stopped when she reached the door and turned back to me with questioning eyes. "Serious answer! Is this a wow dress?"

I looked at her and tried to play it off like it wasn't that big of a deal. The truth was she looked amazing. She took the breath right out of my very lungs. I motioned with my hands to distract her as I caught my breath. "Isn't it a little short?" I managed to say as I smiled.

She walked over to me and smacked me on the head. "That's the point," she said as she turned around and pointed toward her ass. "I have got to flaunt what the good Lord gave me," she said, slapping her butt as she walked back toward the dressing room. She closed the door and tried on another outfit. The rest of the morning went pretty much the same way. She would try on an outfit. I would tell her what I thought, and then she would try on another. I used the time that she was locked into the room to try my best to regain my bearings. I had known this was a bad idea from the moment she walked in my door that morning. I normally wouldn't have agreed to it, but she knew to ask favors of me only when I was drinking. Only then did I agree about a hundred percent of the time. I couldn't say no to her, especially when I didn't have my wits about me. It is a weakness that I have regardless of the situation. It is a weakness I wish I could rid myself of.

She finally had gotten to the bottom of the pile of clothes and had not found something that she liked. I checked my watch, and it was almost noon. It was hard to believe that I had been in this store for almost three hours, and she had not found an outfit. The only proof I had for the morning's endeavors was the fact I had hung up almost twenty outfits on their hangers. That, and the sweat on my palms from clenching my fists each time she walked out of those doors. Finally, she grabbed the final outfit and walked into the room. I sighed a sigh of relief as she walked into the door. "Only one more," I told myself as I heard the lock click behind her.

A few moments passed as she struggled to get into the skin-tight dress she had picked out. After a few more moments of hearing her hit her arms against the walls of the changing room, she finally called out to me. "I could use a little help in here." I heard the door unlock. I stood up and walked toward the door and put my hand against the handle. It was one of those things that seemed forbidden to most, but not me. A man walking into a women's dressing room is one of those things you just don't do, but here I was doing it. I turned the handle and pulled it open. There she was, standing there in the most beautiful backless dress I have ever seen. She stood up as she finished taking off her beat up sneakers and looked over her shoulder at me.

"Do you mind zipping me up?" she said as she held a zipper on her lower back. She didn't have the flexibility to zip it up. I stepped toward her and put my left hand on her back, holding the fabric, and my other hand

9

grabbed the zipper. I took a deep breath as I pulled the zipper up. I swear I could feel her slow her breathing as I reached the middle of her back and hit the final clasp of the zipper.

"Is that good?" I asked as I immediately turned around and walked out of the dressing room. The door swung open as I walked out, and I took a seat on the couch. I did my best to control my breathing, but it didn't help. All I could do was sit on the couch and look at the floor. I counted to ten a few times before I heard the door open again. Before I knew it, there were two perfectly manicured feet standing in front of me.

"Are you ok?" she asked, arms folded. She was obviously confused.

"Yeah, yeah," I said pulling out my phone, pretending to be answering a text. The desperation in my action must have been apparent as I struggled to unlock my device. "Sorry, I had a text from uh, my mom," I said as I pulled up our last text message on my phone. It was from almost two weeks ago. On top of lying, I felt awful that I hadn't talked to my mother in that long. To be honest, I couldn't even remember the last time that I had spoken with my mother. It was something about Thanksgiving, or was it Christmas? I had no clue. The weather made me lean toward Thanksgiving and the possibility that we were having an Indian summer.

All of a sudden, Mae pulled the phone away from my face and put it on the table beside me.

"Tell me how I look!" she said as she did a few poses to show off the new ensemble. To be honest, I didn't think anything could have made her look as good as she did in the first twenty outfits, but this one was different. I can't explain how this dress was perfect, so I am not even going to try. All I can say is it was made for her. Her curves, her figure, and her smile. Everything was perfect. It was as if the dress was really made for her.

"Wow," I managed to say as she stood there in front of me. There was no other word that my mind could think of. It was just stunning. There she stood, this vision of beauty. "I mean, how much does that cost?" I said, trying to change the subject.

"I don't know," she said as she checked the price tag on the back of the dress. She struggled for a bit as she tried to read the tag that was on the back of the dress. I sat and watched her struggle for about ten seconds until I decided to help her.

"Looks like you could use a hand," I said as I stood up and managed to wrestle the price tag from her. I managed to get a look at it, and it read a number that I don't want to repeat. The sad part was that I knew Mae couldn't afford that outfit, and she would be devastated when she found out. I pulled the tag off the outfit without her knowing.

"Wow, I look amazing," she said as she walked up to the mirror to check herself out. "This is the best outfit that I have tried on today, isn't it?" she said again as she twirled around. She looked around for the tag.

"That's for sure the best dress you have tried on today," I said as I stood up and tucked the price tag into my pocket. She sighed as she realized she could not find the price and decided to go get into her regular clothes. She walked into the changing room and closed the door. I took that time as an opportunity to walk to the front counter and pay for the outfit she was trying on. The store manager gave me a weird look as I paid for the outfit. I understood that look. It was the, *she is totally not into you* look. I shrugged it off and pulled out my debit card and swiped it into his iPad and entered my information.

Mae walked up behind me and put her hands on my shoulders. "What are you paying for?" she asked as she placed the outfits on the return cart. She sighed as she placed the final outfit on top of the pile. The store manager picked it up and got ready to put it in a bag. Mae's eyes lit up. "What did you do?" she asked as she looked at the dress, and then me.

I grabbed the bag the store manager had prepared and handed it to her. A smile formed on her face as she realized the contents of the bag. "Are you serious?" she said as she embraced me in a hug. As she embraced me, I looked over at the store manager. He just shook his head in disappointment as he handed me the receipt and I stashed it in my shirt.

"Well, if you bought my outfit, then the least I could do is buy you lunch." She let go of her embrace and quickly exited the shop. The bell rang as she left, then it was just me and the manager. Rather than face another judgmental stare, I just looked at the ground and walked out with what was left of my dignity. When I finally was free from the shop, I turned toward the diner where I knew we would be going. They served the best coffee in town, and it was Mae's and my favorite place to have breakfast, or lunch. Well, basically any meal that we could. I looked up from my shoes, and she was already halfway there. She just stood there tapping her foot and looking at an imaginary watch until I finally caught up.

"Finally! You're the slowest human being alive," she said as she smiled and took my arm. We walked the rest of the way to the diner and walked in and took our usual booth in the corner. The owner, Al, knew us from the thousand times we had been there before. He handed us our usual carafe of coffee and a single menu. Why only one menu, you ask? Well, let me tell you. I had probably had the corned beef hash skillet for the last nearly thousand times I had come to eat here. Mae had the Denver Omelet nearly every time as well. However, she would look over the menu every time as if she was going to eat something different than the norm. After about twenty or so minutes, she would hand the menu back to Al and order the damn omelet...every time.

Well, today was no different, and after the allotted twenty minutes, she begrudgingly ordered the omelet, and we made small talk until our meal arrived. After we had finished our meal and talked about her night classes, we decided to leave the restaurant so Mae could get back home and prepare for her date.

"Ok, I should probably get home and get ready for tonight," she said, walking over to my bike.

"Yeah, I wouldn't want you to be late for the big evening." I reached my bike and wiped some dust from the front of my headlight. Mae was right. This thing was filthy. I made a mental note to get it washed one of these days. I sat down on the bike and prepared to turn it on when I realized what store we were sitting in front of. The liquor store.

"Do you really need another bottle?" Mae chimed in. "You just finished the one you bought the other day. Maybe give it a rest for a few days. You have been more stressed out than usual this past week." It was a sudden sincere moment that I was not expecting. In all the thirty or so years I have known Mae, she usually focuses on one thing at a time, and today that was her date. It wasn't normal for her to break from that routine.

"Yeah, but I will be coming here sober or drunk, your choice." The comment was lined with a bit more malice than I had intended, but I stuck to my guns. "I'll be right back." I got off my bike and went into the shop. I was a regular, so the owner immediately pulled out my usual bottle of shitty whiskey from behind the counter and rang it up. I paid the man as his wife put the bottle of whiskey in a large brown paper bag. She glared at me. I tried not to pay attention. I took my whiskey and left. As I walked outside, I placed the bottle in one of my small saddlebags and got on the bike. Before I started the bike, I stopped and sighed.

"Sorry Mae," I said, as I could tell she was visibly upset by my response earlier. "I'll try to cut it down soon. I have just been so stressed about this commission that I have been working on and I am just a little on edge. Friends?" I tried to sound sincere even though I knew that nearly everything I had said was a lie. I was in fact in the middle of a large commission for work, but everything after that was just false. She looked at me with those enormous blue eyes and smiled.

"Ok, I just worry about you sometimes." She smiled a half-smile and prepared for me to start up the bike. I turned the key, and she gave her usual yell with glee. I walked the bike back into the street and opened her up. After we arrived back at my house, I parked the bike in the garage and reached into my cargo pocket for my pack of cigarettes. I noticed that there were only a few left, and they had been crushed. I reached in and grabbed the least damaged one and fumbled for my lighter. I lit it and took a drag. Before I knew it, Mae was behind me, grabbing it from my hand and following suit. She took a drag and smiled at me as she exhaled.

"What's so funny?" She took another drag. I didn't even know that I was smiling. I tried to think of something off the cuff and failed miserably.

"You have something in your teeth." I managed to say as she handed me the cigarette, panicking.

"Oh my god. For how long?" She frantically looked through the side mirror of my Suzuki. "I don't see anything." She walked back over to me and demanded the smoke.

"You must have gotten it out when you freaked out." I said handing it to her. The truth is, I must have been smiling at her because I was in love with her, and she would never feel the same way. Seeing her standing there next to my bike and smoking a cigarette gave me a glimpse of how things could be. I wanted to grab her and kiss her right there. Unfortunately, there was no chance of that. Not in this reality. I would just have to wait for the poles to shift and go from there.

"Well, you have to get ready for your date." I reached over for the cigarette. She handed it to me reluctantly.

"You're correct sir," she said as she snuck one last drag and handed me a nearly cashed smoke. "I will call you when it is over and fill you in on the details!" She came over to me and gave me a big hug. I held her for a few extra seconds. "Thank you again for the dress. She is going to love it!" I nodded as she let go and started walking toward her little Honda. "See you tomorrow!" were the last words she said before disappeared into her driver's seat and drove off.

I finished off the cigarette and walked over to my saddlebags. I reached in and grabbed the bottle. As I walked into my apartment, I already had it open and went straight to my cupboard for a glass. Nothing was clean, so I rinsed a dirty one off, filled it with whiskey, and took a drink. I walked over to my medicine cabinet and took three sleeping pills when the bottle only prescribed one. I sat on my bed in the dark, waiting for sleep to take me. The sleep that would take me to the life that I loved. To the life where I actually felt like myself. The last thing I remember is hearing some random police siren in the distance. Other than that, all I saw was Mae.

Chapter 2

The alarm clock made a gentle chime as I opened my eyes and took a moment to wake up gently. I looked over toward the alarm clock and saw that it was nearly seven in the morning. The sun was just starting to make its way over the trees across the courtyard. The curtains were pulled back by blue ribbons, inviting the sunlight into our room. A kick in my leg as I stirred startled me, but only slightly.

"Go back to bed, baby," Mae said from the other side of the bed. Her blanket had fallen off during the night, and she laid there. Her body is a thing of beauty, a work of art, and she was all mine. I looked down at the ring on my finger and smiled. Every time I woke up this way, I couldn't believe that there was any other way to do it. I could be alone and hungover or be with the woman of my dreams. Right then, it felt as if there was no other reality but this one. Unfortunately, I knew that was not the case.

"I'm sorry. I need to get to work on that story for my editor. He has been on my case for the past few days." I leaned in over to kiss her. As I got closer, she rubbed the sleep out of her eyes and retreated.

"Oh, go away. My breath must be horrible." She put her hand over her mouth as I got close. I took her hand away and kissed her softly on the lips. As I pulled away, I bit her bottom lip and kissed her once more on the nose.

"Ugh, I hate it when you do that," she said as she wiped off her nose with the blanket. As I stood up, she grabbed me by what was left of my hair and flipped me down on the bed.

"You can't just do that and get away with it. Now I want a little something." She motioned for me to take my shirt off and I did as she asked. I mean, who wouldn't? She kissed up from my navel up across my chest. Goosebumps formed up and down my entire body as I knew what she wanted. I let out a soft moan as she reached my neck and bit into my shoulder.

"Oh my god, where were you last night?" I said as I grabbed her shoulders and slid my nails down to the small of her back. "You know I have to get to work." Her sigh could have probably been heard from space.

"Fine. You can go to work now, but later you're mine," she said as she sat up and put her hands on my chest. She reached over onto our nightstand and grabbed one of my hair ties and put her long curly hair into a messy ponytail. Years of practice paying off.

"Can I use one of these?" she asked as she finished. "You don't really need them anymore."

"Go ahead. You're right. I'm telling you the short hair thing is amazing!" I ran my fingers through my hair and smiled.

"You do look hot!" She kissed me once more and got out of bed and headed toward the closet. She caught me staring as she walked away and immediately became self-conscious.

"Stop staring!" she said as she finally made it to the closet and fumbled for a bra. She finally found one that suited her mood and put it on. She beckoned for me to come over and help her with the strap. I got out of the bed and walked over to her and kissed her neck from behind as I hooked up her bra strap.

"Thanks babe," she said as she turned back around and continued to look through her closet. I decided that maybe it was not her breath that was bad this morning. Maybe it was mine.

"I'm going to go brush my teeth and take a shower. Don't flush the toilet." She grinned at me as I walked out of the room.

"I did that one time!" she said as I made it to our bathroom. I stopped in front of the mirror and turned on the hot water. I splashed it in my face a few times, as was my ritual. I looked into the mirror and the face that stared back at me was not mine. Or maybe it was. The face that was looking back at me was a woman in her mid-thirties. She had short blonde hair that was cropped in a kind of a messy pixie. I had gotten it cut shorter since long hair is just a pain. Mae was upset originally, but I thought she had come around to the style. Not to mention, she did not have to chew on my hair while we sleep.

"Becks, you better hurry or you're going to be late. Don't use all the hot water!" I heard Mae yell from the other room. I decided to heed her advice and took off my shirt and underwear and got into the shower. I turned on the water and was startled by the sudden outburst of freezing cold water. I jumped back and almost slipped.

"That's why I warm it up before I get in," I could hear Mae yelling from the kitchen. She always turned on the water for at least five minutes before getting in. By the time she got in, the bathroom mirror was covered with steam and the windows were as well. I decided to ignore her and step into the water. It had not warmed up completely, but it was bearable to the point that I could stand beneath it. I took my time in the shower and relaxed as I could only do as a woman. Everything just felt better, from waking up to going to bed. The world was brighter, and the future held possibilities. It is too difficult to explain, so I won't even try. Once I was finished with my shower, I wrapped myself in a towel and walked into the kitchen. Mae was dressed already and had a cup of coffee waiting for me.

"Here you go." she said as she handed me the steaming mug and kissed me on the cheek. "What is that article you're working on about? You haven't told me yet, and I am really excited to read it."

I shrugged as I took a sip of my coffee. It was the perfect temperature.

"It's some boring historical piece. If you ever have trouble sleeping, I will read it to you." I readjusted my towel and went into our closet to pick out an outfit. Mae and I were nearly the same size, so our closet had become a chaotic mess. We each had completely different styles of dress. However, she usually used some of my outfits in her ensembles. As I perused through our clothes, Mae's head popped up around the corner.

"It can't be that boring? Can it?" she stared at me while I removed my towel, expecting me to have an issue with it.

"Can I help you?" I said, turning to face her. She looked me up and down and smiled.

"You could have earlier, but you have to work." She pouted as she took one last look and then went back into the kitchen. "Did you want something to eat?" I could hear her looking through the refrigerator. I could hear her trying to quietly open the carton of orange juice.

"You better be using a cup!" I said as I put on my bra. "I bought extra

17

ones so you couldn't use any excuses." I could hear her frantically opening cabinets.

"Oh, totally. I'm totally using a cup." I could hear the clanking of the new glasses I had bought from the secondhand store in town. "These are the ugliest cups I have ever seen, by the way. Just so you know."

"They were cheap, and I love that color of yellow. Reminds me of the fifties." I pulled a tank top from the closet and put it on as I prepared to look for my favorite pair of blue jeans. "Have you seen my library pants?" I said as I rummaged through the closet.

"I think I put them in the dresser. You're always looking for them and I wanted them to be easy to find. Apparently, I failed." She popped her head back in the room and pointed to the bottom drawer. I took a look and there they were. They were the most comfortable jeans I had ever worn, but unfortunately, they stopped making them forever ago and I could not find another pair in this size.

"Thanks," I said as I zippered them up just right. "These pants make my ass look amazing." I turned to look in the mirror to inspect myself, and I was right. I looked good.

"Yeah, they do! I can't wait to take that off later!" I walked into the kitchen, and she was looking at me seductively. "I'm serious about that!"

"Don't worry. I'm just going to hit the library to do some last-minute fact-checking. I want to make sure that this thing is perfect." I rummaged through our living room for my bag with my laptop and some other supplies.

"I'm sure it will be." She handed me a small to-go cup and a small, bagged lunch. "I still can't believe you use strawberry jam and not grape jelly on your PB&J sandwiches. That should be a crime."

I smiled as I grabbed my keys and leaned in to kiss her goodbye. I held the kiss just a bit longer than I usually did and slowly pulled away. "I don't know. I just am not that big of a fan of grapes."

"Ugh, why do you have to do that and just leave. You drive me crazy," she took a sip of her coffee and smiled. "Let me know if you will be home for lunch. I am just going to be working on a paper for business class. I can't believe I only have one class left until I graduate. It has surely been a long time coming."

"Why don't you come with me to the library. We can go grab lunch at the diner together. We can take my bike if you want."

"Really? I didn't think you would want me there while you worked on your article. I don't want to distract you." She walked over to me, making sure to move her hips just a bit extra.

"Yeah, I know, but I really don't want to leave you here all day. I would rather stare at you across the library table while I work. It could be fun."

"Well, then it's settled. Let me get my stuff and I'll meet you outside!" She ran into the other room to grab her school supplies and get a pair of shoes. I could hear her frantically throwing things into her bag. After a few moments, she appeared out of the bedroom and was ready to go.

"Let's go!" she said as she put on some sunglasses. I smiled as I opened the door for her and made sure to smack her on the ass on her way out. She looked back at me annoyed.

"I owed you one, remember," I said as I locked the door and fumbled for my bike keys on my key ring. We walked the short walk to our garage unit, and I opened the door. There in the garage, amongst a thousand other things, was my motorcycle. It had just been cleaned, so it sparkled as the sunlight hit it. Mae jumped on the back of it and jumped up and down as she waited for me to start it. I tossed my leg over the side and made myself comfortable. I started it up and pulled the throttle a few times for show. Mae always loved that. After a few more moments of adjusting my mirrors, I slowly pulled out of the garage and hit the garage door button on my windshield to close it.

"Whoo!" she cried as we sprinted toward the main road. "It's so beautiful out!" she had her hands raised in the air for a few seconds until we began to speed up. She wrapped her hands around my waist for support. Every so often, her grip tightened and loosened as I accelerated and decelerated.

"I love you, Becks," she whispered in my ear as we hit the first stoplight exiting our complex.

"I love you too," I managed to say as the light turned green and I opened up the throttle. In a matter of seconds, we were going about fifteen over the speed limit. I kept it up for a few miles until we started to get into town, and then I slowed it down.

"Awwww," she said as she slapped my leg. "No fun!" I laughed to

19

myself as I drove through the side streets toward the library. I intentionally take these streets to piss Mae off. She loves going fast, and I usually am not in the mood to get a ticket. If I were to stay on the main streets, I knew she would convince me to go faster. She had a way of doing that to me. After a few minutes of Mae trying to convince me to go faster, we arrived at the library. I found a spot to park under some trees, and we disembarked.

"Wow, I haven't been here in forever," she said as she reached for my hand. I took her invitation, and we strolled inside. Her hands were soft, much softer than mine. It was amazing how something so mundane as hand holding could still drive me wild. Every single part of our skin that touched was electric. I had goosebumps running up and down my arm. It could have been the cold, but I don't believe it was.

"Yeah, the last time you were here with me might have been when we still both went to school here at the same time." I looked up at the large towers that were on each of the four corners of the building. We'd had such amazing times there years earlier. I wondered why we ever stopped. I had such fond memories of the building.

"Hurry up," Mae yelled from the top of the stairs. "If she finds out we took the key we are going to get in huge trouble." I climbed the circular staircase for what felt like forever. Mae was in much better shape than I was, and it showed.

"I'm coming." I replied as I huffed. I regretted not putting my hair up prior to going on this little adventure. "My hair is everywhere. Maybe I should cut it all off!" I frantically pushed the hair out of my face.

"No, don't do that." She said as I finally caught up to her. She must have stopped to catch her breath. If that were the case, she would have never let me know. She walked down the few steps to where I stopped and put her arms around me.

"If you cut your hair, what will I grab onto?" She took her hands and wrapped it around my neck and grabbed a tuft of my hair and pinned me against the wall of the stairwell. She pushed her body against mine and kissed me violently. After a few minutes of that she pulled away and let out a deep breath. "So, let's hurry up and get upstairs!" She grabbed my hand and pulled me faster than I really wanted to run. After a few more minutes, we came to a large wooden door. Mae fumbled with the keys and found the correct one. The door moaned as it opened, and we entered. The room was dark and dusty and

covered with boxes. Each large pile of boxes was covered with a large moving blanket and another layer of dust.

"Wow. When was the last time someone was up here?" She walked over to the window and looked out. "We are up so high."

I turned around and closed the door. "Keep it down. You're going to get us caught. I don't want to get kicked out of the library. That's a new type of low." She walked over to me seductively.

"You're scared of getting kicked out of the library? What a nerd!" She smiled as she reached me and put her hands around my waist. "Maybe I can help you take your mind off of it." She pressed her body against mine and pushed me down into a pile of boxes. Dust filled the air.

"Becks. Did you hear me?" She had stopped and was giving me a pretty concerned expression. "Did you just hear anything I said?"

I shook my head in apology. "I'm sorry. I was just remembering that day in the tower." I pointed up toward the area in question. "That was a good day, wasn't it?"

The look of concern faded from her face, and an annoyed look took its place. "Yeah, that was a good day. Did you hear what I asked? I wanted to know where you wanted to meet when you were done grabbing your books? I need to get started on this paper and want to grab a spot before they get filled up and we have to sit next to a bunch of weirdos."

"Let's meet in the nook behind the coffee stand. They have a few power outlets and are a bit more private than the tables. That sound good?"

She nodded in agreement, and took off toward the entrance. She stopped and turned around to give me a kiss. "See you inside." She turned around and she was gone.

I decided to take a moment and enjoy the weather before going in. I took a look up at that tower and felt the sun, warm on my face. I don't take the time to enjoy things like that since I am always on the move. I promised myself that I would try to stop and appreciate those things more often. I decided to not keep Mae waiting and headed into the library.

When I reached the table to put down my bag, Mae was already spread out and chewing on her pen. "How do you do this for a job?" she asked as she shifted through her notes. "I can barely do one of these a semester let alone all the time."

I placed down my bag and peaked at what she was looking at. "I have a deep interest in what I am writing about. Are you really that interested in this?"

She looked up at me and sighed. "Not all of this stuff is interesting. Some of it is just math. I hate math." She looked up at me with a desperate look. "Go ahead and grab your books and come back and keep me company." I nodded and headed over to the section that I had frequented for the past few weeks. I grabbed a small cart and took out several books that I had gone through several times. I had been told by my editor that some of my citations were incorrect, and I wanted to make sure that I at least got through the first few pages that day. After that, I should be in good shape to finish the article on time. I walked over toward the coffee cart and was half-tempted to grab a couple of pastries. Knowing Mae, she would have gotten crumbs all over everything, and I decided against it. When I returned, she was still working on the same page, and this time the pen was a bit more chewed on. She looked up as I walked toward her.

"Did you find what you needed?" She then saw the small stack of books that I had brought with me. "Never mind, you found every book in the section!" She had a look of amazement as I stacked them on the table near where I was sitting. "You read all of these?"

"Yeah. What do you think I do when you're at class or at the gym?" She was amazed that I could read so many books. She was looking at me like I was crazy. "No. I'm kidding. I am just searching these books for facts to cite in my article. This is way too much to read, and to be honest, it is pretty boring." I didn't know if she knew that I was lying through my teeth.

"Ha, I knew it was boring." She had a proud look on her face since she caught me in my little lie. She gave me a look that said, "I win." She then went back to working on her paper. I tried to concentrate on my work but had trouble sitting this close to her and paying attention. It seemed wrong somehow, not paying complete and utter attention to her when she was around. Her very presence was intoxicating, even after all this time. I had known her nearly my entire life, and that one thing had never changed. She was the reason that I was on this earth, and without her, I didn't know if I would exist.

"You're staring at me again," she said as she moved my bag and nudged her way closer to me. "Can I tell you a secret?" she whispered into my ear. Her breath against my neck made me shiver.

"Go ahead," I managed to say as I started to lose focus. "What do you want to tell me?" She got even closer and put her hand on my leg.

"I actually like it when you stare." She pulled away to see her effect on me. She was pleased. "Wow, I still got it don't I?" she said with a smirk.

"Yeah, you really have no clue babe," I was able to say as she put her head on my shoulder and wrapped her arms around mine. We sat there for a few minutes, enjoying each other's company and living in that moment. Suddenly that moment ended.

"Excuse me," said a voice from across the room. It was the librarian, and she was pointing toward one of the columns in the library. We looked over to where she was pointing, and we saw a large PSA about public displays of affection and how they were not allowed in the study area. She didn't seem mad, just a little bit annoyed that two people who were clearly too old to be students were seemingly disobeying library policy on her watch.

"I'm sorry," I said as Mae straightened herself out and continued her paper. The librarian walked away, and we both started laughing. After a few moments of uncontrollable laughter, we decided to sneak one more kiss and continue our work.

That day at the library was one of the better ones that we'd had in a while. Mae and I had an amazing relationship. One that we had maintained over the last thirty or so years. We met when we were young and were childhood friends. We were nearly inseparable through our teenage years and moved in together once I finished college. Only then did our relationship spawn into something much more than friendship. That being said, it was difficult to find things that we enjoyed doing together. This was something that we hadn't done together recently. Maybe I would have to revisit how often we did activities such as this in the future.

After a few hours, Mae had finally made some headway on her paper, and I had nearly finished what I had come to the library to accomplish. We decided that the rest of the work could be finished another day, and I went to check out the two remaining books I needed.

"I'll meet you out by your motorcycle," Mae said as I went to the front counter to check out the books. "Start thinking about where you want to go for lunch."

"Ok. We should go shopping after lunch as well. I want to get a sun dress for our anniversary dinner." She looked at me with a smile.

"That sounds perfect!" I said, and she was out the door. I had completely forgotten about our anniversary. I felt completely guilty. A few moments later, I collected myself and went to the front counter to check out my books, and the librarian that had caught us earlier walked up.

"Hello, young lady," she said with a smile as she took the books from under my arm. "A bit of heavy reading I see." She struggled lifting the two large books.

"Yeah. I am working on an article for a magazine I write for. It's about Lincoln, amongst other things." I handed her my card and she looked down at the name.

"Rebecca, right? Yeah, I see you right here in our system. You come in here a lot, yes?" She must have seen my rental history on the screen.

"Yeah, you can call me Becky. I spend a decent amount of time here fact checking and citing sources." She stamped the rental card and placed them both neatly back in the front cover.

"I remember seeing you, but I have never seen your friend before. Does she go to college here?" Her eyes showed that she was prying a bit, but I was used to being looked at that way. It was just something you got used to after coming out.

"Yeah. My wife and I decided to come together today. She is working on her bachelor's at the local college. She's studying business." When I said the word wife, I could tell she was a bit uncomfortable, but she tried to not let me notice.

"Oh," she said with only a hint of disgust. "That's so nice that you two can spend time like this together. I hope to see you two back here again." She handed me the books, and I had to give her credit—she did a very good job at sounding sincere. She must have had a lot of these interactions nowadays, and at least she was friendly.

"We definitely will be back," I said as I tapped the books and placed them in my bag and smiled. "Take care." I waved and turned to leave. She smiled as I exited the door. I walked down the steps and over to the tree that I had parked underneath, and there was Mae waiting impatiently. She tapped her foot and checked her imaginary watch a few times and sighed.

"Forever...you always take forever." She smiled and came over to help me with my books. The second she realized how heavy they were, she abandoned her effort of chivalry and decided to open one of my saddlebags so I could put them away.

"Thanks, Hun," I said as I zipped up the saddlebag and she got onto my bike. I reached into another one of my saddlebags and looked for my pack of cigarettes.

"What are you looking for?" she asked, looking rather puzzled.

"Oh, nothing," I managed to say as I remembered that I did not smoke on this side of the poles…at least not in front of Mae. "Wait a second, here they are," I said as I pulled my keys from my pocket. "I don't know why I thought they were in there." By the look on her face, she believed the lie, and she patted my seat for me to join her on the bike.

"To the diner!" she said as I put the key in the ignition and started the bike. I checked my mirrors before pulling out into the street. The drive to the main strip was short, and I quickly found a spot near the diner.

"Lame!" Mae shouted as I parked the bike. "I wish that drive was longer."

I laughed as I shut off the bike and we both got off. We turned toward the diner and Mae suddenly stopped and peered through one of the shop windows.

"Wow!" she said as she saw the tight black dress on the store mannequin. "That would look amazing on me!" She pressed her nose against the glass. She slid down until her nose resembled that of a pig. She looked over at me with a goofy smile and laughed as she pulled away.

"Don't you already have a dress like that?" I said, catching my mistake only once the words had left my mouth.

"Are you kidding me? Trust me, Becks, if I had a dress like that you would definitely know about it." She did a little dance that meant she wanted to go inside the store.

"But what about lunch?" I said. "We might not get our usual spot." I pointed toward the diner, and she pouted.

"Fine!" she said as she started toward the diner. She dragged her feet dramatically and looked over her shoulder at me, waiting for me to change my mind. After a few moments, she gave up.

"It looks way too expensive anyway," she said as she walked back over toward me and took my hand in hers. "Let's get something to eat!" She smiled a half-smile, and we made our way down the street to the diner. Once we were inside and seated at our usual table, I decided it was my time to act.

"Oh shit!" I said as I reached into my bag, looking for my pocketbook. "I think I left my wallet on the bike. I'll be right back."

"Wow, you would forget your head if it wasn't attached," she said as she held up the menu. "How about you go grab it, and I will order our usuals. Sound good?" I nodded in agreement and made my way toward the exit. Once I had left the diner, I made my way toward my actual destination... the thrift store.

"Hello!" the manager said as I walked in. "What can I do you for?" he said with a smile.

"I want to buy that black dress in the window. My wife loved it, and I am going to surprise her with it." He chuckled as he walked from behind the counter and made his way toward the display at the front of the store.

"That's very considerate of you," he said as he reached in and took the dress off of the mannequin. After a few moments of struggling, he completed the task and made his way back to the counter. "Here you go!" he said as he laid it down on the counter. "How would you like to pay?" I reached down into my wallet and pulled out some cash.

"Cash should be good. I don't want her seeing how much it cost." I placed the cash down on top of the dress. "That should be enough, right?"

He laughed as he picked up the bills and counted them. "Did I give you a total for the dress?" he said as he looked very confused. "I don't remember telling you how much the dress cost."

"Don't worry," I said trying to find a reason I knew the cost of the dress. "It must have been marked in the window and the number stuck in my head." He looked over the dress once more as he placed it in the bag.

"Yeah, you must be right," he said as he put the cash in the drawer and handed me my change. "You have a great day now! I sure envy your wife. She is surely a lucky one."

"Thank you. That's very kind of you to say." I reached for the bag and smiled. "You have a great day as well." He waved as I left the shop. As I shoved the bag into my purse, I noticed something in the window. It was the shopkeeper looking through the display for a price tag on the dress. He noticed me staring, and his head disappeared from view. I laughed to myself as I walked back toward the diner. The small bell rang as I walked through the front door and alerted Mae to my presence.

"Finally!" she said as I walked in. "You're just in time. Al just brought the food, and it's still hot!" She pointed to the plates on the table. I made my way and sat down next to her and grabbed the mug off coffee that was sitting next to my plate and took a drink.

"Ahh, nothing is better than their coffee." I took a whiff of the mug and took another sip and put the mug down. By the time I had put down the mug, Mae had already eaten half of her plate. She realized I was staring with my mouth wide open and almost choked on her Denver omelet. I smiled as I took a gigantic bite of my skillet, and we both just started laughing. That meal was just like all the others we'd had over the years. We talked about what was going on in our lives outside of us and tried to think of stories that we both hadn't heard about each other. That's the hardest part about a relationship that has been going on as long as ours, surprising each other. Little did she know, I had one of those surprises in my purse.

After the meal had ended, we decided to head on home, since it was getting late in the day. Our brunch had nearly turned into a dinner, and I still had some work to do when I got home. Once we got onto my bike and hit the main road, I could feel Mae tapping on my back and trying to talk louder than the wind.

"Did you just seriously miss our turn?" she asked right before I gave her some gas. I could feel her nails dig deep into my sides as the bike accelerated, and it felt amazing. She always asked me to give the bike a little gas, and I never did. I didn't know why I didn't open her up more often. Maybe it was just like the day before. I couldn't do it because of the way things were on the other side, but here, I could do it without repercussions. I can be who I am and be happy without the feeling of the other shoe dropping. She screamed in excitement as I hit a few straightaways and really got her going. Her head appeared on my shoulder, and I could feel her cheek against my neck. These were the moments that haunted me for literally half of my life. These were the moments that scared the hell out of me.

As we finally finished up our grand prix and turned into the road to take us back to our apartment, my heart was beating at a fever pitch. Riding with her is unlike riding with anyone. Maybe it was just the adrenaline talking, but I just wanted to go inside with her and finish what we started that morning.

"So, I don't know about you, but I am stuffed. I'm thinking we just make ourselves a bowl of popcorn and watch a movie in bed. Sound good?" I said as I fumbled with the garage door. The sensors were not aligned, and you had to press the button about ten times for it to finally close.

"Yeah, that sounds great," she said as she tried her best to get control of her windswept hair. "How about you shower first, and I will go second." We walked up to the front door of the apartment, and I fumbled with the keys. Once the door was open, Mae pointed toward the bathroom. "Get in there. You smell."

I locked the door behind me and walked over to her and gave her a kiss. "Yeah, I do, but you know you love it." I planted a kiss on her cheek and did as I was told and headed toward the shower.

About fifteen minutes later, I exited the shower with a towel around my chest. "Hey, did you make the popcorn?" I said as I opened the door to the bedroom. There was Mae. She was standing in the dress that I had bought her today with a gigantic bowl of popcorn in her hands. She smiled and took a bite of our evening snack.

"Do you really think you can surprise me after all this time? It's cute, but let's be honest. You're getting rather predictable." I walked over to her and took my hand off of my towel to grab a bite of popcorn. The towel fell to the ground and Mae blushed.

"The dress wasn't the real surprise," I said as I grabbed the bowl from her and placed it on the nightstand. "As beautiful as you look in that dress, you need to take it off. I believe we need to finish something that we started this morning."

She shimmied her way free of the dress and kissed me like she hadn't done in a while. The last thing I remembered from that evening was trying to catch my breath. Her head was resting on my chest. I could feel her heart beating next to mine.

Chapter 3

The light hit my eyes as it did nearly every morning, sneaking through a small crack in my defenses and finding its way into my eyes. I tried to reach my hand over to cover them, but it was stuck in the blanket. As I fought the comforter, it finally gave me back my hand and I literally punched myself in the face. I sat up quickly in the bed and let out a quiet grunt. It was quiet, and since my mouth was so dry, I could barely form any sounds, let alone words.

"What the hell," I rasped as I brought my hand to my nose to make sure nothing was broken. I swore I could smell blood. I looked down at my clock and it was nearly nine in the morning. Believe it or not, I did not usually sleep this late. My migraine usually woke me up long before nine. At that point I remembered…the migraine that was hitting me was a bad one. It was what usually happened when I drank too much with my sleeping pills. I was just glad that I didn't piss myself in my sleep. Yes, that has happened. Not my best moment, but a moment of mine just the same.

I got up from my bed and stumbled a bit over some laundry and went to the bathroom to possibly hydrate a bit. I placed my mouth under the sink and turned on the tap. The water was hot, but it slowly cooled as I gulped it down. After a few moments, I decided to try and form a word or two.

"Idiot," I managed to say as I stared at myself in the mirror. The face that looked back at me was mine, but it also wasn't. It was who I am, but it was only part that. The face staring back at me reminded me of a lifetime of disappointment. Not only from my family, but my friends as well.

By now you're probably asking what exactly is going on. Unfortunately,

29

I don't really have a good explanation. I call it a pole shift, but other people might call it…actually, I don't want to think of what other people would call it. The truth is, I have never told anyone. Every night when I go to sleep, I don't dream, and I don't rest. I wake up as her…well me…well you know what I mean. I wake up as Rebecca. As you probably have guessed, I enjoy my life much more there. It has been like this since as far back as I can remember. The two poles are nearly identical, except for the fact that I am her…me…you get the picture.

I decided to put off shaving for the day and get on with it. After about a five-minute search, I found my phone buried beneath the mountain of shit on the floor in my room and realized that it was, in fact, dead. I plugged it into the charger on my desk and went outside for a cigarette. As I sat out on the steps to my apartment, I could see past the field at the college campus across the way. I could see people running around the quad and heading to class. I leaned back on my window and noticed that there was a half empty bottle of beer on the sill. I picked it up and held it up to the light to make sure that there wasn't a cigarette butt in it. When I deemed it safe, I drained the contents of the bottle. It tasted old to me. It must have been from one of my neighbors the night before. It wasn't completely stale, but it was warm.

"Ok. That was disgusting," I heard a voice say from down below. "I sure hope that was yours from last night." Mae must have come over to tell me about her date. I tried to play it off cool.

"Yeah, I must have forgotten to finish it last night before I went to bed. I was having a drink with my neighbor." An obvious lie, but I was hoping she wouldn't pry too hard.

"Well, that sounds fun. Disgusting, but fun," she said as she walked up the stairs toward my apartment door. She came over to the window and leaned against it besides me. She took the cigarette out of my hand and took the last drag. As she exhaled, she looked over toward me and smiled. "So, you haven't asked me about my date." She tried to have one last drag of the cigarette, and when she realized it was done, she handed it back to me.

"Well, I figured you would just start blabbing, so I didn't bother to ask." I took the cigarette butt and placed it in the empty beer bottle. I looked up and she had already gone into the apartment to grab a drink. She caught herself before she drank from the carton and grabbed a clean glass from the dish drying rack. Apparently, I had been in the right state of mind to actually do the dishes the night before. Sometimes I even surprise myself.

"Have I ever told you how ugly your dishes are?" She drained the contents of the glass and then held up the glass to the light. "Like for real, these are awful."

It took me a second to regain my composure. She had never said that to me before. Well, this me. She was constantly saying how ugly the dishes were when the poles changed, but never here.

"Are you ok?" she said as she noticed what I only could assume looked like a mini seizure.

"Yeah, yeah. I'm fine. Just not completely awake yet." I pretended to rub the sleep out of my eyes to bring the lie home. She didn't pay much attention to it and just poured herself another glass of orange juice. She took another look at the glass and shook her head before putting the dirty glass in the sink. She looked up at me and smiled.

"So, do you have anything going on today?" She was already in route to the bathroom to freshen up. I could tell by the way her hair was that she hadn't gone home the night before. The thought of her with someone else put ice in my veins. Unfortunately, I was far too adept at shaking those feelings off. In recent months, she has been out on countless dates, and they usually ended the same way. She would come over to tell me how they went, and I would just sit and be supportive whether they went well or went badly.

"I don't really know," I said as I checked my calendar on the wall by my kitchen table. "I think I have to finish that commission today. The one for the college." As I checked the schedule, I noticed that I was going to be late on a few commissions in the coming weeks. To be honest, I just didn't have the energy or the frame of mind to work on them. Mae had been over a ton lately, and she always got my full attention. As I said before, it was my biggest weakness.

"Anything I can help you with?" she said as she looked over my shoulder. She was using one hand to put her hair into a messy ponytail and the other to peruse my schedule. "It looks like you're kind of busy." When she was done with her hair, she put her bag down on the table and crossed her legs. "So, are you listening?"

She must have asked a few times, and I didn't answer because when I looked at her, she was not pleased. "Yeah," I managed to get out, not really hearing the question until it was too late.

"Really?" she said, sounding surprised. "That's awesome! What can I help with first?"

I finally came out of my trance and looked her way. "Help with what?" At this point I realized that I had messed up.

"Help with your work," she said sounding very annoyed. "You just said I could help you with your work. I am taking it you didn't really hear what I said." She grabbed her purse and stood up. "Seriously, what is up with you? You have been a zombie the last few weeks, and I don't know what I can do to help." She violently pushed the chair, turned, and walked toward the door. When she arrived at the door, she stopped and turned around. She took a few moments to compose herself and then picked up an empty whiskey bottle from the side table near my couch. "I have been trying to be supportive cause you're clearly going through something. Obviously you need some type of help. Is this the one that you bought yesterday?"

I didn't like being yelled at. Call it my Marty McFly reaction. "No as a matter of fact. That one is in the bedroom!" I didn't realize the volume of my voice until it was too late.

"Don't fucking yell at me and act like I am the bad guy here," she said as she slammed the bottle back down on the side table. I'm surprised neither the bottle nor the table broke. "The fact you have a nearly empty bottle in your bedroom does not really help your case here." She began to cry. She managed to compose herself to get one more sentence out. "I love you, and you're just killing yourself. Don't you see?" Seeing her begin to cry made me instantly feel awful. She went and sat down on the couch and continued to cry. I walked over to the couch and sat next to her. I put my hand around her shoulder, and she shrugged me off.

"Mae, I love you too," I managed to say, knowing that it was far truer than she really understood. She took a few deep breaths and looked up at me. Her already day-old makeup was running down her face. She rolled her shirt and tried to wipe off her face the best she could. She looked up at me and the look was something I had never seen before.

"You don't love me," she said as she slowly regained her composure.

"How could you love me if you don't even love yourself?" At this point she stopped crying and seemed to gain some clarity.

"I'm so sorry. I don't know what is going on with me." I said as I noticed my hands were beginning to shake. "I just…I just don't know what is wrong with me." I was literally lying through my teeth. Obviously, I knew exactly what was wrong with me. I was in love with her, and I didn't have the strength to tell her. Even if I did manage to tell her, she would never be with me. As she had joked for years, I'm not exactly her type. If I were to tell her, I would lose her. If I lost her, I didn't know what would happen to me. I didn't think I would recover from that. I put my face into my hands and one thought came to my mind. I am completely pathetic. I am literally the most pathetic person on the planet. Once that thought really hit home, I don't know what came over me. My sadness turned to nothing but rage. I ripped at my hair and just screamed out in aggravation. I stood up quickly and knocked into the table in front of the couch. I knocked into it so hard that everything on the table went flying off and landed on the carpet. I looked down at Mae, and she was no longer crying. She just had a look of terror on her face. Without taking her eyes off me she reached for her purse and got up and made her way to the door. She paused for a moment, expecting me to say something. I gave her what she wanted.

"If you don't like how I am handling myself, just get out. The last thing I need is another parent telling me that I am a disappointment. I am doing the best I can, and if that bothers you, then just go." Her hand fell off the door handle and she cautiously walked over toward me. Her purse slid off her shoulder as she got closer, and she just wrapped her arms around me. I have never laid hands on a girl in my life, but Mae obviously felt as if I was not a threat. My outburst didn't slow her advance. This was not the reaction that I was expecting.

"I don't know what is wrong, but you know you can tell me, right?" she said as she looked up at me. Her face was a mess. Her makeup was everywhere. Her ponytail had fallen out, and she still was the most beautiful thing I had ever seen. "Whatever you need me to do. I'm here." Her hands around me got tighter and tighter until it felt like my ribs were going to break. She had never hugged me like that here, and I didn't want it to end. She buried her face in my chest and kept it there.

"I'm sorry Mae. I just don't think I am ready to talk about it. Not to

33

anyone." I put my hands around her and held her tight. I knew that when I finally did tell her that I would miss this moment just like all the others with her. It would be gone and there would be no getting them back. I would eventually drive her away like everyone else in my life. The question was not if, but when. It was inevitable, and I just needed to hold on as long as I could. She looked up and me and smiled. I could tell it was not genuine. It was to make me feel better.

"Well, when you're ready. I am ready." She took a deep breath, and I could feel her grip on me loosen. I followed suit. She reached down and grabbed her purse and tried to compose herself. "You're my best friend. I can't imagine my life without you. You know that, right?" She wiped a bit of snot from her nose with her hands and wiped it on her skirt.

"I feel the same way, Mae. You literally have no clue." I wiped off my face as well, hoping that she wouldn't notice that I had tears on my cheek as well. Once she had calmed down, she forced out a giggle.

"Well, I am going to get out of here and leave you to your work." She looked down and nodded her head as if trying to convince herself that this was the right course of action. "Let me know if you want to hang out after you have finished your work." She was making a conscious effort to not look me in the eyes. Obviously, my outburst had left her a bit rattled, and she was right to feel that way. Just another reason to add to my mountain of self-loathing. She walked over to the door, and just before leaving, she looked back my way, again without making eye contact. "I'll see you later," she said, and with that she closed the door, and she was gone.

"Great fucking job!" I yelled at myself after a few moments. "Literally the only person in your life that cares, and you just shit all over her." I walked over to my bedroom and grabbed the bottle of whiskey. I opened it up and took a pull. I looked down at the clock as I finished and realized it wasn't even ten in the morning. She was right. I did need help, but it's not like I didn't know that. They say accepting that you have a problem is the first step toward fixing it. That's bullshit. I'd had a problem for years, but I was able to keep it hidden. Now, it seemed that my problems were just coming to a crescendo. I wouldn't be able to go on like this. Not without a bit more effort on my part. I looked down at the bottle in my hands and laughed. "Well, might as well finish it," I said before I drained its contents. Once it was done, I walked over to the trash and threw the bottle away. I walked over to my desk and sat down. I took a moment to think of anything else I could do to procrastinate on my commission, but nothing came to mind. "Well, it looks like it's time to finish this shit." I turned on my computer and put on my headphones. I turned them on full and began my work.

After a few hours of actual work, I decided to stop and make myself something to eat. The high from the whiskey had begun to fade, and it was being replaced with a migraine. I walked over to the cupboard and looked for something to eat. Most of what I had in the apartment was in the freezer and could be simply reheated. I reached in the back behind a few cans of soup and found a bag of dried tortellini. "Nice," I said to myself as I struggled to remember when they were from. The only person that bought me these things was my mother, and she hadn't visited in months. I took a mental note to call her and remembered my mental note from the day before and sighed. She probably didn't want to hear from me anyway. Like I had mentioned, I was quite the disappointment. I dropped out of college for no reason at all. Well, there were reasons, but they were garbage. I would get into them, but you would either fall asleep from boredom or want to punch me in the face.

Either way, I dropped out early and used my one and only talent to get by. Yeah, I always was great at putting pencil to paper, but it was far from glamourous. The only reason I was able to live in the apartment I was in was because I did all the artwork for the landlord's marketing for free. We horse-traded services, and it paid for my rent and utilities. It was a pretty sweet deal. As for my other bills, I really didn't have any, other than my habits and food. Anyway, I poured some water into a marginally clean pot and sat waiting for it to boil. I must have thought to myself a hundred times to go back and do some work waiting for it to boil, but like I said, I was procrastinating hardcore. After about ten minutes, the water was boiling, and I poured the tortellini in and waited some more. After a few more minutes, it was finished. I poured in some olive oil and some parmesan cheese and went back to my work. Yeah, my work might have suffered a bit since I was eating at the same time. I hardly cared since I was so behind on the work. A few more hours passed, and I sat back in my chair and took off my headphones. My stomach didn't feel too great, and I barely made it to the bathroom to vomit. After that, I sat down on the floor of my bathroom and just contemplated every bad decision in my life leading up to that point. Right before flushing, I looked down into the bowl and to my surprise tortellini was not the only contents of my stomach. Inside the bowl, I saw several small bug-looking things. Upon further inspection, the bug-looking things turned out to be cockroaches.

"What the hell!" I said as I thought for a minute. I went over to my desk to inspect the remains of my lunch. I pulled open several of the tortellini and found something that you do not want to find in tortellini. Inside each one, there was a cockroach. After seeing that, I had the sudden urge to lose the remainder of my lunch. I ran to the bathroom to finish what I started. After another few minutes, I leaned back onto the wall and just sighed. Most people would have been mad and called the manufacturer. Myself, however…I just thought it was some karmic payback for my own stupidity, and I convinced myself that I deserved it. For the fight I had with Mae, and for every other bad decision I had made in my life. I pulled out my phone and noticed I had a text from Mae. I opened it and saw that it was just a heart emoji. I decided to give in to my weakness and give her a call. It rang a few times, and she answered. Her tone sounded slightly annoyed.

"Hey there," she said. I seemed to have caught her in the middle of working out. "Did you get your work done?"

"Yeah, I got about ninety five percent of it done. You will never guess what happened to me." I planned on telling her what I had for lunch. She usually found my misfortune amusing.

"That's awesome," she said as it sounded like she was telling someone else to shush.

"Did I catch you at a bad time? Just wanted to see if you wanted to have a drink or sing some karaoke?" A few more seconds of awkward shushing and she responded.

"You know, I am in the middle of something right now. Do you think we could get a rain check?" At this point I could tell that someone was with her. I could hear silenced laughter from someone I didn't recognize.

"Oh, yeah. That's fine. Just have a good night." I waited a second for her to respond, and there was nothing. I hung up the phone and realized what had just happened. After I was such an asshole earlier, she went back to her date's house and hung out.

"Well, that's what you get." I said to myself as I put my phone back into my pocket. "Now that she has someone else, it is only a matter of time before she's gone for good." I took a few moments to collect myself and made an effort to clean up my mess from lunch. I poured the cockroach tortellini into the garbage and took a good look at the pan and didn't think I could eat out of it again. I threw it away with the rest of the meal and laughed.

"If Zane saw this he would be pissed." I smiled to myself as I remembered the macaroni and cheese debacle we'd had right after high school. That was the year that I bought my bike, and I was not the best decision maker in the world. Well, that's a story for another time. "I wonder what he is up to now?" I thought to myself as I cleaned up the rest of my lunch mess and decided to go back to work. I went to put away some of my dishes when I found a nearly full bottle of peach schnapps. I picked it up and remembered when Mae had brought it over. She had taken one sip and said it was disgusting. She left it there for me, knowing that I would drink anything. She was right. I took the bottle back to my room to finish the little bit of work that I had left on my last commission.

After about an hour or so, I was finished and went outside for a celebratory cigarette. I brought the bottle of schnapps with me. I sat there on my steps, watching the sunset, and the only thing I could think about was Mae. She was with my replacement, with someone that would eventually be my undoing. After a few cigarettes and about half the bottle, I stood up and decided that I was not going to let Mae ruin my evening. I made the last-minute decision to throw a couple of beers into my backpack and go and look for some fun. I decided to head down to campus and listen for the first party that I could find. It was a trick that I had used in the past to find somewhere a bit more exciting than my current situation. After about a half a mile, I heard some music coming from the apartments closer to campus. I headed toward the music as I finished the bottle of schnapps and came to a tree line and decided to investigate a bit further.

"Hey there," came a voice as soon as I crossed the threshold of pine trees. "Where did you come from?"

I looked around until I found the source of the voice. It was a guy about ten years younger than me, holding a red solo cup. "Hey man," I said as I tripped over a small shrub and found my footing. "How's it going?"

He looked at me like I had a third eye and took a drink from his solo cup. The contents must have been strong since he winced when he drank. "I asked where you came from?" He pointed toward the line of trees. "Did you just come from over there?"

I looked back to where he was pointing and shrugged. "I have been here for a while. Just decided to go and take a piss where nobody could see. You know how it is."

He looked at me and you could tell he was trying to make a decision on whether to kick me out or not. "So, you went over there to take a piss?"

"Yeah, man," I managed to say as I took off my backpack. I pulled out a beer and handed it toward him. He took the beer with a confused look.

"Dude…" he said as he looked at the beer, realizing it was cold. "Let's play some pong!" he said after a few more seconds.

"Hell yeah, man!" I said as he walked me toward the tables that were set up on the lawn. You could see that there were already a ton of people playing. Somebody had even brought their couch onto their lawn to watch the festivities. I noticed that there were a few girls sitting on the couch. I could see them eye me when I walked up to the table.

"Hey guys," my new friend announced. "This is…?" he looked at me, looking for a name to attach to my face.

I could see he was looking to me to introduce myself. "My name is Chance," I said as I pulled another beer from my backpack and popped it open. I took a drink and held it up. "Cheers!" I said as I took another drink.

"Cheers!" screamed a group from the party who must have been listening in on our conversation. I looked over to a group of people holding their cups, glasses, and bottles in the air. I smiled as I cleared the contents of the bottle and put it in my bag. My new friend from the party handed me a joint, and the last thing I remembered was playing beer pong against a beautiful redhead. She smiled at me as I sunk the last cup. She walked over to me, looking for a rematch.

"So, I don't think I have seen you around here before?" she said, in between trying her best to chug the last bit of watered-down beer.

"Yeah, that's because I probably stopped going to this school when you were in…hmm let me guess, middle school?" I was trying to be charming, but it came out as me just being an asshole.

"Funny, funny." She laughed as she finally finished the cup. "I was going to ask if you were a professor, but…you don't look that smart." She put the cup back down on the table and walked over to me and poked me on the chest. "Anyway, I want a rematch. You have been playing beer pong for like what, twenty years?" Her subtle and playful jab at the fact I was a bit older than her was actually a turn-on. She didn't seem like the frail little girl that she looked like. She had some fire in her, and I really liked that.

"Well, depends," I joked, looking around for something else to drink. There was a cooler filled with some shitty light beer, but beggars can't be choosers.

"Depends on what?" She took the beer out of my hands and opened it. Even though it was shitty beer, she made it look like it was a thousand dollars a can. She finished and smiled. "Don't you have an entire backpack of beer?" She was right, I had forgotten. I pulled the bag off and took out one of mine…they were warm, but I really didn't care.

"Depends on if you want to get your ass kicked again," I said, taking the first sip out of the warm bottle. She walked up to me and grabbed me by the collar.

"You're so on." She went to turn around to reset the table and stopped. She turned around and grabbed my collar again, pulling me down to her level. She kissed me quickly and pulled away. My heart began to race, and the alcohol started to take over.

I remember a montage of beer pong, walking down a sidewalk, and making out in my apartment. The last thing I remembered was her and I in my bed.

Chapter 4

I woke up to a montage of the nights before. I could see Mae struggling to catch her breath, as well as the red head with her hand on my wall. A sudden myoclonic jerk brought me into reality as I nearly rolled out of bed. I was able to catch myself on my nightstand. Unfortunately, my alarm clock was a casualty as I smacked it across the floor. It decided at that moment to start buzzing.

"I'm up!" yelled Mae as she sat up quickly in bed. Her hair was a mess and she had forgotten to take her makeup off the night before. Damn, she made anything look good.

"Don't worry," I said as I placed the alarm clock back on the nightstand. "I just knocked the alarm clock over. Go back to bed." She looked over my way with sleep in her eyes. She nodded and decided to listen and laid back down. She pulled the covers up above her head and was out like a light.

"Better get going," I said as I noticed that the alarm was not an accidental occurrence. I needed to be up early and make sure that everything was in line for my meeting with my editor. He was a real asshole when my deadlines came down to the wire, and I didn't want to have another one on one with him. Before I got out of bed, I went to give Mae a kiss. For some reason, it felt wrong. I kissed her again and the feeling still remained.

"You can't kiss worth a damn when you're sleeping," I said as I poked her in the face a few times. She was out. I lifted her hand up a bit and just dropped it on the bed. It dropped as if she was a corpse. I chuckled to myself as I got out of bed and headed toward the bathroom.

I looked in the mirror and saw bags under my eyes. I pulled out some concealer and began to apply it. A sudden image of the redhead appeared

40

like a bolt of lightning in the back of my mind. I stared back into the face looking at me in the mirror. "Pull yourself together," I said as I slapped my face a few times. Again, like lightning, the redhead popped into my mind, and I lost balance and fell to the floor. My heart was beating out of my chest, and after a few moments of nausea, I was able to collect myself and proceed with my morning ritual. I looked back in the mirror to finish applying my makeup, only it wasn't my face looking back. Well, it was, but it wasn't Becky. I looked down at my hands and they were that of a man, not mine. Mae appeared in the mirror behind me and whispered in my ear.

"Time to get up, Becks!" her whisper was like the sound of a freight train.

"Fuck!" I said as I shot out of bed. My face and chest were covered in sweat and my heart was pounding literally out of my chest.

"Whoa, whoa," Mae said a few times as she tried to calm me down. "It's ok, I just didn't want you to be late for that meeting with your editor." She put her hands on my chest and gave me a hug. "It's ok, you're here with me."

I just looked down at my hands. They were actually my hands. I kicked off the covers and ran into the bathroom, Mae yelling as I pushed her out of the way.

"What the hell, Becks!" she said as she crossed the threshold into the bathroom and looked into the mirror.

"Thank God!" I said as I pulled at different features of my face. "It's me. Thank God!" I put my hands down on the sink and took a big sigh of relief, but then a moment of panic hit me.

"Was that a dream?" I said to myself quietly. "Was that actually a dream?"

I was panicking because I had not dreamt anything like that as far back as I could remember. One of the side effects for my, let's say, condition is that I do not dream. I do not have nightmares or wet dreams or any of it. I simply wake up on the other side.

"You have a bad dream?" Mae said as she appeared in the mirror. I jumped back, startled by the similarity of it all. Mae looked genuinely worried. "Baby, its ok. It was just a bad dream. Everything is fine." She walked over to me and pressed her body against mine and embraced me. This wasn't the embrace of a lover; this was the embrace of someone who was concerned. I hugged her back tightly and began to cry softly into her shoulder. Her free hand appeared on my back and began rubbing it, trying to console her weeping spouse.

"What happened in that dream?" she asked after a few moments. I figured she was trying to let me gain my composure before prying.

"It's nothing…just nothing," I said in between my quiet sobs. "I am just so glad that you're here, and I am so sorry."

She pulled back to look me in the face. "Sorry about what?" she said. "Did you do something in the dream?" She had caught me off guard.

"No, well…yeah," I said, trying to think of something to say. Then without meaning to, I suddenly blurted out something that I would no doubt eventually regret.

"I slept with a redhead," I said, ashamed. Her look of confusion was beyond compare.

"Like in the dream you slept with a redhead?" Her confused look began to take more of a concerned shape.

"Yes, in the dream," I spoke. "I don't know what happened." She pulled herself away and smiled.

"Baby, really? It's a dream. You don't have any control over what you do in a dream. You have nothing to be sorry about." She put her hand on my cheek and wiped a tear from my eye. She slowly brought her thumb down to my lips and leaned in to kiss me softly. A rush hit me, and the feeling of sadness was gone. I pushed her against the wall and kissed her deeply.

"Whoa. What happened here?" she managed to say in between my advances.

"Shut up and get in bed," I said as I pressed her even harder against the wall. I wrapped my hands around her waist. She was still sweaty from being trapped beneath the covers. She always sleeps with so many covers. I stopped my inner monologue when she leaned in close and whispered in my ear.

"Make me." She bit my earlobe as she pulled away and gave me a devilish grin. I picked her up and kissed her again. She wrapped her legs around me and I made my way back toward the bedroom and…well, you get the picture.

"I fucking love you, Rebecca," she said as she bit her lower lip and smiled. We laid in bed looking at the ceiling fan. Both of us were trying to catch our breath. Her hand was placed on my chest just below my neck. I looked over at her and she was already looking right at me.

"Man, that redhead got you really worked up, didn't she." She laughed as she leaned over and kissed me several times all over my chest.

"Oh shush," I said as I wrapped my arm around her and kissed her forehead. "Stop making fun of me." Her words cut deeper than I think she understood, but I couldn't be mad at her for that. She looked proud of herself for the comment, and she slapped her hand on my stomach.

"Well, you're already late, but I think you should get ready and go." She leaned over me seductively and then suddenly blew raspberries in my belly button. I laughed and slapped her on the head.

"Stop it, you know how much I hate that!" I rolled over and put my bare feet against the carpet. I looked around for my shirt. It was hanging from our bedside lamp. I grabbed it and put it on.

"You need to hurry," she said again, this time with a little look of desperation on her face.

"Why are you trying to get rid of me?" I asked. I could tell she really wanted me to leave. She must have seen the concerned look on my face, and she smiled. A few seconds later, I smelled it.

"Really? Was that you? Is that why you wanted me to leave?" She must have let one go without me noticing.

"Stop it. I didn't want you to be around for that one, but since you insisted, I figured might as well." She lofted the covers a few times to spread the smell.

"You're evil!" I said as I looked around the room for something to put onto my lower half. I finally found something business casual and was able to fit into them. They were a bit tighter than I remembered. I went to check myself in the mirror on time before I left and was glad to be greeted by the proper face. I slapped some water on my face, as is my normal routine, and dried it off so I could apply something to cover up the bags under my eyes. Once I had completed my morning-ish ritual, I grabbed my stuff and headed into the office. I decided to take the bike, even though it was a bit chilly. I made sure to wear my leather jacket. Mae met me at the door to give me a goodbye kiss as I grabbed my purse.

"Go get them, tiger," she said as she kissed me on the cheek, and I walked out the door.

43

"I'll do my best," I shot back as she stuck her tongue out and closed the door. I made my way toward my garage and started my bike.

The drive to work was an uneventful one. Usually, I ran into a few assholes that didn't like bikers and tried to cut me off. Too be honest, I was kind of in my own head the entire drive and couldn't even remember one driver that I passed. I could have driven by the Oscar Mayer Wienermobile and probably would not have noticed. I couldn't stop thinking about my dream, or memories, or whatever that morning was. I racked my brain trying to remember a time that I had actually dreamt something but was unable to. The entire morning's events were weighing pretty heavily on me, and before I realized it, I was pulling into the parking lot at the office in which the magazine I wrote for resided. Its logo was on the building, since they were the cornerstone tenant and owned it. I pulled into the motorcycle parking that they had just built and parked the bike. Looking up at the sixth floor of the office filled me with dread. I was nearly thirty minutes late for a meeting with my editor, and he was truly a grade A asshole. I usually tried my best to stay on his good side, but unfortunately, the last few weeks had been a bit rough. He was rather unhappy that I was chosen for this specific article, and he wanted it to go to his nephew, who also was a freelance writer for this magazine. Unfortunately, it was not up to him, and I was chosen. It wasn't the start of our troubles together, but it definitely didn't help.

"Good morning, Becky!" said the security guard as I swiped my badge and went through the turnstile, toward the elevator. "Aren't you late?"

I sighed as I pressed the elevator button and turned around. "Yes Chris, I'm a bit late. Wish me luck!" I crossed my fingers and smiled.

He pointed toward the elevator as it opened and yelled back. "You will do great. Everybody loves you!" He smiled and coughed. I could have sworn that he coughed and said something else under his breath, but I think I was just being a bit paranoid.

"Thanks!" I managed to say as I waved from inside the elevator. The doors began to close, and I withdrew my hand. I waited for a few moments as the elevator music played in the background. I took a few deep breaths as I reached the sixth floor and tried to calm myself down. Hopefully it was not going to be as bad as I thought it would. The elevator doors opened.

"Holy shit! There she is." John, my editor, must have been sitting there waiting for me in the lobby. "You do know you're like thirty minutes late, right? God damn it, this article better be amazing for all the shit I have had to deal with. My nephew is never late for reviews…never." He carried on as he motioned for me to come with him. I couldn't understand what he was saying since he was mumbling and facing away from me. All I knew is that it wasn't good.

"Sorry for being late. I just was…"

He cut me off. "Save it for some who cares, Rebecca, because I don't. All I care about is that your article is worth all of this drama that you bring with it." We reached the conference room, and he opened the door. His nephew Albert was sitting in there waiting for us as well.

"Oh hey," I managed to say as we walked in. "I didn't know you were going to be here." He stood up and reached over to shake my hand. I returned the gesture, and we both sat down across from each other. You see, my editor was an asshole, but his nephew wasn't. He was genuinely a nice individual, and I didn't mind spending time with him. The problem was, his uncle just inserted himself into his business at every opportunity, and it was irritating for everyone else. I could only imagine how bad it was for Albert. He broke the awkward silence.

"You look nice," he said as he awkwardly straightened out his shirt. I smiled a half-smile back.

"Thank you," I managed to mumble as I pulled some papers from my bag and shuffled them on the table.

"Well, you always look nice. I mean, you don't ever look not nice…I mean." He sighed and gave up on the explanation.

"I know what you mean," I said as I finally got my papers organized and placed them down on the table. "I appreciate it."

"Wow, get a room," John said as he slapped his nephew on the back. "I'm just kidding man," he managed to say as Albert gave him a death stare. I coughed to break the silence. John took the hint and changed the subject.

"So, the chief editor wanted Albert in on this because she felt he could learn a thing or two from you." He shrugged his shoulders and leaned back into his chair. "I disagreed. I let them know that Albert is one of our best, but they said that your unique viewpoint on history pieces is something they really enjoy. So, he is going to sit through this with us. You don't mind, do you?" I shook my head.

"Not at all. I love working with Albert. I wish we could…" John cut me off again.

"Enough with the chit chat. I read through what you sent me last night and I must say, it is not your best work." He leaned forward and grabbed a copy of my article and threw it over toward me. I picked it up and started reviewing some of his notes. They were all pretty vague.

"Would you mind elaborating on some of these things?" I continued to look over his notes as he just sat there watching me read them.

"You need me to elaborate?" He laughed a bit and expected his nephew to do the same. Albert did nothing of the sort. "This piece was supposed to be about his life coming up to the anniversary of his death. Not poking holes in his career and conspiracy theories." He pointed out a few spots on the first page. "You quote some Jack White a lot, I don't even know who he is." I took a few moments to compose myself before speaking.

"Is there a problem with speaking about the duality of the man? Lincoln did a great deal of good for this country, but not all of it was rainbows and unicorns. Some of the things that he did for this country had ulterior motives. I just wanted to make sure that people saw that." My voice had raised a bit as I spoke, but I did my best to calm down again. It was difficult looking into John's face as he smiled. He knew he was starting to get to me.

"I think it was great. I actually learned a lot while reading it. Everything she wrote is backed up by fact and…"

John cut him off. "Really? You're taking her side? You know she literally stole this article from you." He leaned back in his chair with a look of disgust. "Basically, begging for it."

I was beginning to get really irritated, but I remembered what Mae had told me. I could hear her in my head as he continued to speak.

"Just don't let him get to you. Be better than him. It's the only defense us women have. Be better than the ones who can't be."

I took a page from her book and took a few more deep breaths. "Why don't we speak to Charlotte about it. I am sure she would have something to say about the way you're acting." Charlotte was our chief editor and felt the same about John as I did. Unfortunately, he was very good at his job when he was not being a complete asshat, and she liked having him around. I looked over at Albert and saw that he was trying to cover up the fact he was smiling.

"There is no reason to bring her into this. Editing this is my job, not hers. You and I can handle this right here. No need to bother her." You could tell he was immediately on the defensive and was about to walk back everything he had just said. To be honest, I was surprised that he tried to strong-arm me at all. If he truly had issues with what I had written, I would have definitely taken the criticism professionally and done my best to correct whatever he had issues with. Unfortunately, for the past few weeks, he'd been throwing crap at the wall hoping it would stick. I'd never really had a conversation with Albert about it, but from his reaction, I could tell that he agreed with me.

"Well, I can see that we both had different ideas on how we thought the article would go. I personally think Abraham Lincoln is a national hero and that there is no reason to tarnish his name. You obviously think otherwise." His accusation was laughable.

"I am not making things up to tarnish his name. To be honest, the things I wrote about in this article make him more human to me. Not just some historical figure that was infallible. He was a good man that also had flaws. What is the problem with that?"

"I agree," Albert managed to say before John spoke again. "I rather enjoyed the article, and like I said. I learned a ton from it." His uncle looked up at him with glaring eyes. You could tell that Albert's continuous support for me was weighing on him.

"Well, I can see that I am outnumbered here. I expect to see the changes made by the end of the day tomorrow. Does that sound fair?" He stood up and hastily placed his papers into his briefcase and stood up. "You two should work on a piece together. Apparently, you agree on everything." With that, he left the conference room. Albert sat there uncomfortably for a few seconds before he spoke.

"So, we should definitely work on something together." He fumbled around with his papers and stood up. He did the act so quickly the chair flung out from beneath him and hit the window. He struggled to silence the chair. When he finally looked toward me, his face was beet red.

"Yeah, that sounds great," I said as I stood up and neatly placed the papers from the table into my bag. "We should grab a quick lunch tomorrow and see if anything we are working on coincides. Sound good?" I stood up and slung my bag over my shoulder. "Coffee?"

I could see him panicking as his face turned even redder. He finally got ahold of himself and took a breath.

"Yes. That sounds great. Just text me when and where you want to meet." He smiled as if he was proud to get the words out unscathed. He reached over to shake my hand. I returned the handshake, and the second our hands touched, it felt like touching a sponge. I withdrew and fought the urge to wipe my hand off on my pants.

"I will definitely do that!" I said, realizing that I was speaking a bit louder than normal. I was preoccupied worrying about how wet my hand was. "I will see you tomorrow." He smiled in return and left the room. He looked back and smiled again and nearly ran into the hinged side of the door. He readjusted, and before I knew it, he was out of site.

"That went well," I said quietly to myself. I took out my phone to text Mae how it went, but once the phone was out, I decided against it. I realized that it was much later than I thought and decided to not head home just yet. The visions of the redhead still were clear in my mind. "Get ahold of yourself," I said a few times prior to leaving the conference room. After a few moments to clear my mind, I decided exactly where I was going to go. The bar.

I walked out of that building as fast as I could. I even heard Chris say something as I left, and I just ghosted him. I made a mental note to apologize to him the next time I saw him. I hopped on my bike and went to the closest bar that I could find. As I got off the bike, I realized that it was a cash only bar, but that couldn't stop me. It was just past noon and the bar had just opened. It was early enough that the bartender gave me a confused look when I ordered a shot and a beer. The fact that Chance was a regular here and I was not didn't enter my mind. I handed him five dollars and downed the shot quickly. I couldn't remember the last time I drank on this side of the poles. I sat there, nursing my beer for a bit, thinking about the day's meeting, about the redhead, and about my dream that morning. I literally could not remember the last time that I had dreamt anything, and the thought was tearing me apart.

I decided to try and take my mind off the minor mid-life crisis and make some of those edits that John had suggested. I pulled out my notebook and computer and spent the next little bit working on making all the changes that I knew I was eventually going to have to make anyways… no matter how hard I fought them.

Before I knew it, the shot and a beer had turned into a bucket and several shots. I sat there with my work in front of me, the news on the television and the jukebox playing random songs. By the time I was barely able to type legibly, I sent out the email with the last bit of revisions made. I celebrated with the last of the shots that had been sitting on the bar. It was warm, and I don't even know if I tasted what kind of liquor it was. To be honest, I didn't really remember ordering it or if it was even my shot. I chased it with a beer nonchalantly and realized I was empty. Before I had a chance to order another round, a finger tapped on my shoulder

"So, the meeting went that bad, eh?" a calm voice came from the darkness. I turned around and it was Mae. God, she was gorgeous. The second I saw her face, all the thoughts about the meeting, the dream, and everything else faded away.

"No," I said as I stifled a hiccup. "It didn't go as planned." I reached over to my beer, but it was already empty. I signaled to the bartender for another one, but Mae must have already paid my tab to cut me off.

"Becks, let's go home." She kissed me softly on the forehead. "You have been here for hours. Let me get your work together and I will drive you home. We can pick up your bike tomorrow." I must have agreed, because before I knew it, we were in Mae's car heading back home. I remember going up the steps to our place and watching the ceiling spin.

"Get some sleep, my love," were the last words I remember hearing before sleep took me. I wanted to vomit, but I just focused on the love of my life squeezing my hand. With her I could do anything…and tonight… anything was not vomiting.

Chapter 5

The first thing I remember was a hand slapping me across the face. The second thing I remember was a blinding headache. I sat up and rubbed the sleep out of my eyes. I looked around the room, and the sun was already pouring into the room. The blackout curtains were moved out of the way slightly. Upon further inspection, it appeared that clothes were thrown at them, and the way they landed allowed for just a bit of light to penetrate the darkness of my apartment. I pulled the blankets off my legs and realized that there was another pair of them tangled amongst mine. I looked to see who they belonged to, and a flood of memories came rushing back to me.

"You weren't so interested in my legs last night," said an unfamiliar voice. "You were more interested in something else." I looked up and it was the redhead. She was being coy and holding the blanket over her naked form.

"Sorry," I said as I rubbed my head. "So, I guess we had a bit of fun last night." I got out of bed and made my way toward my laundry pile to find a pair of underwear and potentially some pants.

"Fun…that's all I get," she said as she got out of the bed as well and wrapped her hands around my chest. "I think we had a bit more than fun last night." She pulled her hands away, and her nails scratched at my skin. I couldn't help but be turned on. She moved her hands down toward my ass and slapped it.

"Ow!" I yelped, not realizing that she was going to slap me that hard. "That actually hurt a bit." She laughed as she pulled away slightly. I could see her looking at me up and down in the mirror.

"How come I have never seen you around before?" she asked. "Do you go to school here?"

This time it was my turn to laugh. "No, I am a bit too old for that. I took some courses, but it never really stuck." I found something that was reasonably clean and put it on. I could feel her eyes burning a hole in the back of my head. "Take a picture, it will last longer," I said as I turned around.

"Funny. I don't want to break my camera." She walked over to her clothes on the floor and started to put on her bra. I took a second to watch her. God damn it, she was beautiful. How could I not be able to have a relationship with a girl like this. She was smart, funny, and beautiful. She was obviously into me, and I was into her as well. Only one thing was wrong. She wasn't Mae. In fact, I didn't even know this girl's name. I had just met her, and I knew nothing about her. Only flashes of images from the night before.

"Who's staring now?" She laughed as she struggled with her bra. "By the way. My name is Sarah. What is yours?"

I laughed as I walked over to her to shake her hand. "My name is Chance." She looked disappointed.

"Wow, a fake name, huh? Classy." She began to hurry and was obviously leaving in a rush.

"Fake name? Chance is my real name." I looked for my pants from the evening before and grabbed my wallet. I pulled out my ID and showed it to her. The second she read it, her face became a bright shade of red.

"I'm so embarrassed." She said as she tried to cover the red in her face with her hands. "I'm just used to people I connect with blowing me off. I guess that's the problem with sleeping with a guy on the first date." She shimmied into her pants and grabbed her purse. "I guess I am just a bit self-conscious is all."

"Self-conscious about what?" I said, obviously taken aback. "What on earth do you have to be worried about?" The thought of a girl like this being worried about her body bothered me.

She pointed toward her stomach. There were faint signs of stretch marks on her stomach and her legs. "I was a bit heavier when I was younger, and I have these to show for it."

I shook my head and smiled. "I would have never noticed these if you had not shown them to me. You shouldn't be worried about that. You're literally a ten. Relax." I walked over to the kitchen and began to make a pot of coffee. I noticed that I was out of coffee grounds, so I decided to use the grounds from the day before. Or was it a few days. I couldn't remember.

"Would you like a cup?" I asked as she made her way into the front room and got ready to leave.

"Sorry, I have to get going. Class is in about an hour, and I can't show up wearing the same clothes as last night. I would catch hell from my friends." She looked down at her shirt and tried to wipe a stain from one of the straps. It didn't work.

"I totally understand. I guess I will see you around?" I said as I got impatient and poured the three ounces of coffee out of the unfinished coffee pot and took a sip. The coffee was hot and weak.

"Yeah, totally." She said as she walked over to my dry erase board and wrote down some information. It appeared to be her phone number and her name. "Just in case you want to call me again."

I went to finish pouring the rest of my cup of coffee when I realized that Sarah was right next to me. She reached in for a kiss, and I wasn't prepared. I kind of moved away and we did some weird kind of dance. She finally hit her mark and pulled away awkwardly.

"Sorry, you just startled me is all. I didn't want to burn you with the coffee pot." She smiled and accepted my lie for the truth.

"No worries. You will call right?" She pointed toward the number on the board. "You don't have any excuses. Don't be another asshole." She smiled and turned around toward the door. She picked up her purse and smiled as she left. Before the door shut, she poked her head back in and pantomimed a phone next to her ear. She mouthed the words "call me." Before I knew it, she was gone. I could hear her speaking with someone outside after the door closed. It was probably just one of my neighbors. I leaned back on the counter and took a few sips of coffee. Realizing at that moment how hungover I was, I decided to stick my head beneath the sink and drink a ton of water. After a few sips I realized how good the cold water felt and just stuck my head beneath the faucet. I let the cold water cascade down my head for what felt like ten minutes. A tap on my shoulder pulled me from my bliss. It startled me so much I lifted my head and slammed it on the cabinet above the sink.

"Whoa there, big guy," I heard a familiar voice say as I tried to open my eyes through my wet hair that had clung to the front of my face. I rubbed the back of my head with one hand as the other freed my vision.

"Oh, hey there," I said. The words sounded a bit garbled since my face was soaked. "I guess the door was unlocked."

"Yeah, I guess your early morning visitor forgot to lock it when she left." I could hear disappointment on her tongue. "She was nice, I guess."

I finally found the kitchen towel and wiped off my face. Apparently, I needed to clean the towel because I could smell something I hadn't eaten in at least a week. I decided to brush it off and finish drying my face. "Sounds like you're jealous," I said, immediately regretting the words.

"Yeah, jealous of some one-night stand? Nobody can replace me so I'm not worried." Those words cut me much more than she had intended, and I could see by the look on her face she realized it as well. "So anyway. Did you get all of your work done yesterday?"

I smelled the towel again and threw it toward my dirty laundry in the hallway. "Yeah, as a matter of fact I did. I decided to go and celebrate and that's where I met…" It was too early in the morning to remember names, and unfortunately hers was escaping me at the moment.

"Sarah?" Mae asked, walking over to the board. "Oooh, she left you her number and her name. She might know you better than she thinks."

"What the hell is that supposed to mean?" Her words, again, cut me like a knife. She immediately took the defensive.

"Don't even pretend like you have actually dated a girl in the past couple of years. You hang out with them until one of you gets bored. That unfortunately is usually after only date one." She wasn't wrong. I didn't think that I had been with a girl for longer than a few days. Maybe a week at the most. Obviously, it had nothing to do with them…well, at least for the most part. I was in love with Mae, and there was nothing I could do about it. I realized my inner monologue was rambling on and Mae was staring blankly at me. I decided this was not the hill I wanted to die on and gave it to her.

"I guess you're right. I just guess I haven't found the right girl is all." I looked around the countertop for my cup of coffee.

"Looking for this?" Mae said as she took a sip from my coffee mug. The mug was one we stole from the local diner. She handed it back to me.

I went to take a sip and noticed that her lipstick was on the rim. I took my shirt and rubbed it off.

"Wow, germaphobe much?" She laughed as she went to the cabinet and pulled out another mug and poured herself her own cup of coffee. "So, I wanted to ask you a favor." She smiled at me, knowing full well I would do whatever she asked.

"What now?" I said, trying to sound comical. I took another sip of coffee.

"I wanted to introduce you to my new friend. You know. My girlfriend." It caught me off guard as I drank, and I decided to just burn my esophagus rather than spitting the coffee all over her. I took a few moments to collect myself. "Are you ok?" she asked, seeing me struggle.

"Yeah, yeah, I'm fine. Just went down the wrong pipe." I wiped the coffee that had dribbled down my shirt. "You want me to meet her already?"

"Yeah. Actually, that's the second part of the favor." She grinned and looked out toward her car.

"She's waiting in the car, isn't she?" I walked over toward the window and peered out. There was, in fact, someone sitting in the passenger seat of her car. I couldn't make out what she looked like, but I could tell she was blonde. "I guess you leave me no choice. Let me get some clothes on and I'll meet you at the diner. Sound good?" I was furious but didn't want to upset her like I had the day before.

"Awesome! You should bring your bike. Becky loves bikes." Taken off guard again, I decided to just put my coffee in the sink before I hurt myself.

"Becky, as in Rebecca?" The name obviously hit home slightly since it was mine on the other side of the poles.

"Why, do you know her?" Mae said as she grinned. "Probably not. She just moved here from Colorado."

"No reason. Just don't keep her waiting, and I will be right behind you." I paused for a moment, and I could see the look on her face and what it meant. "I guess I can bring my bike." She smiled and came over to hug me. This time, I didn't back away.

"Thank you, thank you, thank you!" she said as she withdrew from her hug and ran out the front door. "See you in a few," I could hear her say as she ran down the steps. She had left the door open. I walked over to the door and reached to close it. My hands were still shaking from hearing

Mae say the name Rebecca. I knew it was just a stupid coincidence, but it caught me off guard just the same. I decided to burn a quick cigarette and calm my nerves prior to going out to breakfast with the love of my life's new girlfriend. I sat there on the railing and lit my cigarette and watched them laugh as they pulled away. What was I going to do? Mae might have poked fun at my dating habits, but she wasn't one to talk. She had done exactly the same thing over the past few years. We had everything we needed in a relationship between the two of us, except sex. Obviously, that wasn't going to happen, so it was just a matter of time before she got bored of a platonic relationship with her oldest straight friend.

"What the fuck is wrong with you," I said to myself as I exhaled the last of my Marlboro. "Just call and say you're not feeling good. Call the redhead. Stop doing this to yourself." I quickly quieted down as I realized I was actually talking to myself out loud. My neighbor poked his head out of the door a few seconds later and gave me a dirty look. Seeing as the cigarette didn't do its job properly, I went to the liquor cabinet to grab something stronger. Mae was in my head. She was right, I did have a problem. I took the bottle and placed it back on the shelf. "Too early for this," I said over and over. "Just get this over with, you idiot." I grabbed the keys to my motorcycle and headed out. Come to think of it, I don't even think I locked the door to my apartment.

I got out to my garage and pulled the door open slowly. The bike was still filthy and had seen better days. Unfortunately, those days were far behind her as I got on the bike and turned the ignition. After a few cranks, she reluctantly started, and I pulled out into the parking lot. The drive to the diner felt like an instant. I don't even remember it; I was too far inside my own head. As soon as my thoughts came to the present, I was there. I could see Mae's car; she had gotten a great parking spot. I, on the other hand, was forced to park about three blocks down in an alley. I parked the bike in what looked like a legal parking spot and made my way toward the diner. I walked past dozens of happy couples, just holding hands being happy and content with each other. It made me sick. On one hand, I had what they had...somewhat. When the poles shifted, I bet other people looked at Mae and myself walking like that. Happy and completely oblivious to what it is like to be lonely and miserable. Unfortunately, I had to live in both worlds, and it was far too present for me. I couldn't escape

55

it. I was married, yet single. I was happy and yet alone. I wondered to myself what I had done in some former life to deserve this. Maybe it was better left unknown.

"Hey, there!" Al said as I walked into the diner. He pointed toward the booth. "Looks like you have a rough morning ahead of you. I'll bring you something special to help." I could see the look of pity he had on his face. Everyone that Mae and I spent copious amounts of time around knew the truth. They knew how I felt. Shit, I bet Mae knew as well. I guess people will do anything to not upset the status quo. I looked around and saw them in our usual spot...our usual spot. My heart beat faster as I walked over toward them. Mae was sitting toward me and quickly stood up to greet me.

"Hey there, handsome!" she said as she quickly wrapped me in a hug. "This is Becky, the girl I have told you so much about." I reached over to shake her hand, and it was like looking in a mirror. My headache and heartbeat reached a crescendo as her hand touched mine. It was me. Well, not me, but me from the other side of the poles. Her hair was a bit different, and she over did her makeup a bit, but it was me. I half expected to wake up from another dream right there, but that unfortunately was not the case. I did my best to keep my composure, but I can't know how well I acted for sure.

"Hey there. My name is Chance. I have heard so much about you." My voice cracked as if I was going through puberty. I cleared it to try and mask the reason why...I don't think she bought it.

"All good things, I hope?" she asked as her hands withdrew from mine. She motioned for us to sit, and she and Mae sat down. Unable to sit beside either one of them at the moment, I looked toward a table with an open chair.

"Can I use this?" I asked the lone man sitting with his paper. He nodded that I could, and I pulled it to the open side of the booth. Mae had slid over to the inside of the booth to make room, but she quickly took the hint and moved back toward the center of the booth. Mae said something, but I was unable to hear her over the sound of my head pounding.

"Hey Chance, are you ok?" she asked as she whacked my arm.

"Yeah, yeah. I just need to have another cup of coffee. It's a bit early for me." Just as if his ears were burning, Al came walking over with an extra-large mug of coffee for me. He smiled and pointed toward the mug. I thanked him as he turned and walked away. I took a quick sip of coffee to further give evidence to my lie from just a second earlier. To my surprise, the cup of coffee was about ninety percent alcohol. Not a stranger to the burn of whiskey, I was able to keep my composure and not let Mae or Becky on to the situation. I took another gulp and looked over to Al and gave him a nod.

"Best cup of coffee in town!" I raised the mug, and he smiled in return.

"So, now that you have had your coffee, what do you think?" The look on Mae's face was of utter annoyance. She knew that I had not been paying attention, the thing she didn't know was the reason.

"Sorry, I didn't catch what you said. Was too distracted by the need for coffee." I took another swig of coffee, this time prepared for what was truly in the mug.

"I was going to see if you and your new friend wanted to double date sometime?" She didn't raise her hands to do it, but I could see her air quoting with her hands as she said friend. "I think it would be great for you to get out of the apartment and get your head off your work for once. You seem to never leave that place anymore."

She wasn't wrong. In the past few months, the only times I had left the apartment had been to hang out with Mae, deliver a commission, or restock on my vices. I tried to play it cool, but inside I completely panicked. "Yeah…um…that sounds great. When did you want to do that? I'll have to call…" I couldn't remember her name. It took me a second, but it finally came to me. "Sarah…" I finally said. I pretended to burn myself on my coffee while trying to think of her name. I don't think they bought it.

"Well, I guess that settles it. What do you think, Becks?" she reached over the table and grabbed Becky's perfectly manicured hands. I had a flashback to all the times that Mae and I had done the same thing in the exact same spot, on the other side of the poles though. Her touching someone like she touched me, even here on this side, was truly unsettling, and I had to take another swig of my drink in order to divert my attention long enough to not vomit.

"Well, if Chance and Sarah are down, so am I. I just don't want to intrude." She looked over at Al and motioned to him that we were ready to order. Al came over quickly with his pad and paper, ready to take our order.

The rest of the morning went as normally as it usually did, apart from me sitting there with Mae, myself, and myself. We small talked mostly about work and pop culture. I wasn't aware of most of the things they were talking about. I guess I really had been out of it for a while.

"So, I have to get going in a few," Becky said as she checked her phone and realized it was nearly noon. "I have to prepare for work tomorrow. I had the day off and my place is a mess. Do you mind driving Mae home?" She looked at me right in the eyes, making sure she had my attention. I did my best to match her gaze without spiraling.

"Yeah, I can give her a ride. No problem." I stood up as she did and moved my chair so she could exit the booth. "I will see you tomorrow?" She reached out and shook my hand. Her hands were soft, softer than mine were. I wish I could have asked her what kind of lotion she used.

"Yes, he will," Mae interrupted. "He wouldn't miss it for the world." She walked around me and went to give Becky a hug and a kiss. Realizing how awkward this was, I decided to motion that I was going to the bathroom. I waved at Becky, and she returned the favor. I retreated into the bathroom. I walked over to the urinal and took a piss, breaking the seal for the first time that day. I knew I would regret drinking those few "coffees" in a bit, but right then, I was pretty buzzed. I finished and walked over to the sink and placed my hands down on the wet countertop.

"What the hell is wrong with you, dude? You must hate yourself something awful to say yes to this shit." I turned on the faucet and splashed some cold water in my face. The cold helped my migraine a bit. I went over to the towel dispenser and struggled with it for a few moments. Once I had finally dried my face, I slapped it a few times and got ready to go back outside.

"Good luck man." I heard from the bathroom stall. It was Al, I could recognize his voice.

"Oh, I didn't realize there was someone else in here. Thanks again for the coffee." I saw a quick thumbs up from beneath the stall, and I left it at that. Embarrassed, I headed back to my booth where Mae was sipping her coffee and reading something on her phone.

"I took a sip of your coffee. There is barely any coffee in here." She took the mug and took another sip. "Did you bring this or did Al hook you up?" She placed the mug down on the table. Her lipstick adorned the mug with the prettiest shade of pink.

"Al saw that I was hanging a bit and decided to help me out with a little hair of the dog," I said as I reached over to grab the mug. I purposely spun the mug so that Mae's lipstick sat where my lips would touch. I don't think she noticed, and if she did, she never made any mention of it.

"Well, I guess everyone is enabling you now." She sat back and crossed her arms. "You do know you have to ride me back to my place on your bike, right?"

I shrugged. "I will be fine. I have had enough food this morning to kill a small person. I'll order another cup of actual coffee and we can leave in twenty. Sound good?" My answer seemed to distract her from the actual issue, and she just sighed and rolled her eyes.

"I trust you. Don't make me regret that." She waved over toward Al, and he came over after a few moments. "Can he have an *actual* cup of coffee?" She gave him a judgmental glare and he looked over at me.

"Way to ruin our fun." He laughed. "Sorry, Mae, he looked like he needed it. Meeting your new friend and all." He smiled again and went to the counter to get my cup of coffee.

"What was that supposed to mean?" She said, looking back toward me. "Why should you be nervous about meeting Becky?" At that moment, I wondered whether it was willful ignorance or if she was truly that naïve. I hadn't had enough to drink to answer her truthfully, so I decided to lie.

"I don't know. I guess he knows that if you and Becky keep dating, you and I won't hang out as much. He must know that scares me a bit." I tried not to smile since it was a pretty good lie off the cuff. It appeared to be effective since she just shook her head and looked sad.

"That won't happen. Even if she and I get married, things won't change between us. You're my best friend...you have been for literally my entire life." She reached over and grabbed my hands like she had grabbed Becky's before. More flashbacks of times she had touched me that way flashed in my mind. In all those memories, I was Becky...I wasn't Chance. The hair on my arms stood at attention.

"I want you to be happy. I guess I am a bit jealous is all." I rubbed her hands affectionately, forgetting where I was. I immediately stopped. If she noticed how uncomfortable I was withdrawing my hands, she made no mention.

59

"I know you do. That means a lot. Hey, maybe this…I mean Sarah might be the one?"

I hoped she could not differentiate between real and fake enthusiasm. "I can't wait for our double date." The words just poured out and there was no stopping them. She smiled from ear to ear.

"Good! Well, it's about time you took me home.

"No problem," I said as I took a look at the check. Mae quickly grabbed it out of my hands.

"Let me take care of this one." She bit her lip slightly as she took a look at the total. She dug through her wallet and pulled out one of her many credit cards and walked over toward Al and paid. I could see the look of surprise on his face that she, and not I, paid the bill. He took her card just the same, and a few moments later, she was beckoning me to leave.

We walked to where my bike was parked, and Mae gave me the usual business regarding how dirty my bike was and that it needed to be cleaned. She usually said these things as she noticed how much dust rubbed off onto her when she mounted it. I said the usual same excuses I always did and started up the bike. I revved her a few times and made my way the short distance to the apartment where Mae lived. Driving to Mae's from downtown always was a pain. She lived in a loft above one of the shops at the end of the strip, and it took forever to drive down main street. Every block had a stop sign, traffic light or a crosswalk, and I was mad at myself for not telling her to walk. She made such a big deal about me drinking, you could tell how much she didn't want to walk because she didn't think of that solution herself. I pulled off into a metered spot and put my leg down. She quickly jumped off the bike and went around to the front.

"Are you sure you're good? You can come up and have some real coffee if you would like." The truth was, I hated going up to Mae's place on this side of the poles. All the things from the other side were there, and it just was too weird being around that stuff.

"Yeah, I am fine. I might actually go home and call…" her name escaped me again.

"Sarah…her name is Sarah." The look on Mae's face was more disappointment than anything else. She and I had danced this dance before.

"Sorry, still a bit early in the morning for names. Like I was saying, maybe I'll call Sarah and see if she wants to hang out." I went to pull out my phone only to realize that her number was not in there. It was neatly written on my board at home. I put the phone away smoothly. "I'll wait until I am home, that way we can talk longer if she wants to." Mae gave me a weird look.

"Well, you two have fun. You deserve it, Chance. Give yourself one." She smiled at the pun and blew me a kiss. "See you later?"

"Yeah, see you later." I returned as I put the bike in gear and pulled out onto the street. I made my way home up North Avenue and saw the students walking down the street. It felt like a hundred years since I had walked those sidewalks during the day. Unfortunately, if I walked those sidewalks now, it was because I was too drunk to drive. Not because I was heading to class. Not anymore, at least. I pulled the bike into my already open garage and grabbed a small towel from the corner. I wiped the dust off the bike as best as I could and took a few steps back. I pulled out my cell phone and took a few pictures of it, trying my best to not catch my reflection in any of the surfaces. I don't really know why I did this. Maybe as a way to show Mae that I did wipe it off from time to time. I was also thinking about selling it. I had been for a while. The only reason I still had it was because Mae loved it so much. The insurance was very expensive.

I closed the door of the garage and made my way into my apartment. Once inside, I shut the door behind me. Realizing it was already a bit past noon, I decided to grab a beer from the fridge and have a cigarette. I went over to my table where my cigarettes were left from the day before and saw Sarah's number on the board. I decided to put it into my phone quickly since I'd actually had a decent time the night before.

"Maybe she and I could have some fun," I thought to myself as I put her name in the phone. *Sarah Redhead* was officially in, and I shot her a quick message.

"Hey there. Just saying Hi. This is Chance btw." I said the words out loud as I typed to ensure they made sense. I took another swig of the beer and went out to the porch for a smoke. I put the phone in my pocket and waited for a response. After two cigarettes and another four beers, I got a call from Sarah.

"Just getting out of class for the day. Did you want to watch a movie or something? I am a bit too tired to go out." You could tell by her voice that she was not lying. We had drunk a lot of alcohol the night before and stayed up pretty late, well…you know.

"Yeah, I have a couple of movies we could watch." My heart fluttered slightly. Was I excited for her to come over, or was I just horny from my breakfast slash lunch with Mae? "I'll leave the door open."

"Sounds good, see you in about ten. Bye." She hung up and I stowed the phone. I walked outside to light another cigarette and took a look at the horizon.

"Today is dragging on," I said to myself as I exhaled the first lung full of smoke. Once the day's activities were drawing to an end, all I wanted to do was cross over to the other side. I was an addict. It was all I could wait for and all I wanted to do. It was one of the major sources of my unhappiness as well as my depression. "Maybe this girl can change that," I said to myself as I took another drag. "Maybe she is different." I took a swig of beer and realized it was empty. I sat there to finish my cigarette when Sarah pulled up to the parking lot. She drove a beater, some small mid-engine two-seater from the late eighties. It was tiny, and so was she. The similarity was amusing.

She waved as she grabbed her purse and what looked like a small bag out of the passenger seat. "Hello there," she said as she approached the steps to my deck. "It doesn't look like you have changed either." She came over to me and gave me a quick kiss. This time I didn't flinch.

"Yeah, I had a brunch thing with an old friend." Being purposely vague I hoped she wouldn't press any further.

"Well, I was able to stop by my house this morning to grab a change of clothes." She held up the bag. "I also grabbed some pajamas, hoping you would call and want to hang out."

"Well, looks like I better change," I said as I opened the door and let her in. She went straight to my bathroom and shut the door. I went into my room and quickly put on some sweatpants and a clean shirt. Mine was covered in dust from the bike. I sat down on the futon and turned on the television. A few moments later, Sarah appeared in a pair of very short shorts, and a baggy T-shirt. She jumped into the spot next to me and looked at the screen.

"That one!" she said, pointing toward a horror flick I hadn't seen yet. "It's so cheesy it's awesome."

"Let's do it," I said as I clicked the play button on the remote. I leaned back against my wall, and she placed her head on my lap. Her hand gently rubbing my thigh as we sat and watched the opening credits. After a few minutes the rubbing stopped, and I could hear her snoring.

"Wow, you were really tired," I said as I rubbed her head. I reached over to one of the glasses of warm whiskey on my nightstand from one of the past few nights and took a sip. I closed my eyes and said a quick prayer. "Please, help me change," I said, taking another sip. I looked down at Sarah and suddenly felt guilty about Mae. Not from this pole, but from the other side. I had slept with a ton of women since her and I got married. I had never felt anything for them. This was the deepest feeling I'd had in a long time for someone other than Mae. I laughed to myself, since that morning I'd struggled to remember her name.

"Sleep well," I said as I continued rubbing her head. She was right, the movie was cheesy as hell. I watched the entire thing, just stroking her hair as she slept.

Chapter 6

"Ugh" was the only word that I could muster as my eyes opened. Even before the light hit them, my head pounded as if it had been inside a ringing bell. I reached over, and Mae was not there. I could hear her tinkering in the kitchen.

"There she is," she said quietly as she turned the corner into our bedroom. "How are you feeling, Becks?" She came and sat down next to me. I grabbed her by her shirt and pulled her in close. I hadn't realized she had two cups of coffee in her hands. "Whoa!" she said as she struggled to keep them from spilling. She managed not to spill any, and she placed them on the nightstand. Once the risk of third-degree burns was gone, I pulled her in again. I kissed her like I had not seen her for months. I pulled away.

"I love you so much. Do you know that?" I said, tears starting to form.

"Whoa, I didn't take care of you that much. You just had a rough day. No reason for the waterworks." She rubbed the tears off the side of my face with her hand. I looked into her eyes and saw that they were a bit moist as well.

"I just love you." I placed my head on her chest and squeezed her tight. "I never want to let you go." She smiled as I released her. She reached over to her coffee and blew on it before taking a sip.

"Just have a cup of coffee. I think you're still drunk from last night." She stuck her tongue out at me and made a goofy little face.

"Yeah, well, pass it over here," I said as I sat up. I realized I was only wearing underwear and a shirt. "Did you get me naked?" I joked as she handed me the coffee. I took a cue from her and blew before taking a sip.

"Yeah, well, you were a bit out of control last night. You kept apologizing

64

for that redhead from your dream. You also mentioned something about coffee with Albert. What's that about?"

"Oh shit!" I said, the yelling made my head hurt, and I grabbed it in agony. "I am supposed to grab a coffee with him to discuss a project he wants to work on." I reached over to my phone and saw that it was nearly nine in the morning.

"Hey there. Calm down," Mae said, rubbing my head as I cycled through my phone to see when I had penciled it in. "Just say you're going to be a bit late. It's not like he is your boss or anything."

I took a sip of my coffee and relaxed a bit. She was right, Albert was a colleague and not someone who could really get me in trouble. I decided to text him that I would be a bit late, and that I hoped he didn't mind. I sent the message and felt an instant sigh of relief. "Thanks." I took another sip of coffee. It still needed a few more minutes until it was cool enough to drink.

"Oh, I know I am right," Mae said as she took a large gulp. She poured creamer in her coffee, and that helped cool it down. She always finished her cup long before I was able to start mine. Sometimes she would put an ice cube in the mug, but that just ruined it. I preferred patience. "So, what is this date about?" She laughed as she realized her mug was empty and left the bed to go refill it. As she got up, she grazed her nails across my legs down to my feet. Once she reached them, she scratched on the bottom side of my foot, tickling me in the worst way possible. I nearly spilled my coffee.

"Are you trying to kill me?" I said as I shook my leg free of the torture. "You're going to give me burn marks, and a stained bed sheet."

"Stop changing the subject," I could hear her say from the other room. I could hear the sound of coffee filling up her mug. "So, this secret Albert project. What is it about?" She rounded the corner back into our room and tried to tickle my foot again. I was too quick for her this time.

"I actually have no clue. I know that he has been wanting to work on something together for a while now. I suspect he believes that working on something together will keep John off both of our asses." I tested the coffee once more with my lip. It had cooled down enough to be tolerable.

"So, he hates John as much as you do?" She sat down on the bed next to me and put her coffee down on the nightstand. "I still have no clue what that man has against you." She motioned for me to scoot over so she could lean up against the wall. She positioned her pillow so that she was comfortable and grabbed her coffee to take a sip.

"I don't know. I just don't think he likes my writing. Either that, or he loves my writing and wishes he could write like I can. Either way, he's a dick and even a week without him breathing down my neck sounds amazing." Mae scoffed and shook her head. She stared down into the mug of coffee and then down at the nightstand.

"Well, you better get going," she said as she handed me my phone. "Apparently Albert is already at the coffee shop." I took the phone and unlocked it. She must have seen the message appear on the lock screen, since she was correct. He had just gotten there and said he would wait.

"Fuck!" I said as I struggled to climb over Mae to get dressed. "I hate being late to shit." I put the coffee down on the nightstand, and it spilled all over my alarm clock. "Great, just great," I said in a panic. I went over to the closet to find a bra.

"Chill out. I'll clean it up after you leave. Just get dressed and don't hurt yourself." She got out of bed and walked into the kitchen. Probably to grab some stuff to clean up the coffee mess.

"Ugh," I said to myself as I tried to find something to wear. "I hate business casual." I pushed several dresses and skirts aside to find something that wasn't too provocative. You see, I had always suspected that Albert had a thing for me, and well…he knew that I was married but didn't know that I was gay. I tried to keep personal stuff like that to myself. It was hard enough being a woman at the office, and I didn't need any extra attention.

"Wear that!" Mae said as she walked into the room and reached into the closet. "This is hot!"

"Hot is not the look I am going for. You know what I think about Albert." I took the outfit that she suggested and held it up. It was one of my better ones.

"Yeah, I love the fact that others think my wife is amazing. Makes me appreciate you a bit more." She laughed as she took the hanger from my hands and held it up to me. She made a few provocative faces and smiled.

"Funny, you're so funny," I said as I finally reached the boring outfits.

"A pantsuit, really? Who are you, Hillary Clinton?" she shook her head and sat back down on the bed. She pretended to be holding a box of popcorn at the movie theater. It reminded me of the Michael Jackson meme...anyway.

"Well yeah. I have had issues with this in the past, and I don't want to exacerbate the situation. Albert is a work friend and a really nice guy. I don't want to be an asshole." She continued to watch me as I got dressed. I may have wiggled into the outfit a bit more than I needed to in order to get her going. When I finally got the pants on, I looked at her and smiled.

"Wow, you suck," she stated as she stood up and walked over to me provocatively. She placed her hands on my waste.

"I don't have time for that," I said as she continued to wrap her hands around me. "Come on, Mae," I said as she motioned me toward the bed.

"Wow, such a prude." She made a sad face and pulled away. "You're such a tease."

I walked over and kissed her on the cheek as I buttoned up my top. "I'm sorry baby, I just really need this meeting to go well. Having John off my back for a bit will really help me out. He has just been such a dick lately."

"Don't worry," she said, pulling away. "You can make anyone love you." She winked as she went into the living room. I followed her and went to go look for my bag. When I turned the corner, she already had my bag and keys dangling from her hands.

"Thank you," I said as I took them and took a deep breath. I shook my head a few times and made sure I had everything I needed.

"Don't worry, Becks. Everything is fine. Go wow him like you wow everyone." She kissed me on the cheek and smacked me on my ass.

"Wow, so aggressive," I said as I smiled at her and made my way for the door. Before I closed the door behind me, I blew her a kiss, and she caught it in her hand and rubbed it all over her face. I chuckled to myself as the door locked behind me.

I made my way to my car and threw my bag in the back quickly. I started up the old stick shift and was on my way. As I navigated the roads to the coffee shop downtown, I tried my best to contain myself. I was still severely hungover from the night before and was struggling to pay attention to the road. I would have been screwed if I would have taken my bike, but thankfully the manual transmission helped me focus. I had been driving a manual since as far back as I could remember. Before I knew it, I was pulling into the parking lot of the coffee shop. It was just a few doors down from where I...well yeah, I guess you could say that. Where I had bought the dress for Mae a few days earlier. It was just a small shop that only served coffee, tea, and some small baked goods. It wasn't my favorite place, but Albert talked about it all the time, so I figured it was as good a place as any. I parked and walked inside. Albert was waiting for me.

"Hello Rebecca," he said as he saw me enter the coffee shop. I didn't see him until he stood up and waved. I walked over to the table and put my stuff down.

"Hey Albert, I'm so sorry about not being here on time. I had a...let's say I had a rough day." Albert laughed.

"I went home and had a few beers after that meeting as well." He smiled. It was the first genuine thing I think I had ever heard him say.

"What do you mean?" I said as I tried to collect myself. I sat down and waved toward the barista to come and take my order.

"Your bike is still across the street in the parking lot...the parking lot of the only good bar in town.

He must have been able to see my face turn bright red because he immediately backed off.

"I...I...you caught me," I managed to say as the barista finally came to the table to take my order.

"Vente coffee black," Albert said with literally no hesitation. "Also a blueberry scone." The barista shook her head in affirmation and was gone.

"Wow," I said, flabbergasted.

"Did you want something else?" he said, his face looked as if he was afraid that he offended me.

"No, that's literally what I was going to order. How did you know?"

"Well, you only drink your coffee black, and the only time that you eat blueberries is in scones. This place just happens to have the best of both in town." He paused for a second as if contemplating if he should speak again. He chose to ignore his inner thoughts. "I'm sorry for ordering for you. I don't want to seem like that kind of misogynistic guy. I just feel like I knew what you were going to order."

I laughed it off since he was one hundred percent spot on. "Yeah, maybe wait for me to order next time. In all honesty, that's exactly what

I would have ordered if you would have given me the time." My smile seemed to put him at ease, and he relaxed in his seat a bit.

"Thanks. As you can see, I don't really get out much." He laughed for a second until he realized the truth to what he said. He seemed somewhat sad afterwards.

"Oh, don't worry. Other than hanging out with Mae and writing, I get out just as much as you do." I only realized what I had said once the words left my lips.

"Mae? Who's that?" he said as he took a sip of his coffee. He was distracted for a second by one of the employees of the coffee shop waving at him. He must have come here frequently. After he regained his focus, he asked again.

"Sorry about that. You mentioned Mae? Is that a friend of yours?"

I struggled to find a word that would fit into my mouth. On a better day, I would have been a bit more agile with my word choices. Today, struggling with my hangover and a pounding headache, all I could say was.

"Uh, she's, my wife." I saw the words leave my mouth, and there was nothing that I could do to put them back in. They were out there, sitting at the table next to Albert's cell phone and his cold cup of coffee. There was an awkward pause for a few seconds until the silence was finally broken by the barista bringing my coffee and scone.

"Here you go," she said as she placed the items down on the table. "The coffee is hot, so I suggest giving it a minute." She smiled and walked away. I took the coffee, and without even thinking, took a swig. It was not nearly as hot as the coffee had been that morning, but it was hot, nonetheless. After my swig, I took a bite of the scone in an attempt to cool my mouth down. It helped a little.

"Your wife?" he asked again, acting as though he might not have heard me. "I don't care that you're...well...you know." Society has turned adjectives to describe people like me into some sort of slur.

"Gay?" I said, suddenly taking the defensive. A million emotions were flooding me all at once. My face must have been the darkest shade of red. I stumbled a few more words out. "Yes, I am gay. What about it?" I didn't realize it at the time, but I was talking a bit louder than I normally would have. I took another sip of my coffee and put it down on the table.

I couldn't take my hand off the cup, and after a few moments, they started to burn.

"Rebecca, are you ok?" Albert asked. He must have asked a few times before, I just didn't notice. There was genuine concern in his voice.

"I'm sorry, I don't know why I just blurted that out. That was actually none of your business. I'm just having a rough week, and the other night...I mean last night was just a mess. I just..." Albert interrupted, he reached over the table and put his hand on my arm.

"Rebecca, why are you apologizing?" He patted my hand and withdrew to take another sip of coffee. "I don't care about any of that. I was just trying to make small talk. I didn't mean to pry." He put his head into his hands and sighed. "I always do this. I just...fuck things up."

My anger began to fade as I realized that he was not trying to pry any information out. I was just hungover and spiraling a bit because of everything going on. "It's ok...I just...I don't know." Another series of words decided to release themselves from my inner psyche. I couldn't help it. It was as if I was no longer in control of myself. "I thought you kind of had a thing for me, and since you were the only person in the office that I got along with, I didn't want you or anyone else to know about Mae." The look he gave me was something straight out of a movie. His look of embarrassment slowly turned into that of disappointment as he shook his head.

"You thought I was into you? Like wanted to date you?" A smile slowly came across his face. "Rebecca, everyone knows that you're gay." Now it was my turn to be embarrassed.

"What do you mean?" I said, noticing my face getting flushed. Hopefully he didn't notice since it was already red from being so angry earlier. "Everyone knows?"

"It wasn't that hard to figure out. You're always talking to your friend, and sometimes you say you love her before hanging up. I guess I just didn't know her name. Also, you can tell by the look on your face when you're talking to her. That's no ordinary friend." He reached over and put his hand on my hand as if to comfort me. I pulled my hand away.

"So, you just all let me think I was keeping up some ruse. I feel like such a fucking idiot." I stood up and grabbed my bag. "I just...I appreciate you telling me...but I need to go." I took out my wallet from my bag and threw down a few dollars on the table for the coffee and scone and walked out of the shop. The slurry of information that was swimming around my head was just unbearable. I needed to get away. I needed to leave all of this behind. *My bike!* I thought as I stumbled around my bag for my key. I pulled it out and started walking toward the bar I had been at the night before.

"Rebecca, wait!" Albert said as he left the coffee shop. By the time he decided to come after me, I was already a few blocks away. I turned back, and I could see him looking down the street to look for me. I ducked into a nearby alley and waited a few minutes. I took out my phone to text Mae. Once it was out, I decided against it and continued my way toward the bar.

"How could they just pretend they didn't know?" I said to myself as I walked down the street. I was so fucking pissed off I didn't care who saw me talking to myself. In my panic, I suddenly replayed every conversation I had ever had with my Albert in my head. I thought I was being smooth and keeping my homosexuality a secret, but apparently, people just pitied me and pretended to let me get away with my little secret. Fuck, that pissed me off. After a few minutes of walking, I had to actually check the street signs to see where I was. I was so angry I couldn't even pay attention to where I was. I regained my bearings and continued toward my bike. After about fifteen more minutes of looking like a maniac talking to myself, I reached my motorcycle. I laughed to myself quietly as I saw how terribly I had parked. "Wow, someone was in a mood yesterday," I said to myself as I wiped a few leaves off the gas tank and straddled the bike. I inserted the key into the ignition as I had a flashback of riding the bike with Mae... only I wasn't myself. Well, not this myself. I could feel her nails pressing into my legs and her arms around my waist. I looked back to see her hair blowing in the wind as I snapped back to reality.

My hand released the key suddenly as I came back to this reality. "Fuck," I said to myself as I sat up and ran my hands through my hair. After a few moments, I shook it off and started the bike. I put the bike in neutral and backed it up into the lot. It was early, and the lot was basically empty, so it was simple. Once I was clear of the curb, I put the bike in gear, and I was off. I turned onto the main road and decided to take the turn that took the long way to my apartment.

After a few minutes, I finally hit the main country road that ran parallel to the main street and decided to put on my sunglasses and open her up. As the bike accelerated, something took over me. I couldn't stop and continued to keep my hand on the throttle. I just let the wind blow my hair into a rat's nest as I leaned back and screamed at the top of my lungs. If anybody had seen what I was doing, they would have thought I was losing my mind. Maybe I was. I hadn't felt this out of control on this side of the poles since I was young and I had gotten my first period. For that time on the bike, I didn't care whether I lived or died, and even if I died…would that really be the end? Who cares, it didn't matter one bit. I was enjoying myself, and that was all that mattered. The only problem was that I forgot about the stop sign up ahead, and I didn't notice it until it was too late. The honking of an oncoming car's horn woke me from my daze.

I screamed as I pressed on the brakes just in time to slow my advance. The semi-truck that had the right of way had seen that I was not planning on stopping at my stop sign. His horn probably saved my life. As I stopped suddenly, my rear tire began to swerve. I was able to keep control of the bike, just barely. As I passed the intersection, I looked down at my speedometer and noticed that I was going over a hundred miles an hour. I took my hands off the handlebars and coasted for a few moments. As I leaned back and steered with my legs, I put my hands on my head and let out a sigh of relief. "What the hell are you doing?" I said to myself as I put my hands back on the handlebars and decided to head back home. I slowed the bike down and made a quick U-turn and headed back to the road that led back to our apartment. After about five minutes, I reached my parking lot and didn't even park my bike in the garage. I pulled right up next to Mae's car and parked. Before I knew it, I ran into the apartment. All I could think about was Mae and how much I needed to see her. While trying to pull out my keys from my bag, Mae opened the door.

"Hey Becks," she said as I nearly tackled her. "Whoa whoa, what's wrong?" She managed to push me away and look into my eyes. "Why are you crying?" Up until she mentioned it, I didn't even realize that I was.

"I'm sorry. I am just a mess right now," I said in between the sobs. I was holding her close. The smell of her shampoo was comforting, and her hair was damp. She must have just taken a shower.

"What happened with Albert?" she asked as she put her hand on my cheek and wiped off a few tears. "You weren't gone that long."

I looked into her eyes and felt like such a fucking idiot. This life I had been living just felt like such a lie at that moment in time. Everything from my job to my nonexistent friends and family all the way down to my marriage with Mae. It was like the feeling that I'd had something stuck in my teeth my entire life, and everybody pitied me too much to tell me. All my lies I told to keep my business my own. Every time I made an excuse, they all knew I was lying. All I wanted to do was bury my head in a pillow, or the bottom of a bottle.

"Hey there, Becks?" she said, the words breaking my inner monologue. "Netflix and chill?" I nodded as she motioned for me to take a shower. "Get in your comfy pajamas," she said when I eventually got the hint and started walking toward the bathroom. Even though I had put on some semi-clean clothes that morning, I could still smell the stench of last night's drinks all over me. The smell of the cigarettes that I had borrowed from someone still lingered on my hands. I turned the shower on and went to the mirror, only the person staring back at me wasn't me. The five o'clock shadow and unkempt hair of my other self was smiling back at me. I raised my hand to touch my face and so did he. I looked at my reflection in amazement as he just started laughing, then suddenly he punched the mirror, and it shattered all over the bathroom. I flew back and hit the wall, slipping on the bathroom mat that sat outside the shower. I hit the wall, and then the floor hard. A few seconds passed as I sat in the fetal position on the floor.

"Becky, are you ok?" Mae said as she ran into the bathroom only to find her wife crying on the floor.

"I broke the mirror, I'm so sorry Mae. I don't know what happened." Her hand was on my shoulder. She looked up at the mirror.

"The mirror isn't broken. What are you talking about." When her hand touched my skin, I could feel my hair standing on end. "Here, let me get you in the shower. You just had a bad day and still must be hungover pretty bad." She took my hand and helped me up. I looked over at the mirror, and it was unbroken. The reflection staring back at me was my own, even though this girl staring back at me didn't look like herself. It was, in fact, the correct reflection.

"Watch your step," Mae said as she helped me into the shower. "Do you need me to clean you as well?" she said, partially joking, but I knew she would if I asked her to.

"No. I'm fine now, sorry," I said as I stepped into the water. I had turned it on way too hot, but it helped snap me back into reality.

"Stop apologizing, babe." She laughed as she looked at me with a concerned look. "You owe me one, though. Maybe I'll get drunk tonight and make you take care of me tomorrow." She stuck her tongue out at me. I turned over to her and grabbed her by her face and kissed her. This was not just a peck on the lips. This was a kiss that was supposed to show her how much I loved her. It was a deeply passionate kiss that, to be honest, felt like the last time I would kiss her. I felt as if my world was unraveling around me, and I couldn't take it. She pulled away.

"Well, I am definitely taking a shower too," she managed to say through my constant attempts to keep the embrace. She took off her shirt and shimmied out of her pants. In an instant, she was in the shower with me, caressing my body and holding me close to her. We cleaned the stain of the day away, as well as a few other things. That shower melted away all the regret and despair from that afternoon.

The night ended with her and I cuddled up on the couch with a single whiskey-filled mug shared between us as we watched re-runs of *The Office* on Netflix. I took one last sip of the mug and laid my head onto her chest, the events from earlier today still fresh in my mind. I fell asleep to the sound of her heartbeat, and the sound of her breathing.

Chapter 7

I woke up to the sound of something I don't normally hear…cleaning. "Well, good morning," Sarah said as I got up off the couch. "Your futon sucks." She dried her hands on a paper towel and walked over to the garbage can to dispose of it.

"What are you doing?" I laughed as I walked over to her. She greeted me with a kiss. Even though she had morning breath, it was nice.

"You were out cold, so I wanted to do something nice for you. Did you watch that whole movie?"

I rubbed the back of my head. My headache was a bit worse than it normally was. It most likely had something to do with me sleeping sitting up. "Yeah, I was too comfortable to move. You were sleeping so soundly." She walked over to the coffee pot and grabbed one of my yellow mugs.

"Wow, I love these. They are the perfect color of yellow." She said, pouring me a cup. She brought it over to me, but before giving me the mug, she took a sip. She handed me the mug and her lipstick remained on the rim. It almost made me smile. I walked back over to the futon and sat back down.

"So, plans for the day?" I said as I blew on the mug to cool the coffee. It was very hot. The fact that Sarah had been able to take a sip was surprising.

"Nothing much. I have a class this afternoon, but other than that, I am free. Why? Aren't you sick of me yet?" She poured herself a cup of coffee and came to sit next to me. She snuggled right up beside me and put her head on my chest. "If you are, don't tell me. Now I am too comfortable to move." I kissed her head as she snuggled.

What the fuck is wrong with you? Why are you even leading this girl on?

75

Should you tell her about Mae, or would that scare her off? I felt infinitely guilty at that moment because even though I had done nothing wrong, I would have chosen Mae over Sarah in an instant. If Mae walked right through the door and told me she wanted to be with me, I wouldn't have even hesitated. What did that say about me? I had never had much luck with women in the past. They were either too boring, too exciting, verbally abusive, or anything in between. Let's just be honest…they weren't Mae. Here was someone who genuinely wanted to spend time with me, and I was just thinking about someone else…I was so angry at myself in that moment that I nearly started to cry.

"Are you ok?" Sarah asked as I came back from my inner monologue. "You look angry." I looked down at her face and was saddened infinitely more. I was lucky that I was an amazing liar, because I was able to get myself out of anything.

"I bit my tongue," I said as I pantomimed having a sore in my mouth. "Coffee really aggravated it." She laughed and nearly spilled her coffee.

"Well, be careful next time. I don't like seeing you frown. You look way more attractive when you smile." She took a swig of her coffee and retook her position on my shoulder. A sudden vibration in my pocket brought me back from cloud nine. I reached into my pocket and saw that I had a few missed messages and calls. One from my mother, who I really needed to call one of these days. There were several texts from Mae, as well. She usually sent about ten messages at once and gave little reason for a response until the last one. I waited for the last text to come in before responding…I wish it hadn't.

"Who is that?" Sarah asked, suddenly realizing it was none of her business, and she took a swig of her coffee.

"Just a friend, she wants to know if we wanted to double date tonight?" The conversation at the diner the other day was fresh in my mind. I vaguely remembered her saying we should go on a double date, but I didn't think she was serious. Apparently, this time she was. "She wants to see if you want to go to the bar tonight. She wants to meet you."

"Oh wow. You tell your friends about me." She laughed and turned her head. I could see her ears raise up as she was trying to hide her smile.

"Yeah. Her name is Mae. She saw you leaving the apartment the other morning."

"Wait a second. That girl I passed by. She was coming to your place?" She bit her lip. "Why was she stopping by so early in the morning? Should I be worried about her?" She bit her lip again to show that she was being playful, but I could see the truth in her eyes.

I laughed and tried to play the question off like it was way off base. "She doesn't exactly swing for the same team that you do. If you know what I mean. She wants to double date...her and her new girlfriend."

I could see the slight panic in her eyes slowly disappearing. "Oh, well that doesn't matter to me. I wasn't worried about her. I just haven't heard you mention her, so I didn't know."

"Yeah. I have known her literally as far back as I can remember. She is my oldest and closest friend. I can't wait for you to meet her. You two will definitely hit it off." The last bit of what I said was a lie for sure. Mae and Sarah already seemed totally opposite of each other. I just hoped that in this situation, opposites truly would attract.

"Well, I don't have anything going on tonight...so, I am down if you are? Unless you don't want me to go?" I could see the doubt in her eyes.

I squeezed her tight so she couldn't see the expression on my face. "Of course I want you to meet her." Again, I could see her ears raise up, signaling that she was smiling. She slapped me on the leg and drained the contents of her mug.

"Well, then I need to go to class and wash up. I want to impress your friends." She kissed me and stood up. She went to grab her stuff and came back one final time. "Are you sure you're good with this?" The look of worry returning to her face.

"Yeah." I stood up and embraced her in a hug. "Trust me. We should have a pretty good time."

"Thanks!" she said as she gave me one last kiss. "Text me the details!" A few moments later she was leaving through the door. She went over to my window and breathed some fog onto the glass. She took her finger and drew a heart...and then kissed the center. She smiled, waved, and was gone.

"What the fuck are you doing?" I asked myself. This time out loud. "This is a mistake, this is a mistake." I repeated the words a few more times, getting quieter every time. I pulled out my phone, partially to text Mae that I wasn't feeling good. I needed to find a way out of this. While pondering what to do, I went to the fridge to find a beer. I opened the bottle and chugged it. The second I was finished, I lit a cigarette and went to stand on my porch. As I inhaled and exhaled the smoke, I could feel the phone in my hand vibrating. I knew who it was, and I knew what she wanted. I decided to finish the cigarette, knowing full well that answering this text message was a complete and total mistake. Eventually, I tasted filter and decided it was time to seal my fate. I pulled out my phone and told Mae both Sarah and I were in for tonight. I asked her to text me details and shoved the phone into my pocket. "I need another beer," I said as I walked back inside. I pulled a few bottles out of my fridge and went to go lay down in my bed.

Several hours passed as I watched random shows on Netflix and YouTube. One drink turned into far too many one mores, and before I knew it, it was starting to get dark. The dark room lit up as I received a text. I was terrified to see who it was. It was Sarah.

"Fuck," I said to myself as I saw that the message read that she was on her way. I texted her back that I just got out of the shower and took the last sip of warm beer from the bottle between my legs. I got up and headed toward the shower. I stumbled slightly as I walked through the door and hit my head on the door jamb. "I guess I had a few too many." I laughed to myself as I corrected and walked into the bathroom, my head aching. "Well, you deserve to let loose every once in a while," I said to reassure myself. I turned on the water and didn't even get undressed. I just walked into the shower completely dressed. There was a knock at the door, and I panicked.

"Once second!" I yelled as I could hear the door open. I really need to start locking the door to my apartment. I quickly took off all my clothes and made sure that every inch of me was wet. The water was freezing and most likely did me some good since I'd had too much to drink, and we hadn't even gone to the bar yet.

"I thought you were just getting out of the shower?" I could hear Sarah say from the living room.

"Well, I found some soap that I didn't get out of my hair. I wanted to make sure I didn't embarrass you tonight." I said back...again my ability to come up with solid lies on the spot held up.

"Well you need to hurry up. You told me we had to be at the bar in almost twenty minutes."

She was right. I had napped and watched videos the entire day. While people were working and being productive members of society, I'd learned how to survive a night in subzero temperatures by building a survival shelter out of snow and pine trees. Fuck, I felt useless at that moment.

"I'm done, let me get dressed real quick," I said as I grabbed for a dirty towel on the ground. I wrapped it around myself quickly and headed out into the hallway toward my bedroom.

"Hold it right there hot stuff," Sarah said as she walked over toward me. She put her hands around my waste and pulled back suddenly. "You're literally freezing right now. Are you good?"

"Hot water is having issues. I already called the landlord about it. I didn't want to smell too bad for our date, so I dealt with it." I took the towel off my waist and dried my hair.

"Whoa, whoa!" she said as she covered her eyes. "So much hair. I wasn't ready to see any of that in the light." She took and moved her fingers aside, pretending to peek.

"Ah shut up," I said as I walked into my bedroom to try and find some clean clothes to wear. She followed me into my room.

"Seriously. It looks like you're wearing pants, there is so much hair." She walked over to inspect my rear end and put her hand over her face to hide her laughing.

"Wow. What a nice thing to say to the guy you just started dating." The words just came out.

"Oh. So, we are dating, eh?" She walked over to me and put her arms around me. She could tell I was excited well...because she could see it. "Just get dressed there, sasquatch. We need to get going." She kissed my chest and left the room.

I got dressed, and quickly threw my wallet into my pants pocket. I grabbed my keys as well and heard laughter from the other room.

"Yeah, I think I am going to drive. I can tell you had a few before I came over." She took her keys and swung them around on her newly manicured finger.

"What do you mean?" I said, trying to sound genuine.

"I took that trash out this morning dummy. It's filled with Miller Lite bottles. No judgement, but it looks like you needed a day off." As I pulled the shirt over my head, I could hear her foot tapping. "We are going to be

79

late, and you're going to make your new girlfriend look bad." Her words hit me hard, and I am glad the shirt was covering my face. I wasn't used to hearing labels like that. Especially since I was in love with someone other than the person saying those words. To be honest, it was usually the sign of the end of the relationship. I took a breath and finished dressing myself.

"Yeah, I wouldn't want to do that." I took my keys out of my pocket and threw them on the counter.

"Don't you need those?" she said as she heard them hit the Formica.

"These are all I need," I said as I walked over to the front door and grabbed my cigarettes off the table I had put there for my keys...obviously that worked well, since they were residing about two feet from my kitchen sink.

"Wow. You don't lock your door when you leave?" She looked baffled.

"I don't lock my door when I am home...I don't really have anything of value here. Plus, I have a knack for locking myself out of my apartment. So I just stopped locking the door." I went over to the futon and sat down to put on my socks and shoes.

"Well, from now on, when I stay over you need to lock your door. It gives me the creeps." She laughed and went to the door and opened it. "Let's go, Mr. Dangerous."

I put on my second shoe and pulled the tongue tight. I stood up and checked my pockets for the necessities. Wallet, lighter, smokes and phone. "Ok, let's go," I said as we both walked out the door and headed toward her car. As we walked toward her car, I expected her to unlock it with her key fob. I just kept following her until she stopped besides this mid-engine two-seater from what looked like the eighties.

"Ready for the best ride of your life?" She laughed as she struggled to get the key into the door. "She might be old, but she has heart." "Well, let's just hope she gets us there in one piece without starting on fire." She finally got the door open and sat inside the surprisingly low bucket seats. She reached over to manually open my door, and I followed suit.

"Oh, so you know about Fieros?" She put the keys into the ignition and turned the key. A few moments later, the car came to life...even though it took several attempts.

"No, I have never been in one of these in my life. I'm more of a Chevy guy." I buckled my seat belt as I struggled to make myself comfortable.

"They make cars for people over five foot ten." I smiled at my joke. Sarah didn't.

"Oh, you mentioned fire. I thought you knew about their issues." She pressed down the clutch and put the car in reverse.

"What do you mean their issues?" I said, suddenly alarmed.

"Oh, no, nothing," she said, completely ignoring the questions and pulling out onto the street. She looked over at me and stuck out her tongue. "See, no fire yet."

"Well, we've only just started." I panicked slightly as she accelerated.

The bar that Mae and I frequented was only a few miles away from my apartment. This was done by design, since I usually was not good to drive after one of our nights out. Other than some playful banter back and forth, nothing really was spoken in the car. I could tell that Sarah was nervous to meet my friends. I, on the other hand, was terrified of spending any prolonged period of time with Rebecca. Her very presence called literally half of my life into question, and she just bothered me, I guess. There was nothing that she had done, she was actually quite nice...but she was me. The only thing worse than that was the fact she would be intimate with Mae. If I knew one thing about Mae, it was that she didn't care about people seeing her be herself. She would kiss whoever she wanted or do what she wanted, especially when she was drinking. I feared that my ability to hide my emotions might not be as effective with Sarah with me. I feared that Mae might have actually found someone who would take her away from me for good.

"Whoa, serious face much?" Sarah said as she parked the car. "You ok?" She looked at me, puzzled. She had already been a bit hesitant about coming tonight. I guess I hadn't really done anything to ease her mind, other than tell a few lies.

"Yeah. Maybe I did have too much to drive. Thanks for noticing."

She smiled and put the car in park. "Any time." She reached in to kiss me. This time I didn't panic, and I returned the gesture. The small kiss ended up turning into a bit more, and a few moments later there was knocking on the glass. It was Mae and Rebecca.

"Oh hey, I didn't mean to break up something," she said, pretending to avert her eyes. I quickly pulled away, embarrassed for God only knows what reason. Sarah did her best to recover, and she smiled as she took a deep breath and exited the vehicle.

"Nice wheels!" Rebecca said as we both got out. "I haven't seen one of these in ages." She ran her hand along the side of the vehicle, obviously enthralled by how retro it looked.

"Thanks. Fieros are my absolute favorite. I have owned way more of them than I can count. My father used to restore them for some club he was in." She put the key in the lock and motioned for me to lock the passenger side manually. "Thanks babe," she said with a wink as I clicked the lock.

"Babe? Be careful, Sarah, you might scare him off." Mae didn't realize how true her words were. I know she was just playing around, but it immediately put me on the defensive. I might be a creature of habit, but I have been told I am predictable.

"You're definitely one to talk," I said under my breath...apparently, I was a bit more inebriated than I had originally thought.

"What did you say?" Rebecca shot back. Not in an angry way. Just in the way that a friend would say when they didn't hear you.

"Nothing, I just stubbed my toe on the tire." I said as I pretended to limp a bit. Not my best lie, but it was noisy on the street, and the music from several apartment parties filled the air and drowned out my true words.

"Hurry up!" Mae said as she jumped up and down slightly. "We need to get our seat!" She grabbed Rebecca by the hand and pulled her down the sidewalk.

"Are you ready?" Sarah said as she gestured for my hand. I took it and said a quick prayer in my head for this young girl's heart. I was about to break it, and she had no clue. I obviously had no intention of doing such a thing, but I knew myself and I knew that with Mae in my life, I would never have a true meaningful relationship. She had destroyed so much of my life. She had estranged me from both of my parents, from every other friend that saw how much I cared for her. Every girlfriend that I had that even stood a chance would eventually see that our relationship was toxic, and they would always play second fiddle to her. Sarah would eventually catch on and leave, just like everyone in my life had. Mae was the one thing in my life that made it worthwhile. She was also the person that single-handedly ruined it…I guess that was unfair to say. I ruined my life…for her. A quick tug pulled me back to reality.

"Uh, yeah," I said, thinking back to the last question I was asked.

"Uh, yeah?" She laughed. "Let's go get fucked up, and then go back to my place." The seductive smile she gave me and her biting her painted lips was all anyone could ask for…anyone but me.

We walked down the sidewalk until we finally reached a bar that Mae and I frequented. It was the bar I had just been at the other day…well, on the other side of the poles. It was a cash bar that had good beer, strong liquor, and bad house music. They also served pizza, so it was obviously a pretty popular hangout. Over the past few years, they had adopted a following for the local hockey team, and memorabilia had suddenly started adorning the walls…

Shit, I thought to myself. *Do I really drink at a sports bar?* Truth is, up until this moment I really hadn't noticed. I was usually too focused on Mae and what was going on with her, or what she was wearing, to notice the state of the bar…at least on this side of the poles.

"ID?" the man at the door asked me as we finally reached the building. I reached for my ID when the man finally recognized me. "Ah, you're good, man. I didn't see your face."

"Come here often?" Rebecca said, jokingly.

"Once and while," I said, trying to defend myself.

"Nah man," the bouncer chimed in. "Most days, he is here when I get here. He's a regular." I don't think he realized what he was basically saying to my group. I just laughed and slapped him on the shoulder.

"Funny man." I walked into the doorway, completely forgetting the group. I headed straight to the back corner of the bar where Mae and I usually sat. After a few moments, the rest reached the seat and put their belongings on the bench seat.

"Looks like I am dating a VIP," Sarah said as she took off her sweatshirt and placed it on the back of one of the seats. Everyone laughed again, this time a bit quieter. I think the joke was already starting to lose some of its humor. For that, I was grateful.

"So, what are we having?" Sarah said once we were settled in. "First round is on me!"

"I'll have a whiskey neat!" Rebecca and I said, in perfect unison.

"Jinx!" Mae said jokingly. "Are you two twins, or what? I told you that you two would get along." She went over and kissed Rebecca on the cheek. "I'll go and help Sarah with the drinks." Sarah and Mae both retreated into the crowd, which was slowly trickling into the venue. There was an awkward moment of silence between both Rebecca and me, until she finally broke it.

"So, I think it is really cool that you and Mae have been friends for so long. Most people really don't hang out much when they get older."

I know she was just trying to make conversation, and I appreciated that. I just didn't really know how to interact with her yet, so I must have seemed like an idiot.

"Yeah, I guess," I managed to mumble. "We have known each other forever, and I guess we were each too obnoxious for anyone else, so we figured we might as well keep each other company."

She looked over at me and smiled. "That can't be the only reason. She talks about stuff you two have done all the time. I am actually jealous of that relationship. I hope the two of us can have some cool stories to share like the two of you do." She played with a loose piece of fabric on her shirt. I could tell that what she was saying was the truth. She was extending an olive branch to me. I just didn't know if I wanted the branch at all. This girl was actively trying to take Mae away from me, whether she knew it or not.

"What are you two talking about?" Mae said as she and Sarah came back with their hands filled with our drinks. "We ordered a pizza as well! I hope you guys are hungry."

Sarah handed me my drink and leaned in for a kiss. I returned the favor and took a long hard drink from what she handed me. She had gotten me good whiskey. I hated good whiskey.

"Thank you!" I coughed as I recovered from the drink. Its quality actually hurt more than the rotgut whiskey I was used to. I looked over and Rebecca was just sipping hers. If it burned, she didn't let me know. For what seemed like an eternity, we all just sat there drinking our drinks. The silence was better than anything that would follow. It felt as if we were sitting on powder kegs and not bar chairs. The house music was rather loud, so that might have been the majority of the reason for our silence, but let's be honest. We all knew the reason, or at least I did. Of course, Mae was the one to finally break the silence.

"So, do you guys want to play darts or pool or something?" She motioned over to the game of pool that was just ending. "I have some quarters in my purse." She started rummaging around in her purse, looking for the change.

"I really don't play pool," I said, taking another drink. "Not really my kind of game."

"Oh, come on!" Sarah said, standing up and grabbing my arm. My drink almost spilled, and I was beginning to get irritated. "Please?" She looked at me with puppy dog eyes and bit her lip. "How about I play Mae or Rebecca, and you can just watch me bend over the table?" She grabbed her drink and walked over toward the pool table.

"Ok, I definitely like her," Mae said as she followed suit and prepared to go play a few games of pool.

The very reason that Sarah gave is the very reason that I do not like playing pool. I actually am very good at shooting billiards, but I only ever hung out with Mae. That meant I had to watch her bend and lean all over the table when trying to make a shot, and then jump up and down and want a hug when she actually made a shot. I used to play a ton of pool with her, but I had to stop, so I just told her that I didn't like playing anymore.

"I guess we are playing pool," Rebecca said as she drained the contents of her glass and reluctantly stood up. I could see that she was just as enthusiastic about her girlfriend playing as I was about Sarah wanting to play. She reached for my hand to help me up. "I hate it as well, but look how happy they are. Let's just go and get this over with." I shrugged as I took her hand and she pulled me to my feet.

"You're right. I am being a stick in the mud. I'm sorry, I just am not being myself tonight." I went to go toward the pool table. Rebecca tapped me on the shoulder.

"Do you want to have a cigarette before we do? Mae said that you smoke." She pulled out a pack of cowboy killers out of her purse and then produced a small pink lighter.

"Yeah, I guess we could have one before we go watch them play pool." She smiled slightly and looked around the bar for the smoking exit. I saw her confusion and motioned her toward the back door. We walked past the bathroom and left through a large metal door, and we were alone in an alley. There was a small picnic table against the building with the normal coffee can filled with cigarette butts. I pulled out my half-smashed pack and found one that was still good. I pulled out an old lighter that was a gift from my grandfather. His initials were etched into the side of it. I struck it a few times until the wick caught and lit my cigarette. I could see that Rebecca was struggling with her lighter in the wind, so I reached over to light hers. She took the hint and lifted her hair out of the way so I wouldn't start it on fire. She took a drag of her cigarette. I could see her lipstick on the filter.

"Thanks, this lighter sucks." She took another drag of her cigarette. I did the same.

"Yeah, this thing always works really well in the wind." I handed her my lighter. She took it and manipulated it in her hands.

"This is really cool. It looks old." She handed it back to me, and I placed it in my pocket.

"Yeah. It was a gift from my grandfather before he died. Those were his initials on the side. I will never get rid of it." I took another drag and held the smoke in my lungs.

"So how long have you been in love with Mae?" The question hit me like a sack of bricks. There was no playing it cool. I exhaled instantly and coughed as the sudden rush of smoke back through my esophagus caused a harsh burn. I continued to cough for a few moments as I suddenly regained my composure.

"What do you mean?" I struggled to say. By her body language I could tell she wasn't buying it.

"Chance. It is obvious you're in love with her. Don't worry, I don't think she knows, and obviously you're not my competition. I just don't know why you do this to yourself. I have only known Mae for a short time. She is amazing, and obviously you know that. I just can't understand why you put yourself through this torture." Once she finished her little rant, I could tell that she regretted saying anything.

I must have been white in the face. I couldn't even manage to look her in the face. I just continued to smoke my cigarette, hoping that what was happening was, in fact, made up in my head. After a few minutes of silence, she walked over to me and put her hand on my shoulder. I pulled away, surprised by the affection.

"Chance, it's ok. I'm not upset about it…unless you were trying to do something about your feelings?" It was a question that needed to be asked, and I didn't blame her for it one bit. The pressure in my head was building, and I could feel a few tears running down my face.

"Of course not," I finally managed to say through my head and my heart beating heavier than they ever had. "I just need her in my life, in whatever capacity she will allow me." I sat down on the bench. My hands began to shake to the point that I put out the cigarette in my hand. I reached for the lighter in my pocket and tried to relight my cigarette. After a few attempts, I was successful.

Rebecca sat down beside me and put her hand around my shoulder in an effort to comfort me. I couldn't believe how understanding she was being regarding the entire situation. I felt like a complete fucking dumbass and a fool. How the hell was she so calm and rational? Was she truly that good of a person? I can easily say, on the other side of the poles, I definitely was not. That began to turn my panic into anger. I stood up and shook her arm off me. I paced a few times and finished my cigarette.

"Don't pity me," I said, the words not truly formulating, so they probably just sounded like gibberish. I repeated them again to make sure she understood. "Don't pity me. The last thing I need is anybody else's pity."

Rebecca stood up and walked over toward me in the most non-threatening way possible. "I'm not pitying you, Chance. I just want this thing between Mae and I to work, and I also want to be your friend. This isn't something I want to get in the way of that. I just wanted to let you know that I know. I didn't want to upset you. I'm so sorry." She finished her cigarette, threw it into the can and began to walk inside. She had been kind and comforting, and just like usual, I was an asshole. I called out her name.

"Rebecca, wait," I said as I walked over toward her. "I'm sorry. You don't know me...I can be a bit abrasive. I appreciate you being so rational, but I just am in a really bad place right now. Mae has been my best friend for my entire life and has never given me any reason to believe we would ever be together. I have accepted my role as her friend and nothing more. Just try to understand how much that has fucked my life up."

She interrupted. "That's not her fault, though, you know that right?" Her voice was raised higher than normal. "Your obsession is your problem, not hers." I put my head down and sighed.

"I know that. Also, for the record, I am not obsessed with Mae. I am in love with her, and I always have been. I'm her friend, not some creep. I have never even tried to cross that line…I know she will never feel that way about me, and I have accepted that. Let's just go inside and get back to them. They probably are wondering where we are." Rebecca opened the door to go back into the bar. When the door opened, Sarah was standing there with wide eyes. Those eyes were crying.

"What the fuck did I just hear?" she said softly. "You're in love with Mae?" I tried to walk over toward her.

"Sarah, let me explain. Please?" As I reached for her, she stepped back and bumped into some casino-style game that was mounted on the wall.

"Get away from me," she said as the tears ran down her face. "Just leave me alone." She turned and started walking toward the pool table. As I followed her, Mae was giving us a look of confusion.

"What's going on?" she asked as she put down her pool cue. "Sarah, what's wrong?" Sarah just blew by her and grabbed her purse. She looked over at Mae. "I'm sorry, but I just need to go." She did just that, pushing herself through the crowd. Mae looked over at me in disbelief. "What the fuck did you do to her?" She looked over at Rebecca. "What happened, will someone please tell me what happened!"

Rebecca looked over at me, and then back at Mae. "Sarah heard Chance saying something and it really upset her. Too be honest, I think I am going to get a ride home from Sarah. Chance, do you want to explain to Mae what happened?" They both looked over to me. This was it. This was the moment I always knew was going to come eventually. I just had no clue that it was going to literally happen on our first time out. I looked over at Mae, and my world stopped. Yeah, she was pissed off, but she didn't hate me. It was truly as if time stopped at that moment. I tried to remember everything about this moment. Her hair, her eyes, and her face. Everything came crashing back to reality and all I could hear was…

"Explain what?" Mae said. When I regained my composure Rebecca was already gone and Mae was standing there in front of me. I looked at her in the eyes and said what I had needed to say since we were teenagers.

"I…I…Mae, I am in love with you." The words were out, and they could not be put back. A rush of some kind of calm rushed over me…that was until I saw her face.

"What the actual fuck are you talking about, Chance? You're in love with me? What the hell does that mean?" She stood up straight and ran her hands through her hair and looked as if she was going to hit me.

"Mae, I don't know what to say. I just, I…"

"Shut the hell up, just shut the fuck up!" she interrupted. A few people around us at the bar started to notice the commotion and started talking amongst themselves. The bouncer at the bar began to make his way toward us to stop whatever he thought was going on. I looked over at him and waved him off.

"Don't worry. I'm leaving," I said as I turned around toward the rear exit of the bar. Mae was screaming something that I couldn't make out over the sound of the slot machine on the wall. I slammed my body against the door and was met by the smell of the dirty alleyway. I walked over toward the table and pulled out my pack of cigarettes. I lit one as I started walking toward the main street that would lead me back to my apartment. I heard the door slam open and turned to see who it was. Of course, it was Mae. She looked around the alley until she saw me walking and yelled out to gain my attention.

"You can't just say something like that and just leave. What the fuck is wrong with you, man?" She was trying her best to walk in her shoes. I hadn't noticed whether she was wearing sneakers or heels. That wasn't something I normally noticed on this side of the poles. "Chance, just stop!"

"Mae, I don't know what you want me to say," I said as I turned around. The second I did, she embraced me in a hug.

"Chance, you're my best friend. I'm sorry I got angry, but how could you tell me that after all this time? Are you expecting…" I interrupted.

"No, Mae, no," I said as I continued the embrace. "I just needed to finally tell you how I feel. You have never given me a hint that we could ever be together. I just…I just…can't get over you. I don't think I ever will, and it is literally starting to ruin my life." The words I chose were not the correct ones.

"Ruin your life?" she said as she pulled away. "I ruined your fucking life?" She started hitting me over and over, tears swelling in her eyes. "Ruined your life, how fucking dare you say that. You're my best friend. That's the worst thing anyone has ever said to me." She continued hitting me and this time was sobbing uncontrollably. I tried to catch her hands as she began to fatigue. I finally was able to catch her hands and pulled her in. She was exhausted and was just sobbing uncontrollably. She eventually stopped resisting my grip and wrapped her hands around me once more… it was short lived. "No!" she yelled as she pulled away. "Fuck you, I'm done. I can't even fucking stand to look at you right now. Go the fuck home. I have to go see Rebecca."

She wiped her tears on her arm. The makeup on her face was running and was a mess. I reached over to touch her shoulder and she pulled away as if I was a leper. "Mae, don't…" She stopped me.

"Don't what. Lie to your best friend for thirty years? Try to undermine her first real relationship in her life? Sit in the shadows and wait for what, me to get drunk and sleep with you?" Her words were calculated. They were meant to hurt me. It was her retaliation for what I had said moments earlier. "Go home." She turned around and started walking back to the bar. "Don't fucking follow me." I watched her as she walked back to the bar. For all I knew, it was possibly the last time I would ever see her. If it was, could I blame her? I said a few choice words to myself as I started to walk down the alley. I was obviously not dressed appropriately for how chilly it actually was. I folded my arms and continued walking toward my apartment.

The streets were packed, and once I got out of the alley, it was a fight to make my way down the sidewalk. I normally didn't walk around the town at this time of night. I was either at home drinking…or nestled somewhere else drinking. Walking amongst all those happy fucking people was not really my scene. I tasted filter on my cigarette and tried to light another one, but in the hustle and bustle it was too difficult. I finally was able to get the lighter to catch and brought it toward the cigarette in my mouth.

"Hey, watch where you're walking," some fucking potato said to me after he hip checked me nearly into the street. I turned and took a drag.

"How about you fucking watch where you're going, prick," I said as I regained my bearings. Suddenly, a large man, about two inches taller than me, turned to face me from the crowd. His girlfriend was holding onto his arm trying to stop him from confronting me.

"Look at this old man," he said as he walked up to about three feet away from me. People passing us in the street parted like water against a rock, trying to avoid what they thought was an inevitable and unnecessary street fight. "Come on, you think you can take me? Just move out of my way next time, and maybe I won't knock your fucking ass down." At that point in time, two more fucking oafs walked out of the crowd coming to back up their friend. I did some simple math and decided getting the shit kicked out of me that night wasn't really in my best interest, and I decided to walk away. I hadn't had enough to drink to give me the courage to do that. I decided to fix that.

"Fuck you," I said as I turned and took a drag. "Just look where you're going next time." I exhaled as he screamed profanities and some other insults my way. For the most part, they were all spot on. I was a loser on all fronts...I just needed to get to the other side of the poles. That was all I cared about. The walk back to my apartment was about thirty minutes, and I couldn't wait that long to be drunk...I needed to make a quick stop.

"Hey, there," the man behind the counter said as I walked into my normal liquor store and went directly toward the discount whiskey and grabbed a fifth. "I don't normally see you this late." He laughed as he walked over to the register.

"Yeah, it's been a bit of a different evening," I said as I walked over and pulled a twenty from my wallet. "This should cover it." I walked away as he reached for my change. By the time I hit the door, the bottle was open.

"What about your change?" he said, holding up a dollar and some change.

"Keep it. Have a good night," I said as I held up the bottle. "I'm going to." I left the building and stood in the doorway, taking another swig from the bottle. I could feel it warming my entire body from my core to my extremities. The feeling instantly made me feel better knowing that soon I wouldn't fucking care about this life anymore. I would be back where I belonged. Back with Mae...I took another long pull, and I started the long walk home.

Chapter 8

The light from the living room window burned my eyes as I opened them. The dust from the old curtains that Mae refused to get rid of lit up in the beams as they danced around the carpet. I reached down and grabbed the blanket and pulled it around myself and reached my hand up to see if Mae was still there. I think I poked her in the eye.

"What the hell, Becks?" she said as she grabbed my hand and kissed it. She reached down and tried to poke me in the eye in response.

"Ow, I did it on accident. Are you trying to blind me?" I grabbed her hands and we wrestled for a bit. I turned around and got on top of her and held her down to tickle her.

"Becks, what the fuck! Stop it!" she yelled in between bouts of laughter. Flashbacks from the evening before hit me like a hammer. I could see her screaming at me in the bar. I could see the tears running down her face, mixed with foundation and emotion. "Seriously Becky, I'm going to piss myself!" I continued the onslaught for a few more seconds and then let go. I shook my head a few times to get the previous images out of my mind. I could see her sitting there playfully, and it brought me back to the present. She pretended to try and hit me, but I caught her arms mid swing. I pinned them down over her head against the couch and leaned in for a kiss. I pressed my lips against hers and took it all in. How could it be that I was so miserable just a few hours ago, and now I was the happiest woman alive.

"I love you," I said to her over and over again. "I love you, I love you, I love you." Part of me wanted to hear her say it, part of me needed to hear her say it.

"I love you too Rebecca." As she clearly grew tired of my sappy romantic attitude, to lighten the mood, she slapped me on my butt. "Damn, my wife is hot." She laughed as she pushed me off her and shimmied her way off the couch. She was wearing my old volleyball shorts, and she wore them infinitely better than I ever did. Something about the way her panties snuck out of the bottoms sometimes when she got up from sitting down. I only ever wore them with spanks.

"Well, at least we agree on something." I laughed as I tried to be as sexy as her getting up. I hit my shin on the coffee table struggling to get free from the blanket and let out a few expletives.

"Klutz!" She sneered as she walked over to make some coffee. "What do you have to do today?" she asked as she reached into the cupboard for our can of coffee. "Can we do something? Maybe go see a movie?"

I thought about it for a minute. "Let's go to the park. We used to go all the time, why did we stop?" I limped over to the window and opened the curtains.

"How does it look outside?" Mae said as she pressed the button to start brewing a pot of coffee. "Let me check outside." She walked over to the door, opened it, and walked outside, accidentally slamming it as she left.

"Wow, way to slam the door. The damn thing is going to come off the hinges." I walked over to the cupboard to grab a few coffee mugs. A few moments later, Mae walked in with a big smile on her face. A sudden vision of her walking in hit me like a hammer. She was drunk and crying. She walked over to me and put her arms around me and kissed me deeply. I reached my hands over and ran them through her hair. I could literally taste the alcohol on her lips. I looked at my hands and there weren't mine… they were his.

"Becks, are you good?" she asked as she walked over to me. I took a few steps back and eventually ended up backing into the countertop.

"Sorry, the sun was in my eyes. How was the weather?" I pretended to block the literally nonexistent sun from my eyes, and she seemed to buy it.

"Weird." She laughed as she noticed there was no sun that deep in the kitchen. "Well, the weather looks nice. We might need a sweater for a bit, but other than that, we can definitely go for a walk." She ran into her room to get her things ready. I followed suit and went with her. As I walked in the door, she was taking off her pajamas in order to start picking out her clothes. She retreated into the closet for a few moments and popped her head back out with a yellow sun dress. "I'm finally going to be able to wear this?" she said, smiling with a childish glee.

"I remember that one. That rummage sale a few towns over, right?" I walked over and touched the fabric.

"Yeah. There really hasn't been a nice day to wear it since then." She hugged the dress and put it over her head. "Do you mind zipping me up?" She turned around and moved her hair out of the way.

As I zipped up the dress, I slowly kissed the skin on her back and her neck. I could see her get goosebumps as her hair began to stand on end. Once the zipper had made it all the way to the top, I kissed her neck on last time and embraced her in a hug, placing my hands across her waist and my head on her shoulder. We stood there for a moment, spooning and rocking back and forth. I breathed in the moment the best I could and took a long hard breath of her hair. A vision struck me like lightning.

She and I were lying in bed, covered in sweat. My hands were rubbing across her body. She looked back at me, I could tell she had been crying since her makeup was all over the place. She looked back at me seductively, albeit a bit intoxicated, and grabbed the hair on the back of my head and forcibly pulled it toward hers and shoved our faces together in a rather messy but sensual kiss. "Is this what you wanted?" she said, almost out of spite.

"Rebecca, is this the one you wanted?" Mae said, holding up an aquamarine dress that I have literally had.

"Uh, yeah," I said, gaining a bit of composure. "I'm sorry, I was just mesmerized by how good you look in that dress." I didn't think she believed me on that one.

"We can just stay home and hang out. I know you have had a rough couple of days." She put the dress down on the back of my desk chair and came over to give me a hug. I grabbed the dress quicker than she could embrace me.

"No, let's go have a nice walk in the park." I spun around and took the shirt off over my head and threw it on the ground. I put the dress on. It was a bit snugger than I remembered, but it eventually went down and I walked over to the mirror on the closet door to took a look. This was definitely one of my favorite dresses, but it just didn't look right. I looked over at Mae and she smiled.

"Looks like the last few days have taken their toll on you." She walked over to me and helped me zip up the neck of the dress. She wrapped her arms around me and put her head on my shoulder. "Just more of you to love, I guess."

"Wow, that's an awful thing to say to your wife. You're too mean." I turned around and kissed her quickly. "That's the last one you get for a while. We are fighting."

"Fuck you!" she joked. The vision hit like a train. We were back at the bar, but it was raining inside the building. We were the only two people there, and it was a downpour.

"Fuck you!" she said again as she stood there in the rain. "Why the fuck would you let me do this?" she repeated herself over and over. I tried walking toward her, but I just couldn't move fast enough to get to her…it was as if I was on one of those belts at the airport. I just couldn't get to her.

"Why the fuck would you let me do this?" she said again. I snapped back to reality.

"I'm sorry, what did I let you do?" I looked up at myself in the mirror, and my face was as white as a ghost. The blood slowly started to return, and my normal color returned.

"You don't remember last night? You told me to respond to my mom's text messages." She brought her phone over to me. She must have checked it while I was spaced out. "I responded to her text, and now her and my dad are coming out here and want to meet up for some reason." The panic in her face was pretty apparent. Her and her parents really hadn't spoken much since she came out. Come to think of it, my mother and I didn't really talk much anymore.

"Well, when are they going to get here? Maybe they can just meet us at the park. You know, a public place." I walked over and took her hand. "Don't worry. Everything will be alright. Maybe they just want to see you and say hi."

"Yeah. I highly doubt that, Becks. We only really exchange pleasantries and pictures of her cat. We haven't really spoken about anything substantial in…in forever." She looked as if she was trying to figure out that last time they had really spoken.

"It was senior prom," I said, remembering the day very vividly. Her parents knew we were close and knew that we were going to the dance together. They just didn't know we were going…together. They were under the assumption that we were each going solo and just wanted to hang out. When I showed up to her house with a corsage, we told her parents that she was gay together. It was as if she was someone completely different. They were never really religious or conservative about those kinds of things. Mae and I thought it was going to be a great and happy occasion. Her mother really showed us that we were dead wrong. Her father initially wasn't upset; actually, he looked rather relieved that she had finally told them. I guess he didn't want to disrupt the marriage and eventually towed the line with her mother in order to keep the ship from rocking too much. After getting her head bit off and a ton of finger wagging, we left for prom and Mae moved into my place for a few weeks until school ended. After that, we got a place together, and that was that. As for my mother, she was pretty accepting when I came out. She just moved far away to be closer to her work, and I didn't talk to her as much as I should. On the other side of the poles, I had zero relationship with my family, but that was another story.

"Oh wow. Yeah," Mae said awkwardly. She remembered the day just as well as I did. She just didn't like letting me know that it bothered her as much as it did.

"Yeah, that was a long time ago," I said as I finished looking at myself in the mirror. My hair was a mess, but it was windy out. I figured it would get messed up anyway.

"Well, are you ready to go?" Mae asked. "You're so slow." I looked over, and in the few moments we were talking, she was one hundred percent ready to go. Makeup, shoes, and matching purse. The works.

"Wow, I guess you're always waiting on me," I said, smiling. I went and grabbed my purse and we were off. She held my hand as we walked down the sidewalk toward our car. It was something small, but it made my entire body tingle with happiness.

On the way to the park, we stopped by one of our favorite sandwich shops in town. They had this bread that had oats and stuff inside of it and the crust tasted slightly of honey. Mae always got some foamy caramel monstrosity, while I always got a plain hot green tea. Yeah, it was simple, but it was what I liked. We grabbed the sandwiches and a couple bags of potato chips and put them in Mae's bag. Our usual walk through the park revolved around the lake and a small bike path that surrounded it. The path broke out several times and had small walkways through the forest where the trees formed what almost felt like a tunnel. The sound of wildlife and the wind whistling through the trees was always a welcome feeling. I used to go there and write years ago but got tired of idiots from the college coming there and ruining it. The world was going to hell, but not today.

"We're here!" Mae shouted with glee as we pulled into the small parking lot meant for the park. They must have been mowing the grass somewhere because a large truck and trailer were taking up the majority of the spaces. When we exited the car, my suspicions were also confirmed by the smell of freshly cut grass.

"I love that smell," I said as I reached into the back seat for my bag. I shut and locked the door, and Mae came running around the car to give me a hug.

"Let's go!" she said, jumping up and down impatiently. We were still hugging, so it was terribly awkward.

"Ok, let's go," I said, trying to pry her off of me. "You need to let go of me first." She finally released her death grip, and we started walking toward the main path.

The path around the lake was just as serene as I remember it from years earlier. There was no wind at all, so the lake itself looked like a large piece of glass. The only thing that disrupted it was the occasional jumping fish or landing duck. There were a few people who must have brought their paddleboats, since they were quietly paddling on the other side of the lake.

"That looks cool!" Mae pointed toward the couple. "We should do that sometime." She grabbed my arm and held it tighter. We continued to walk and decided to take the first forest path we saw. The first few minutes, it was far too quiet, and I could tell Mae was disappointed. She always was such a fan of the wildlife and the symphony of sound that transpired during our walks. Unfortunately, something had happened in recent years, but the forest was void of life, or so it seemed. Once in a while, we would see something skitter into the grass. Most likely a chipmunk or squirrel, but unfortunately, the birds weren't singing today. I spent the majority of the walk wondering why.

"Let's go back to the lake," I finally said, knowing that the silence in the forest was likely making Mae somewhat sad. This was one of the reasons we stopped going there years earlier. Not necessarily because of the asshole students or the lack of wildlife, but the disappointment Mae felt when the time she had been looking for didn't go quiet as planned. She took things like this hard, and there was really nothing I could do about it.

"Yeah, let's eat those sandwiches. The shop smelled so good I can't wait." I nodded in agreement, and we took a detour that took us back toward the lake. Once we made our way through the clearing, we made our way toward our usual bench. Fortunately for us, it was empty. As we approached the bench, I heard Mae's text message notification, and her heart immediately sank.

"You know, you don't have to answer it if you don't want to." I put my bag down on the bench and sat down. Mae just stood there holding her phone in her hands. I motioned for her to come join me on the bench. She looked over and smiled and took my advice.

"I just don't want to ruin today. It's been such a nice morning so far. Her meeting us here and saying whatever she is going to say is just going to make things worse." She placed the phone on her lap and put her head on my shoulder and sighed. "What do you think she wants?"

I pondered the question for a few moments and eventually could not come to any conclusion that made sense. I shrugged my shoulders and kissed her head. "I don't know Mae. She could want anything. I think the best thing to do is just answer the text and let her know where we are. Whatever she has to say, we can face it together." She looked up at me and smiled.

"You're right." She pulled out the phone and read the text. "She's here and she wants to know where I am." She began typing her response.

"Let her know where we are." I said, exaggerating the word "we." She looked up at me and grinned.

"Don't worry. I already let her know that you and I were here together. If she has a problem with that, then she can leave. I want to spend a nice day with my wife, and there is nothing she can do to ruin that."

I smiled and pulled her in tight, kissing her on the head yet again. A few moments later, I could hear the sound of her text sending.

"Well, it's done. Let's see what she has to say." She put her phone in her pocket and laid down on my lap. She put her legs up on the armrest of the bench and closed her eyes. The sun was to our backs, so her face was nicely shaded. I put my hand into hers and did the same. I closed my eyes and breathed in the afternoon air deep. Rarely did I get moments like these, even on this side of the poles. Here, I was usually moving and working and trying to do my best to provide for Mae and myself. On the other side, my life was just chaos. This was a small glimmer of peace and tranquility in an otherwise hectic world. We sat down on that bench listening to the water and the wind, to the sounds of nature. Dogs barking and the patter of runners passing by. I was nearly asleep when I heard a woman clear her throat. It had been years since I had seen or spoken to her, but I knew exactly who it was.

Without even opening my eyes I greeted her. "Hello Steph," I said, trying my best to sound unhappy by her presence, but also nice enough not to start the conversation on a bad note.

"Hello, Rebecca, you know how I hate being called Steph. Can you please refer to me as Stephanie." I opened my eyes and there she was. The years had not been very kind to her, but you could see the resemblance to Mae. Thankfully, she got most of her kinder features from her father.

"I was so happy to hear that you were going to be joining us on this little talk." If she was truly happy about my presence, you could never have told. Her face held on to just a hint of disgust as she said the words. Her smile was only slightly apparent through the disdain. The words woke Mae as she sat up and rubbed her eyes.

"Hello. Mother," she said, taking a page from my book. I wondered at that point if she really had been sleeping, or if she was just playing possum. "It's nice to see you." Again, she said it so genuinely I could not tell if it was fact or fiction.

"It's great to see you too, Margaret. You're looking very pretty in that dress. It's nice to see you in something other than short skirts or jeans." Obviously, she had been paying attention to her daughter's social media accounts. Mae had a tendency to wear clothes that her mother wouldn't approve of. She joked about it all the time when shopping.

"Mom, please don't call me Margaret. Everyone calls me Mae. We have been over this a thousand times." She stood up and went in to give her mother a hug. The two embraced in what looked like someone attempting to hug a cactus. After a few odd pats on the back, they separated.

"Would you care to take a walk and have a quick chat?" her mother said. She looked over at me with a sideways glance. "Alone, if possible."

I could see Mae tense up as she was going to try and defend my honor. I decided to step in.

"Actually, I have some work emails to catch up on. Feel free to leave me here." Her mother gave me a look which was the closest thing to gratitude I had ever received from her. She looked back at Mae and nodded.

"See, your wife…" she stuttered at the word. She coughed and tried again. "Your wife doesn't have an issue with it. Let's just try and get this over with." She made a gesture showing Mae which way she was intending to walk.

"Thanks, mother. What every daughter wants to hear when having a talk with their mother. Let's get this over with." Her tone was a bit annoyed, but still respectful…she was trying to keep the peace.

"You know what I meant," her mother said quickly in response. "I just want to get what I have to say out." Mae nodded in agreement, and the two went on their way. As they walked away, I could see her mother begin to speak, and Mae's arms were firmly crossed as she walked. Obviously on the defensive. As they faded from view around a wooded bend of the path, I could see Mae drop her arms. I guess whatever her mother was saying was at least nice enough to have Mae drop her guard. I decided to do as I said and pull out my phone to check my email. It was the first time that I had done so since my last interaction with Albert. I was expecting a bunch of texts and emails, but when I opened my phone, I just had a single email from him. It read simply:

Rebecca.

I am so terribly sorry about yesterday. I didn't mean to make you upset. I was only trying to make you more comfortable around myself and others. I thought about how our conversation must have made you feel. I am so sorry to be the cause of that. I know you're under a lot of pressure right now, and I don't want to be the cause of adding to that stress. Please take care.

Albert.

I was thrown back by how nice he was in the email. He was a super nice guy, I just expected him to be angrier about the way I reacted. In the light of day, what he'd said wasn't that bad. He was just trying to reach out to me and let me know that he accepted me for who I am. I had treated him so terribly, and now I just felt sadness. I sat on the bench nearly in tears for about fifteen minutes until I saw what looked like Mae and her mother coming around the other side of the lake. They were still pretty far out, so I had time to pull out a small mirror and fix my makeup that had started to run while reading Albert's email. By the time I was able to collect myself, they were just within earshot. I could hear them talking, not yelling. As they approached, I could tell that Mae wasn't crying and didn't look upset.

"Hey Becky," Mae said as she walked up to take my hand, gesturing for me to get up off the bench. "My Mom has something to say to you."

I stood up and walked over to her. You could tell that she was uncomfortable but trying to be civil. It was surprising to see her somewhat vulnerable. Usually, she was just yelling with a scowl on her face. She finally met my gaze and just said it.

"Rebecca. I am sorry for treating you so badly all these years." She took a pause as she took a deep breath. Once she collected herself, she spoke again. "I just didn't understand yours and Mae's...situation. I can see that you are truly happy together, and that's all I want for my only daughter. Happiness and someone to share her life with. Obviously, you're that person, and I have treated you so horribly. Can you forgive me?" She was beginning to sweat and reached out her arms to embrace me in a hug. I returned the gesture and we hugged. It must have been infinitely more awkward looking than her and Mae had looked earlier. After the long embrace, she pulled away and fixed herself. Once the apology was completed, she slowly retreated back to her normal persona.

"Well, I must be going now. I need to speak with your father." She gave Mae a quick hug and a peck on the cheek and waved as she left. A few moments later, she was gone. Mae came over and sat down on the bench. She slapped it a few times, signaling for me to do the same.

"What was that whole thing about?" I asked. "It apparently went well." Mae just sat there for a minute with a bewildered look in her eyes.

"Hand me my sandwich and I'll tell you while we eat." I reached into the purse and grabbed each of our sandwiches, and as promised, she told me what her and her mother had talked about. Apparently over the past year or so, her mother and father had grown apart for several reasons. For starters, his relationship with his daughter had suffered greatly since she had come out as gay. Her father had tried to keep the peace for years, but he found it easier to sneak behind his wife's back in order to talk to his only daughter. Well apparently, he had grown tired of the charade and decided to give Mae's mom an ultimatum. Either make up with Mae and me, or he was going to leave her. If you knew anything about Mae's mom, you would know that she was a very old-fashioned individual and could never imagine getting divorced. Mainly because she looked down her nose at anyone who had gotten divorced, amongst other things. This must have been the main reason she decided to come and make peace with her daughter and her wife…to save her own marriage. By the time the story was complete, we were just finishing our sandwiches and bag of chips.

"Wow. Just wow," I said as I wiped the crumbs off my dress. "So that just happened, like during your walk?"

"Yeah, I couldn't believe it either." She followed suit with the crumbs and wiped some mustard off her face with her hand. She looked down at her dress and decided to just wipe it on the interior of the dress.

"Really?" I laughed as I caught her wiping her hands on her outfit. "What a pig." She laughed and almost spit out the few remaining pieces of sandwich from her mouth. She put her hand over her mouth to shield me from potential debris.

"Shut it," she said while finally swallowing the last bite. "Let's just get out of here. I think I want to go and get a drink with you for a change. After that talk, I could definitely use a drink." She started packing up our impromptu picnic and stood up quickly. "Well, what are you waiting for?" she reached out her hand to help me up, and I took it.

I looked up, only it wasn't Mae, it was Sarah. She was holding her hand out for me to get out of the car. We were parked on the street. I looked around and Mae and Rebecca were waiting. She pulled me up, and I gasped.

"Becks, what's wrong?" Mae asked. I was back in the present, sitting back on the bench. "Why did you recoil like that?" I looked at my hand,

and the hairs were standing straight up and my heart was racing like a freight train.

"I'm sorry. I guess I could use a drink as well." I stood up on my own. Mae was still holding her hand out to help me up. She slapped it down to her side and shrugged. "We should drive to your car so you can pick it up and drive it home. Then we can take the bus to the bar." That way we don't have to worry about driving.

"Yeah, that sounds like a good idea. I don't feel like getting a DUI after such an amazing afternoon." She smiled and took my hand. We walked the short walk back to the parking lot of the park. During the walk, Mae was talking about something that I unfortunately was paying very little attention to. I would throw in a few words of affirmation to try and pretend that I was listening to her. She was used to short responses from me, so my brevity didn't upset her in the slightest. After a few minutes, we arrived at my car. I blew a kiss towards Mae as I jumped out and started up my old stick shift. After another quick drive, Mae and I were walking into our apartment. I went over to the refrigerator and checked the bus schedule and saw that we had about thirty minutes until the next one would make its stop. Mae saw me waiting and went to the liquor cabinet to pull out a bottle of whiskey she had gotten me for my birthday the year before... the bottle was nearly half full. Noticing that, I smiled for more than one reason. Normally, I was a half glass empty kind of girl, but I didn't think of it like that today. Also, the fact that a bottle like that would last longer than a day or so showed what side of the poles I was on and how different my life was on either side.

Mae poured a few glasses, and we sat out on the stoop and drank while waiting for the bus. We didn't really talk about anything specific, just what was going on in the news and the weather. Simple things like that. After our glasses were empty, we decided to grab our things and head toward the bus stop. Thankfully, it was only a few minutes away

"One second," I said as I grabbed Mae's glass and ran back into the apartment to put them into the sink. When I turned around, Mae was standing in the doorway. "Did you forget something?" I asked as she walked toward me slowly. She pressed her body up against mine and pushed me into the countertop. She grabbed the whiskey and took a long drink from the neck of the bottle. She smiled and kissed me deeper than she had in a while. The burning sensation from the whiskey and the taste of her lipstick made a sweet medley of flavor in my mouth. I couldn't get enough of it. I grabbed at her back, pulling the zipper of her dress down and touching the small of her back. Once the zipper was down, I pulled the straps of the dress down around her shoulders and kissed the freckles up into the nape of her neck. Mae took this opportunity to take another swig from the bottle and handed it to me. I took a hint and did the same. We continued to kiss until both she and I were only in our bras an underwear.

"What is going on?" I asked as she kissed up and down my body, finally giving up and taking my hand into the bedroom.

"I can't wait until we come home from the bar. I want you now." She tugged hard and drew me into the bedroom. I managed to grab the bottle and take one final swig before she nearly pulled my arm off.

"I'm coming." I said as we entered the bedroom and she laid down on the bed. She seductively moved backwards and laughed.

"Already? We haven't even started." She bit her lip and curled her perfectly pedicured toes on our sheets. She patted the bed with her hands and then slowly started to slide the covers over her legs. Ruining a perfectly good view.

"Shut up," I said as I took a final swig of the bottle and put it down on the nightstand. "Slide over, you're taking up the whole bed." She slid over and lifted the covers so I could join her. Her legs were warm, but her feet were freezing. She turned toward me and wrapped her legs in mine, I could feel her legs slide smoothly against mine. The rest of what happened that night is better left unsaid. A good girl doesn't kiss and tell. Like most nights on this side of the poles, we fell asleep, drenched in sweat and holding each other tightly. The last thing I remembered was looking into her eyes right before falling asleep.

"I love you, Mae," I said as I pulled the hair from her eyes and put it behind her ear. She snuggled quietly against me, and I fell asleep. Her hand soundly in mine.

Chapter 9

My head pounded as my eyes opened. It appeared that I hadn't been asleep too long since there was still a cigarette smoldering in the ashtray next to my bed. I picked it up and took a drag from it. The taste was off, so I pulled it from my mouth and noticed the lipstick on it. Mae's lipstick. The events from last night rushed into my head, similar to how they hit me across the poles.

Mae was standing there in my doorway. She had been crying and her makeup was completely messed up. She was soaking wet, it must have started to rain. Her words echoed as if said by someone else.

"You're in love with me?" she said, standing in my doorway. "Chance, I love you. What do you want from me?" She was shivering. I stumbled over to get her a blanket to keep her warm. She threw it on the ground. She bit her lip, walked up to me, and kissed me. The taste of cigarettes and vodka were apparent. I pulled away.

"Mae, you're drunk. We are drunk. What about Rebecca?" It was weird hearing myself say the name to her. She looked down at my pants and grabbed me. To my knowledge, she had never done this before to another man, so her movements were clunky and forced.

"Do you really want to know about her, or do you want me tonight?" I knew what I wanted to say. I wanted to run away and hide. I wanted to tell her that this was a mistake and that she should sleep in my bed and I would sleep on the couch. I knew what I wanted to say…what I should have said. I said none of those things. I wish I could blame it entirely on the alcohol, but to be honest, I know exactly why I said what I said next.

"I've wanted you every night for my entire life, Mae." I put my head down and sighed. The feeling of her soft fingers lifting my chin caught me by surprise.

"Then have me," she said, taking my hand. She closed and locked my front door and pulled me into the bedroom. My vision kept skipping between the events of both evenings from both poles. She led me into my bedroom and started taking off her wet clothes. Once she was done, she laid down in my bed. Visions of her from both poles were overlapping as if put together by a highschooler in a film class. She pulled me into the bed and took off my clothes. We both lay there naked for a few moments to take a deep breath. It was as if both of us wanted to stop what was about to happen, but neither of us did. Neither of us knew how to start the act. It was either that or we were too afraid. I pulled her close to me and…

I snapped back to reality. I was up in my bed and panicked.

"What the fuck did you do, Chance?" I said as I got up. I looked around the room and Mae was nowhere to be found. I got up, completely forgetting that I was naked and walked around the apartment. Mae's purse and shoes were still there. I walked around the corner to check the bathroom and heard the crying before I saw her. The door was cracked open, and she was in the bathtub crying. She heard the door creak and looked my way.

"Just come in. Who the fuck cares anymore." It was a tone I had never heard from her. It was sound of regret…and that regret was me. I walked into the bathroom and the light hit me hard. My eyes, struggling to adjust, could barely make out her silhouette in the bath.

"Mae, I don't know…"

She interrupted. "You don't know what? We had sex, Chance…us… me and you. What the fuck don't you know?" She shook her head and put her face into her palms. "What the fuck do we do now? What the hell do I tell Rebecca? Oh my god, I fucked everything up." She began sobbing quietly. I reached over to put my hand on her shoulder like I had done thousands of times, and she recoiled as if my hand was as hot as a branding iron. She just sat there crying, and there was nothing I could do to make her stop. I just sat there thinking to myself. How could I do this to her? How could I do this to Sarah? Everything that I touched just turned to shit, and now I had taken the one thing that kept me sane and completely destroyed it. The feelings were welling up inside of me like nothing I had ever felt before, until…I leaned over to the toilet and vomited the contents of the night's debauchery. The torrent of bile was relentless as it poured out of me like a hose with air in the lines. As the acid burned my mouth and the compressions from my stomach burned, all I could think of was how much I deserved this. If I had an aneurism from the strain of this, everyone that I knew would be better off. Mae could forget that I ever existed and go back to being happy with Rebecca. Sarah would most likely never know until she ran into Mae on the street. Yeah, she might be saddened a bit. Hopefully her anger at me would help fuel the grieving process into nothing more than a bad night of drinking.

"Jesus," Mae said as she poked her head from the shower. "How much did you fucking drink?" Even though I could hear her through the spasms, there was no way that I could answer. I could feel her eyes burning holes into the back of my skull as the fit slowly started to taper off. Once what seemed like the last spell hit, I leaned back and reached for some toilet paper to wipe my mouth. Once I was finished, I threw the toilet paper in the general direction of the toilet. I don't know if it even landed in the bowl.

"I don't know. I remember leaving the bar and stopping at the liquor store. By the time I got home, the bottle was nearly empty…hell, it could have actually been empty." I leaned back over to the toilet bowl, thinking another round of vomiting was coming. I burped and the feeling subsided. I leaned back against the wall.

"So, how much of last night do you actually remember?" I guess the sound of me sick helped her become a bit more serious than a few minutes earlier. She motioned over to me to hand her a towel, and I did just as she asked. I reached over and was able to grab the corner of the towel and pull it off the rack. After a few missed attempts, I was able to free it from the towel rack and it came whipping into my face. I grabbed it and handed it over to Mae without looking. The only way I knew she had grasped it was the sound of her hand leaving the water, and the small bit that her finger grazed mine as it grabbed the towel. I turned away as she stood up and wrapped the towel around her chest. She didn't even ask me to move as she stepped over me and walked out of the bathroom and into my bedroom. I waited a few minutes and finally felt good enough to stand up. I placed my hands on the toilet seat and pushed myself up. Once I was up, I managed to get myself in front of the mirror. I looked like shit. The reflection staring back at me didn't look like anyone that I knew. The large black bags under my eyes and the facial hair that was slightly longer on one side from a bad shave job the other day. My hair was slowly starting to show the signs of aging as I could see grey in both my hairline as well as my eyebrows and stubble. I reached under the sink and washed the blood off my hands… wait, blood? I inspected my knuckles on my right hand and most of the skin was scraped off as if I had hit a brick or something. I shrugged it off, knowing that I would find a hole in a wall later that day and know the cause of the injury. I finished washing my hands and rinsing my mouth and limped into the bedroom. Mae was sitting in a pair of my pajamas on the corner of my bed. She was able to wash off the running makeup in the shower but not her demeanor.

"I'm sorry. I threw up on my clothes this morning when I woke up." She pointed toward the small pile of clothes next to my laundry basket. "I'll clean it up." Though I could hear the inflection in her voice, her face showed nothing but the look of complete and utter devastation. I tried to lighten the mood.

"Don't worry. Most girls I'm with end up vomiting one way or another." I was trying to be self-deprecating, but apparently it was too soon.

"Do you think this is funny?" she said. The sadness receded and turned into anger. "This isn't fucking funny." She pulled at her hair in an act of frustration and just sighed.

"I'm sorry, Mae. I just don't know what to say. I came home and then you were here. We were both drunk and upset." I walked over and sat down next to her. There was a bottle of whiskey next to my bed, the one from my birthday last year…wait, no. Not that bottle…I shook the memories from the other side of the poles out of my mind and picked up the bottle to inspect it. It was simply the remains from the bottle I had bought the other night, or the night before…who cares. It has just about enough whiskey in it for a swig or two. I took a small swig and handed the remnants over to Mae. "Hair of the dog?" I asked as she looked at me with rage-filled eyes. She must have been hanging just as much as I was because she eventually shrugged and finished the remnants of the amber liquid and handed me back the empty container.

"Can't hurt," she said, placing her hands over her eyes. "My head is just pounding like nothing I have ever felt before."

"I know the feeling." I sighed as I leaned back farther on my bed until my back was up against the wall. "I just want to go back to bed." I yawned. Once I was comfortable, I closed my eyes and tried to clear the events from the night before out of my mind. For some reason, everything that I had ever wanted on this side of the poles seemed like the worst thing to happen to the both of us. Would this effect our relationship? Would we ever be able to go back to the way things were? I guess I will never know what she was thinking. Just as that thought crossed my mind, I felt something rest their head across my lap. I opened my eyes, and it was Mae. She had curled up on the bed and was using my legs as a pillow. I reached over and rubbed her head. Her hair was soft, and when I did, she nuzzled in a bit more.

"Can we just pretend yesterday never happened?" she said as she turned to look at me. I could see a few tears welling up in her eyes. I could also see that the spot where she had laid her head on my pajamas was also wet. I reached down with my other hand and wiped the wetness from her cheek.

"I really hope so, because I can't imagine my life without you in it." She turned her head back to face the other side of the room, but I could see her ears move a bit toward the top of her head. That was usually a good indication that she was smiling. Her smile just wasn't her face…it was with her entire being. The room and the situation seemed a bit brighter once she smiled. After a few minutes of tangling her hair, I heard the faint sound of snoring. I stopped and reached my head over. Mae had fallen asleep on my lap and looked too peaceful to move. I managed to reach my television remote to turn on some Netflix and watch a documentary or something. I flicked through the screen to run through my options and ended up settling on something about tanks during World War Two. After about thirty or so minutes, I started to space and daydream. Before I knew it, I was asleep.

"Wake up, Chance," I heard Mae say as she shook me awake. Her voice was quiet, as if she was trying to evade detection. There was also a hint of panic in her voice.

"What up, where am I?" I said, not used to falling asleep in the middle of the day. I was still me, well…you know.

"Sarah's here...she's knocking at your door." I could feel the panic set in.

"Fuck!" I said. "She must have seen your car. Fuck, we are so fucked." Mae put her hair on my shoulder.

"Calm down. I took the bus here. I was in no shape for driving last night. I was completely hammered." She was surprisingly calm. I looked around the room, and it was nearly pitch black. There was no way she could have seen Mae and I sleeping in the bed. The curtains were blackout curtains, and they were wider than the window, so there was no seeing through them and into my apartment.

"Ok, well. What should I do?" I was whispering as well.

"Well, you should go tell her you're just hungover and want to stay inside. Just don't let her in." she got up and peaked out the curtains. "She's not going anywhere."

As if to illustrate some cosmic point, she chose that moment to get aggravated. Sarah pounded on the door and yelled. "Chance. I know you're in there. I can see your shoes through the window. Just answer the door, I want to talk to you about last night." She pounded a few more times and leaned up against the railing to light a cigarette.

"She smokes?" Mae said as she poked her head back from looking out the window.

"I didn't know she did. She must be pissed. Let me go out there." I collected myself as best as I could and stumbled to the door. I was still pretty hungover but was embellishing it a bit for effect. I walked over to the door and noticed Mae's purse. I took it and placed it behind where the door would block when it was open and unlocked the lock. I opened it to find a very upset Sarah.

"What the hell took you so long," she said as she rushed in to give me a hug. She regretted it. "Wow, you smell like stale cigarettes and whiskey. What the hell happened to you last night?" I smelled my shirt and thanked God that my ordinary smell was outperforming Mae's perfume.

"I walked home after the bar and grabbed a bottle of whiskey from the liquor store. I don't remember much else. My phone died on the walk, I guess. Did you call?" I rubbed my eyes and let out a fake yawn.

"Yes, I called, Chance. I called about a hundred times. I felt so awful about last night. I mean, you're an asshole, but it's not like anything happened between you and Mae…you aren't exactly her type." She looked me up and down. "Yes, definitely not her type. Can I come in?" I was ready for the question, so I reacted quickly.

"I would rather just be alone today. I have been throwing up randomly and am really hungover…I'm surprised I don't need to get my stomach pumped. How about we just have a quick smoke and talk, and I then I can go back inside and die." I closed the door and reached for her cigarette. She gladly gave it to me and pulled out her pack to light up another.

"So what was last night about?" she said as she took her fist drag. "You were outside with Rebecca and then all hell broke loose." I took a moment to collect my thoughts and told her how Rebecca had confronted me about Mae and my feelings toward her.

"She wasn't angry?" she said, a look of surprise. "I guess she didn't really feel threatened. Again, you aren't Mae's type." That phrase was beginning to become really irritating.

"Yeah, so I've been told," I shot back. She could tell that I was getting annoyed by the comment. "Mae and I are just friends. That's all we will ever be. I just have been lonely for so long and I guess I developed feelings for her. She has never led me on in any way, and this is all my fault, not hers." Sarah must have been done with her cigarette and gave it one final drag before walking over to my window and finding an empty beer bottle to squash it into. She walked over to me and wrapped her arms around me.

"I'm sorry I reacted that way. I mean, I am still really pissed at you for not telling me the truth, but you didn't do anything wrong. You two have been friends for so long, and I shouldn't get jealous of something like that." She looked up into my eyes. "I really like you, Chance, and I don't want to let this go. I also don't want you to lose your best friend over this as well." She placed her head back into my chest. "Let's just forget this ever happened."

I shook my head slightly at the fact that I had heard that phrase too many times that day. It's easy for a guy like me to forget stuff like this, simply because I am kind of an asshole and will most likely drink and smoke those memories away. I, on the other hand, didn't think I could ever forget the memories of Mae and I the night before. What if it wasn't just a one-night thing? What if it could be the start of something that would happen whenever we got drunk? Would I even want a relationship like that? Would Mae? I snapped back to reality.

"Yeah, let's do that," I said, trying to sound as affectionate and as sincere as I could. "Let's talk tomorrow, though, because today I feel like shit and want to go to bed next to a bucket." She giggled at the thought of it, and I could feel her smiling against my chest.

"Sounds good," she said as she squeezed me one more time. "Get some rest." She gave me a kiss on the cheek and grabbed her purse from the railing and waved as she walked toward the steps that led down to the main path. She put her hands to her lips as if something was off but decided not to say anything.

"I'll call you tomorrow," I yelled as she turned back and waved one more time. She nodded in agreement and then gave me a thumbs up. A few moments later, she was in her little two-seater and was gone. I shook off the stress of the moment, put my cigarette butt in one of the empty bottles on my window, and went back into my apartment. I walked toward the refrigerator and pulled out a beer. Pulling the bottle opener from my refrigerator handle, I opened the beer and took a long swig. How the hell could that girl like a guy like me? She was literally amazing, and there I was just being a gigantic pile of shit. After all that drama the night before, she had come over to check on me to make sure that I was ok, and then she forgave me for keeping my true feelings about Mae from her. Not knowing Mae was inside after a drunken night of regret. Mae interrupted my inner dialogue.

"Is she gone?" she said, poking her head out from my bedroom door. "Holy shit, that was close. You're a really convincing liar. Makes sense." Those last few words were a bit harsh, but I deserved all of it and more.

"Yeah, I guess," I said, pulling another beer out of the fridge. I opened this one as well and finished about half until Mae came over and tried to take the bottle away.

"Drinking? That's how you deal with this? Chance, you need to face this sober and not just get drunk again." She reached a few more times, but I was able to keep the bottle from her grasp. Once she pulled away, I finished the beer.

"Yeah, after the night we had, I am surprised you're not joining me." I wanted to go and fall asleep again, but it was almost three in the afternoon, and Mae and I had slept basically all day. I was wired and too full of energy. I thought about taking a few sleeping pills, but Mae would definitely disapprove. A knock at the door startled us both. Mae ducked into the bedroom once again and hid. It could have been the UPS guy for all we knew. I took the chance to grab another beer from the fridge and a handful of sleeping pills from the cupboard above. I shook out a few and chased them with the beer. Now I was ready to answer the door. I walked over and unlocked it once more only to find Rebecca on the other side. She looked as if she had been crying. Her hazel eyes were puffy, and her hair was unkempt. I was all too familiar with that look...well, on the other side, I guess.

"Hey, Chance," she said. Her voice was quiet and hoarse as if she had been yelling. "Have you talked to Mae?" I took a sip of my beer and shook my head.

"No, I haven't," I said confidently. "I only just woke up a bit ago. Apparently, I drank an entire bottle of whiskey walking home from the bar last night." I reached in my pocket for another cigarette. My pockets were empty. "Once second," I said as I opened the door slightly to reach my emergency cigarettes in the bowl next to my door.

"Well, we got into a huge fight last night when we got back to my place. She left on foot and I think she took a cab or a bus. I can't find her anywhere and her phone is dead." The tears were welling up in her eyes as she explained what had happened after the bar last night. Apparently, her and Mae had gotten back home, and Mae had had a couple of drinks. Mae was normally a happy drunk, but the events that had transpired had turned her bitter and angry.

"I'm sorry to be the cause of all this trouble," I said, finally getting the shitty lighter to work. I had washed it a couple of times, and it was a little worse for wear. "Both you and Mae don't deserve to have to deal with me and all my baggage." I took a long drag from the cigarette. The cigarette was stale since it had been sitting there open for probably a few weeks. I was just getting enough of a buzz to not care. I took another drink from the bottle in my hand.

"Wow, drinking again?" Rebecca said, sounding surprised.

"A little hair of the dog," I said, holding up the bottle as if I were giving a toast. "I'm surprised it took until three for me to start drinking after last night."

"Yeah, I guess last night was rough on you as well." She fidgeted a bit and finally decided it was time to go. "Sorry to bother you. Feel better, and let Mae know to just come home. Tell her I'm sorry for bringing this up, and that I love her." Seeing her say those words, seeing me say those words, hurt. Mae and I had thought all morning that last night had been the end of the world for us, and we were just too selfish to understand that other people would be hurt by this act as well. If it was even possible for me to hate myself any more in that moment I would have, but my normal self-hate was nearly maxed out on a regular basis.

"I will tell her next time I see her." I finished the stale cigarette and shoved the filter in my pocket when I noticed that both bottles on my ledge were full. Rebecca smiled and said thank you as I walked over to the ledge and grabbed both bottles, intending to throw them away.

"Hey, Chance," she said right as she started walking away. She looked over her shoulder and smiled. "Sarah is a really special girl. You would be an idiot to fuck that up. Do yourself a favor and give her a call." I nodded my head and smiled. Rebecca returned the favor, turned, and left. Here she was, still thinking about other people. I hoped at that moment that what Mae and I had done wasn't going to completely ruin their relationship. I watched her as she walked away. My vision slowly started to blur as the sleeping pills finally started to take effect. I decided to get inside and throw the bottles in the trash. I decided to finish the one in my hand and leave it on the ledge for the next day. I locked the door behind me and walked over to my trash can. Turning toward my room, I saw Mae just standing there crying.

"Chance. What did we do?" She ran over to me and hesitated before hugging me. She finally gave in and wrapped her arms around me. She began crying uncontrollably into my shirt. Her tears and snot left trails as her body convulsed from each fit of crying.

"Mae, calm down," I said, trying to ease her suffering. I rubbed her back and held her close. "Both Sarah and Rebecca don't know what happened. There is still a way to fix this." My words hit a nerve.

"Yeah, what. Just lie to them like you do all the time, apparently? Some of us aren't just natural-born sociopaths like you." She pulled away and was clearly on the defensive. "You come in here thinking everything is ok. It's not ok. I'm gay, Chance. I'm gay and I got drunk last night and had sex with my best friend...who, if you don't know...is a fucking guy!" She was beginning to spiral. "Now, I cheated on the best thing that has ever happened to me, with you of all people!" The sadness was quickly replaced by rage. She was pacing frantically, and her face was getting red.

"Mae, I'm sorry. I don't know what to say. I came home and you came here. You were drunk and confused. I was drunk and..." she interrupted.

"Yes, you were drunk, but you weren't fucking confused," she yelled. Her words were more right than she knew. "You wanted this, and you fucking got it. How does it feel?" She stood there expecting an answer, but I didn't have one. She was right. This was all I had ever wanted...but not like this. I didn't want to ruin the only real relationship I'd ever had in my life. Even if it was a toxic and codependent one that was the reason every other relationship in my life had failed.

I really didn't know if it was the pills or the beers or both. I was tired of this shit. I was tired of my life revolving around her. I was tired of the way the last thirty some odd years had gone. I was no good for her, and she was no good for me. Fuck, I hadn't even talked to my own fucking mother in God knows how long because I was so caught up in her drama and her life. Yes, we had needed each other growing up, but maybe we were done, and we no longer needed that crutch. The only thing I could do was hurt her. That's what I did to the people I cared about. That's all I know how to do...hurt people. The words came out before I knew I was even thinking them.

"It fucking felt great," I said, my voice no longer quiet. "I finally got to have you, even if for one night. My whole life I have been in love with you, and the thought that maybe our relationship was something special was what kept me going. I have alienated everyone because they confronted me about how I needed to move on and let you go. My parents, my other friends...literally everyone. So you dare to ask me how it feels to finally be able to be with the woman I love. You might not have known, but you knew. You knew every time you came over and woke me up. Every time we laid together on the couch and watched a movie. Every time we hugged, and my heart would nearly jump out of my throat. Every dance, every date, every night out, every morning after. Fuck you, Mae. You came here looking for something last night too, and I refuse to take all the blame for that." By the time the rant was over, her face was void of any blood. The tears had stopped, but it might have been out of fear rather than anger. I was sweating, and my face was red. My head ached from yelling, and I could feel the veins in the side of my head protruding from my skin. It was her turn to be speechless. She just stood there for a few minutes with her jaw open. She slowly regained her composure, and the anger returned slightly.

"You know what? You're right. Some part of me thought that maybe you were different. Maybe I was unhappy all these years because the person I never saw like that could have been the best thing that ever happened to me. How could I have been so stupid?" She shook her head slowly and sighed. She walked over to the door and pulled her purse out of the corner. She found her shoes under my side table and put them on. "I'm going home to clean all of this regret off me. Then I am going to call Rebecca and apologize. I am going to kiss the fucking ground she walks on, because she is amazing, and I don't deserve her. I suggest you do the same for Sarah." She opened the door and walked out. I followed her out onto the steps, and she never turned back...not even once. She walked all the way out to the bus stop. I wanted to go after her, but she was right. We had done something terrible, and it would be a mistake to go after her. If I was smart, I would never talk to her again. I would let her be and let her have the amazing life she deserved.

"Fuck!" I yelled as I slammed the door. A picture of my family fell off the wall and bounced on the carpet. I walked over to the kitchen and grabbed another beer out of the fridge. There was an old wine cooler in there as well, so I took that out too. I chugged them all and followed them with another handful of sleeping pills.

"Fuck this," I said to myself as the first series of pills started to really hit me hard. The ringing in my mouth, the dryness that always happened with those pills was becoming rather apparent. After finishing the beers, I went to the sink and put my mouth underneath and drank until my stomach felt like it was going to burst. I stumbled into the bedroom and fell down on the bed. I was barely able to stand by the time I was in my room. I turned the television on some random station to have some noise in the background. I laid my head back on my pillow as the room began to darken. It was as if I couldn't even keep my eyes open. "Maybe I took too much?" I thought to myself. What I was feeling was not the normal drowsiness. "Fuck," I remember thinking. "I think I did take too much." The last thing I remember was the feeling of terror as I slipped to sleep.

Chapter 10

I woke up to the sound of my text message ringtone humming. I groaned as I turned over and faced the other way...it rang again.

"Turn that shit off," Mae said as she pulled her pillow over her head. She turned over and exposed her back. I pulled the blanket up and realized that we were both, in fact, naked. I sat there admiring her body until she turned over and laughed. "Wow, what a creep." She came over and nuzzled her head on my chest. Her head was slightly beneath the covers. Suddenly I felt a hand creep up somewhere it shouldn't have been.

"Hey there, what are you doing?" I said as I jumped. I moved so suddenly that I hit my head on the headboard. A picture from my nightstand fell off and bounced off the carpet. Suddenly, I was seeing the fight with Mae last night. The picture frame hitting the floor, the look in her eyes and everything that both of us had said. Whatever good mood I was in that morning suddenly faded.

"What's wrong," Mae said, expecting me to play along to her foreplay. Instead, I just rubbed my head and got up from the bed. I grabbed my phone and walked into the bathroom.

"Sorry, I have to pee," I lied as I closed and locked the door. I went over to the sink to throw some water into my face. "Fuck," I said quietly to myself as the cold water gave me goosebumps across my body. They came across me like a wave. I looked into the mirror and saw the woman staring back at me. She didn't look like me anymore. It didn't feel like me anymore. I reached my hand to my face and pulled on my cheek...it did just as I intended and matched every movement I made. I felt like Peter

Pan fighting with his shadow…I was half expecting it to do something completely different, like it had done the other day.

"You ok in there?" Mae said from outside the door. I could see that she was trying to get in. "You never lock the door."

"I'm sorry. I just need a minute. My stomach is kind of crampy. I think I'm getting my period." I tried to sound sincere.

"Well, you know where everything is. Feel better, babe." I could hear her footsteps going into the kitchen, most likely to make a pot of coffee.

I continued to look in the mirror at Rebecca's face. That's what it felt like…her face, not mine. "This is your face," I said to myself over and over, as if trying to convince myself of the truth. "This is you," I finally said as I started feeling a bit more accustomed to the reflection. I decided that I needed to shower the last few days off me and opened the shower curtain.

Mae was sitting in the bathtub crying, her makeup was everywhere. I knelt down to put my hand on her shoulder, and she looked at me and screamed.

"Fuck," I said as I shot backwards, the sudden outburst catching me completely off guard. Suddenly, the tub was empty and dry. I shook off the vision and turned the knob to warm up the shower. I actually had to pee a bit, so I answered nature's call and hopped in the shower. Once I was done, I went into the bedroom to try and pick out some clothes for the day.

"Coffee?" Mae said from the other room. I could smell it from the bedroom.

"Yes, please," I said as I looked in my drawers for a sports bra. I really wanted to go for a run that morning. I never wanted to run, but I felt as if I needed to get out of the apartment for a bit. I threw on the first sports bra I found and an old shirt from high school. I found a pair of running shorts, and I was ready to go. I walked out into the kitchen to claim my coffee.

"Oooh, someone getting ready for a run?" Mae said as she poured me a mug. She gave me the first cup of the morning. It was appreciated.

"Yeah. I haven't gone for a run in a bit, and I should start up again. My pants are getting a little tight." I patted on my stomach to emphasize that I was getting a bit pudgy.

"Funny, if you want to run that's cool. You definitely don't need to lose any weight." She poured herself a half cup since the pot wasn't completely done. She went over to the little kitchen table that we had and sat down. She motioned for me to do the same before my run, so I obliged.

"What are your plans for the day?" I asked as I blew into the mug. I took a sip, and the coffee was too hot to drink. I sipped on it anyway.

"I have some homework to do. I didn't really get much done yesterday, thanks to you. I emailed my professors, though, and let them know that I was sick yesterday. Hopefully they don't mind." She pretended to cough a bit in jest. We both chuckled at her sad attempt at humor.

"Well, good for you for doing what you're supposed to do...only a day late." I blew on my coffee some more. We had a small discussion while our coffee cooled and talked about our plans for the weekend and into the next week. For some reason, the next week felt so impossibly far away. I tried to think why, but I was unable to think about it. As I tried to think about what I had done the night before, it was as if there was a mental block. I suddenly got immensely tired, and Mae noticed me struggling to stay awake.

"You ok, Becks?" she said as she came over to me and caught me as I nearly fell out of my chair. She put me on the ground, and I felt as if I hadn't slept in a year. "Oh my god, are you ok?" she said, panic in her eyes. My vision suddenly began to go black. As if it was closing in around me from the outside in.

"Mae, what's happening?" I said, my words slurred as if I was drunk. Was I having a stroke? Wait...I remembered what I had done the night before. The terror I had felt as I had fallen asleep the night before. It was all too much, the pain of what I thought was happening. I was too afraid to even think of the word. I was dying. The pills and the liquor, that's what would do me in. Mae would come over to find me cold and stiff, laying in my bed. She would tell Sarah, and she would be devastated. She and Rebecca would most likely grow closer, and my presence would no longer strain their relationship. One final good deed for the woman I loved. I looked up into Mae's eyes as they closed forever. "I love you," I said, or at least I tried to say, as things went dark.

I was alone sitting in a dark room. I was too afraid to move, I was too afraid to do anything. I held my hands up to my face, and I couldn't see them. "Hello," I said. No echo or any response. I sat like that for what felt like an eternity. It might have been only a few minutes. Crying in the darkness, completely alone.

"Becky, wake up!" I could hear Mae like she was right next to me.

"Mae, I'm right here!" I yelled as loud as I could. "Help me!" I screamed that over and over as loud as I could until I could barely breathe. I couldn't see anything, I couldn't feel anything. I was terrified.

"Please don't leave me," she said again. She was crying uncontrollably. It was all too much. I was leaving her to be alone, and it was all my fault. This wasn't some tragic death where it was an accident or was beyond my control. I caused this. I committed suicide. I was such a fucking idiot. Suddenly, out of nowhere, I could feel my stomach churn.

"Oh fuck, I'm going to be sick," I said out loud for no reason. Nobody was here to hear me. "Fuck!" I managed to say before I vomited out into oblivion. I couldn't hear it land. All I could hear was the poison exiting my body. Beer, whiskey, and pills, that was all I tasted.

"Mae!" I heard her scream as I vomited all over her. I was back in the kitchen with Mae. Her entire shirt was covered, and she was just smiling ear to ear. I was laying on the ground against the cold tile. I pushed myself up and was barely able to support my own body weight.

"I...I...what happened?" I mumbled, spitting the remnants of God knows what onto the floor. I took the bottom of my shirt and wiped my face off. I knew exactly what had happened, and I couldn't believe it. Something on the other side of the poles made a difference on this side. What did that mean for me...the other me. Was I still alive and laying in my bed, covered in vomit? Was I dead, and this was the last bit of neurons in my brain firing all at once? I knew what was happening, but I couldn't tell Mae. How would I even begin to explain that to her.

"Becky, what was that? Are you ok?" She reached over to the table and grabbed a few paper towels to wipe off my face. The amount of bile that had exited my body was surprising. It was void of any food or solid bits. It was most likely the drinks from last night as well as whatever else was sitting in my stomach. "Do we need to take you to the hospital?"

"No, no. I'm fine," I said as I shook to keep myself upright. Mae wrapped her arms around me and helped me stay sitting. "I need to shower. Then I can help you clean up." I tried to stand, and she stopped me.

"Rebecca, you need to relax. You just passed out and puked everywhere.

121

Give yourself a minute." She put her hand on my back and began rubbing me. After a few moments, she was holding me tighter and tighter. "I thought I was going to lose you," she said, her voice faint. She was trying to keep from crying.

"I'm sorry I scared you. I just think maybe I ate something bad." I tried to think of the last thing I had eaten. It was the sandwich at lunch yesterday. Not wanting to ruin that place for Mae, I kept it to myself.

"You and I usually eat the same thing. Maybe an allergy?" Her mind was going a thousand miles an hour trying to figure out what had almost killed her wife. Not knowing that her wife was the culprit. "I think we just need to get you cleaned up and take a chill pill." I laughed awkwardly, thinking another pill was the last thing I needed. Mae looked at me as I laughed but decided not to say anything. She helped me up, and I limped to the shower. With every passing moment, I could feel the strength returning to my limbs. Once we were in the shower, I started laughing. "What is so funny?" Mae asked.

"I just took a shower," I said through my soaking wet shirt as I tried to take it off without letting the disgusting shirt touch my face. Mae assisted in the effort and placed the shirt neatly in a plastic bag she had grabbed out of the closet where we keep our towels on the way into the bathroom. She then helped me take off my running shorts and did the same thing with them.

"Well. I guess I am coming in with you," she said as she began taking her clothes off as well. She unfortunately was the recipient of the majority of the bile, and her entire shirt was soaked. She took that and her pajama pants off and placed them in the bag. Both of us, smelling disgusting, were standing in our bathroom in our underwear.

"Sexy," I joked as she reached in and turned on the water. She shook her head.

"I love you, Becks, but there is no fucking way in hell we will be doing anything other than cleaning ourselves in here." She waited a moment and reached her hand into the shower. Apparently, it was warm enough for her, and she removed the rest of her clothes and jumped in. Needless to say, I joined in, and she was right. We cleaned ourselves, and that was it. Apparently, watching her wife almost die, and me nearly almost dying myself, really wasn't something that would put either of us in the mood.

The shower was almost platonic. As if we were sisters, sleeping on a hotel bed and going through the motions. We spent about thirty or so minutes in the shower, and I don't think I even looked at her body unless it was in the way of the soap or the loofah. We took turns in the hot water since there was really only enough room for one person under the faucet. One of us would soap up and scrub ourselves down while the other took time rinsing off. We were both pretty disgusting, so the fact that we took such a long shower wasn't completely out of the ordinary. Once the water started to get colder and we realized that our unit was running low, we decided it was time to get out and get dressed.

I couldn't help but think about my fate once I slipped to the other side of the poles. What would I find? Was this my last day here on earth, or was it just another trial I had to overcome? The sad thing was, if this truly was my last day on earth, I was surprisingly calm. All I ever wanted was to live on this side of the poles forever. My other life, whether real or fantasy, was something I had to overcome and endure in order to get to where I truly belonged. Where I truly wanted to be. I handed Mae her towel and grabbed mine as well as we both stood in the bathroom in complete silence. The silence was like a freight train in my head. Causing all these thoughts to manifest and fill my head with doubt and panic. That day, however, the panic had subsided, and only questions remained. I did my best to dry my hair off using the damp towel from the morning's shower. I then took the damp towel and wrapped up my body in it. I always struggled with this since I really wasn't well endowed, so I had to tuck in the extra piece in tight in order for the tower to remain in the proper position. Mae looked over as I struggled and laughed.

"Having trouble there, kid?" she said as she easily wrapped the towel and loosely tucked it in. She was a bit more well endowed than I was, and as much as I liked looking at them, I was jealous all the same.

"Wow, I nearly die, and you're already poking fun at my body. Nice, Mae," I smiled to let her know that I was kidding once I realized she felt bad about the joke.

"I'm sorry," she said as she walked over to me and hugged me. "Who said you almost died? You passed out and threw up." Her mind was already formulating a story that she could comprehend so it would be easier for her to cope. I shrugged and nodded in agreement as I went into my bedroom for the second time to get ready for my day. It wasn't even nine thirty, and already, our day had too much excitement. We were both exhausted from the ordeal and quietly put our clothes on. I decided that jeans and a t-shirt were good enough for me. Mae decided that putting a new pair of pajamas on was her best option. We then walked into the kitchen, noticing the mess on the floor. Too be honest, I had completely forgotten about it. I looked at her and sighed.

"Well, I can clean this up. You go start your homework." I grabbed the paper towels and did my best to soak up the remnants off the tile floor. We were lucky that nothing had gotten soaked up in the carpet…losing our security deposit was the last thing we needed that day.

"Ok, are you sure?" she said as she stepped over one of the puddles and onto the carpet where it was safe. "I can help."

I looked over at her and smiled. "My mess, I can clean it up." She walked over and grabbed a bottle of cleaner from under the sink. She had to untangle a few grocery bags from the spray handle, but eventually she succeeded. She reached over and handed it to me.

"Here you go," she said. "I am going to go and start studying. Call me if you need me. She gave me a look as if she was looking at me for what could be the last time. I guessed after what happened, I'd better get used to that look.

"I'm fine. Go ahead and get to studying. I want to be a stay-at-home wife, so you need to study up and make the big bucks." We both laughed, and she grabbed her bag and went to sit down on the sofa.

It only took about fifteen or so minutes to clean up the rest of the mess in the kitchen. The tile that we had was already stained from previous tenants, so that made cleaning a bit more difficult; however, it went rather quickly. Once I was done, I went to wash my hands and put a warmer-upper in my coffee. The coffee in the pot was still rather hot since it had never been turned off. I poured Mae a small cup as well and brought it to her in the living room.

"Thank you," she said as she peered at me through her librarian-sized reading glasses. That was an odd thing about this side, she wore reading glasses. I always wondered why she didn't wear them on the other side. I never asked her since…well, you know.

"How goes your studying?" I said, trying to annoy her a bit.

"Well, I just got started, but it's going, I guess." She licked her finger and flipped the page of the textbook. She looked over at me and smiled. "Are you feeling ok?" The look of concern came over her face again.

"I'm fine. Stop worrying. Whatever that was is over and I feel great. I am thinking about going out to grab us lunch. It will give you a little peace and quiet and give me something to do other than work on that article."

"Are you sure you're up for it?" she asked. "I don't need you crashing the car and dying."

"Don't worry. What do you want to eat for lunch?" I pulled out my phone and started looking up some of our favorite places. "I can get tacos, Chinese, pizza? Any of those sound good?"

"Actually, a big burrito sounds amazing right now, and that place is within walking distance. You can get your exercise in, and then we can eat a ton of Mexican food. Sound good?" Her idea checked all the boxes. Exercise, I didn't have to drive, and we got burritos…perfect.

"Sounds like a deal," I said as I put away my phone and stood up. "Text me what you want, and I'll order it on the way." I went into the bedroom and grabbed my wireless headphones. I walked over and grabbed some cash out of my wallet and gave Mae a kiss. Before I knew it, I was out the door, cutting across the large field to the main road. I put in my earphones and turned on one of my alternative rock stations and hit shuffle. The music flowed into me, and I instantly felt better. The morning had been incredibly stressful for both Mae and me, and I really had no clue what to expect after the day was done. I just wanted to get mine and Mae's lunch and sit and relax with her.

I finally hit the main street, and it was about a half a mile more to the taco place just off campus. It was a pretty nice morning, so a ton of the students were walking about. Whether they were going to class or coming home, I didn't know. I remembered when I was still in school and was just so focused on what I was doing. I was going to be some bigshot writer, and people would know me. Well, people did know me, but it usually wasn't a good thing. I laughed as I tried to think of all the pieces I had written for this small newspaper and how nice of a life that work had provided for both me and Mae. Even though that life was comfortable, we could always use more. Mae knew how much I wanted to write stuff for myself. Publish a book or a series of short stories. I had tons of pieces I had worked on over the years and she knew how much I wanted to publish them. Unfortunately, a self-published book is a tough thing to make money on. I think that's one of the reasons that she decided to go back to school…to help me have the financial stability to pursue some of my dreams. It kind of hurt that she had to do something like that in order for me to be happy. I hate being a burden, and that was just how I felt at that moment. She was going to school, and I was having a mid-life crisis. Getting drunk, having vomiting spells, coming home crying uncontrollably. I made a mental note to be a better wife to her, or at least do my best to be a better person. By the time all these thoughts had run through my head, I was approaching the restaurant.

"Hey there, Rebecca," I heard a familiar voice say. Albert was running from the Stop N Go a few doors down. He must have seen me coming and made his way to intercept. I waved, and once he realized I noticed him, he stopped running.

"Hey, Albert," I said. He finally caught up with me. He was panting as he stopped to catch his breath. "Working out?"

"Funny," he said. He put his hands behind his head to open his airways. "Yeah, it's obvious that I don't work out much. I just saw you and wanted to come apologize."

"You don't have to apologize, Albert. I overreacted the other day. You were just trying to let me know that I can be myself, and I took it badly." I could feel my face getting red. I don't mind if he saw…I was embarrassed. I had overreacted completely to a nice guy who just wanted to make me feel more at ease about who I was. I had actually no clue why I reacted that way, other than that I was just being emotional.

"No, seriously," he said, color starting to return to his face. "I just feel bad that I blurted that out. I was so nervous about talking to you about anything other than work. Obviously, I am not really good at talking to women." He put his arms down as if he were presenting himself as a prize in a game show.

"Well, let's just agree to disagree," I said as I motioned that I was going inside to order. "Well, time to get the wife a burrito." He laughed at the statement.

"Well, I will let you get dinner and have a great rest of your day. We miss you in the office. Well, everybody but my uncle. We all love it when you show him up. For some reason, you're the only person that isn't afraid of him." He smiled as he waved and started to walk back to wherever he was parked.

"Well, how about a taco? I think I owe you one for the way I acted the other day." I motioned inside and opened the door for him. "Well, I have never been one to turn down a taco." He smiled and went inside the restaurant. I walked in behind him, and we were greeted with all the amazing smells from the kitchen. We walked over to the counter and ordered our food. The lady behind the counter mentioned that it would be about a thirty-minute wait. "Care to get a drink while we wait?" Albert said as he motioned toward the small four-seater bar that sat against the back wall of the place. I nodded in agreement, and we walked over to sit on the empty stools.

"I think I can just have one. Apparently, I drank a bit too much last night, and I shouldn't have more than that." I said as I put down my purse and sat down in one of the high stools. Albert was a bit taller than me, so it was easier for him. My legs just dangled form the stool and couldn't even reach the foot support attached to the bar.

"Well, hair of the dog," he said as he motioned to the bartender and she came in from the other room. "Two margaritas, please." He pulled out a twenty-dollar bill and handed it to her. She gave us both a dirty look for drinking so early, but she took the money just the same. Business is business, I suppose. As the bartender went through the process of mixing our early-afternoon margaritas, we sat there awkwardly; that is, until Albert spoke.

"So, what did you want to work on together? Or did I blow my chance at working with you one-on-one?" He fidgeted with the watch that was on his wrist.

"Stop it," I joked. "I'm sorry for overreacting. I would very much like to work with you on something. What did you have in mind?" He continued to play with his watch for a few moments and then looked up at me.

"I want to expose my uncle." His words came out just as the margaritas hit the counter. I took the margarita and took a gigantic drink. The cold hit me like a knife, and I took a few seconds to recover from the brain freeze. Albert just sat there sipping his drink. After a few moments, I recovered.

"What do you mean, expose him?" I said with my mouth open

wide. "What is he doing?" At that point, I realized that Albert was very uncomfortable but needed to get the information off his chest. I needed to make sure he was able to.

"My uncle. He isn't as innocent as he looks. A few years ago, I suspected that he was into some illegal dealings with some political figures. I mentioned it vaguely in conversation, and he really blew up at me. Since then, he has been extremely nice, and I think it is because he is trying to keep me quiet. A few nights ago, I received a tip from someone I have been working with, someone who had evidence." He reached out to grab his drink and take another sip. The words coming from his mouth seemed dry and forced.

"Evidence? What kind of evidence?" I said, literally hanging on his every word.

"He is taking extremely large bribes from some political figures to make up lies about political rivals as well as silence stories that could hurt the people he is working with. I saw the bank statements and the check stubs. There is even a video with my uncle in a meeting with..." He stopped and turned to look around as if he thought we were being watched.

"Don't worry. I doubt anyone here is listening to us idiots drinking this early in the morning." My words put him at ease a bit.

"The governor...the fucking governor." He paused and his face began to lose all its color. "I am a journalist, but he is also family. I just don't know what to do. What should I do?"

I took a few moments to think. Was he really asking me to help put his uncle in jail? At the very minimum, lose his job and basically become a pariah. Why would he do this? Did he want his uncle's job? No, that couldn't be it. There were a hundred people more qualified that would get the job. I doubted he wanted to piss off his family. He always spoke of them fondly. I doubted that there was any familial interest in any of this. I finally just decided to ask him the question.

"Why, Albert? Why do you want to do this?" He answered me with silence for a few seconds and then answered.

"What he is doing is wrong, Rebecca. Like, really friggin' wrong. I can't in my right mind let him keep doing this. I need to stop him." I could begin to see the inner turmoil in his eyes. He was weighing his options, and one of those options seemed to be to pretend it was a joke and leave.

Knowing that I wasn't stupid enough to believe a lie like that, he took the other route. Doubling down. "I need you to help me."

"Me?" I asked, my mouth suddenly dry again. I was surprised that it had even made a noise. I took another swig from the drink and could feel the alcohol start to hit my extremely empty stomach. "Why do you need me to help you?"

"Because you're the only person at the office that stands up to him. You're the only person at the office who sees what I see. Yeah, everyone hates him, but they respect him. They would never believe me if I brought this to their attention. They would only tell my uncle, and then I would be done for." The rant was a little more than both of us expected, and he took a few deep breaths. "This is what I wanted to tell you the other day before I fucked it all up. We have to take him down." He added special emphasis on the word "we."

"Well..." I began to say before I decided to trust my judgement. "I need to talk to Mae. If I choose to do this, it will affect more than just myself. It could mess up her life as well. Being the target of a major political campaign as well as actually risking my career and reputation if things should go south. You understand right?" He took what I had just said in for a moment and nodded.

"Of course I understand. I don't want to unhinge your life at all. I just can't do this by myself. I don't have the strength." He finished his drink and placed it on the counter. He motioned for one more but was ignored. I drained the contents of my glass and looked over toward the counter. The person was just bagging what looked like our food and looked in my direction. She gave me a nonverbal cue that it was, in fact, our food and walked it over to us at the bar.

"Here you go," she said with a thick accent. "I hope you enjoy."

I looked at her and smiled. "We most definitely will. Where else can you go to get a burrito the size of your head?" I took the bag and handed Albert the small box with his order.

"Thanks for lunch," he said as he opened the box and smelled the food. "Go talk to your wife and let me know what she says." He finished off the last few drops of his drink, and I did the same. The alcohol was definitely affecting me now. I could feel the blood rushing to my cheeks.

"I will," I said as I put the glass down on the counter. "Albert, please don't do anything crazy until we have a chance to talk again, ok? Get all of that information together and keep it close." I grabbed my purse off the back of the bar chair and slung it around my shoulder.

"I will," he said as he reached in for one of the most awkward hugs I had ever had. Once it was over, he turned and walked toward the exit.

"What the hell?" I said to myself as I just stood there for a moment trying to understand what had just gone on. I looked at the bartender and motioned for her. She walked over reluctantly, and I ordered a shot. She begrudgingly listened and reached for the bottle.

A few minutes later, I was walking back to the apartment with a few bags of chips and Mae's and my burritos. The walk was must more enjoyable now that I had a little buzz. The air seemed cleaner, and the sky seemed brighter. The events of the morning had already faded into obscurity, and I felt pretty amazing. Well, I guess part of it might have been the fact that John was a corrupt journalist, and I could possibly end his career. Was it bad that I was actually happy about that? What did that say about me? Before I knew it, I was back at the apartment, and I was walking up the steps. Mae heard and met me at the door.

"What took you so long?" she said as she opened the door. "You didn't answer my texts." She came over to me and hugged me. I guessed I should get used to her worrying after our morning.

"I ran into Albert...we had a drink while waiting for our food." I held up the bag.

"Drink? As in alcohol? Are you fucking stupid, Becks? After what happened this morning, you're out drinking before noon?" The look of disappointment was pretty extreme, and she was right. She was still wondering what had happened that morning, and I already knew. That was why I wasn't worried.

"I'm sorry. He was stressed and ordered for me. I had to wait a bit for the food. I guess I should have ordered when I was walking there. I just got lost listening to music. I'm sorry Mae..." I tried to use puppy dog eyes to make her less mad. It worked to a small degree.

"I was just worried about you," she said as she put her arms around me again. "Let's forget about it and eat some burritos. I am starving." I nodded in agreement, and we walked over to the table to set up our lunch. As I pulled out the food, I told Mae about the interaction that I had with

Albert and what he had said about John. I explained how it made perfect sense that John treated Albert so nicely. Apparently, from what Albert told me, that was a new development since had John found out Albert had information regarding his wrongdoings. Nepotism was a crazy thing. Here John treated this person like shit for years, and only when it was beneficial for him did he start giving Albert preferential treatment.

"Albert has been John's favorite for years?" Mae said, stuffing a guacamole-filled tortilla chip into her mouth. Crumbs poured onto the plate where her burrito resided. "Why is that?" Her inquiry made sense. If he had only started being nice to Albert recently, then why did it not feel like that from the outside? I made a mental note to ask Albert at our next meeting. I doubt that I would be going into the office until I got my next assignment anyway. John left it up to Albert and me to decide what to bring him next...it might be his undoing.

"I don't know. I wish I did." I quickly went into my bag and grabbed my notebook and a pencil. I quickly started jotting down questions that I would want to ask Albert the next time I saw him. I added Mae's to the list.

"Good Idea. Get everything down on paper so you don't forget what to ask him." She stuffed the burrito into her face once again. God, she was beautiful, even with a face full of carne asada. I jotted down a few more notes to discuss with him and then dug into my lunch as well. I didn't realize how starving I was until I took that first bite. Losing the contents of my stomach that morning had not been something I intended, and I had been too preoccupied to realize that I was both starving and a little intoxicated. Hopefully the food would help in remedying both of those issues.

We both sat there for the rest of the afternoon and talked a bunch of small talk. Mae would do a bit of homework, and I would sit and watch her. Once she began her homework, she really focused on it, though. I think she was trying to distract herself from everything that had happened that morning. Neither of us wanted to really go into great depth regarding the events that had taken place so far that day. To me, it seemed like Mae didn't want to think of it mainly because she had witnessed my episode firsthand. I, on the other hand, didn't really want to think of it simply because I was afraid of what was happening to me on the other side of the poles. I had almost died; well, at least it felt like it. What should I expect on the other side…darkness? Would I wake up to find that nothing was wrong? Would I even wake up at all? These were questions that I didn't want to think about, and Mae did a great job at keeping those thoughts out of my head for the time being, but I knew they would creep into my psyche eventually and I would have to face the ramifications for what I had decided to do the night before.

"You ok?" Mae asked as she must have seen that I was starting to spiral. "I'm so full from lunch, I don't want dinner. How about you?"

I smiled. "How are you even thinking about dinner?" I said, looking at the clock. "Holy crap, it's almost two o'clock!" I hadn't realized that Mae and I had literally spent the entire afternoon lounging about doing nothing." Mae scoffed.

"Well, you might have been doing nothing. I was doing my homework like a good student. Didn't you have any work to do today?"

I thought about it, and other than what Albert was planning, I really didn't. The Lincoln paper had been turned over, and I had been paid for it. That was going to pay the bills for the next little bit. I started really thinking about Albert and his predicament. It was really the first time that I had given it any thought. I caught Mae off guard with my question. "What should I do about Albert?"

She looked over at me and smiled. "What do you want to do?" It didn't feel one hundred percent honest, but it was what I would have expected from her.

"It doesn't matter what I want to do. This will affect us both. I want to make sure you have a say in it. This isn't just my decision, it's our decision." I wiggled over closer to her and put my arm around her. "I could lose my job over this." Those words were weird to say. It was the first time I had even thought of it going wrong for me.

"How could you lose your job over this?" Mae asked. "He is the one doing illegal things. How can that mess up your career?"

"Well, newspapers or magazines might not want to hire me knowing I am a whistleblower or whatever. Not to mention, we know that he is doing illegal things, but he might get away with them and still be in charge. That would not end well for me."

"I wish we had some savings so we could take the chance and not be totally screwed." She sat back and sighed. "That's why I am going back…"

I interrupted her. "I know, honey, but this shouldn't be on you. You're almost done, and I am super proud of you. We will figure something out."

We both sat on the couch for a few hours and discussed how we could make it work without being too overzealous. It turned out we had a little over a month's worth of savings, and Mae was about six months from graduation and finding a job. That meant we would need a good chunk of money in order to get by in case I lost our only source of income. After we had exhausted all options, like selling clothes, trinkets, and collectibles, there was only one option.

"Mae, I think I have to sell the bike." I knew what her reaction would be and how she would feel about that. She loved that bike, honestly a bit more than I did. I also had another one on the other side of the poles, so it didn't bother me too much.

"Nooooo," She whined as she heard the words leave my mouth. "You can't get rid of the bike. I loooove that bike." Even speaking the words, she knew that they were in vain, and she also understood that it was the only way to protect ourselves.

"I know, but it's the only thing we have of any real value. That and the car, but you need that to get to school. Also, the bike is worth way more than the car. I will go out tomorrow and clean it up and then put it up for sale online." I put my hand on her shoulder. "If nothing happens, I can just buy another bike. This way, we are covered no matter what happens." She frowned and put her head down.

"I wish this had happened in six months. Then I would be able to be your sugar mama for a bit, and you would get to keep your bike." She bit her lip at the mention of a sugar mama.

"Sugar mama, eh? Is that all I am to you?" I took the book from her hands and threw it on the coffee table. I made sure not to lose her page by throwing it cover up. I pushed her down on the couch and started tickling her. "Yeah, if that's all I am to you then I am going to make you suffer!" She was in hysterics as I placed my fingers in all the spots where I knew she was ticklish. After only about thirty seconds, she could barely breathe, and I decided to give her a break. After she caught her breath, she smiled and grabbed me by the collar.

"Get your ass over here," she said as she pulled me in to kiss her. Her hands were all over my body, and mine were all over hers.

"One second," I said as I got up and went to close the blinds. As I returned to the couch, I removed my shirt and then my bra. Mae did the same. I jumped on her like it was the last night of my life.

After, we both sat on the couch, drenched in sweat. Her head was on my chest, and she was snoring loudly. I pulled the cover off the top of the couch onto both of our bodies. Thank God we had a large couch and both of us could fit comfortably on it with little issue. I laid back and said a little prayer to God.

"Please don't let this be my last night on earth." I looked down at Mae and I thought of one more request. "Please don't let me hurt her any more than I already have." I started to cry softly as I felt sleep take over me. I was exhausted, both mentally and physically. Not just from the last thirty or so minutes, but from the day as well...well, from the past few days. I needed rest...real rest. I hadn't had that in what felt like forever. I was constantly at odds with even the thought of respite. My eyes began to close, and I wasn't able to fight it any longer. The last thing I did was reach over to my phone and text Albert two simple words. Two simple words that I hoped didn't begin the end of my career and my and Mae's life together.

"I'm In"

Chapter 11

Before my eyes even opened, all I felt was pain. My head was pounding harder than it had ever pounded. The second thing I noticed was the smell...vomit.

"He's awake," a familiar voice said. It was Sarah. I tried opening my eyes, but I was weak. Why was she here? Where was here?

"He is?" said another familiar voice. It was Mae. I tried to reach my hand out, but again, I was too weak. I decided to try and speak...my mouth was dry, and it was rough. I managed to get a few words out.

"Where am I?" I managed to say. It felt as if dust came out of mouth. It was course and quiet.

"Where the fuck do you think you're?" asked Mae. "You're at home in your bed...you know, the one you apparently tried to..." Sarah interrupted her.

"You're at home in your bed, Chance." I felt her hand touch my forehead. Her hand was cool and soft. It might have been one of the best feelings I had ever felt. She kept on rubbing my head for a few more moments, and then I felt a hand on my shoulder. I tried again to open my eyes and the light in the room was blinding. Sarah must have noticed, because I heard the blinds close, and the light dimmed.

"Sorry about that," she said quietly. "Try again now." I did as she said and opened my eyes. They were stuck together with sleep and didn't want to open, but after a few moments, I was laying in my bed with both Mae and Sarah looking down at me. Mae was pacing back and forth frantically, and Sarah was sitting on the bed beside me. I looked down and noticed that I was not wearing what I had been when I had laid down the night

135

before. "Yeah, we had to change your shirt and remove your bed sheets. They were covered in puke, and well…pills."

It was all coming back to me. Further and further was last night with Mae on the couch fading away, and the remnants of my fight with Mae in my apartment and what I had done after came more into view. Both of them knew what had happened, but only one of them knew why.

"How did you guys get into the apartment last night?" I managed to say. I could feel some strength returning to me, and I managed to push myself up to lean against the wall.

"That's all you have to say to us?" Mae said. She began shouting but her voice slowly lowered its volume. "I have a spare key, idiot."

"Mae, calm down," Sarah said, her voice soothing and calm. It was the exact opposite of Mae's. "I came over last night because I couldn't stop thinking about you. You were acting so funny, and I wanted to see what was up. When I got here, the door was locked, and you weren't answering your phone or the door. I went to look through the window and I saw you on the bed…you were…I thought you were dead. I didn't know what to do, so I called Mae." I hadn't even realized that they had exchanged numbers the other night at the bar.

"Yeah, and then I had to come over and get the door open. We found you, and you were barely breathing. Why would you do this?" I could see that she was crying, and I could see that her state had caused Sarah to begin crying as well.

"I don't know, I think I took too many sleeping pills last night. I was…" I paused because I knew the next thing out of my mouth would basically expose what both Mae and I had done the day before. You could see that she was hoping I wouldn't say anything that would expose the both of us. "I don't know. I think I just got drunk and didn't realize how much I took." It wasn't my most convincing lie, but then again, I had almost died the night before, so I was hoping for the benefit of the doubt.

"Well, I would say we should take the bottle of pills away…but you took nearly all of them." She held up the bottle and shook it. I could only hear a few pills rattling around in the container. "You seemed fine yesterday after I left, what happened to make you want to go to sleep that badly?" The look on her face told me that the lie I had told just moments earlier was believed and that she didn't expect that Mae and I had done anything. The fact that she still cared for me after all I had done to her made me want to just blurt it out so she could save herself…instead, I was selfish and tried to keep up the ruse.

"I just was upset about the night before. I guess I just…" Mae interrupted.

"I called him, and we got into it over the phone." She looked at me straight in the eyes. "I said things I didn't mean, and I'm sorry." A softness returned to her face, one that I hadn't seen in a few days. I could see the apology wasn't just meant to keep Sarah off the scene of our betrayal, but it was also one that was real. One that was from the heart. If I was capable of crying, I probably would have at that moment.

"I said…and did things I didn't mean to, Mae. Can we please just forget this whole thing happened? I am obviously ok, and I just want to put it all behind us." This time it was my turn to give Mae the eye.

"You might be ok, but we need to talk about what happened last night…Chance, last night you tried to kill yourself." The words were not something I was expecting. I looked at her with surprise, and Mae did slightly as well.

"I didn't try to kill myself, Sarah. I just, I guess I just took too many sleeping pills. I…I just…" Sarah interrupted.

"Took too much? You literally took the majority of the bottle. I didn't really count as I cleaned them off your unconscious body and clothes and sheets…too much? No, that's not what happened. Whether you want to believe it or not, you were not just trying to go to sleep." She was beginning to cry. I sat up and put my hand on her shoulder to try and comfort her. She brushed me aside and put her face in her hands. She began to sob. I looked over at Mae, and she just shook her head and walked over to Sarah and put her arms around her. Sarah didn't brush her aside; in fact, she embraced Mae and just sat there crying for a few minutes. Mae was giving me looks that made me wish that I had not vomited up the pills the night before. She just sat there holding Sarah and looking at me. The look on her face was that of someone who was being tortured. Mae knew deep down that I hadn't tried to kill myself, or at least didn't intentionally do it. I had problems with substance abuse regardless of its type. Liquor, drugs, sleeping pills, one-night stands, and cigarettes, I was addicted to them all. I couldn't stop unless I was happy. On the other side of the poles,

I was. Or at least I told myself I was happy. I thought about the way I had treated Mae over the last few weeks on the other side. I was acting crazy, getting drunk, smoking, and randomly crying and acting like a complete mess. She didn't deserve that…especially on both sides. I couldn't take it anymore and just wanted out. I looked over at Mae and she gave me an understanding eye. She knew I hadn't tried to kill myself, but the truth was…maybe I did.

"I need a cigarette," I said, getting out of the bed and walking into my kitchen. I opened the freezer and pulled out one of my old packs and shook it. There were still a few left in the pack. I walked out toward the front steps and grabbed one of the lighters in the bowl by the door. I leaned up against the railing and lit the cigarette. I coughed violently, as I had forgotten how dry my mouth had initially been. I decided to just take the abuse and finish the cigarette…I needed a bit of pain right then. Every one of my extremities felt asleep, and my head was groggy. It was just like any other hangover, just like any other night. Unfortunately, it wasn't. Mae and Sarah came walking out to join me, or to leave, I didn't know which yet.

"Hey," Sarah said, coming over and standing next to me. I wanted to reach out and put my arm around her but feared another rejection, so I just continued smoking my cigarette. I decided to extend an olive branch and see if she wanted a drag. She grabbed the cigarette and took a long drag and handed it back to me. I looked at the cigarette in my hand and noticed that she had left some lipstick on the filter. I smiled as I inhaled another lung full of smoke and tasted her lips.

"Wow," Mae said as she looked as us both. "You two really are perfect for each other." She reached into her own purse and grabbed a cigarette of her own and began lighting it.

"What do you mean by that?" I asked while she tried to light her own cigarette. She had a knack for washing lighters as well, so I handed her mine, and she was able to finally light her smoke.

"I don't know. The way you're sitting there, it just makes me wish you both were smiling. I don't ever see you smile anymore." She took a breath and blew the smoke out of the side of her mouth.

"Yeah," Sarah responded. She looked up at me and peered into my eyes. "I found a reason to smile, but…" She looked down and sighed. "I don't think he is ready for it." She took one last drag of her cigarette and put it out on her shoe. She reached up to my face and grabbed my face in her hands. She stood up on her toes and kissed me on the lips. She lingered there for a few, and I could smell her breath. It smelled sweet, it smelled like it should smell. "You should call me when you want to smile. I don't think this is going to work out unless you really want it to. After last night, I don't know if I can handle whatever it is you have going on. If you ask me to stay, I will, but I am pretty sure you won't." She put her face in my chest and nuzzled it for a moment. She pulled away and smiled. "Take a shower, you smell." She backed up into the apartment and grabbed a bag off the couch. She slung it over her shoulder and walked out of my life. I just sat there finishing my cigarette like a fucking coward.

"What the fuck was that?" Mae said as Sarah reached her car got into it. "Fucking go after her."

"I'm not good for her, Mae. I'm not good for anybody." I pinched off the cherry of my second cigarette and placed the butt in my pocket. I walked inside and over to the sink. I grabbed a dirty glass and filled it with water and drank the entire glass, I repeated the task a second time. It barely felt like I drank anything. Mae came storming in.

"What do you mean by that? Are you stupid?" She came over and stood next to me in the kitchen. "Up until recently, you were pretty damn good for me. You're the reason I am even here at this point." She wasn't yelling, but she wasn't just talking either.

"What do you want me to say? I didn't want anyone to show up last night. Why couldn't you have just let me be, everyone would be better off." My last words stunned her, and she didn't even have a response. After collecting herself, she spoke, and this time she was yelling.

"Wow, what the fuck! So you wish you would have died last night? Are you serious?" She took a few more seconds to pick the right words. "Chance, did you really try to kill yourself?" I looked at her dead in the eyes, and I didn't have an answer. To be honest, I don't really know, myself. I think we can all agree that I have issues, but I never really thought they were too much. Even if things sucked here, I always had the other side of the poles to look forward to. I remembered taking the pills, that part wasn't a lie. What I didn't remember was how I was feeling when I took that second batch of pills. Usually, it was just go to bed and see Mae on the other side. Just like an addict, I would do anything to get my fix. Anything

139

to get that thing that I wanted…Mae. Now, she was here, looking at me with a look I had never seen from her: disappointment.

"Well?" she questioned again. Apparently, my blank stare was not an acceptable answer. "Are you even listening…" I interrupted her this time.

"I don't know, Mae. I just don't know. Can you not see that I am miserable? Can you not see?" I was starting to get angry again but didn't want to lose my temper. This was an argument that could be the end of things between us. "I just don't know where to go from here. How do we go back to where we were before? Before we were lying to people who care about us? Before we stopped being friends and not just people who are used to each other being around." I could see that those last few words hit home a bit deeper than I had intended. "I just…I just…I just want to be done, Mae. I don't want to do this anymore, and I don't know what else I can do to make you understand. I love you, more than you will ever know, but I think it's time we maybe were apart for a bit. Maybe long enough for me to get over these unrequited feelings that I have." I was shaking, and I could feel the hot tears rolling down my face. "I think you should go. Go start your life with Rebecca and forget about me. I will only ever hold you back, and I can't imagine being the person who does that to you." I was lightheaded and had to sit down, but I powered through. The kitchen counter was the only thing keeping me standing.

"So you want me to leave, is that it? Just go and leave you to try whatever this was again?" She slammed her hand down on the counter for effect.

"Yes, just go!" I shouted. "I just need to get my shit together, and it's really hard to do with you here." I walked up to her and took her hands. The way she flinched slightly when I reached for them killed me a bit inside. "Mae, you're my best friend. You have known me longer than anyone other than my parents. You're smart, and funny, and beautiful, but you will never love me the way I love you. I need to learn to get over you, and I literally have no idea how to do that." Her hands were soft, and her fingernails long. They dug into my hands as she held them tight.

"I don't want to leave you right now. You need me here, with you." Her grip tightened, and her posture loosened.

I had to say the next sentence, and I had to mean it. I had never meant it before…but this sentence might have been the most important thing I had ever said in my life. "Mae, I need you to go home. I don't want you to…but I need you to. Right now, you being here is not helping me, it's hurting me. When I figure shit out, I will give you a call, and maybe we can salvage whatever kind of relationship this is, but right now, you need to go." She pulled her hands away, and they were shaking. She looked up at me, and I could tell that she was biting her tongue so hard that I was surprised there wasn't any blood. She went over to the table and grabbed her bag and walked to the threshold of my front door. She turned around with sad eyes and a sad smile.

"Ok, Chance. I'll leave. Just know this. You don't think I can love you the same way that you claim to love me. You're wrong. If something happens to you, I will never be happy again. Figure your shit out, and I will be waiting." With that, she walked out of my door, and what I thought was out of my life forever. I took a deep breath and sighed and broke down into tears. I was able to make it to the kitchen table as I sat and cried for what felt like an hour. My head was ringing from the strain, and my entire body felt weak. Whether it was from the mistake I had made the night before or Mae leaving, I didn't know. One thing was for sure; I needed help. I just sat there looking at the blank screen of my phone as I wept. Who would I call? If not Mae, who would come to my aid in what was likely the most vulnerable state I had ever been in? I thought back to the dozen or so times that my mother had either called or texted. I decided to reach out and see if she could help me in ways she had tried to help before.

The reason my mother and I didn't talk much was the same reason that everyone in my life stopped talking to me…Mae. From an early age, my mother knew that Mae would be trouble. When she found out that she was a lesbian, it made matters infinitely worse. It had nothing to do with Mae and her choice of partners. It had everything to do with my mother knowing how much I loved that girl and had spent my entire youth and adolescence pining over her. My mother was always very protective of me and voiced her concerns about Mae often. I just got tired of my mother calling the woman I loved names and telling me I had to get over her. In my heart, I always felt that if I was here long enough, maybe Mae would fall in love with me the way I fell in love with her every time I saw her. Unfortunately, with each passing day, that became more of a dream than a reality. I really didn't remember when I started shifting to the other side of the poles at night. To me, that world was just as real as this one, but the feeling always lingered that it wasn't, and I was stuck in some type of fantasy. Even at a young age, I knew that what was happening to me wasn't something I should talk about. I remembered voicing opinions in school about my other life where I was a girl and I was happier. The Catholic school where I went didn't feel like these episodes were good and sent me to various types of punishments. Whether those punishments were for lying or storytelling, I didn't recall. I just knew that what happened to me every evening must be kept a secret, from everyone…even Mae.

I pulled out my phone and looked at the text chain from my mother, checking in. She had probably texted me twenty times to my one response. Noticing this, I instantly felt guilty. My mom was a great person who did everything she could to raise me right, which was hard, considering that I had never known who my father was. She never spoke about him, and at a young age, I had learned to stop asking. I wanted for nothing growing up, and she was the one who had made that happen. I shot her a quick message to see if she wanted to grab lunch and put the phone down on the table in order to go and see what the laundry situation looked like after the night before. Knowing my mom, she would want to come over after we ate to see how I was keeping up with the place. She had always been much cleaner than I was, and my habits didn't really leave a lot of time for cleaning. Usually, the only time I would clean anything up was when it became a bother or an inconvenience to me. Dishes pilling up or nothing clean to wear…you know, stuff like that. I didn't own a real vacuum, so God only knows what was in the thick carpeting in my living room. My bedroom had shorter carpet, and I had one of those push broom/vacuum hybrids that I had found at a garage sale one time. Needless to say, I should probably have invested in a vacuum. I spent the next hour or so cleaning up the place and placing my vomit laundry in a garbage bag to do later. Mae and Sarah had been kind enough to rinse it off, so it wasn't that terrible. Closer to noon, I heard the familiar sound of my phone vibrating on the kitchen table and went to go see who it was. Of course, it was my mom. She said she was free for lunch and that we could meet at one of her favorite restaurants in town. They were known for their Italian beef sandwiches. I told her I would be there in about thirty minutes, and she said she would probably beat me there. I put the phone back on the table and went to go find something less disgusting to wear.

An exhausting thirty or so minutes later, I was pulling into the parking lot. I was going to take my motorcycle, but it started raining, and I didn't feel like trying to kill myself twice in one day. As I walked into the parking lot, I noticed an unfamiliar vehicle with a familiar license plate. I walked around the vehicle, taking a look at its condition.

"Really, mom? This thing is a beater," I said to myself quietly as I realized how bad the car was. I looked back at mine and laughed. It really wasn't much better than hers. I shook my head and continued into the restaurant. I blew past the hostess, knowing exactly where my mother would be sitting. She, like myself, was a creature of habit, and when we had these little lunches however infrequently she sat in the same place every time. God help the people who sat in that booth when she came in. It hadn't happened yet, so I wondered if she called ahead to reserve this specific booth.

"Chance," I heard her say right as I turned the corner to the back area in which her favorite booth resided. "You're late." She stood up and walked toward me to greet me. When we were close, she wrapped her arms around me in a hug and lingered for a bit. "It's good to see you," she said, her voice strained slightly. It could have been her emotion, or her allergies. Whichever one it was, she made no mention.

"Hey there," I said as she released the hug and we both slid into the booth. "Have you been here long?"

"Not really, only about ten minutes or so. Just long enough for the waitress to forget that I am here and not bring me my coffee." She peaked around the back room to see if she could locate the waitress. It was as if we were in a zombie movie, there wasn't a living sole in site. "Well, she has to come back here eventually." I laughed.

"Some things never change," I said as I looked down at the menu." New menus, eh?" I held it up and realized that nothing on it seemed familiar.

"Yeah, you didn't notice, did you?" She pointed around the restaurant and laughed. "They were bought out by someone else. The place has a different name." She held up the menu and showed me the front page.

"Wow. Yeah, I didn't even notice." I started realizing that the entire place was decorated differently. You could still see some of the old paint and wallpaper peeking out from the corners. "When was the last time we were here?" I asked as I decided to take a look at the menu and see what I actually wanted to eat.

"I don't know. Probably the last time you texted me to come to lunch." She picked up her menu and began looking it over. "Probably about four months. They did a pretty good job remodeling in that time. I'm impressed." She peaked over and gave me a quick glance from above the menu.

The conversation was just like that for about ten minutes or so until the waitress finally came from around the corner and gave a look as if she had completely forgotten we were there. A few moments later, she came running up to greet us.

"Hey there, I didn't see you back here. What can I get you to drink?" Without skipping a beat, my mother answered.

"You could get the cup of coffee I ordered nearly twenty minutes ago." She looked over at me. "He will have a whiskey and coke." The lady looked at me as if she was going to ask for my ID. Apparently, I looked a bit long in the tooth, and she decided against asking. I was a little upset that my mother had ordered for me, but that was exactly what I was going to get, so I let it slide.

"Wow, am I that predictable?" I said as the waitress wrote down the drink order and left quickly, most likely to not invoke any more of my mother's wrath.

"Well, yes, and well, yes," she said, continuing to look over the menu. "So I might as well ask. How's Mae doing?" I looked up at her from the menu and acted surprised.

"Wow, it only took about fifteen minutes. That's a new record." We both pretended to laugh and hide that we were both hurting inside. "She's good, I guess. She is dating someone, and it seems serious." My mother perked up.

"Oh, you don't say?" She sat up in her seat and took a bit more notice to what I was saying.

"Yeah, we actually got into kind of a fight." I looked around for the waitress. My drink could not come fast enough.

"A fight about what?" If her interest was genuine, the question didn't feel like it.

"I finally told Mae, well…I guess Rebecca confronted me, and Mae found out how I feel about her." My mother gave a look like she was stunned.

"What? You're in love with her?" She exaggerated her gestures in an attempt to poke fun at Mae. "Chance, everyone knew you were in love with her…but her." She shook her head and went back to reading the menu. "Let me guess, she didn't take it well and you two are quarreling over it." I took a moment to calm down and check again for my drink. Both of which didn't seem like they were going my way.

"Yeah, she didn't take it well. We got into it at the bar, and I got drunk and went home." I took a moment and thought about whether I should say what I wanted to say. I guess I never really expected to see Mae again after that day, at least not on this side of the poles. *I might as well get this off my chest and tell my mother*, I thought…maybe our relationship could be bettered for it. "She came over later that night drunk as well…and we…" I didn't even have to finish the sentence, and my mother was on it.

"No…there is no way she would…Chance…what did you do?" I shook my head.

"What did I do? She came over and threw herself at me." I realized at that point that I should have just shut up.

"She's gay, Chance, and you thought maybe she would like it and be not gay? Are you stupid?" I waved my hands and motioned that I wanted the conversation over.

"You know what. Forget I mentioned anything. I thought I could vent a bit, and I thought you would be excited that Mae and I are fighting."

"No!" she insisted. "Why would you think I would be happy to see you unhappy?" For the first time that day, I felt as if she was being genuine. "Wow, you must really resent me if you could say that. I am your mother and want nothing but the best for you. You just don't want anyone telling you their opinions, especially if they include Mae." She took a deep breath, and at that point, we realized that the drinks had arrived. The waitress stood there awkwardly and just put them on the table. I motioned to her that I would like another drink, and she quickly slipped away. I took a long sip form the glass. There was a ton of ice, so I had to use my finger to block it in order to not have ice slap me in the face. Before I realized it, my sip turned into the entire drink. I placed it down on the table and wiped my face. I looked up, and my mother was just shaking her head.

"What?" I responded, knowing exactly what she was upset about. Aside from Mae, my drinking was one thing that she really didn't care for. Which in this case was funny, since she had ordered my drink. I guess people catch themselves enabling the ones they love, even if they know that what those people are doing is hurting them. "You ordered it for me!"

She continued shaking her head and sighed. "Yeah, to drink over a period of time. I didn't order you a shot, Chance." She shrugged and took a sip of her coffee. She didn't like her coffee too hot, so she and I had that in common.

"Yeah, well. The last few days have been a bit rough. I just want to go to sleep for a year." I leaned back into the booth and held up the menu again. I just needed something light. I decided to try their French onion soup...that is, if the waitress ever came back. My mother reached across the table in a rare moment of sincerity and put her hand on top of mine.

"Chance, are you ok? I guess I am used to seeing you look tired and depressed, but today is different. You haven't shaved in days, your eyes are bloodshot. It looks as though you haven't been eating at all, and...well, believe it or not, I am your mother and I worry about you. I try to reach out when I can, and you're just living your life. I just want to be a small part of it." She paused for a second, and then as if trying to slip back into her regular persona, she snickered and took another sip of coffee. "Well, with Mae out of the picture, I guess I am the only girl in your life now." The words left her mouth, and I could see that she regretted saying them. It was meant to be a joke, but the argument with Mae was still too fresh. I decided to let sleeping dogs lie and pretend that the comment wasn't as hurtful as it was. When she realized that I was taking the high road and avoiding the comment, I could see a look of appreciation on her face.

"Well, what can I get you two to eat?" the waitress said, scaring the shit out of me. I guess I was so focused on the conversation that I completely missed that she was standing there. Truth is, I think my mother saw her and chose to ignore her. I had to give her credit, she could be a real bitch if she wanted to.

"I'll just have the house salad with whatever your house dressing is." She handed back the menu without even looking at the waitress.

I looked up, and she was nervously smiling at me. "I will just have the bowl of French onion soup, if you don't mind. Thank you." I handed her back the menu. "My drink?" I asked as she took it.

"It will be right up. Sorry, we are a bit short-staffed. New owners didn't like the idea of having so many servers for lunch. My apologies for being a bit vacant." She smiled and grabbed my empty glass and was gone. For some reason, I didn't realize how attractive she was until she smiled.

"Wow, are you really checking her out?" my mother asked, apparently forgetting what kind of person she had raised. "Aren't you pining over someone else?"

"I never mentioned someone else, who are you talking about?" She caught me by surprise with the question.

"Mae...Mae...you know the girl you have been chasing for your entire adult life..." She looked at me as if I was crazy. "Wait? Is there someone else as well?" I guess even though we didn't see each other as much as we should have, she still knew how to read her son like a book. "Oh wow, there is someone else, isn't there?" She sat back and shook her head.

"Yeah, I guess there is," I said, scratching my head.

"You guess? Well, I guess that about sums it up." She just looked at me like I was nuts. "You have so much potential, but you just waste it. Here you are, pining for a woman, and then one falls into your lap and you're just clueless with what to do and how to handle the situation. What did this girl say when you told her you and Mae...you know." Though she was comfortable talking with her son about this stuff, she didn't really like using the vocabulary necessary.

"Well...she doesn't know. The Mae and I thing only happened the once, and it won't happen again. Mae and I are taking some time apart, and she is going to fix things between her and Rebecca. Hopefully, I can do the same with Sarah." The waitress could not have picked a better time to bring my drink over. She had learned from the previous encounters and quickly left. Prior to her leaving, I made sure to give her the hand gesture for another drink.

Ignoring the fact that I had ordered another drink, my mother clapped excitedly. "Sarah, is that her name? I'm glad you remembered a girl's name other than Mae's. Is this Rebecca Mae's, uh…partner, or whatever they call it?"

Her backhanded remark about Mae's partner and the word they kind of pissed me off. Even on this side of the poles, I didn't like that kind of talk. "They?" I tried to convey with my tone that I was not happy with her choice of words. "To answer your question, yes. Rebecca is Mae's girlfriend. They have been seeing each other for a few weeks." I took a drink. This one was a bit stronger than the first.

"Well, that's great for them. I hope it all goes well." She paused for a second, realizing that what she had said was just a canned response. "Well, you know what I mean. I hope things go well, after all of this…well, drama." She kind of hid a sideways smile. She definitely was my mother… she loved drama. I, on the other hand, hated it, but unfortunately it seemed to follow me wherever I went. She continued to sip her coffee and tried and hide her satisfaction in the matter. I could see the look on her face change slowly from satisfied to depressed as she realized that she was, in fact, taking great pleasure from the pain of others, including her only son.

"Well, let's change the subject," I said as I took another sip. My mother decided it was far easier to follow suit and sip on her coffee a bit as well. After trying to change the subject, we sat there in an awkward silence until the food came. During the meal itself, nothing of substance was exchanged as well. The most we did was comment on the quality of the food. Obviously, my mother had issues with the amount of dressing on the salad as well as the lack of fresh ground pepper. The meal could have been made by a five-star chef, and she would have found a dozen reasons to complain. If I was going to be honest, the soup wasn't very good, and the only reason I didn't complain was the fact that my mother had treated the waitress fairly badly, and I didn't want to add insult to injury.

"Well, that was fun," my mother said as she grabbed the bill to pay. Even if I'd had the money, I wouldn't have bought the meal anyway. My mother had come into some money recently, which was one of the reasons I wondered about the condition of her car. I thanked the waitress and my mother for the meal, and we walked out of the seating area and into the parking lot. As we walked by my mother's car, she slapped the back of it and smiled. "Got this from an auction. It's a classic."

"What happened to your other car? That thing was pretty nice." I looked through the windows at the condition of the vehicle and shook my head. "I can't believe you're actually driving this thing."

"Oh, shut it. I still have the other car. I wanted to drive this today. I am taking it in next week to have it restored." She walked over to the driver's side and pulled out her keys. I guess it shouldn't have come as too much of a surprise. I didn't know where my mother got her money. My guess was a good investment or two, but we never spoke about it, so I never really asked or cared enough to ask.

"Well, I hope this thing actually makes it to the shop," I said as I walked over to my mother to give her the hug I knew she would inevitably ask for. The second she realized what I was doing, she came in as well and we embraced for a moment. As I tried to pull away, I could feel her grip slightly tighten, letting me know that she was not ready to end the affection.

"I am glad you called," she said, her voice breaking slightly. "We need to do this more often. Maybe if you fix things up with this Sarah girl, we can do something like that." She pulled away and grabbed me by my shoulders. "I just want you to be happy, Chance. You're my only child, and you deserve happiness, whether you believe it or not." She looked as if she was going to say another thing, but she bit her tongue.

"What were you going to say?" I took her a bit by surprise as she looked at me with eyes that told me I was not going to like what she had to say.

"I am glad you finally decided to attempt to get over Mae. She might be a good friend, but she is not good for you. It is not healthy to obsess over someone like that for so long. It's time to move on, and I am proud of you for trying." She smiled and walked over to the car and got in. I didn't want to let her have the last word, but I could tell that it took a lot out of her to be heartfelt. Even if it had a jab at Mae in it.

"Thanks," I said as she sat in the seat. She looked back and smiled.

"Get out of the way, or I'm going to run you over." She laughed as she put the keys into the ignition and put the car in gear. She backed up a bit and rolled down her passenger side window.

"Chance. You need to shave." She smiled and put the car in drive, and then she was gone. I shook my head and laughed, hoping that maybe we would get together more. She was my mother, and yes, our relationship was a bit odd, but she did care for me. The way a mother always cares for her children, no matter how old they get. It was moments like that when I felt terrible for how our relationship had suffered over the years. It was as if I was sober for the first time…obviously a metaphor. Without Mae on my mind, I was already beginning to see clearer. She was really like a drug. I guess it was all still pretty new to me, since it had only been a few hours since we had last spoken. We would see how I felt in a couple of days, and we would see if the detoxing hit me hard.

I walked over to the car and got in. I started her up and drove back to my apartment. The ride home was just as boring as the ride there. It was only made a bit better by the buzz that I had going on a bit from lunch. That second drink had been strong, but the food had started to kill it a bit. When I got home, I walked into my apartment and closed the door behind me. It was quiet…too quiet. I walked over to the fridge and grabbed a beer out of the box that was on the bottom shelf. There was only one left.

"Fuck," I said to myself. I looked through the cabinets, and all the bottles that I had were empty. I went to the nightstand where I'd left the bottle the other night. It was gone as well. I noticed that Mae and Sarah had probably cleaned up as they waited for me to regain consciousness. They most likely even got along a bit. Mae would have been extra nice since our transgressions the night before. When she felt guilty, she was infinitely less confrontational. I sat down on my computer and turned it on. The fan on the back of the tower buzzed as if something was stuck in it. I kicked it slightly, and the fan realigned and stopped its complaining. I checked my emails and noticed that I had a ton from the past few days. Most of them were customers looking for me to bid on work or some people complaining that the work they had requested was coming close to being due. I pulled out my notepad and made myself a list of what I had to accomplish in order to get paid and actually pay my bills this month. I had started to run out of cash over the past week, and it was time to get some work done.

I spent the next hour or so cleaning my room in order to concentrate on my work. For some reason, I needed the room to be clean in order to be productive. Without a clean workspace, I was completely useless. Once the immediate area was clean, I slowly sipped my beer as I worked on finishing a few projects that would bring a bit of money in. I worked until night set in and I had to turn on one of my desk lamps in order to see what I was doing on my keyboard and stylus pad. Once I had turned in the last of my commissions, I invoiced the customers and sat back in my chair. I pulled out my phone and noticed I had a text message. I unlocked it and quickly went to my messages. I was disappointed to see that it was my mother thanking me for meeting her for lunch. I responded and threw the phone back down on my desk.

"What now?" I said to myself as I sat there completely alone in my room. I turned on the TV and went to the cabinet for a bag of chips and sat and watched some crime show I had never seen before. Before I knew it, I could barely keep my eyes open, and I began to drift off. I leaned back into my bed and closed my eyes. I couldn't wait to see Mae. To touch her and to kiss her. To taste and smell her. I was an addict through and through, but all my other vices just masked the one…Mae. I fell asleep staring at the ceiling fan above my bed and thinking of her.

Chapter 12

Before I opened my eyes, I could feel Mae's body against mine. She was sound asleep and was snoring softly. We had both fallen asleep on the couch, and the covers had slidden off. I was freezing. I reached over and grabbed the covers and pulled them over my head. I most definitely didn't want to get up, but I guess we had turned off the heat and the entire apartment was freezing cold.

"Go back to bed," Mae said. Her words were barely understandable in her sleeping state.

"Aren't you cold?" I said, trying to get myself comfortable. I couldn't understand how the hell I'd slept like this. I reached over to check my phone and realized that it was still dark out. The phone said it was only around quarter after five in the morning.

"It's so early. Stop moving," Mae said again, her words clearer this time. She must have started to wake up. This was not a good thing. Mae before seven in the morning was not a pretty site.

"Go back to bed," I said as I tried to get off the couch without waking her. After a few moments, I managed to get off the couch and onto the floor. The room was dark except for the few nightlights we had scattered around the place. I bet if I could really see, I would have seen my breath, that's how cold it felt. After stepping on literally every item that was in my way, I managed to make it to the thermostat to turn the temp up a bit. After a few moments, I could hear the heater kick on and air start to move in the apartment. It was surprisingly cold, and I needed to make sure we both didn't die of hypothermia. After that, I went to go put some actual clothes on. As much as I loved walking around in just my underwear, it was rather chilly. I threw on a shirt and a pair of flannel pajama pants and thought about going and laying back down with Mae. The truth was, I was pretty wide awake and felt pretty well-rested, as well. I decided to grab one of the blankets off our bed and put it on top of Mae to help warm her up. She smiled as she pulled the blanket up close to her face and nuzzled up into the armrest of the couch. I smiled, knowing that she was a bit more comfortable. I walked over to the kitchen and made a pot of coffee and watched some videos on my phone. A few minutes after the coffee was done, I sat down to drink it, and I received a text message from Albert. It was a very enthusiastic text asking where we could meet up to discuss our little coup d'état we were planning. I thought about it for a minute, sipping my coffee. I responded that we could just meet at the diner and discuss things, but only if we were both keeping it on the down low. I didn't want any random strangers hearing about what we were planning to do. I sat there sipping my coffee until the sun started to come up. I only noticed it because of where I was sitting. It was literally the worst spot in the apartment. It seemed that at least six hours a day, the sun shone or appeared to shine right through the window and right into your eyes. I struggled for a few minutes and then decided to move to the chair next to the couch. My phone vibrated again, stopping the video about fossils that I was watching. I swapped over to my messages; again, it was from Albert. He wanted to meet that morning before he headed into the office. I looked down at my old ratty t-shirt that had coffee stains and paint splotches on it.

"You should just go like that," Mae said as she poked her head out from the side of the couch. "You look sexy as hell in your flannel." She reached over and put her hand on my leg and ran her fingernails down my shins. Ever hair on my body stood at attention. "Is that Albert?" She continued to rub my leg, placing her hand through the bottom of the leg in my pajamas to touch my actual skin. Once she realized that I had goosebumps, she smiled and kept going.

"Yeah, he wants to meet about his uncle. I still can't believe that he wants to go through with this. This could potentially ruin his uncle's life." I put the phone down and moved over to the couch and sat by her stomach. I leaned back extra hard to try and squish her. She was not amused.

"You're going to crush me," she joked in between pretending to suffocate. I pretended to hit her for the jab at my weight. I knew I had gained a little bit recently, but she knew it bothered me. She was a fan of making fun of someone for what bothers them to help them get over it. It was still early on, and I was clearly not over it.

"You're lucky I love you so much, or I might really crush you when you talk like that." I jumped around a few times, bouncing on the couch for good measure. Mae made a quiet strained grunt every time I landed. We both laughed for a moment at how silly we were acting. We hadn't had a moment like that in a bit, and after the day before, it was nice.

"So, where are you meeting him?" she finally asked, knowing it was on my mind.

"Where else would I have breakfast…" I said, pausing for effect. In unison we both answered the question.

"The diner!" She laughed as she finally realized that she was no longer going back to bed, and she struggled to get up from her supine position.

"Make sure he pays." She smiled as she yawned. "Least he can do for risking your neck on this whole thing." The words left her mouth, and I could see the look of worry slowly return to her face. A second later it was gone. I hated making her worry, which was funny because apparently that was all I had done the past few days…I wasn't proud of that.

"So, I guess I should go and get ready. Can't show up for a coup in pajama pants and an old t-shirt." I put my hand on her leg and put all my body weight on it as I got up. She groaned as I stood and pretended that her leg was broken. "Not funny. I'm serious. You're going to give me some kind of eating disorder."

"Sorry, I couldn't help myself," she said, rubbing her calf where my arm was. I couldn't tell if she was just faking, or if I put too much weight on it and she was actually in pain. I felt less bad since she kept calling me fat. We said a few more pleasantries, and I went to take a shower and get dressed. I got undressed and took a look in the mirror and took a look at myself. Mae was right, I had gained a bit of weight. I guess I was getting older, and I needed to start taking better care of myself. Although I still felt young. It was beginning to show. I turned on the shower and let it warm up, and I continued to look at myself in the mirror. I pulled on my face to get a more detailed look. I could see wrinkles and blemishes where there used to not be any. I thought of Rebecca on the other side of the poles and didn't remember her looking like this. In fact, she looked younger and in way better shape. I shook that thought out of my head. We may have looked the same, but we were two completely different people. I was not her, and she was not me. I finally gave up feeling sorry for myself and stepped into the shower. The water was hot, and it felt amazing. I took an unusually long time in the shower. Normally, I was an in-and-out kind of girl, but today felt different. I needed it more than I usually did, for some reason. After I was done cleaning myself, I just continued to do it again and again. A knock at the door disrupted my routine.

"You ok in there, Becks?" Mae said from the other side of the bathroom door. "You have been in there forever."

"Sorry!" I yelled back through the curtain. "I'll be right out." I decided that four times was too many to wash myself and rinsed myself a final time in order to exit the shower and begin my day. As I dried my hair in my towel, I thought about exactly why I had taken such a long shower. Was I dreading this talk with Albert that much? Was I procrastinating in order to be late and screw things up? I wasn't one to upset the status quo, at least not on this side of the poles, but was I really chickening out subconsciously? I shook off the idea and wrapped the towel around my chest and tucked the last corner into itself to hold the towel in position. I walked to the mirror to check it one last time. The same familiar face was staring back at me. I remembered the other day, and chills came rushing down every inch of my body. I checked one last time, just to be sure.

"Hey there," Mae said as I opened the bathroom door and walked into the living room. "Enough hot water left for the rest of the apartment complex?" She was up, cuddled up with a cup of coffee on the couch. Her glasses were on the tip of her nose as she was reading something. I didn't see whether it was a schoolbook or one of mine from the shelf. Mae didn't own any of her own books...as she said, since we were married, all my books were half hers anyway. She would only read one or two a year, about a page at a time. She always complained that she could never remember the books when she read them and that was why she really didn't like to read. I had tried to explain to her that if you start the book and then a year later finish the book...that's why you can never remember anything. The same thing happened with some of my writing. I usually had to go back and read a few pages, if not chapters, to get back in the groove. I guess it really depended on how long it had been since I picked up my laptop to write.

Work was much different. I did so much damn research on what I was writing about that I usually remembered the story for months and months afterwards. If it was just an article, I was known to recite entire pieces a few months later. Each word was carefully chosen, since some columns only allowed a certain size of article to fit in the magazine or paper. My personal writing was much different. That was usually why Mae didn't like reading it. She said it was just like listening to me talk, but about other people. She didn't care for it.

As I walked into the bedroom and got dressed, Mae and I had a bit of banter back and forth about random things. We talked about my work and her school. We talked about the future and what she wanted to do with her degree when she finally got it. We may have mentioned a house and maybe kids and a dog. I loved the idea of having all those things with her, it just was weird planning anything. On the other side, I could barely get through the day, let alone think about the next one. Here, I was happy, and that might have had something to do with it. I made a mental note to plan some things on the other side. Try and make my life better in whatever way I could. Not having Mae in my life didn't scare me as much here as it did over there. I guess it was because she was just in the other room, and over there she most definitely was not...especially now.

"Becks?" I heard her say. I must have been lost in thought and hadn't heard her.

"Oh, sorry. What did you say?" I tightened up my pants, obviously unhappy as to how they were fitting.

"You're going to be late." She was handing me a pair of socks. I had completely forgotten about socks. I hated going anywhere barefoot. Even on this side, where my feet were nice and not disgusting. I looked down at chips in the paint. Maybe Mae and I should have a spa day soon.

"Thank you," I said as I grabbed them and hopped around on one foot to put the first sock on. I repeated the process with the second foot and finally stabilized myself.

"Oh wow, you're so graceful." Mae laughed as I realized she had taken a quick video on her cell phone. "I have definitely got to save this."

"Thanks, I thought you were supposed to love and support me." I fixed my socks to make sure they were not twisted and gave her an evil look.

"Yeah, support you in life, not support you when you're about to fall over putting on socks. I should have put something about videotaping you during embarrassing moments in our vows." She stuck her tongue out at me as she watched the video a few times and smiled. I am sure I would be seeing a lot of that video soon enough. Mae always liked to send them to me via email or post them on social media. Though I was not a big social media person, Mae was, and so were our friends. Yeah, we didn't see them often, but I would most likely get the random text from one of them in the future saying how funny the video was.

"Well," I said as I finally stood up fully dressed. "Wish me luck." I looked around for my car keys for a minute and then decided to take the bike.

"Awww, you're taking the bike without me?" she said sadly. "Are you sure that I can't come with?"

I shrugged as I threw the keys up and caught them in the other hand. "I think its best that whatever information he gives me stays between him and me. God only knows what is going to happen with all this stuff." I reached over for the backpack that I used while riding and started to put some notepads as well as my laptop into it. I looked over at Mae, and she just looked at me with her puppy dog eyes. "Fine, maybe I can take you out for a ride after I get back. As long as the weather holds up. Sound good?" A smile immediately returned to her face when I mentioned a ride, and she jumped up and down on the bed excitedly.

"Maybe we can grab lunch or something. If your date doesn't last too long." She got up from the bed and walked up to me as if she was going to give me a kiss. At the last second, she pulled away and walked right by me into the living room.

"Cold!" I said as my heart melted a bit with her proximity. "I guess I will just have to make sure I get my kiss on this date." I turned around, and she was right there to give me a kiss on the lips. It was more playful than anything, but a few moments later, our lips parted.

"Can't have you going out there looking for kisses. That's my department," she said with a devilish grin on her face. "There's more where that came from when you come back...with that bike." She added the last part as she brushed her finger along the bottom of my chin.

"Fine, I guess I have to come back to get that second kiss...and maybe a third?" I walked by her and into the living room to find my shoes. I needed to make sure I wore shoes that were good for riding a bike. That meant I couldn't wear anything cute.

"Getting a bit greedy, aren't you? I guess I can see what I can do when you get back. Also, it depends on where we go on that bike. It better be someplace nice." She sat down on the couch and picked up her book and opened it to the page she was on. I could tell that she wasn't really planning on reading, but she wanted me to know that she had other things to do that day. I smiled at how predictable she was. God, I loved this woman.

"Alright, I'll see you later," I said as I waved goodbye. She smiled and did a cute little half wave as if I was bothering her. That was something she did often. I walked through the door and made my way to my motorcycle. As I walked, I tried to put my hair into some type of braid to hold it up. It was just long enough to put into a hair tie. By the time I reached the garage, my hair was up, and I reached into my backpack and pulled out my sunglasses that I used on my bike. They fit really tight and held on while riding nicely...they were also very expensive. I smiled as I slung my leg over the bike and turned the engine on. Even though I played off that I didn't like the bike that much, I had to say...I loved the thing. I revved the engine a few times and put up the kickstand and was off. I decided to take the long way to the diner by taking a left out of our little apartment complex. It was really only a few minutes longer, but there was a long curve that I really loved taking fast. As I hit the main road, I hit the throttle and sped off like a bullet, faster and faster as I realized that nobody seemed to be on the road that morning. I took the opportunity to move around the lane a bit, ducking from the right side to the left side in a serpentine pattern. It was something I had been taught during the class to get my license. They called it exploring the road, even though that sounded dumb as hell. Basically, learning the road and your limitations on the bike. You would normally do this if there was a bit of water or rocks on the road, and you wanted to make yourself more comfortable while riding. I sometimes did this on new roads, but I hardly ever drove on roads that I didn't know very well. Let's be honest, though, I usually did it because it was fun and looked cool. I wound side to side until I reached the large turn that I loved, the reason that I had taken this way. I made the turn and excelled up until the road started to curve. The curve wasn't sharp enough to have to worry; it was long and perfect. I leaned the bike in toward the turn and used my body to keep the bike upright. I turned the throttle slowly and kept the bike at a single constant speed…fast. I whipped my face into the wind and shook my head. This feeling was one of the greatest on either side of the poles, but unfortunately, I really only enjoyed it on this side. I think it had something to do with the hair, which means that I might be mistaken about a long summer in my twenties on the other side when I had hair down to my elbows. Mae didn't let me forget, since she had several pictures of me on her phone and computer. I bet she had deleted them by now. No matter, nothing could get in my way. I may not have had her there, but I definitely had her here. That was all that mattered. I finished off the remainder of my ride on the straightaway that led right into the main street a few blocks south of the diner. I did the usual tricks that I normally did alone. I rode a few miles with no hands and steered the bike by moving side to side with my upper body. If you have ever ridden a bike, you know exactly what I am talking about. I was able to do this for long stretches since my bike had an aftermarket cruise control, something that was usually only available in choppers. Right outside of town, I began to slow down and pay attention for cops; they liked to hide down the alleyways and side streets. I usually was pretty good at getting out of tickets if I got pulled over, puppy dog eyes and a pouty lip were all that was ever needed. Mae hated it because she was never able to get out of them. I, on the other hand, was an expert. I found a spot only a block from the diner and decided to park the bike there and walk the short distance. By the time I walked into the diner, I could see Albert sitting in the corner, looking as nervous as possible. I swear to God, if you walked in and I asked you who looked the most suspicious you would have picked him eleven times out of ten. I waved to the waitstaff and motioned that I was going to sit with him. A young woman server I had never seen before just waved me over.

"Good morning, Rebecca," Albert said nervously. He looked genuinely disheveled, like he hadn't slept in a night or two. "Thanks for meeting on such short notice." He ran his hands through his hair and took a sip from the mug at the table. He grimaced as if it was something stronger than coffee. Come to think of it, he smelled a bit of liquor.

"Hey there, Albert," I said as I pulled out one of the chairs across from him and sat down. I held up the empty mug at the table and looked for the waitress. She waved that she understood the gesture and she came over in an instant with a hot pot of coffee. She poured it nervously, and a few drops landed on my arm. She apologized quickly and was gone.

"Wow, must be her first day," Albert said, half laughing. It looked like he was trying to lighten the mood.

"Yeah, I guess. Are you ok?" I asked as I noticed that he was fidgeting a bit.

"Yeah, I am just nervous about this whole thing. I am not a problem starter, but I just feel like I have to do something…right?" He took another drink from the mug and took a deep breath. "Are we doing the right thing?"

I blew into the hot mug and took a small sip. "Yeah, I mean, we are journalists, right? We have to uncover things like this, it's what we are for." I took another sip and followed suit by taking another deep breath. He was so nervous that it was actually making me more nervous. "This could be our one chance to uncover some serious corruption in this state. Really help people see these crooks for what they truly are. Don't you want to do that? I definitely do." I took another deep breath and paused. I could see the thoughts working around in his head. My comments looked as if they were making him a bit more comfortable, and he started looking a bit less nervous. Another sip from his mug and it was clearly empty. The waitress came over quickly and asked him if he wanted a refill. He motioned that he was good. After she left, he pulled out a fairly decent-sized flask and poured some more of its contents into the mug. He looked over at me and shrugged.

"I just am a mess." He laughed awkwardly. "I just…I just need this right now."

I shrugged. "You don't have to explain that to me. I am no stranger to needing a bit of help coping every now and then. Maybe even a bit more than that." I smiled and tried to make him comfortable. He nodded and took another sizeable sip from his mug and reached for his backpack. Prior to pulling anything out from his bag, he looked around the place suspiciously to make sure that nobody was, in fact, watching him. Once he felt comfortable that he was not being spied on, he pulled out a fairly large binder. It looked like the scrapbooks my mother used to make at the local hobby store. It was crammed full, and you could see picture corners and documents hanging out. He motioned for me to come sit next to him and I did without hesitation. As I sat next to him, he leaned in close and opened up the binder and flipped the pages slowly. The damn thing was filled to the brim with severely incriminating photos of not only his uncle taking bribes with the associated bank statements, but a ton of other predominant political figures, including the friggin' governor. It was amazing how much information was in this binder. Too be honest, it seemed a little too good to be true how much information was in there and how well-laid-out the information was. Whoever had given this to Albert had bigger things in mind than just a small-time newspaper editor.

"This is crazy," I said as he pushed the binder in front of me and sat back, taking another sip from his drink.

"Yeah, I can't believe it myself. There is just so much information here that can incriminate so many people. I almost just want to burn it and forget it even exists." Once his mug was empty, he didn't even try to keep up his little farce. He took the flask out and just started drinking straight from it. The waitress came over and went to refill his mug.

"Wait, are you guys talking about scrapbooking? I used to love doing that!" She looked over at the mess before him. "Well, we all have to start somewhere," she said as she smiled awkwardly and walked back to behind the counter. Albert sat back and relaxed a bit. This woman just walked right up to him and had no idea what he was so nervous about.

"Yeah, maybe all this cloak-and-dagger shit is all in my head." He seemed to finish the contents of his flask and picked up a menu. "I should put something in my stomach. Do you want anything to eat? My treat." I smiled and nodded as I picked up the menu. I was a bit hungry.

Albert and I spent the next few hours going over each page of the binder, and I took notes on everyone. Some of the photos were labeled with the names of the figures, some of the figures you could identify just by looking at them, and some of the people we actually had to Google. From what it looked like, half of the entire state senate was in this binder. People from both sides of the aisle clearly either taking bribes, performing illegal acts, and even worse. I used nearly an entire legal pad prior to the waitress coming up to us and asking if could clear the tab since she was leaving for the day. Albert gladly paid and asked to open up another tab since we were clearly going to stay for lunch.

The hours flew by as the pile of notes in front of me grew. Page by page, his disheveled binder became an organized piece of evidence that could incriminate dozens of people. One of those people being his uncle, who seemed to play second fiddle to the majority of crimes in there. After we ate lunch and a second helping of dessert, we decided that enough was enough and called it quits.

"Wow, I can't believe what time it is!" I said as I yawned and took a sip of extremely cold coffee. I grimaced at the taste but needed the caffeine.

"Yeah, I feel a bit better now that we have a bit of order to this whole thing. Thank you again for meeting me and helping me organize my thoughts. It really means a lot that you would put yourself on the line for me." You could tell that the look on his face was sincere, and it looked like a bit of the stress on his shoulders was beginning to dissipate. That was a good thing because he was either going to die of a heart attack or a hangover.

"That's a good thing. You're not going through this alone. Just remember that." I patted him on the back as I picked up my bag. For some reason, my bag always felt heavier when I had taken a bunch of notes, and I definitely took a bunch of notes that day. I was going to have to do a ton of research that night in order to get my thoughts around what path we were going to take with this thing. With every page in that damn binder, another controversy unfolded. With each controversy, were half a dozen guilty individuals. It was nothing short of a bombshell. This single binder would disrupt so much more than the little newspaper that we wrote for. This wasn't just Albert's uncle, this was the state's government. I just couldn't wrap my head around it.

"You good?" Albert said as he threw some more cash down on the table and smiled at the waitress as she came and thanked him. "You look like I felt this morning." He took a deep breath and took a step. You could tell he was worried about the amount he drank, but in reality, it had been several hours and a ton of food later. He took a step with little issue and instantly looked more confident.

"Yeah, I am fine. I just think that there is a ton of information to look through. Do you mind if I take this home with me and take a look at it some more?" I grabbed the binder and held it up.

"I guess, just make sure you don't leave it anywhere or lose it. That thing is a curse." He laughed awkwardly as I held it up. I put it in my bag and zipped it up.

"Don't worry. This isn't going to leave my sight. You have my word." I slapped the bag where the binder resided. He seemed to smile, and he started walking toward the exit.

"Alright," he said as we walked through the door and were about to part ways. "Seriously. Thank you for everything." He came in for an oddly attempted hug. I decided to just go with it and not make him feel worse than he obviously was already feeling. "Have a good evening." Were the last things he said and then he walked off down the street toward the setting sun.

I pulled my phone out of my pocket and texted Mae that I would be home soon. She texted back that dinner was almost ready. I smiled as I put the phone back in my pocket, lucky to still have her in my life. Mae was a terrible cook, but she usually stuck with the basics, like spaghetti, mac and cheese, and large oven casseroles that we bought at the local market. I started walking toward the spot where I had parked my bike and looked into the windows of the shops on the street. The liquor store where I had bought a bottle was brightly lit, and the clerk that I knew very well was behind the counter. Of course, he didn't know Rebecca, he only knew Chance, so I didn't stop and say hello. Plus, I knew that we had beers in the fridge and a bottle in the cabinet, even if it was old.

I arrived in my bike and quickly got her started. I drove home the short way since it was getting dark and I didn't like driving at night anyway. In about ten minutes, I was pulling into the garage in my apartment complex and walking into the apartment. I put my key in the lock and was greeted to the smell of pasta. I wasn't that surprised. Like I said, she was a terrible cook.

"Hey, Becks!" she said as she turned around. An old "Kiss the Chef" apron was around her waist, and from what it looked like, a stained white tank top. She saw me looking down at the shirt. "Yeah, I had a bit of trouble opening the pasta sauce, but most of it ended in the pot...I swear." She turned around and continued to mix the contents of her pot.

"Smells good, Mae," I said as I walked into our room and placed the backpack down by my desk.

"Funny, it's noodles and sauce. Can't smell that good, can it? I just wish I knew how to make meatballs or something. Oooh, turkey meatballs sound pretty good." She looked over at me and shrugged.

"Yeah, those do sound good," I said as I rubbed my stomach, showing that I was hungry. I walked over to her and kissed the back of her head as I reached for two plates and some silverware from the strainer next to the sink. I went over to the table and pushed some papers and mail over to the side and set the table for dinner. A few moments later, Mae came over with the pot of spaghetti and a potholder to place down at the center of the table.

"Dinner's ready!" she said as she jumped up and down. She really loved pasta. She went over to the refrigerator and grabbed two beers and the parmesan cheese, drawing special attention to the fact that it was grated and not shredded. She walked back to the table and set down the contents of her expedition. She handed a beer over to me, and we both popped the caps at the same time.

"Cheers!" I said as I put up the bottle. She gladly accepted the gesture, and our glasses clinked together. After we took the customary swig from the bottle, I picked up the serving utensils and served both of us.

Dinner was nice, just the two of us. Mae hadn't attempted cooking in a while, and it felt like things were slowly getting back to normal. I guess "normal" wasn't the right word to use, but things were going a bit better. The day spent with Albert seemed to be beneficial to both of us, since we had gotten a ton of work done on this project. I guess "project" wasn't the right word for it. Too be honest, it just felt like regular old work, but this was actually exciting. I was excited to start writing…it had been a long time since that had been the case. Mae and I just spent the next hour or so talking about random stuff. Mae mentioned that she'd talked to her mother today and that it appeared that she really does want to patch things up. I was happy with that since it had really been something that Mae took a ton of responsibility for, so the fact that her mother still was reaching out after their talk the other day was a good sign. I told her about my day with Albert and how he was struggling with the decision to have us write this article. She kind of understood the dynamic with a family member that's a complete asshole, and she discussed the similarities between John and her mother in great detail. Though the relationship between her and her mother were beginning to repair itself, she wasn't very kind when describing some of the emotions that her mother had conveyed to her over the last decade or so. The conversation continued as we finished dinner, cleaned and dried the dishes, and made ourselves a giant bowl of ice cream to both share on the couch while watching some unnamed romantic comedy on our TV. It was using the apartment complex's tv antenna, so we couldn't just click information like you would normally do with cable or streaming services.

"So, you really think this article could be some crazy career-making story? The way you describe it, I would be expecting to be dragged out of the apartment with a black bag over my head." We both giggled at the thought, but actually taking a second to think about it sent chills down my spine.

"I don't even think it will get picked up by any news stations. Either they will be too scared to broadcast it, or they will do what the news does...basically glaze over the details of the meetings and suppress the information." I sighed and got instantly depressed that I had become so jaded about the news media lately.

"There is no way they will just ignore it. From what you're telling me, this could be a pretty crazy story. You don't think anyone will be held accountable?" She seemed frustrated, but she was still hopeful for the world. I, myself, was not.

"Only time will tell, babe," I said as I took a scoop of ice cream and tried my best to look sexy while eating it. I felt a cold drip of spillage fall into my top. I looked at Mae, and she was laughing.

"You need help eating that?" She smiled as she took a spoonful herself and presented it to me. Right before I took the spoon in my mouth, she made train noises as if I was a baby. The sound caught me off guard, and I nearly did a spit take. I managed to not spit ice cream all over her face, but just barely.

"Wow," I said as I barely kept my composure. "You have no clue how close you were to a face full of ice cream."

"Promises, promises," she said as she took the last bite of the bowl. She walked over to the sink and placed the bowl inside. "We can clean that up tomorrow. Come to bed with me." She held out her hand and wiggled her hips.

"Yes ma'am," I said, clicking the television off and following her into the bedroom. I looked back at my backpack and suddenly because terrified of its contents. I laid down beside Mae, and she turned around so her back faced me.

"I want to be the little spoon tonight," she said as she took my arm and placed it between her hands and her chest. I fell asleep to the sound of her breathing and the smell of her hair.

Chapter 13

I woke up, staring at the same ceiling fan in the exact same position as the night before. I instinctively reached for my head ready for the first pain of a hangover, but none came. I laughed a bit as I struggled to remember the last time that I had woken up on this side of the poles without a pounding head and a dry mouth. After a few moments, reality set in, and I realized that I may not have had a hangover, but I was, in fact, alone. I sat up and brushed the potato chips from the evening before off my shirt and went to check my phone…nothing.

"Fuck," I said softly as I realized that the phone itself must not have charged and the phone was dead. I inserted the cable and removed it several times, thinking maybe there was something stuck in the phone causing it not to charge. After a few failed attempts, the little charging icon came onto the screen, and I carefully placed it down on the nightstand to not disrupt the cable's orientation. I sat down on the edge of my bed and looked around at my bedroom. It was cleaner than it has been in recent memory, which wasn't saying much. Looking around the room, I noticed my stomach was grumbling something awful, and I decided to see what was in the fridge. Usually, I was sick to my stomach about now, so a cigarette and a shot fixed the nausea, but that wasn't the case this morning so I thought food was a good choice.

I walked into the kitchen and opened up the fridge. There was a carton of eggs from a few weeks before when Mae and I had gone to some farmers' market. I reached for the carton.

"Why are we buying eggs from a farmers' market?" I asked as I picked up some doodad from a table across the lane. "They aren't even refrigerated."

167

"Duh." She said as she pointed over at the sign on the table. "They are farm fresh eggs. They don't need to be refrigerated." She looked over at the lady behind the sign. "They don't have to be refrigerated, right?"

The lady nodded and smiled. "They haven't been washed yet. If you wash them, they will need to be refrigerated." She held up a bowl of eggs, and I walked over and looked into the bowl. The colors were beautiful.

"So she's not trying to poison me?" I said as I picked one up and held it in my hand. "It's warm."

"No sir, she isn't trying to poison you. When the chicken lays the eggs, we don't wash them. The natural film protects the egg until it's washed." She smiled as she saw the look on my face when I put two and two together and put the egg back into the basket. Mae laughed as she reached into her purse for some hand sanitizer and gave me some.

"Thanks," I said. "Sorry, I am not really used to this farmer stuff. I'm not really from around here. When I need eggs, I go to Walmart."

The lady laughed and handed Mae a carton of a dozen eggs. "A dozen eggs for the happy couple. Might I say, you're one lucky guy." She said as she took the cash from Mae's hand.

"Well…"

Mae interrupted. "Yes, he definitely is. This morning, when we woke up, I said, 'Baby, let's go to the farmers' market,' and he didn't complain one bit. Did he?" She looked over at me. Her eyes were begging me to keep up the ruse.

"Yeah…babe. Whatever you want to do, we do. It's why we make such a good couple." I put my arm around her shoulders and tried to not look completely awkward doing it.

"Well, you two are adorable. You remind me of my husband and I when we were your age. Hold on to that. It only fades over the years if you let it." She put the money Mae handed her in her till and handed Mae back her change.

Mae took the money and handed me the carton of eggs. "Thanks, honey," she said, not knowing what her act was doing to me. We thanked the lady, and she wrapped her hand in mine and we walked off down the street. Once we were out of eyesight, she laughed.

"Sorry, I didn't feel like explaining anything to her. Not today, I am having way too much fun." She smiled as she pulled out two cigarettes and lit them. She handed me one, and I nodded. "You're pretty amazing, though.

Letting me drag you to this place. Definitely grade A boyfriend material." She smiled and exhaled her cigarette. I did the same, but for different reasons.

I smiled at the memory and closed the refrigerator door. I placed the carton on the counter and opened it to find three eggs left. I hated odd numbers, but I figured I might as well cook all of them. I filled a pot with water and tossed the eggs in. I turned on the stove and walked toward the front door to go out and have a cigarette.

I stood outside, remembering both Mae and Sarah walking away. I had just let them leave and hadn't done a damn thing. I am a fucking coward. Now, here I was just smoking a cigarette and missing them both. Maybe I should call Sarah to see if we could grab coffee. Or maybe I should have texted Mae and told her that I was wrong and I missed her. I couldn't do that to them. They were better off without me...but what about me? Mae and Sarah both seemed to think that I deserved some type of happiness, why didn't I think that? Maybe it was because I had never had happiness, or I had never had what I really wanted. I struggled with it growing up, not able to get to where I wanted in life. I used to play the drums and play guitar, but I never was really good. I practiced a ton but didn't have any real natural talent. I ran track in high school but never made varsity. I was just as good as the kids running varsity, and I still never got the chance. Maybe the coaches saw something in me that I didn't see in myself...weakness. Hell, when I played fantasy games, I always played a friggin Bard...the jack of all trades but master of none. I finished the cigarette I was smoking and decided to light a new one off its butt. I remembered hearing that what I was doing was the literal definition of chain smoking...lighting the new one off the old one. I laughed as I remembered the person who had told me that. Just another ex-girlfriend who I would never speak to again. Another person who was better off without me.

The sound of the water boiling over the pot woke me from my daydream. "Fuck," I yelled as I ran into the apartment and turned down the heat and the pot began to boil without going over the edge. I stood there for a minute until the smoke alarm started blaring. The cigarette in my hand had set it off. I jumped up and took it down with one quick grab and threw it at the wall. It smashed into a dozen small pieces and the alarm slowly turned off. The reaction even startled me. My hands were shaking, and my heart was racing. I thew the cigarette into the sink and ran some water. I splashed it on my face and could feel the stubble. It felt rough on my hands, and I didn't like it. I missed my smooth complexion on the other side of the poles. I missed everything about the other side of the poles. "Fuck!" I screamed as I fell to the floor in defeat. I sat there crying for a good while. It came out of nowhere, and I just couldn't stop. I could see my neighbors leaving to start their days, walking past my door and peering in. I must have looked like a fucking mess. I was a fucking mess. I had never really talked to any of them, so they just walked by and continued their day. After about four of them, I got up and slammed the door. I went over to the stove and turned it off. The eggs must have been overcooked by then, but I didn't care. I just needed something in my stomach.

I sat on the kitchen floor, peeling the eggs on a paper plate, and ate them in silence. They were extremely overcooked but tasted just fine. After I was done, I folded the paper plate and the broken eggshells and threw them in the garbage can. It was a good thing that it actually went in the can, because if I had missed, it would have made a real mess. Aggravated at myself for the entire situation, I decided to try and take my mind off it by drowning it in work. I did have a ton of commissions that were delinquent or about to become delinquent. I went to the fridge, looking for some beer. There were two brand new twelve packs in there with a sticky note attached to one of them. What was written on it was simple. A heart with an S in the middle. I took two bottles out of the top of the box and shut the door. A few magnets fell, and I could hear a few condiments fall from the inside of the refrigerator. I took the bottles and went over to my desk to work.

I spent the morning into the afternoon working diligently...well, not totally diligently. Every forty-five minutes or so I made another trip to the fridge...then another...and then another. By the time noon rolled around, there were just over a dozen empty glass bottles adorning my desk. Every once in a while, I would get a bit overzealous with my mouse movement and knock into one of them. They would topple around like bowling ball pins for a few moments and then settle. A few minutes later, I would do it again. After about twenty or so of these occasions, I got tired of listening to the noise and grabbed a handful of them to threw them in the garbage can next to my desk. I then took the remaining bottles and did the same. The garbage can was full.

"Wow," I said to myself, not realizing how much I had actually drunk.

The sound of my own voice and how the words sounded made it quite apparent. I looked at my computer screen at what I had been working on. It looked like shit. My normal level of quality was not amazing, even on a good day. People liked my work because I was just good enough to pass as talented. That was not really portrayed in that last thing I had worked on. It was sloppy and rushed. "Fuck it," I said to myself as I saved the work and decided that four hours was more than enough work for the day. I went over to the bed and sat down. I looked down at the nightstand and saw that my phone had apparently finished charging. The little battery icon was completely full. I pulled it from the charger and pressed the power button on its side. A few moments later, it chimed to life and spent a good thirty seconds getting signal.

"Finally," I said quietly to myself as the device registered that it had signal. I held it in my hand for longer than I normally would have. I needed someone to text me…I needed someone to want to talk to me…nobody did. I had pushed them all away. I just sat there like a fucking idiot holding my phone wishing for someone to call me. Suddenly, the phone sprang to life and began to ring. I looked at the screen and it was just a spam call. I laughed slightly and wiped away the few tears that had been forming on my face. As quickly as the phone began to ring, it stopped. "Not even the spam callers want to talk to me right now." I threw the phone down on the nightstand and decided to eat something to maybe help with the fact I was drunk again by noon.

I went to the kitchen and searched my cabinets for something to eat. The only thing that I could find was an old box of cereal. I hadn't even remembered that it was in there. I opened it and took a handful of its contents and shoved them in my mouth. The cereal was stale, but not bad, so I just grabbed it and sat at the kitchen table. Just a man, a beer, and his cereal. I sat and ate the entire box of that stale cereal until there was nothing left in the bag but dust. I stared into the darkness of the box when I knew it was completely empty and actually thought about pouring the dust into my mouth. I had done this before, and it usually ended with me getting cereal in my eyes, so better judgement prevailed.

"Fuck this," I said as I brushed off the cereal from my shirt and decided to do something other than fucking mope alone drunk in my apartment. I got up and went to look for my wallet and keys. "I'm going to go enjoy myself." I slurred as I put on my shoes and headed for the door. Once outside, I lit a cigarette and headed toward the nearest bar I could think of.

I stumbled down the sidewalk in broad daylight, drawing attention from everyone that I passed. A few people even made rude comments as they walked by. I guess I understood what they were looking at. It didn't bother me at all. I was used to people staring at me doing stupid shit while being drunk. Hell, I was drunk most of the time that I was in public anyway. It was one of the reasons that I liked working for myself. It wasn't the best lifestyle, but it afforded me all the things I liked doing. I could sit at home and drink until I couldn't work anymore. I would fall asleep and then rinse and repeat. It was, in a sense, a routine, but it gave me the ability to feed my habits and make enough money to live, and then feed my habits even more. The job enabled me, just like everyone in my life enabled me. Enabled my addictions and my fantasies. Now with Mae gone, I didn't know what to do. I was an addict without my drug. I was going into withdrawal, and I feared that the other side of the poles was the only way I was going to get my fix. It was the only way I would be happy, and I feared that it would ruin both worlds. Until then, I just needed to forget her. I just needed to get over her, and when getting over one drug, another takes its place.

I reached the bar and walked in to my usual spot. It was early enough that they weren't even checking for driver's licenses at the door. When I hit the bar, I ordered a 7 and 7 and asked for a menu. The barback obliged, and in a few minutes, I was sipping on a drink and looking to see what garbage I could fill my face with.

"Deviled eggs?" I asked the barback. He gave me a sideways glance.

"Yeah, they are a new menu item...I haven't tried them yet." He hesitated a bit as he spoke. I'd had just enough to drink to be overly curious about the quality of deviled eggs at a towny bar at around noon on a weekday.

"Well, now I have to try them, since you gave such a great recommendation." He could tell I had already been drinking, most likely by my demeanor.

"I'll put that order in for you in a moment. The guys in the kitchen just started their shift." He tried to reach over to take the menu. I put my hand on the bar and stopped him.

"I might need this for later. I plan on being here a while." I slowly pulled the menu back from under his hand and he just shook his head, annoyed.

"Sounds good," he said as he walked over to the other side of the bar to continue what he was doing, obviously a bit farther away from the only person at the restaurant.

After a few minutes of trying to listen to the news that was playing on the television behind the bar, I pulled out my cell phone. Without even thinking about it, I pulled out my messages to the last thing Mae had sent me. It was a message she must have sent when I was comatose. I typed out a long and desperate message about maybe meeting for a drink...I deleted it. After that, I wrote out a long message about being sorry and regretting everything I had said before. The problem was, I really did mean it, and I needed to be away from her. I deleted that message as well and just sat there looking at my phone until my appetizer came. I laughed to myself since I forgot I'd had eggs for breakfast, and now I was going to have eggs for lunch. It was really a good thing that I was going home and sleeping alone.

"Is there an issue?" the barback asked. He must have seen me going through the thought process in my head.

"Oh yeah, everything is fine." I pondered whether to tell him about the eggs that morning, but I figured he really didn't give a shit and wanted to get on with the rest of his afternoon. Half a dozen fairly decent deviled eggs later and one or two cocktails...I lost count. I was feeling pretty good with myself, and people were starting to walk into the bar to have lunch or meet with friends. It was weird seeing people gather there during the day. I rarely came in this early, and it was a completely different place. In the evening hours, they moved most of the small tables in the larger area of the bar to make room for dancing and such. I looked around and found it odd that I had never seen this place with so many of these tables set up. The transformation was actually rather impressive. I sat at my little perch at the bar listening to people converse about random topics, wishing that I could interrupt and join in. I was starving for attention from anyone, and I guess it showed. Every now and then, the bartender would come and check on me to see if I needed anything else, and I would bother him with small talk. I bet he worked for tips, because if he didn't, then there was zero reason for that poor man to listen to any of the words coming out of my mouth. I would say at that point, I would have actually been considered drunk, and all the deviled eggs in the place wouldn't have been able to change that. He played along as I looked in the corner and saw that they had one of those jukeboxes that you could access with your phone and play music. Another place in town had a similar one, and I just so happened to have the app on my phone. I pulled up the screen and played Piano Man by Billy Joel and waited for the introduction to start. I sang along quietly as the bartender poured me another drink, this time with a shot of fireball. The place was getting louder by the minute as the late lunch crowd began to shuffle out. He mentioned it was from a group of people over in the corner. As he pointed them out, I immediately recognized them as some old coworkers from back in the day. We had all worked together at a local hobby store and almost became friends. "Almost" being the key word. I looked over as I took the shot, and they waved me to go over to their table. I slammed the shot glass down at the bar and grabbed my drink and headed over to their table. A few bumped chairs later they were scooting over to make room. I grabbed a chair from an unoccupied table and sat down.

"How are you guys doing?" I asked as I placed my drink down on the table. "Long time no see?" The three of them laughed and giggled about something. It took me a moment, but I slowly was remembering their names. Jessica was the tall brunette who I always felt had the hots for me but never acted on it. Then there was Heather, the short redhead who I was pretty sure always hated my fucking guts. Last but not least was Ally. I am pretty sure she was the only reason that Heather and Jessica actually hung out. She was just a great person who seemed to hold people together like glue, even if they had zero things in common. She was always great to work with, but the other two had made hanging out with her back then a bit of a chore.

"Well look what the cat dragged in," Jessica said, smiling at me. "I haven't' seen you in ages. I barely recognized you with all that facial hair. You were always so clean-shaven." She looked around the bar and then back at me. "Where is Mae? Aren't you two connected at the hip or something?"

I reached over and took a drink and shrugged. "She is somewhere else, obviously. Probably with her girlfriend." The three of them looked shocked.

"Her girlfriend?" Heather said, sounding rather disgusted at the thought. "I didn't know...well...you know."

"What, that she's gay?" I was a bit blunter than I would have liked, but I was also a bit drunk.

"Well, yeah," Ally chimed in. "We always thought you two..." Now it was my turn to laugh.

"Wow, that's actually pretty funny," I said, taking another drink to try and hide my aggravation. "You thought her and I...yeah, that's not the case at all. We are...were just friends, you know." It felt as if it was getting a bit hot in the bar.

"Oh, you two don't talk anymore?" Jessica asked, seeming rather intrigued by the fact I had used a past-tense word in my description of our relationship.

"Oh, I'm sorry," Ally said, putting a hand on my shoulder. I hoped she didn't notice, but her touch gave me goosebumps up and down my arm.

"Yeah, it was just recently." I tried to sound indifferent about the situation, but I don't believe I sounded that convincing.

They kept the conversation on me and Mae for a surprisingly long time, and another round of drinks was ordered. It appeared that they had ordered and eaten lunch already while I was feasting on deviled eggs at the bar. They mentioned that I had looked sad sitting at the bar, and they had grappled with the idea of asking me to come sit with them. Jessica had finally gathered up the nerve to buy me a shot, and, as they say, the rest was history.

We continued to talk about our old job and how much we missed it. It was a weird sort of nostalgia, since the company we worked for sucked it was an odd thing to miss. I really think the reason I missed it so much is that it was just a simpler time. I was able to get art supplies cheap before everything went digital. Mae and I had lived together, and we all went out with the group that I worked with nearly every other night. It was truly remarkable how much I had known about these individuals when I worked with them. I knew their boyfriends, family, interests. I knew what they wanted to do with their lives and what they loved and hated the most in this world. Though I was sitting there with those three women, it was if I was meeting them for the first time. Nearly a decade had passed, and their lives had changed literally in every way possible. They were all just in town for a mutual friend's wedding and had decided to get back together for a late lunch and evening of shenanigans. It was kismet that I was sitting there lonely at the bar across from them this very night.

We continued to go around the group, and they described to me what their lives were like now. I sat there, excited for my former friends, but feeling sad for myself. Here these three women had taken their lives and done something with themselves. Jessica was a saleswoman at a large pharmaceutical company and lived in California. Heather still lived close to home, but she was engaged to be married to the guy she had been dating back then. I couldn't remember his name, and even if she had said it during her story, I still couldn't recall it. Ally, on the other hand, had finished school and traveled abroad for her career in politics, and when she had returned, she had opened up a coffee shop on the east coast. It was really quite impressive all around. When the table's discussions finally got to me, I was at a loss for words, and for me, that was a difficult feat in and of itself. After my sad description of the last decade, Jessica could tell that I was feeling sorry for myself and quickly changed the subject.

"So, shots?" she asked as both Heather and Ally raised their hands. "How about you two get this round, I got the last one." They both agreed and went to the bar. I looked over toward where they went, and they were already lost in the crowd. I looked back at the table, and Jessica had come and sat closer to me.

"Sorry about that. I could tell you were getting a bit uncomfortable." She put her hand on my arm.

"Yeah, it's fine. You three have just done so much, and I feel like I have done nothing." I reached over and took the last sip of my drink.

"Chance, don't feel like that. You're an artist and self-employed. That's really cool. I actually follow you on social media and your stuff looks really good." I could tell she was being overly nice, and I wasn't a fan of being felt sorry for. I was beginning to get aggravated until she spoke again. "Actually, I really am glad we ran into you tonight. I had such a huge crush on you back then, but thought you and Mae were an item, so I never said anything." I looked up into her hazel eyes and smiled.

"So, I'm not crazy," I said, smiling. "I actually thought you did, but never really liked the idea of dating someone I worked with. It never ends up well."

"Yeah, you're definitely not crazy," she said, this time digging her nails slightly into my arm. I looked down and she gave me a devilish grin. Just then, the other two returned to the table.

"Who's ready for shots?" Heather said as I realized both her and Ally's hands were filled with multiple shots a piece.

"Holy shit!" Jessica said as she stood up and helped them place the shots down at the table. "You do know that there are only three of us. Why did you get ten shots?"

"Well, we haven't seen Chance in forever and you said you wanted to have a great night!" Heather said as she passed Jessica and me both a shot. She made sure to give herself and Ally one of the remaining shots. She counted to three, and we all took a shot. It was funny to watch the three of them grimace at the taste of whatever the hell Heather and Ally had gotten. I, on the other hand, was pretty gone to begin with, and it didn't hit me as hard as it did them.

"Wow, Chance. Did I give you a shot of water?" Ally joked as she saw me down the shot without any issue. "You should take another one to prove you didn't just get a dud." Jessica reached over the table and slapped her on the arm.

"Ally, he's had plenty, let him be." She looked over at me and winked. The night's drinks were slowly starting to get to me, and usually when multiple shots were purchased, that was the end of the fun and the beginning of the end for me.

"Nah, I'm fine," I said as I took one more shot. I placed the shot glass neatly on top of the other one, upside down in a wet spot on the table.

"Chance, don't go too crazy," Jessica said. I could feel her hand reach under the table and grab my leg. She scratched her nails up and down right above my knee.

Like lightning, the image of both Mae and Sarah doing the same thing hit me like a hammer. I looked up, and it wasn't Jessica sitting across the table, it was Mae. I looked over at Heather and Ally and it wasn't them either. It was Rebecca and Sarah sitting there laughing at me.

"Are you ok?" Mae asked...but it wasn't her, it was Jessica. My vision started to blur, and I had to stand up.

"I'll be right back," I said as I started walking toward the back alley.

"Oh shit, Chance, are you ok?" Jessica said, getting up and preparing to follow me.

"I'm fine, I just need a bit of air," I said, doing my best to not alarm her or the others of my minor episode. "I'll be right back." She sat back down, but the look of concern on her face didn't disappear.

I walked straight through the back door into the alley behind the bar that people usually used for smoking. When I stepped outside, I was surprised by how dark it was, and I checked my phone for the time. I had several missed text messages, but I was more concerned about the time. It was nearly seven, and I had been at this bar for the entire afternoon. "Fuck," I said as I pulled the crushed pack of cigarettes out of my pocket and put one between my lips. I lit the cigarette and leaned against the wall as I inhaled the smoke into my lungs. I held it there deep for a moment and then exhaled a long breath. I repeated this process until the panic attack or whatever it was ended. A few people passed by on their way home, and they looked at me awkwardly since I was just sitting in an alleyway swearing. I nodded as they passed to show them I wasn't psychotic, and they went on their merry way. I finished my smoke and threw it in the coffee can near the door and headed into the bathroom to throw some water in my face. I went in the single occupancy bathroom and locked the door behind me. I looked in the mirror and the man who looked back at me looked aged and worn down. I felt every wrinkle and grey hair that showed in my reflection, and I turned on the faucet. Somehow, I thought, I could just throw some cold water in my face and rally like I used to do when I was younger. I repeated the process until my head stopped pounding and looked at myself once more. This time the face looking back at me felt much better.

"What are you doing to yourself?" she asked me. Her soft features made me feel at home, and her voice was soothing, reminding me of happier times. It was me, it was Rebecca.

"I don't know," I said, my voice trembling as if I was about to start crying.

"Well, it looks like you're about to go fuck Jessica." The reflection didn't look happy. "You're just going to forget Mae and Sarah that easily? This is why when you use the word 'love,' nobody believes you. People that love someone else don't make decisions like this. People can't love someone without loving themselves first." I put my head down and started to cry softly.

"I'm sorry, I just…I want to be done with this shit. You don't get to talk down to me. You get to have Mae, I don't. You get to be with her every day, and I get to miss her." I grabbed a paper town and wiped my face and blew my nose.

"Look who you're talking to," the voice said. "Look at me." I looked up into her eyes. "What do you mean you don't get to be with her. You get to be with her every single fucking night and it's not enough for you. You can't go a single day without her…you're fucking sad." She was…I was right.

"I don't know what you want me to do. She is better off without me, and you know it as well. I need to let her go, I need to get over her." I was beginning to calm down a bit, and I splashed water in my face.

"Yeah, it totally looks like you're getting over her," the voice said as I looked up.

"Fuck you!" I said as I looked back up at the mirror. The reflection was just me staring back. My face was red, and you could see that my eyes were a bit bloodshot from my crying. "Fuck you," I said one more time silently as I dried my face one final time and tried to make myself presentable to the others. When I felt like I could pass for just drunk, I took a piss, washed my hands, and left the bathroom to go back to the table. By the time I got back out, there it was just Jessica sitting there awkwardly. She saw me walking up and waved.

"Thought you bailed on us," she said as I walked up. "The others went to go get some fries or something. I don't think shots were such a good idea. Are you ok?" she said, sounding genuinely concerned.

"Yeah, just got a bit claustrophobic is all. I have had a bit too much to drink and a bit too little to eat is all." I shrugged and forced a fake laugh. It looked like the bought it.

"Well, we don't have to drink anymore," she said, smiling. "By the way, we never got to finish our little conversation earlier." Her hand returned to my leg.

The last thing on my mind was sex, especially after my little conversation in the bathroom, if you could even call it that. I didn't want to be an asshole and just reject her. I had been giving her the same signals the entire night, so this was my fault. Part of me just wanted to invite her back to my place and then she would leave in the morning and return to California. I wouldn't even have to make up some excuse. It was the perfect arrangement. She was looking for a one-night stand, and so was I. It was harmless, wasn't it? Jessica said something I didn't hear since I was preoccupied with what was going on in my own head.

"I'm sorry, what did you say?" I actually had no idea how long she had been talking, but I must have been nodding along because she kept talking.

"I was asking what you're doing tonight?" She blushed, not knowing if I was just being drunk or put off by her comment.

I tried to play it off like I was unaware of her advances, either because I was stupid or just too drunk to notice. "Most likely just going home and hitting the sack. I have some work I have to finish tomorrow so I can pay my rent. What are you up to?"

"I was just thinking it was getting late and I didn't want to drive back to Heather's place. Plus, I have had a bit to drink, and you said you lived pretty close, right?" She was pressing hard, but I didn't want to give in. Mae and Sarah's memory from earlier was still fresh in my mind, and my reflection was right. Was I really going to bring this girl home after telling Mae I loved her? After treating the nicest girl I had ever met like shit? Sarah didn't deserve that. If I ever wanted to make things right with her, I need to get up and leave right now...Jessica had other plans.

"Chance, I am just going to be blunt with you because you seem to be too drunk to get what I am hinting at. I am going home tomorrow night and wanted to have some fun tonight...with you." This time, her hands started traveling further up than just my leg. I receded back into my chair and shrugged.

"Jessica, I'm sorry...but...I don't think I can do that." I felt instantly better once the words had gotten out. Her hand instantly retreated, and her face got extremely blushed.

"Fuck, listen to me," she said as she slowly started to gain composure. "You must think I'm just...that I just...God, I am embarrassed." I put my hand over hers and tried to sound as sincere as possible.

"Jessica, you're amazing, and trust me...any other day and we would already be halfway home, but I just have been going through some stuff since Mae and I stopped talking. I also just kind of got out of a relationship, and I really need to make things right with her." The red on her face slowly disappeared and was replaced with understanding.

"Wow, that's not what I was expecting to hear." Her eyes began to water a bit. "I'm sorry, I just thought you...you know...were into the whole hit it and quit it lifestyle." Her words were not meant to be hurtful, but they hurt nonetheless. The look on my face must have let on to how it felt.

"Yeah, I guess. I just don't think I want to be that guy anymore. I..." she interrupted.

"Chance, you don't have anything to explain. At least not to me. Maybe that girl you were talking about, maybe explain it to her?" She shrugged and took a sip of her water. I hadn't realized she swapped her mixed drink for a water with no ice and a coffee.

"I think that ship has sailed, unfortunately. I think my little change of heart came a bit too late." For some reason, I wanted to tell her all about what had happened. My confession to Mae at the bar. The night after and what had happened with the pills. This was, unfortunately, not the time or place to go into such morbid details, and I decided to take the high road and just take my leave. I was tired and I was drunk, and I didn't want to upset Jessica any more than I already had. Both Heather and Ally had taken the most unfortunate time to show back up, and their entrance was as awkward as you could imagine.

"You two going to get a room?" Heather said sarcastically. Ally slapped her when she saw the look of rejection that apparently was on Jessica's face. A look only another woman could see.

"Actually, I have to get going. I have a ton of work to do in the morning, and I don't want to take up the entire night of your reunion." I stood up and shook Jessica's hand. It wasn't the affection that she was hoping for, but she took it, nonetheless.

"It was a ton of fun reminiscing, Chance. I still have your number. If you're ever in California, you should hit me up. We might be able to scrounge up some fun there, as well." She smiled, and our hands released. I looked over at Ally and Heather and reached out for a hug.

"Awwww, take care Chance," Ally said as we embraced. Heather was a bit late and just kind of hugged Ally with her hands slightly around me as well. Like I said...awkward.

"Thank you for entertaining me this evening. I really needed a fun night, and you guys made tonight the definition of a great night out." I made a small mock bow and said goodbye. I walked up to the bar and quickly paid my tab and headed for the door.

I got out into the evening air and didn't realize how much cooler it had gotten. I thought about stopping at a liquor store and grabbing a small bottle for the walk home but decided to light a cigarette instead. I pulled out my phone and saw the few missed text messages from earlier and noticed that one of them was from Sarah. It was just a simple one-word text, but it made my heart jump. "Hey" is all it said, and it made me happy that she had not written me off completely. The decision to go home alone seemed infinitely better in my head now. I responded a simple "hey" back to her and saw that the other texts were random spam messages from my phone carrier telling me I had forgotten to pay my bill. I made a mental note to do that tomorrow and started the long walk home.

For some reason, the walk home seemed infinitely better than the walk to the bar. I had a flutter in my chest that hadn't been there in the afternoon. Sarah had messaged me and given me hope that she wasn't completely out of my life. I had stopped myself from making a terrible mistake and I hadn't texted Mae at all. I felt pretty good about myself, even though I still felt like shit and had drunk way too much. All I can say is a win is a win. I made it home in record time and closed the door behind me. I walked straight to the bed and fell into it. I don't even think I was awake long enough to hit the pillow.

Chapter 14

I woke up to the sound of my phone buzzing. I looked over at the clock and saw that it was early and tried to go back to bed, but unfortunately, I was unable to. I just laid with Mae and closed my eyes. I smelled her hair and touched her skin. I kissed her shoulders and her neck. Each time I did this, her body reacted, and I could see her goosebumps forming wherever our bodies touched. This was the time I got my fix. Being on this side of the poles didn't mean that I was not an addict. It was just the time I can act without fear of her rejecting me. I took my hands and ran them down her back and back up again. I could literally have sat there all day with her. The phone buzzed again, and I finally decided to just take a look at the texts. They were from John.

"Who keeps texting you," Mae said sleepily. "Tell them to shut up and let's go back to bed. I'm still tired, and it's too early for this." She rolled over and pulled the covers over her head to block the small amount of sunlight in the room.

"It's John. He wants me to come in to the office." A sudden burst of panic hit as to why he would want me in the office. He hated me. Why would he want to see me?

"Well, fuck him. Just come back to bed." Her answer seemed so vague that I bet she wasn't even really awake. I looked over at her and laughed slightly.

"Well, I guess I should go in to the office later and talk to him." I messaged him back saying I would be in as soon as I could, and he sent back a simple message saying that he had acknowledged the message.

"Ok. I love you," Mae said, turning around and pursing her lips. I think she was looking for a kiss or dreaming about taking a selfie. I hoped it wasn't the latter. I kissed her quickly and got up to get dressed.

I always hated going and meeting John. He always gave me weird vibes, and now they were even weirder. I knew a lot of dirt on him now, and it was going to be hell to dance around that the entire meeting. Hopefully it would be quick, and I could just be on my way. I showered quickly and got dressed. I made myself a to-go cup of coffee and placed it in my favorite thermos. I grabbed my bag and saw that it was far too heavy. I removed Albert's notebook from the bag and placed in one of my drawers on my desk. Hoping that would keep it safe, I grabbed my things and left the apartment.

The drive to work was short but full of anxiety. Why did John want to see me? A planned meeting with him was stressful enough, but one just out of the blue? I was driving myself crazy, and I bet it showed. I brushed my hair and my teeth quickly. I could still taste the toothpaste in my mouth, since I didn't rinse enough. I didn't put on any makeup or even attempt to. I guess I didn't normally wear that much makeup, but for a meeting with the editor, I usually put on some eyeliner and concealer. This was so last-minute that I was pretty sure I was wearing two different-colored socks. Thankfully, they were ankle socks, and the sneakers I slapped on covered them up almost entirely. Needless to say, I didn't really look my best, or at least I didn't feel my best. Not the way I usually went in to the office.

I pulled into the parking lot and took a few moments to collect myself. I looked in my glove compartment for my spare cigarettes. After a few seconds, I found them and popped the cigarette lighter in my car until it popped back out. I opened the door and lit my cigarette. I leaned against the car and smoked the stale cigarette until the anxiety that I felt began to fade. Replacing the anxiety was unfortunately the smell of stale cigarettes. I pulled some lotion and body spray from my back and applied it until I felt that I didn't smell like an ashtray and thew them back on the seat. I hurried into the building and was met by the security guard, Chris.

"Hey, Becks, I am so sorry to hear about Albert." The look on his face told me everything I needed to know.

"Albert, what happened? I just saw him yesterday." I walked up to the desk where he was standing. He looked down and fidgeted with his hands.

"He was in a really bad car accident last night coming back from dinner. Apparently, it was a hit and run or something. He is in the hospital. He's in pretty bad shape." He just shook his head and sighed.

"Wow, I was at dinner with him. We were working on something pretty much all day. Fuck, man." I usually didn't swear at work, but I was pretty taken aback by the news.

"Yeah, we got him a card when we heard. We already sent it up to your office. Make sure you sign it if you have the chance." The thought of the kind deed brightened his face up; only by a little, though.

"I definitely will, Chris," I said as I swiped my ID and waked through the gate. I stopped when I passed him and put my hand on his shoulder. "He will be fine. He's nerdy, but he's tougher than you think." The gesture felt forced but was sincere.

"Thanks, Becky. Have a good day, I am sure that John is pretty upset. Go easy on him today, will you?" We both smiled knowing that he was kidding.

"I'll try," I said as I continued on toward the elevator. I rode the elevator up to the office, and when the doors opened, you could immediately see that there was a somber attitude in the air. The normal ambient noises of calls going on and paper being shuffled were still there. There just was a dark cloud that was cast over the entire building. Nobody was trying to hide it.

Walking over toward John's office, I could hear some of the office gossips talking about the accident. There was even a group of people talking like Albert was one of their best friends. I don't think I had ever seen those people speak to him, let alone hang out with him outside of work. I guess neither had I until recently, so who was I to judge. Once I reached John's office, I took another set of deep breaths and knocked on the door.

"Come in," he said immediately. I could tell that he was not in a good mood to begin with, but his outburst made opening the door that much more difficult. "Close the door, will you?" He was pacing back and forth behind his desk. His hair was unkempt, and his clothes were not as neat as they normally were. There was a large mug of hot coffee steaming on his desk, and next to it, there was what looked like a nearly empty glass of scotch. A quick glance at the bookshelf behind his desk showed that he didn't hide the second bottle nearly as well as he thought. Another small bottle of scotch peaked out from behind a set of books. It was a nice bottle, probably worth more than I made in a week.

"You wanted to see me, John?" I just stood there awkwardly, holding my bag around my shoulder and fidgeting with one of my rings on my right hand.

"Yes...yes of course. Please take a seat." He motioned toward one of the chairs in front of his desk, and I did as he asked. I placed my bag on the chair beside me and sat down. He took a deep breath and did the same in his chair. "Obviously, you must have heard about Albert, it's really a shame, just a shame." He took a swig of coffee and wiped a bead of sweat from his brow.

"Yes, Chris told me downstairs, and I just can't believe it. Him and I..." John interrupted.

"Yes, I know that he asked you to work on a project with him. Can I ask what the project was about?" He looked me dead in the eyes when he asked me, which was not normal. Usually, he didn't give people the satisfaction of pretending to pay attention to them. I found it off-putting and decided to lie.

"Yes, he asked me to meet him yesterday to talk about something, but he never showed up." I really hoped that he had not talked to Albert before the accident, because he would have definitely known I was lying. Hopefully, if he had, Albert knew enough to keep his mouth shut regarding our encounter at the diner.

"He mentioned he did want to work with you last time you and I spoke. He was excited about it. I just...I just didn't know if you two had actually started on something." He went back to fidgeting and drank the remaining contents of the mystery glass.

I thought quickly about what I could say to change his mind. I felt as if he already knew the answers and was just toying with me. The way that he carried himself spoke otherwise, since he was a literal mess. He was looking for some information, but I didn't want him to get it from me. Also, I had no idea what it was. He was about to let me know, though. "Yeah, I wish I could tell you more. If that's all, I would like to go visit Albert in the hospital and maybe drop off some flowers. I just feel awful about what happened." He waited a second and then answered.

"Yes, yes...go and see him. He is pretty beaten up, but they expect him to make a full recovery." He motioned for me to leave, and I didn't complain. I picked up my bag and headed for the door.

"Actually, Rebecca. There is one thing you could answer for me." He turned around and got oddly calm. "Albert used to keep a small binder with some things he was working on. I know he would hate to have his accident cause any stories to be delayed. Do you know where that binder is? He didn't have it in his car, or at least the police couldn't find it." He looked at me over his shoulder. Even though he was not looking directly at me, it made my skin crawl. This fucking guy knew exactly what he was looking for. It was the proof Albert had against him. I lied harder than I had ever lied before.

"Binder? Albert never had a binder with him when we worked together, just that stupid yellow legal pad he carried. I wish I could have been more of a help. If there is anything you need for me to help with, let me know." I waited for him to respond so it didn't feel like I was running out.

"Yes, of course. That damn legal pad. He carried it with him everywhere. I was given that with his things. Just…forget about it, Rebecca. Go and visit Albert, and we can worry about work tomorrow." I nodded and quickly left.

I walked as fast as I could to the elevator and didn't talk to anyone. Once I was in the elevator and the door was closed, I nearly broke down. He knew, he knew everything, and he had just lied to me to try and get the evidence Albert had. For all I knew, he could have been behind the accident itself…or maybe worse. One of the politicians could have been behind it. I looked down at my shirt and sweat had stained underneath my arms, and I felt like I had just taken a shower. The air in the elevator was stifling, and I could barely breathe. The second the door opened, I nearly sprinted until I got outside. I waved at Chris as he said goodbye to me, but there was no time. I ran out the door and immediately vomited in the bushes next to the entrance. My world was spinning, and I didn't know what to do. I wanted to go see Albert, but would someone be watching? I wanted to go back home and just destroy the fucking binder, but then what? All of this would have been for nothing, and Albert was hurt for no reason at all. What the hell was I supposed to do? I suddenly became very aware of my surroundings and stood straight up. I looked around trying to act like I hadn't just thrown up outside of my place of business. I collected myself and walked straight to my car and got in the driver's seat. I started the engine and drove straight back home. This time, the drive seemed like an eternity. Every person that looked at me was someone that knew what I knew. Every single vehicle that stayed behind me for longer than a few seconds was someone tailing me…possibly to run me off the road like they did to Albert. Well, at least what I think they did to Albert.

After the longest ten minutes of my life, I was home. I pulled into the driveway and put the car in park. I looked around and there was nobody watching me. I left the vehicle and power walked back to the apartment. When I walked in, Mae greeted me with a smile and a hug.

"Hey Becks, wow, that was fast. What the hell did he want?" I went into the bedroom and retrieved the binder that Albert had given me.

"This, he wanted this." Her jaw dropped open, so I assumed she understood what I was trying to say.

"He knows. Holy shit, what did Albert say?" I went over to the window and closed the curtains, and bolt locked the door.

"I don't know…he's in the hospital in a coma or something. Someone hit him with their car last night and drove off." She was putting the pieces together in her mind, and I saw the moment lightning struck.

"Fucking John? You think he did this to Albert? His own family?" Her mind was just as much of a hurricane as mine was. I didn't know what to say to comfort her. I had no clue what I could do to make this right. I didn't think that there was anything that could be done. I looked at her with panic in my eyes.

"I think if he did, it was unintentional. He was a fucking wreck when I went to visit him. Maybe someone else did this, and he is just as surprised as we are." I held the binder close to my chest and took a deep breath. "We have to give this thing to someone else. What if we are next? What if they know we have it?" She nodded and went to sit down on the couch.

"Can't we give it to like the news or someone? Wouldn't they know what to do with it?" I had never thought of that. What if we could get rid of the notebook as well as not have Albert's injuries be in vain?

"That's not a bad idea," I said to Mae as I looked through the book. "This way we can kill two birds with one stone." I flipped through the book and took a look at my notes. It seemed that so many people were in this thing from both sides of the aisle, finding a news station that would take this seriously might be difficult.

"Only question is, who do we give it to?" Mae asked, peering over my shoulder as I flipped.

I took the next few hours looking through my notes and doing research on who I could send it to and have it be taken seriously. As I did my research, I made sure Mae went through the entire book and wiped it down for any fingerprints or anything that could trace it back to either Albert, myself, or worst of all, Mae. It seemed like a bit much, but after what had happened to Albert, I couldn't take any chances. After the entire book was clean and I had a good idea as to where to send the book, the only thing left to do was actually get rid of it.

Mae sat there the entire time while I scrolled through what seemed like dozens of news stations and researched different times when big leaks like this had happened in the media. From what it seemed like, everyone involved in the scandal suffered...including the journalist reporting it. That made the decision to just get rid of it that much more appealing. I couldn't imagine anything else happening because of this stupid binder.

We decided to take a break and eat some lunch. Mae attempted to make grilled cheese sandwiches, and she burned mine something awful. Instead of making her feel bad, I decided to eat the sandwich with zero complaints. She knew that I would eat almost anything, and because she made them with everything going on, I decided to just eat the damn sandwiches.

Once lunch was done, we debated shipping the entire binder or just some of it. That way, if one news organizations decided to not cover the story, we would still have some of the information. I just wanted it gone but went back to my notes and found the top three stations that we wanted to send it to. One was a national news station, and the two others were more regional. We divided the binder into three groups of photos and notes, Mae found some old yellow envelopes, and we stuffed them full of the photos and notes.

"What about a return address?" Mae said as she started to write the addresses of the news stations on the front of the packages. "We can't write ours on there?" She was batting a thousand today. I hadn't thought of that and most likely would have written our address on there in panic.

"Wow, good call, babe. Let's just write the addresses of random places. Go look up three addresses online and we will wright those in." Mae nodded and went over to my computer desk and started looking up random places. "Make sure they have nothing to do with us." I said, thinking of all the places she was probably looking up. I knew what she was thinking, looking up random places that we know of rather than completely new places that have never seen our face. A few moments later I had finished what I was doing and was getting restless.

"Did you get the addresses yet?" I walked over to her and peered over her shoulder.

"Yeah, I am just checking postage. How many stamps do we have?" I went and checked our junk drawer where we always kept our stamps. I pulled out a brand-new roll that might have had fifty or so stamps on it.

"Enough," I said as I unraveled the roll of stamps and showed them to her.

"Good." She looked over my way and gave a half-smile. "We are going to need all of them."

About thirty or so minutes of a therapy session later, we had both of the packages with all of the information on them and a ton of stamps each. We went over the amount we had researched online just to make sure that the packages didn't get returned to us. Once it was gone, we wanted to make sure we never saw it again until we saw it on the news.

"I think we are ready." Mae said as we put on the last stamp. "The stamps almost took up the entire package." We both laughed a nervous laugh. She was right, the package did look a bit silly with all the stamps on it the way we had them.

"Ok, I will go and walk them to the drop box by the leasing office. You just stay here and lock the doors." I tried to sound stern, but I was terrified. I could tell that Mae heard it in my voice, but I was trying to be brave. Truth was, it was me that had gotten us into this mess by underestimating what people would do for information like this. I thought we would be ok because I usually believed that people were naturally good. Apparently, I was wrong, and the people we were dealing with were not. They would hurt us to get this binder back, and they didn't care who it was that got in their way.

"Ok," she responded after thinking about it for a few seconds. I stood up, grabbed the packages, and headed out the door. Mae poked her head outside to watch me as I walked. Even though the walk to the leasing office was short, and it only took about a minute, it felt a lot longer to me. I tried to be casual and just walk at my normal pace, but when I did that, it felt like I was sprinting. So I must have looked goofy, walking with a weird Monty-Python-like silliness. Once the packages were safe in the mailbox, I turned and walked back to the apartment. A few moments later, I was back in the doorway.

"So..." Mae said as I walked through the door and shut it behind me.

"I don't know. I put them in the mailbox and came back." I peered out the window half expecting someone in a suit and a tie to be reaching into the mailbox. Obviously, I had seen too many spy movies.

We both stood there for a bit, looking out the window like idiots. After we felt as though we were crazy, I decided to go and make something to eat. I walked over to the fridge and looked inside.

"Wow, we don't have anything to eat," I said, peering into a nearly empty refrigerator. "We should go shopping." Mae walked over and looked in the freezer as well. Apparently, we had been so busy over the last week or so that we hadn't even thought about groceries. We had plenty of coffee and beer, but that was it.

"I'll go shopping," Mae said as I closed the refrigerator door. "You should go and see Albert, I know that you're dying to." She did make a good point. What could happen to me at the hospital? I could go and see Albert quickly, and nobody would suspect anything odd. He and I worked together, and he had been in an accident.

"Yeah, you're right," I said. "Ok, you can head to the store in the car, and I will take my bike to the hospital. It's only about fifteen minutes away." I took a moment to think about what had just transpired. Was I really going to let Mae go to the store alone and then go visit Albert, myself? What if someone would try to do the same kind of thing they did to Albert? "Maybe we should just order in and not go out. I'm just worried that something could happen if we go out. How about we just order Chinese from Wu's and stay in and watch a movie."

"Thank God," Mae blurted out. "I didn't really want to go anywhere. I just wanted to stay inside." She burst into tears and just wrapped her arms around me. I could tell that she was so worked up over everything, and

I just stood there holding her for a bit. It was nice. With the end of such a hectic day in sight, hugging Mae was just what was needed. From the first minute I had woken up that day, it felt like I had a rock in my chest and something was terribly wrong. From the second I had seen that text from John, to walking into his office. To hearing about Albert and then coming back home to see Mae and shipping out the evidence. I just...I just couldn't help it.

"Are you crying, too?" Mae said when she heard me start to whimper.

"No..." I lied as I pulled away and we both looked into each other's eyes. They were both wet, and we smiled as we both reached up to wipe the tears from each other's cheeks.

"Liar." She laughed as she pulled away and took my hand. She led me to the couch and handed me her phone. "Just order dinner so we can eat, I'll pick the movie." I did as she asked and called our favorite Chinese place in town, Wu's. The second I called, the owner recognized the number and asked if we wanted our usual. I laughed and said that we need our usual plus another appetizer platter.

"Rough night?" the owner said on the other line.

"You have no clue." I half laughed. I paid with a card and threw the phone down on the couch.

"Be careful with that," Mae joked as she picked up her phone and pretended to check for damage. I sat down next to her, we cuddled up on the couch, and she scrolled up and down the lists until she got to her favorite movie.

"Becks, it's back on Netflix!" She jumped up and down as she saw the old black-and-white film.

"*Casablanca*? We have that in the other room." I pointed toward the bedroom, but she just shushed me.

"Not with director's commentary, we don't." She went through the settings, and low and behold, this version had an option for the director's commentary.

"If we are going to watch this, can we just watch it regular without the commentary?" She sighed and turned the commentary off.

"Fine, but you owe me." She smiled. I leaned back and covered up with a blanket. She curled up beside me and pressed play on the movie. We sat and watched the movie until we heard a knock at the door. I checked through the peephole, and it was, in fact, the usual delivery driver. He handed me the food, and I signed the receipt. I ran back and we spread all the food out on the living room coffee table. I went and grabbed us each a cup of water and some napkins. We were, in fact, messy eaters. We sat on the ground with our feet underneath the table and gorged on the takeout. Every once in a while, Mae would quote the movie with a mouthful of noodles or rice. One time, she sounded so funny I nearly spit out the contents of my mouth all over the living room. We eventually finished dinner and moved back to the couch where Mae instantly fell asleep while I rubbed her head. I just sat there, looking at her face in the low light of the room. The black-and-white film was all the light I needed to see the lines of her face and how beautiful she really was. I felt like I took this side of the poles for granted too often, especially now that Mae and I were not talking on the opposite side. I sat there and sighed.

"Rebecca, what is wrong with you," I said softly, feeling completely and utterly guilty for everything that I had put her through and then suddenly angry for everything that she herself had put me through. It was an odd form of cognitive dissonance, being with her. Here, she was my wife, my partner, and my friend. She had literally always been there for me, and I for her. On the other side, it was almost the same. We had been there for each other through the most difficult times in our lives. I was there when she had come out to her parents and was there through her first heartbreaks as well as all the good stuff. I just...couldn't be with her how I wanted. I had just dealt with it for so long, it felt as if it was the only way. Like any addict, I wasn't able to see how much worse I had actually become. I thought back to every conversation I'd had with a family member, a friend, or anyone really. I had acted so shitty to them, and they were only trying to help me. My relationship with my mother on both sides was strained simply because of Mae. She was a fucking drug that I couldn't get enough of, and if I couldn't have her, I needed to dull the pain in any way possible. Here, at least, she was mine, but there...I couldn't have her...and if I did, I would lose her. Guess what? That was exactly what had happened. I had her for one night, and I had lost her for the rest of my life, so it seemed.

I was distracted from my inner dialogue by a text from Chris, the security guard at my work. I looked down and saw that he had messaged me that Albert was awake and coherent. My heart started to race as I read the message. I had nearly forgotten about the entire day, sitting here with Mae, like a true addict. I texted him back that I would go see him tomorrow. Chris instantly messaged a smiley-face emoji and said goodnight.

"Who was that?" Mae said, half asleep.

"It was Chris, he said that Albert is awake and coherent. I am going to go visit him tomorrow, do you mind?" She turned her head back toward the tv and closed her eyes.

"No, but I want to go with you." With that statement, she was out again. I smiled as I turned off the TV and slid out from under her. I placed a pillow where my lap was and covered her up so she wasn't cold. I cleaned up the dinner mess and maybe ate a few bites more. Once the mess was cleaned up and the leftovers were placed in the refrigerator, I went over to my desk to look over my notes and work for a bit. I hadn't really done anything work-related in a few days, and I felt as if I was falling behind. There I was, expecting to disrupt the entire state and its politics, and now I was just going to go back to my normal routine and work on the next article I had been given. Usually, these came via email or on our work's employee portal. It is amazing how fast you can switch gears in your life. Hopefully tomorrow, well...not tomorrow, but you get it. Hopefully I would be able to talk to Albert and let him know what had happened, maybe find out what had happened to him. He was an innocent victim of this whole thing, and I wanted to make sure that I was doing right by him and myself, as well. I just hoped he understood that I couldn't let anything happen to Mae...I just couldn't.

The night went on, and I looked through my portal and took note of all the work they were looking for people to do. The magazine that we worked for did kind of a groupthink, and John and his cronies put up articles that might be of interest for future editions. We then posted feedback on each one and let John's team know that we were interested. I guess with what I had just mailed, the status quo might change a bit in coming weeks, but that I guess is another story. Nothing I could do about it now but wait to see if anyone would be braver than I was and write the story in its entirety.

I jotted down some notes, deleted some old work emails, and paid a few outstanding bills. Once that was done, I heard some movement coming from the living room. My hair was standing on end until Mae came walking in from the kitchen with a half-empty glass of water.

"Go to bed, Becks," she said, her words mumbled with the mixture of being half asleep as well as half filled with water.

"I will, babe," I said as I turned off my computer and went to lay down beside her. Normally, sleep came rather easily for me on this side of the poles, but not that night. I felt like I was back in the car that morning driving to work, unsure of what the day would bring. For some reason, I didn't want to go to sleep. I didn't want to be Chance…I wanted to stay Rebecca for a little while longer. I wanted to be with Mae for just a little while longer. Like they say, all good things must come to an end. As the saying goes, so did my day. I fell asleep staring at my alarm clock on the nightstand.

Chapter 15

"Ugh," was all I could say when my eyes opened. I'd had too much to drink, and what I had drunk was outside my normal shitty whiskey... so it was much worse than normal. I winced my eyes as they came into focus, and I realized that the curtains were wide open. The sun was higher in the sky, so I am assumed I had overslept. I rubbed the sleep out of my eyes and yawned. "Fuck," I said as I tried to sit up. I was a bit sorer than I usually was from walking to and back from the bar. I was definitely out of shape. I looked around for my phone and realized that it was in my pocket. I pulled it out and checked it and there were no new messages. I guess Sarah had gone to sleep before I sent my message. It had been pretty late at night when I had texted her back, and I didn't really expect to get a response immediately. I decided to try and be productive that day since I had already spent an entire day getting drunk and making questionable decisions, so I guess I had to make up for it.

I stood in front of the mirror and decided to shave. I hadn't shaved... well, at least shaved well, in quite a while. I took the small brush that I had been given as a birthday gift about ten years earlier and ran some water over it. Mae had thought it would be funny to buy me a vintage shaving kit from a thrift store we had gone to, and I actually loved it. I was not a fan of the single-blade safety razor, but the little brush and lather kit was actually amazing. I hadn't used it in forever and usually just got lazy and used the canned shaving cream that I had laying around. My facial hair was long, and it was difficult to shave with my little disposable razor. I played around and gave myself a few different shaves. My favorite was the Wolverine-looking beard, but I decided to just stay with a mustache. Mae always hated me with a mustache, so I guess there was nobody to complain about it now. I thought about cutting my hair, but that never ended well.

Since I was covered in facial hair and shaving foam, I decided a shower would help as well. Again, I couldn't remember the last time that I had taken a shower that was just for normal hygiene. I usually had to shower because I had vomited everywhere or a similar reason. I took my time and cleaned myself properly. The water felt good on my pounding head, and I actually enjoyed the process for once. I wasn't a fan of showers normally since I had grown up in a house that didn't have a shower until I was nearly in high school. I was more of a fan of baths, or as Mae called it, making Chance soup. She gave me tons of shit on this side of the poles, or at least she used to. Mae wanted to take baths all the time with Rebecca.

"Stop it!" I said. The outburst actually caught me by surprise. "Just stop it!" I had to stop thinking about Mae on this side. She was gone, and it was a good thing. She needed to move on and get on with her life and so did I. The only question was how the hell could I continue my life here and get over her when every night I went to bed, and Rebecca got to be with her. It was like an alcoholic getting drunk every other day and saying that they are sober, it just doesn't fucking work.

I stood there in the shower, aggravated at myself for not being strong enough to not think about her every fucking minute of the day. I was frustrated, but it felt more like withdrawal than anything. Yeah, I wasn't seeing her every day and spending time with her every day...but she was literally all I thought about every second of every day. Just like an addict thinks about his next fix. He joneses for his high, his release. Every time I felt as if I was getting better, I would just go to sleep, and it repeated the cycle. I stood there for a few minutes and let the water just run down my head and down my body. The water was hot, and I could barely stand it, but I guess it was what I deserved. A little bit of pain never hurt anybody, and for some reason, I needed my pain that day. I felt that if anything was going to get me through this entire ordeal with Mae and Sarah, it was my pain.

When the torture session was completed, I went and got dressed. I took a bit more time that day to get ready in the hopes that Sarah would want to get together and talk. I felt as if I had so many things to say to her, and it felt odd since we had only known each other a short while. I didn't think

197

of her like I thought about Mae, but she was creeping into my thoughts more often than a girl normally would. I guess that was a good sign, the fact that I had slept with this girl and still wanted to hang out with her. That thought made me fucking angry at myself. I was just a piece of shit, and the fact that Sarah wanted to be with me still should have been a sign that I needed to change. My negative thought spiral was interrupted by the sound of my phone ringing from the other room. I picked it up as soon as I saw that it was Sarah calling.

The phone was silent for a few seconds until I heard her voice. It was faint, and you could tell she wasn't completely sure she should be calling.

"Hey, Chance," was all she said, and my heart was racing. "You there?"

I swallowed my tongue. "He...hey Sarah. How are you?" My excitement must have made me sound out of breath. I actually might have been yelling, as well.

"I'm good. I was glad you texted back last night. I didn't think you would want to talk." Her voice gained a bit of confidence but was still lacking.

"Why wouldn't I want to talk to you, Sarah?" The fact that she still felt even remotely at fault made my blood boil.

"Well, you know. I left the other day. I didn't know if you were mad. You just let me go. I figured you didn't want me to stay."

"Sarah, of course I wanted you to stay. Why wouldn't I? I just don't want to bring you down. You're amazing." I felt like I had a thousand things to say, and I couldn't think of them. It was as if the words were on the tip of my tongue, and I couldn't say them.

"Chance," she said softly. "Can I come see you?"

The words took me by surprise, and I didn't know what else to say. It had only been two days and it seemed like she was feeling just as down as I was. Should I tell her to come over? Should I just go and meet her somewhere? Her apartment, maybe? Fuck, I was desperate to see her and maybe salvage some semblance of a relationship with her. The only thing that stopped me from meeting her right then and there was the fact that I had cheated on her with Mae. I could rationalize it as much as I wanted, but I had cheated on her, plain and simple. It just wasn't fair to her to be dishonest with her. Before I could think another word, I spoke.

"Yes," I said softly. Even my subconscious was hesitant for her to come over. If she came over, I had to tell her about Mae and me and let the chips fall where they may. The only thing was, I was too much of a fucking coward to do that. I shouldn't have answered the phone. I should have let this poor girl just get over me and get on with the rest of her life. Instead, I had to answer the phone, tell her to come and see me, and possibly break her heart all over again. Break her heart...listen to me. Like anyone could ever love a guy like me. If anything, she would be out of commission for a week and then jump right back into it. I was nothing special. I was just some fucking train wreck, some sinking ship that wanted to take down as many people as I could while I fucking imploded.

She paused on the phone for a second, and I could hear her mood improve once I told her I wanted to meet up. "Ok, where should we meet?" she asked. Her voice sounded excited and more like her usual self.

"I can come pick you up on my bike?" I said, thinking she wouldn't want to go riding. The only person I ever dragged around on my bike was Mae, and other than that, I hated riding it.

"Yes!" she said. I had to pull the phone away from my ear to not go deaf. Apparently, she was excited.

"Ok, just send me your address and I will be there in a half hour?" She paused for a second before answering.

"Make it an hour, give a girl a chance to get ready. Bye!" she said as she hung up the phone. A few moments later, her address came through in a text message.

"What are you doing, Chance?" I said again, only to myself. "You're not ready for this." I took a few deep breaths to calm myself down. I didn't want to hurt this girl any more than I already had, I just didn't know how. I needed someone, anyone, here to think of me as something other than a piece of shit. Sarah was that person, and all I had done was desperately try to prove her wrong. If I did tell her about Mae and I the other night, she would leave for sure. On the other hand, if I didn't, I was almost certain this girl would follow me to hell and back. I wouldn't deserve her, though, and she would eventually find out. I looked down at my phone and just wanted to call it off. Wanted to tell her to run and not look back, to leave me be because I was nothing but trouble. Again, I was just a fucking coward and grabbed my keys to leave. She only lived about ten minutes away, but I figured I would do something that I had been meaning to do for a while...wash the bike.

Mae had always asked me to, and it would have made her happy to see it clean. I never did, because why would I? Why would I do something genuinely nice for someone without expecting something in return? I thought about that single thing the entire way to the car wash, and by the time I was there, I was whipped up in a fervor. I put a few quarters in the machine and the brush started to bubble up with soap. I wasn't going for perfection here, just enough to get the dust and dirt off it. I scrubbed everywhere that my ass wouldn't touch and proceeded to turn the dial to the spray setting. The bubbling brush stopped its bubbling, and a spray nozzle attached to some hooks in the wall started to spurt a steady stream of water. Knowing the drill, I picked that up and rinsed off the soap. The bike was a bit hot from the drive, so it steamed a bit when the water touched it, but nothing too much to worry about. The wash station was close to the apartment, so it didn't have a chance to get too hot. Once I was done, I walked it out into the sunshine and let it dry. I pulled out a pack of cigarettes from my pocket and lit one up and sat down on a park bench near where my bike was.

"Nice bike!" some kid said as his mother drove out of the automatic washing stall. He had rolled his window down to tell me, and his mother was frantically yelling at him to close the window to not let all the water drip inside. He smiled and waved so I returned the favor and the tinted window closed.

"Clean clothes, a clean shave, and a clean bike. Things are looking up," I said to myself, trying to sound reassuring. I sat there finishing the cigarette, watching my bike dry for a good ten minutes. When I felt comfortable to drive it again without leaving a giant wet spot on my ass, I started her up and started the quick ride to Sarah's. She lived in the student housing on the other side of campus. It was a much nicer side of campus than mine. Not as many liquor stores and fast-food places. The main street separated the nice part of town from the not so nice part of town. The main street kind of downtown area was a good mix of both. There were nice shops, the diner, a few bars, and a bunch of not so nice shops. I always wondered why people would rent or buy a shop only to just leave it looking like a piece of shit. I guess it came down to money or something.

I could never let a building I worked in rot. Of course, I wasn't a business owner or a landlord so what the hell did my opinion matter. Anyways...

I pulled into the complex parking lot a bit earlier than she was probably expecting me and decided to stop at the convenience store to see if I could get her something nice, like a flower or something. Mae always loved it when Rebecca bought her stuff like that, and to be honest, I liked it also. I walked into a 7-Eleven and looked around the place. It was pretty much just snacks and drinks. Nothing really of value anywhere to be found. I went over to the clerk.

"Hey there, sir. Do you have any flowers or anything like that?" He nodded and shook his head. He walked around and beckoned me to follow. He led me to an aisle that had some home baking goods and pointed at a small half-pound bag of baking flour. He gave me a thumbs up and then returned to the area behind the counter. I laughed as I picked up the bag.

"Maybe Sarah will find this funny," I said to myself as I made my way toward the counter. I bought the flour, a pack of cigarettes, and two small bottles of whiskey...just in case things didn't go well. I tucked the bottles of whiskey into my small saddlebag as well as the flour and cigarettes. I made my way toward her apartment complex about five or so minutes early and pulled out my phone to text her that I was there. Right before I hit send, I heard my name called out from a window. I looked up and it was Sarah. She was waving and signaled that she would be right down. I decided to have another cigarette as I waited, and before I was halfway done with it, she came running out of the entrance to the building.

"Right on time!" she said, pointing at a pretend watch on her hand. "You shaved, too, who is this man coming to take me away on his motorcycle?" I smiled as I handed her the cigarette and she took it. She looked amazing, and as the wind blew, I noticed that she smelled amazing. It was intoxicating.

"Can I have that back?" I joked after she took a few drags. She handed it back to me, and I finished it off. Her lipstick remained on the filter, and it reminded me of Mae. I tried to stop the thoughts like that from trickling in, but it was no use. I made a mental note to hit myself later for it.

"You ok?" She must have noticed the brief pause.

"Yeah, I'm fine. Where do you want to go?" I said, slapping the passenger seat of the motorcycle. I have half a tank of gas, so we can go basically anywhere." She thought for a minute and smiled.

"I want to go on a first date. Something not too cliché, but also fun. We never got a first date." I saw what she was trying to do, and other women had tried this before. They tried to make fun of the fact that we skipped all the first date stuff by sleeping together on the first night we met. It usually didn't work, since I was not interested in the girl performing the charade. I thought in this case, it just might work.

"Well then, somewhere not too cliché but also fun. How about a walk in the park, and then we can go see a movie?" She nodded her head in agreement and did a little jump.

"I guess that could work," she joked as she hopped up on the back of my bike and bounced with excitement. My ex used to have a bike, and I love them." The second the words left her mouth, she regretted them. It was refreshing to see that she was having trouble keeping someone else out of her mind as well.

"Don't worry about it. Mae used to love riding the bike as well." She took my little olive branch and smiled.

"Sorry, it's only been a few months. I have trouble...you know." I nodded and walked over to her on the bike. I put my hand on her face.

"Don't be sorry. Trust me." She smiled, and it lit up her face. Fuck, she was beautiful.

"Ok," she said as she wiped a small tear from her cheek. "To the park!" I handed her a pair of sunglasses that I usually had reserved for Mae and got on the bike myself. I took the filter from the cigarette and shoved it in my back pocket, started the bike, and we were off.

"Whooo!" Sarah yelled as we hit the main road toward the park. I sped up and her nails dug into my sides just like Mae's did. Her legs and body up against mine, just like Mae. Fuck, this was going to be harder than I had thought. I didn't want this to be something to take my mind off Mae for a while. I needed to get over her, and I needed to get over her for good.

"Hold on!" I said as we started to hit the winding road that led to the park. It was adjacent to some baseball and soccer fields. The area was pretty well kept, and the trees blocked the sunlight to make the shadows dance on the road. I had to slow down because the last little bit was cobblestone, and I didn't feel like giving Sarah a concussion or a broken neck. We reached the parking area, and I looked back at her. She was smiling from ear to ear, and apparently her hair tie had gone missing, so she was struggling with her hair a bit.

"Here," I said as I reached into my saddlebag. I pulled out a small container of hair ties and scrunchies.

"Wow, you're prepared." She laughed as she pulled one out and quickly put her hair back in a messy ponytail. "Let me guess, Mae's?" This time, it looked like she was a bit more understanding.

"Why do you say that?" I asked. "My hair not long enough for flower scrunchies?" I pretended to throw my hair around like that one model who did the butter commercials. She thought it was much funnier than I had anticipated and snorted a bit when she was laughing.

"Stop it, you're going to make me snort again." She finally had regained her composure and handed me back the container. I placed it in the saddlebag, and she must have been looking inside. "Did you bring whiskey to our date?" She reached into the saddlebag and pulled out one of the bottles. "Sorry, correction. You brought really shitty whiskey on our date." Here it was, she was pissed. I looked down and got ready to start apologizing when I heard a sound I wasn't prepared for. The bottle opening. I looked up, and she was sitting on my bike with her leg up, taking a pull from the bottle. It might have been the sexiest thing I had ever seen on this side of the poles.

"Wow," was all I could muster. She smiled.

"Well, glad you brought something for me. I would totally give you some, but you have to drive us back. Maybe if you're really good, you can have a sip." As she walked by, she shook the bottle in my face and started toward the prairie path we had come to walk. I said a quick prayer and followed her into the wood line.

We walked and talked for a while. It was nice to speak to her sober. That sounds like an odd thing to say, but with some people, you need to be drinking to talk to them. The night before had been a good example. Those girls and I used to have a ton of fun with Mae, but to be honest, they were kind of annoying back in the day. The whole valley girl mentality that they had was a bit of a drag. I guess Jessica had gotten to go out to that area to live the life of a valley girl. I smiled at the thought of her with a ton of fancy rich people all talking like that.

"What are you laughing at?" Sarah interrupted. My thought process must have shown on my face.

"Nothing. Us talking like this is just refreshing. Is that stupid?" I reached out for her hand. She took it happily.

"Not at all. There is a whole lot more to you than meets the eye," she joked. "Wait, are you a robot in disguise?"

"Funny. You're really funny," I joked as the grip of our hands tightened. We continued like that for a while. We talked about our lives and our families. Lost loves and heartbreaks. She talked about how she had always wanted to write and that she was too afraid to show anyone anything she had ever written. I was far too familiar...well, Rebecca was far too familiar with that experience, so I felt as if I had something to add. I told her how difficult it was...for my friend to do the same thing. How putting a piece of art, poem, or a story out there is like putting a piece of yourself out there for the entire world to see. They might not like it, and that fear is really debilitating.

"Wow, this friend of yours. What did they do?" The look on her face showed that she was truly interested.

"Well, that friend had someone who inspired them to try new things. Inspired them to believe in themselves. She is a writer now, full time. Works writing for some local places." I was saying too much and started to back down. I had never mentioned the other side of the poles to someone... never. There I was, talking about Rebecca like she was someone I knew, not actually me. The entire conversation started making me a bit uneasy.

"Well, that makes me feel good. Hey! Maybe you can be that person who inspires me?" She looked up at me, and the sun lit up her face. She smiled and turned her head to look back down the path.

I told her about my mother and how overbearing she was. I also told her that it was mostly my fault. She didn't ask about Mae at all, but I found myself talking about her a lot. I talked about the first time we met when we were kids and how we were instantly drawn together as friends. How difficult it was for her to grow up in her house and how difficult coming out was. I had ostracized myself because of my relationship with Mae from everyone that ever cared about me. Mae had been ostracized for just being who she was, and that was it.

"So you don't talk to your mother at all?" A genuine look of sadness came across her face.

"I do, I actually had lunch with her the other day. It was nice to see her, but it was very difficult to see her as well." I explained, in a bit more detail, how it had been growing up and how my feelings for Mae had really trashed a ton of my relationships throughout my life.

"You really do love Mae, don't you?" Sarah said, the look of sadness leaving her face and a look of acceptance replacing it. I stopped walking, and Sarah walked a few steps farther before turning to face me.

"Yes," was all I could muster the strength to say. Now it was her turn to be pensive. She stood there for a good while, thinking of her next words to say. She reached into her pocked and pulled out the bottle of whiskey. She was giving herself strength to say what she wanted to say next.

"You slept with her, didn't you. The other night after our fight. That's why you...you tried..." She couldn't even finish the sentence. The liquid courage gave her the strength to start the thought, but nothing can help you with the strength to finish something like that.

I just stood there, not knowing what to say. I guessed that the look on my face said everything. I looked up at her, and she never took her eyes off me. "Yes, she came back over that night...I was just about blackout drunk and so was she." Tears were welling up in my eyes, and Sarah came over and handed me the bottle of whiskey.

"Well, this isn't what I was thinking about when I told you that you could earn a sip. I think you have earned it all the same." I reached over and took the bottle from her hand and took a long sip. Fuck, she was right. This was shittier whiskey than I was used to.

"Sarah, I...I don't know what I am doing." The thought of what must be going through her head was unthinkable. To think that she knew that we had slept together already and she still wanted to come out here either meant that she was stupid or that she had already truly forgiven me. I was afraid to ask her which one.

"Chance. I knew the second that I saw you that morning. You think you're a pretty decent liar, but I feel like I know you a bit more than you think." She reached over and took the bottle from my hands and finished its contents. She put the cap on and put the bottle back in her pocket. "I know that your relationship with her is important to you. Hell, it might even be the most important relationship in your life. Just know this. I can't even begin to think of starting something with you if there is a possibility of that ever happening again." The tears were becoming present in her eyes now as well. "Fuck, I just wanted to have a fun day. I don't know why I even said all that. Chance…" She was about to apologize.

"Don't you dare apologize," I said, walking closer to her. I reached out and embraced her in a hug. "You're fucking amazing, and I am a class A fool. You never have to apologize to me." I pulled away and had both of my hands on her shoulders. "I just want to make it right. I want to be someone you deserve, but as you see, I am pretty fucked up."

"You think I don't know that, Chance?" She was half crying, half laughing. "Fuck, the first night we met you just randomly walked out of some bushes with a backpack full of beer. You were already drunk, and you clearly are about ten years older than anyone else at that party." She wiped the tears from her eyes. "I don't know why I was so drawn to you, but…I was, Chance. The way you're drawn to Mae, for some reason I am drawn to you like that." She walked over to a log on the side of the path and just sat down, defeated. I walked over to her and sat down next to her. She put her head down on my shoulder and sighed.

"I don't deserve a woman like you, Sarah. I really don't." I just put my head down in my hands.

"Maybe you don't," she said, her voice quivering slightly. "Shouldn't you let me decide that?" She was right. There I was, trying to make decisions for her, and she was a grown-ass adult. She had met a guy, started dating that guy, and found out that he had cheated on her with his lesbian best friend…and she was still there with me. Thinking of it just made me want to vomit. I pulled out two cigarettes and lit them both. I handed one to her, and she reached over and grabbed it.

"Chance, can you promise me that shit with Mae will never happen again?" I couldn't see her face, but I saw the exhale of smoke as she spoke.

"It will never happen again, Sarah. Mae and I are done. We have never been good for each other, and I think we both finally realized it." I took a drag and exhaled. "We have basically ruined our lives by having them based around each other. She has never been able to have a real relationship with anyone because of me. I haven't either. I don't talk to any of my friends anymore, and if I do, they just make me feel fucking stupid. Our relationship was the most codependent and toxic relationship you can imagine." I took a second to collect myself. I was starting to get upset, whether it was about this situation or the fact that I really thought I had lost Mae for good, I didn't know at the time.

Sarah got up and looked at me. Her eyes were bloodshot, and her makeup was running. "She is your best friend, Chance. You can't just give up on that. Is the relationship not worth saving?"

"I just don't know, Sarah. Maybe someday, but definitely not now. She fucking hates me...she hates herself as well. What happened was never supposed to happen, but it did, just the same." I sighed and finished my cigarette. I saw that Sarah was finished as well and I took her cigarette butt from her and placed them in my pocket. "I am an addict in more ways than one, and it's time for me to get over it. Finally, I have a reason to." I put my hand on hers and gripped it tightly. "I feel like you're the first person that could help me walk away. Believe me when I say that." She looked at me and cocked a half-smile.

"Yay," she mocked halfheartedly. "I just...I just can't go through the last two days again. Chance, I need you to promise me." She held up her pinky and put it in front of me. "Pinky promise me. I take these fucking seriously." I wrapped my pinky around hers and made the promise. At the time, I really wanted to keep it, I really did. She hugged me, and we just sat there for a moment in each other's arms in complete silence. The only sounds around us were the birds and the wind blowing through the trees. If I hadn't just put this young woman through a traumatic experience by being a complete and total piece of shit, it might have been a nice little moment together.

She looked up at me in a way I don't believe anyone on this side of the poles had ever looked at me. "So, we were going to see a movie, right?" She wiped her nose on her arm and then her arm on her pants.

"We can skip the movie, I think I have some popcorn at my place. We can just pretend and maybe go out another night if you want." She perked up a bit.

"Yeah, I was hoping you would say that. I don't know if you knew this, but I am kind of going through something with my boyfriend right now, and a movie theater might not be appropriate."

Her ability to crack jokes even when confronted with this situation was admirable, but it might just have been a front. She was hurting, and I was the one that had caused it. She might have been holding on, but for how long? I said a quiet little prayer for her in my head, hoping that I could be a better man and not destroy this poor girl's heart. I stood up and reached down for her hand.

"Let's get going," I said, reaching down to her. She took my hand, and I pulled her up. We walked back to the bike in silence, our hands never unclasping, not even for a second.

The ride back to her apartment was a quiet one. She had asked for me to drop her off so she could drive her own car to my place. I didn't argue since at this point she could punch me in the face and I would still apologize for it being in the way of her fist. She was either completely insane or mature way beyond her age; or mine, for that matter. She had forgiven me immediately and still wanted to try and make this work. Hopefully, I could keep my end of the bargain.

I arrived at the apartment first and tried to tidy up a bit before she got there. She and Mae had cleaned the place up, and like a normal slob, I had done a pretty good job of untidying it rather quickly. About fifteen or so minutes after I finished cleaning, there was a knock at the door. I answered and it was obviously Sarah with a six pack and her overnight bag. I smiled as I let her in and went into my cupboard to give her the flour from that morning.

"You bought me flour?" she asked as she held it in her hand. "I don't bake." She was obviously confused.

"Well, they didn't have flowers, so I bought you flour. I thought it was clever." She looked at me slightly annoyed and put the bag on the table.

"Thanks," she said, realizing that she was being rude. Her tone changed slightly.

"I guess it is a bit stupid," I said, feeling a bit self-conscious at the gesture. It was obviously wasted on that day since events had taken a bit of a turn at the park. I should have just thrown the damn thing away.

"No, it's sweet. I just..." she trailed off.

"No, I totally understand." I took the flour and put it on the kitchen table and threw the open bag of popcorn in the microwave. Sarah sat down on my futon and turned on the television. She went through movies we could watch while the popcorn popped. I popped a second bag since I usually just ate one by myself anyways. I poured their contents into a large metal bowl that I had gotten from my grandmother. It had been used only for popcorn for as long as I could remember.

"Thanks," Sarah said as I put the bowl of popcorn between us and sat down.

"No problem. What did you want to watch?" I asked. She just kept switching between movies and didn't seem like she could make up her mind.

"I don't know. You can pick something if you want. I...I just can't make a decision." She handed me the remote and put her feet up on the futon. She leaned back and started to eat some popcorn. I could tell the change in her demeanor from earlier. This day hadn't been what either of us had planned, but I was glad it had happened. This girl was extremely strong and had infinitely more heart than me. She was adult enough to see something and then confront it with no fear. Knowing full well that what she was going to find out would hurt her for sure. She knew that she wouldn't be able to live with not knowing one hundred percent. I envied her to the point that it made my bones hurt. She sat there looking at the television until I picked the sequel to the horror movie she had chosen a few days earlier. She looked over at me and smiled as the movie started.

The eighteen inches between us seemed like a canyon that might as well have been uncrossable. She needed her space, and all I wanted to do was show her how much I cared. How sorry I truly was. I chickened out and let the movie run its course. She fell asleep about halfway through the movie and was snoring so loudly that I decided to just go to bed. I moved the popcorn and stretched her out on the futon. I placed a pillow under her head and covered her in the blanket from my bed. I wanted to lay down next to her and hold her tight, but I was too much of a pussy. I placed a pillow on the floor next to her and fell asleep. Just before I faded to black, I felt her reach her hand down and take mine. I fell asleep smiling.

Chapter 16

I woke up a few minutes before my alarm went off. I laid there staring at the countdown until I had to get up and start my day. Honestly, I was a bit terrified to go and see Albert. For starters, I had given away the evidence that would potentially have skyrocketed our careers to some other news station to take all the credit. Secondly, I was terrified of leaving the house. After the previous day's cloak-and-dagger escapades, I didn't want anything to happen to us like it had happened to Albert. Just as I felt Mae starting to stir, the alarm sprang to life.

"Shut that thing off," Mae mumbled. "Can't we just sleep forever?" She pulled the blanket over her head and laid there for a few more minutes. I decided to let her try and get a bit more sleep and get up for the morning. I went into the bathroom and washed my face. I had forgotten to take off the bit of makeup I had put on the day before, and it was all over my face and most likely all over my pillow, as well. I used some of Mae's facial moisturizer wash and splashed water in my face a few times. I looked up in the mirror and saw a familiar face, only it was a bit more haggard than usual. Just as I was thinking it, Mae walked in behind me and took the words out of my mouth.

"You look like shit, Becks. Did you even sleep last night?" I would have argued with her, but she was right. I had big black bags under my eyes, and my eyes were bloodshot. My skin even seemed blotchy.

"Thanks, honey," I said halfheartedly. "You really know how to make a girl feel special." She came over and gave me a kiss on my cheek.

"Hey, you're using my face scrub, aren't you?" She sniffed me another

210

time. "Wow, it smells good on you." She smiled and left the bathroom with me just standing there.

"Complimenting me isn't going to get you out of hot water, Mae. I'm still mad at you." I could hear her making a pot of coffee in the kitchen.

"Get over it, honey." Her voice was playful, but still had a bit of sarcasm to it. It usually wasn't like her to say things like that. I decided to brush it off and blame it on a lack of coffee before starting anything with her this early in the morning. I contemplated taking a shower for about five minutes while watching stupid videos on my phone while using the toilet. I decided that I had showered enough over the past few days, and all the hot water in the world wouldn't make me feel better and I should just get started with the day. I went and got changed to go visit Albert in the hospital and went to meet Mae in the kitchen. She was sitting on the kitchen table with a cup of coffee in her hand and an old magazine in her other hand. Noticing that she hadn't poured me a cup of coffee, I went to the cupboard and grabbed my own…again, a little unlike her. Usually, whoever poured the first cup poured them both. A little unwritten rule in our home.

"So, did you still want to go see Albert today?" She looked up at me from my magazine, annoyed.

"I don't know. I really don't know him that well and think that maybe I wouldn't be welcome. Especially given the circumstances." She went back to reading her magazine.

"Oh, ok," she responded, taking a small sip of my coffee. "You said last night that you wanted to go, that's the reason I am asking." She took another few seconds to respond, this time never taking her eyes off the magazine.

"I don't remember saying that last night." She took another sip of coffee and looked up at me. "Sorry, babe."

"No worries. I can just go visit him quick and then come home. What did you want to do tonight?" She paused and put the magazine down.

"I have some homework to do, so I might just stay in and do that. Just want to finish school and finally get a job." She put the magazine down on the table, got up, and refilled her cup of coffee. She walked by me and stopped like she was going to say something. It looked as though she decided against it and then kept walking into our room.

"What's up with her?" I said quietly as I took another sip of coffee. I sat there for a few minutes, thinking about going in there and talking to her, but I decided against it. Sometimes people are not having a good day, and there is no reason to pry. I knew I was the last person in the world to give Mae shit about having a bad morning...or afternoon...hell, a bad anything. I'd had my fair share of those over the past week or so. I decided to let sleeping dogs lie and go see Albert. I got the last of my things ready and threw on a pair of sneakers and left. I didn't say another word to Mae, and it just felt off.

As I drove, I continued to think about Mae and how she was acting. Actually, come to think of it, she was acting a lot like Sarah was on the other side. The only thing was, Sarah had a reason to be angry at me and Mae didn't...

"Fuck," I said to myself as I pulled out my phone to check the date. "Today is our anniversary." I wanted to call Mae and apologize, but I figured the apology would be better in person. I thought about all the subtle hints she had dropped over the past few days, and they all started to make sense. "Wow, Becky, you fucking suck." Here I had told myself to be a better wife and partner to Mae, and I screwed it up at the first chance I got. We had been together officially for thirteen years and married for ten of them. How could I forget that? No wonder she was pissed. If I were her, I would be angry too.

I stewed about it the rest of the drive until I reached the small community hospital in the next town over. It was a small regional hospital, and it barely had an emergency room. It was the closest place to bring someone in an accident, so it was no wonder that they had brought Albert there. I sat in the car for a few minutes, prepping myself for what I was walking into. I was terrified to step foot inside that hospital. Not only because of the whole situation with Albert, but because of the fact I was terrified of hospitals to begin with. They smelled of death and decay mixed with a general cleaner. The thought of people dying within the walls of this place just gave me chills. I gathered up my nerve and grabbed my bag and headed into the hospital.

Walking in, I was greeted with the exact same smell I was expecting... death. I walked up to the counter, and the lady pointed at the sign-in roster for me to sign my name. I started filling it out until I got to the part where

I filled in Alberts name. I had no idea what his last name was. Wow, what kind of shitty person was I? I had been working with him for years and his name just escaped me. I decided to take a look at the last few pages to see if anyone else had visited him. The day before, I saw that Chris, the security guard, had stopped by and saw that Albert's last name was Roberts. I applauded myself quietly for my ingenuity and finished the sign-in sheet. The lady put on a pair of thick reading glasses to read the paper.

"Oh, ok. You're here to see Albert Roberts. How do you know the patient?" She peered up at me, and from my perspective, her eyes were magnified, making them huge. I stifled a chuckle and responded.

"He is a coworker, and we are friends, I would say." It was weird explaining my relationship with someone to a complete stranger, but I guess it checked the right boxes for her. She filled out a name tag and handed it to me.

"Through the door on the right and all the way down the hall. He is in room 181. If you need directions, ask a nurse." She then went back to ignoring me. I thanked her, and she didn't look up from her crossword. She just repeated herself one more time until I started walking down the hall. I dodged patients and nurses walking through the hallway. Each time I passed them, it brought the fresh stench of death that hospitals always seem to smell like. I held my breath as best as I could when I passed linen baskets and tried to keep my eyes focused entirely on the door numbers as I passed. The lady at the front desk was not wrong, he was nearly the last door down the hallway, and when I finally reached it, I took a deep breath and prepared myself for the worst. I pressed the door open and crept inside slowly.

"Hey, Rebecca!" I heard a familiar voice say. It was Albert. He was sitting up in his bed with a tray of food on his lap. "Breakfast is served." I walked in and past the curtain I didn't notice that John was also there, sitting in the corner of the room.

"Oh, hey, John," I said as I walked up to the bed. Albert looked pretty beaten up, but he didn't seem to be in a bad mood.

"Hello, Rebecca," John managed to say as he stood up and reached out to shake my hand. For some reason, he was on his very best behavior. "Sorry about that meeting yesterday. I was very upset about Albert, and I knew that binder had all his notes for something he was working on."

I paused at the mention of the binder. He knew I had it, I just knew it. I didn't know what to say, and I could tell that Albert could tell what I was thinking due to my demeanor.

"Yeah, he was looking for my notes binder. I had just finished something for him the evening before the accident, and he needed to polish it up to publish." Whether Albert was lying or just covering for me, I didn't know. The confession made John lighten up a bit.

"Deadlines are deadlines," he joked as he held up a small binder. "Well, now that I have this and you're here. I am going to head in and finish this piece. Thanks Albert, and goodbye Rebecca." He reached over to the chair and grabbed his coat and quickly left.

"Phew, I thought he would never leave," said Albert as he pushed the empty breakfast tray away and motioned for me to sit down in the chair where John had been sitting.

"Yeah, it was a bit of a surprise to see him here," I stated as I sat down and tried my best to relax. The cushions on the chair felt like sitting on a Little Tike's bench.

"He came in looking for my binder. I didn't know what he was talking about at first. I thought he knew about the...you know...binder." He looked around the room again to make sure nobody had walked in. "Speaking of which..." I interrupted.

"Albert, what happened with your accident? Did it have anything to do with the pictures?" I was not beating around the bush. I needed to know what we were up against.

"Rebecca. I fell asleep at the wheel and went into the ditch on the way home. It was nobody's fault but my own. Thank god I had all of that food in my stomach, or I probably would have blown over the legal limit, and I'd be handcuffed to this bed." He held up his hands to show them free of restraint.

"I thought...I mean, you were freaking out about the pictures. I don't know..." Albert interrupted with a laugh and a smile.

"Dear God, no. I just fell asleep and that's it." He took a second. "Wow, you really thought someone tried to kill me?" He laughed for a second, and then the laughing stopped. "Oh fuck, you really did, didn't you? What did you do with the binder and pictures?" I shuffled around in my seat, not knowing how to answer.

"I panicked, Albert, I just...I panicked." I repeated myself over a few times. I could see that Albert was getting a bit impatient.

"Did you burn them?" he asked, his eyes wide open.

"Oh no, I didn't burn them...I did something else with them. I divided them up and sent them to three major news outlets." I paused, and the room was quiet for a few moments after I told him the truth.

"So, it's done, huh?" he said as he grew rather pensive regarding my decision. "I guess we were planning on doing it ourselves." He sat back in his bed and took a few deep breaths.

"I'm sorry, Albert, I just thought that someone tried to kill you, and I didn't want anything to happen to Mae. I was thinking about my wife." I reached over and put my hand on his leg. "I didn't know what else to do."

He put his hand on mine and just shrugged. "Well, it is what it is. Maybe they will approach my uncle, and he might be able to be cooperative and help put the real criminals behind bars." He sounded like he believed his words, but I do not think he did. I had sealed his uncle's fate. "I was just rethinking the entire thing after seeing how upset my uncle was. I know he is a real son of a bitch, but he was genuinely concerned about me. I mean, just last night, they thought I would be in a coma for a while. I woke up late last night to a room full of very surprised people." He sat back in his bed again and sighed. "Well, what's done is done."

I paused for a minute before asking my next question, since I knew that it was going to determine mine and Albert's entire relationship going forward. Once I knew I had to ask the question, I did. "You're regretting it now, aren't you?" He fidgeted a bit, and I had my answer.

"Yes. I regret it. I think we made a mistake." He began to get upset. "I just...he was so concerned...he has been here all night with me. He isn't the greatest uncle, but does he deserve what is coming? I have to warn him." He paused, and I realized what that would mean. I knew he wouldn't say it, so I did.

"He would know that you turned him in." I put my head down. "That would ruin your entire relationship, wouldn't it?" I looked back up at him, and his face said it all.

"It's too late, isn't it?" He started to get fidgety and was getting nervous. His heart rate on his monitor was going a bit crazy to the point that a nurse came in. They came in and gave him a once-over. They eventually thought

215

that I was the culprit and asked me to leave. I apologized to Albert, but he wasn't paying attention. He got upset to the point that I think they were about to sedate him. The nurses looked at me again and asked me to leave…I did as I was told. The door closed behind me, and I sat there in the hallway with all of my greatest fears around me.

"What do I do?" I asked myself, looking down the hall and then at the floor. I started to panic. "Fuck!" I yelled as I started sprinting down the hallway back to the front desk. I blew past the receptionist as she yelled at me for running and sprinted out to my car. I managed to pull my keys out prior to getting to the car. Once inside the car, I got her started and rushed back home. I drove a bit wilder than I usually did, but I had to get home in time. In time to catch the mailman. I pulled the car into the parking lot of the apartment complex, right by the leasing office and ran in.

"Has the mailman come yet?" I said, panting as I spoke.

"Well, good morning. How can we help you today?" The receptionist must not have been listening because she took some headphones off prior to speaking to me.

"Has the mailman come yet?" Again, panting like a lunatic.

"Oh no, they haven't come yet," she said with a smile. He usually comes around noon." She nodded and went to put on her headphones again, "Is there anything else?" she asked before doing so.

"No…that's it," I said, trying to catch my breath. "I'll just come back around noon." I walked out into the parking lot and laughed. I had rushed and risked getting a speeding ticket, and he wouldn't be there for at least two more hours. At least I was going to be able to catch him. I checked my phone and then set an alarm for about thirty minutes before noon and decided to go and wait up in the apartment. When I walked up to the door, it opened, and Mae greeted me.

"What were you doing down at the leasing office? I heard some tires squealing and came to see who it was. Didn't expect to see my wife running into the office. Are we that late on our rent?" She smiled at her off-the-cuff joke and seemed pretty proud of herself.

"No. I went to go see if the mailman had come yet." She looked at me, puzzled.

"Because you wanted to make sure the packages mailed?" She looked worried, as if there was something else she should be afraid of.

"No, not that either. I talked to Albert, and he is regretting throwing his uncle under the bus. When I told him that we already mailed the packages, he started to panic, and they asked me to leave. I thought I could come back here and grab the packages and stop this whole thing from happening." I stopped to catch my breath, and Mae just looked confused.

"So, what caused the accident? Did someone try to hurt him?" She looked to the left and right and half retreated into the doorway. She signaled for me to come inside.

"He fell asleep. He said it was his own fault, and that's that. Nobody tried to hurt him, we were just letting our imagination get the best of us." I walked inside as I spoke and closed the door behind me. "He wants to bring the evidence to his uncle, I think, and let him decide what to do with it. Maybe turn himself in or use it as some kind of leverage." I shrugged, and I could tell that Mae was not pleased.

"So yesterday was completely just you panicking and freaking out about nothing and then making me freak out as well?" She crossed her arms and was not pleased.

"I'm sorry, Mae." Her demeanor was not normally like this. I guess she was right, I did overreact. What else would she have me do, just not give a shit about her? I was beginning to be irritated but remembered my promise to myself...be a better wife and partner. I decided to honor that and just took her abuse.

"Wow, ok," she said as she went back into the apartment. I wondered what had happened to make her this irritated with me. The day before had been rough, but we had done it together. We overcame it together. Now it felt like we weren't even getting along. Something must have happened, and I decided to give her a bit of space. Maybe then she would come to me with what was bothering her. I went and grabbed a cup of coffee from the pot, but it was cold since Mae had turned the pot off. I threw it in the microwave for a minute and then went outside to wait on the mailman.

I hadn't really sat outside the apartment alone in some time. I had grabbed my notebook, and I jotted down some ideas for stories and maybe a few poems while I waited. I hadn't even done any free writing like this in forever. I kept talking about being some hotshot writer, but it appeared that I didn't even want to put in the legwork. I liked writing, and I was good enough for small articles and such, but I didn't really think I had it for the published world. Nobody would even think twice about publishing someone like me without a bit more of a resume. I had nothing to show for it. A ton of half-finished projects, and even if I went back and started to finish them, they would already be outdated and basically ancient compared to how pop culture had gone. I wanted to write something powerful, something that would last the ages. I laughed, probably because every other writer wanted to do the same thing, and to rise to the ranks of literary canon, you had to be truly exceptional. I was mediocre at best. Hell, Mae said last year that I should make it my goal to finish my first book by our anniversary...

"Fuck!" I thought out loud, suddenly remembering our wedding anniversary. I had completely forgotten that I had forgotten our anniversary. I got out of the chair and went inside. Mae was sitting there in our bedroom, watching something on the television. She looked at me when I came in. She could tell by the look on my face.

"Remembered, didn't you?" she said with a half-smile. "Well, it's too late. I hate you." She folded her arms and leaned back against the wall. I jumped into the bed and wrapped my arms around her.

"Fuck, Mae, I am so sorry. I can't believe that I completely forgot about our anniversary. I am the worst wife in the world." She resisted at first, but then I could feel her arms wrap around me as well.

"I was really mad at you and thought you would get it...but then you didn't, and that made me madder." She kissed the side of my head and squeezed one tighter hug before withdrawing.

"You're such a fucking cliché, do you know that, Mae?" She blushed a little bit and then realized I was right.

"Fuck. I have been so shitty to you today. Now I'm sorry." She put her head down and looked up at me with a guilty look.

"Let's just say we both suck and move on. Didn't we want to go out to dinner? You wanted to go to the place where they cook in front of you, right?"

"Chori Shanata's!" Mae said gleefully. "That's my favorite place ever! You remember that place, but not our anniversary...shame on you."

"Well, I didn't know the name, you did." I felt a bit relieved that the quarrel was over and that she had forgiven me. Too be honest, I was a bit pissed off at her for being so passive aggressive, but I knew her, and that was how she was. When you love someone like Mae, you take all the bad in with all the good. You love all of her or don't love her at all. This woman I could honestly say was the love of both of my lives, and I wasn't going to let some little fight get in the way of that. Especially now that I only had her on this side of the poles.

"Well. Don't you have a mailbox to rob? I still do have a ton of homework to do." She pointed toward the door and gave me a devilish grin.

"Fine, and for the record. I am not robbing it. I am taking back what is rightfully mine...well, Albert's. You know what I mean." I suddenly noticed that I had been inside and wasn't watching for the mailman. I just left Mae sitting there and sprinted out of the front door. The mailman had just arrived and was walking up to the post box. I ran like a bat out of hell down to where he was, and by the time I reached him, he was just starting to pull packages out of the box.

"Hey, sir!" I said, panting as I finally reached him.

"Oh, hey there, young lady." The mailman was a bit older, maybe in his late fifties. He was surprised to see a young woman running up to him.

"Sorry," I said again, trying to catch my breath. "I must look like a lunatic. I mailed three packages to some places, and I need to have them back. It's an emergency."

The man shook his head and apologized. "I'm sorry, I can't give you any packages back unless you have proof that they are your packages." He shrugged and continued to unload the bin.

"I can't prove it because we didn't put our names on the boxes. We also used stamps, so we don't have a receipt. I can literally describe everything about the boxes to you, including their destination. Like I said, it's an emergency." He put the bag down and smiled.

"Well, I have been doing this a long time and have never come across this situation before. How about I make you a deal. If you can give me exactly what the boxes look like and what's on them, I will consider giving you them back. Just know, that what I am doing is kind of against policy and I can get in a lot of trouble. You seem nice enough, though, and it also looks like you're in a bit of a pickle." He finished unloading the bin and took his bag into the back of his truck. He used the door to hide the contents. "Alright, young lady, what am I looking for."

I explained the three packages as best as I could. I also described the stamp situation as well as the locations that they are being mailed to and from. He was a bit concerned about how suspicious the packaging was, and too be honest, he looked happy when I was finished.

"Well, I don't think you can give me much more proof than that." He smiled as he handed me the three packages. "Now, this will just be our little secret, you understand?" He made a hand gesture for me to be quiet and gave me one more smile and then closed the doors to his truck. He got in the front seat and a few moments he was gone.

I walked back up to the apartment with all three packages in hand. "You did it!" Mae said happily. "What did you give him? I am assuming you just broke some kind of mail law or something."

"I didn't give or do anything. I just gave him exactly what was on the packages, literally everything. He felt comfortable enough to give me the packages after that." She raised an eyebrow.

"Wow, well. That's good, I guess. Much easier than I thought." I handed her the packages, but she turned away. "Don't touch me with those, I want nothing to do with them.

We both laughed as she recoiled, and I placed them on the table by the front door. I went over to my phone, and I texted Albert. I hope he is happy that I was able to retrieve them. I let him know I would bring them back to him tomorrow. I didn't expect an answer right away, seeing as I had nearly given the poor man a heart attack at the hospital earlier. When I was done, I went to go and join Mae over on the couch.

"Turn on the television or something, babe. Just keep it low so I can keep on doing my homework. Then we can go have our special dinner." I did as she asked and sat with her for a few hours. Unfortunately, I was watching one of my favorite cooking competition shows, so I was working up quiet an appetite. We sat there until the late morning turned into the early afternoon. The early afternoon turned into early evening, as it usually does. I nearly dozed off a couple times, but that never usually happened. No matter how tired I got on this side of the poles, I couldn't really nap. I don't know why.

"Well, I think I am about done with my homework. I'm going to go and get ready for our dinner!" She jumped up and down and went into the shower to get ready. I, on the other hand, just sat there and waited. I had showered enough in the past few days...on both sides, and I wanted to give Mae time to relax. I sat there and finished the show I was watching and could hear Mae doing her thing in the bathroom. I decided I might as well try to get dolled up for her as well and went to go and find something that wouldn't embarrass her. I went through my entire wardrobe, trying to find something, and settled on a dress I had bought for a wedding a year or so before. It wasn't too flashy, but I thought I looked amazing in it. I shimmied into it and tried my best to do my hair. Unfortunately, Mae was still in the bathroom and so were all the hair products. My hair was still short enough that it needed styling, but I usually just used moose and hairspray. I could hear Mae getting out of the shower and grabbing her towel. She barged into the bedroom, soaking wet.

"You going to dry yourself off?" I joked as she looked up at me while drying her ears.

"Funny, you can go and do your hair and stuff now. Time for this girl to get into her anniversary dress." I smiled, as I had completely forgotten the dress that I had bought her about a week earlier. She looked amazing in it. I left her to get ready, and I went into the bathroom to finish up myself. The mirror was covered in steam, so I wiped it off and got to work on my routine. I didn't usually wear a ton of makeup, and that day was no exception. Once in while I would, but I really didn't like it. Maybe a bit of eyeliner, but that was it.

I finished my hair and makeup and went back into the bedroom.

"Can you zip me up?" we both said as soon as we saw each other. We laughed and each said "Jynx!" We shook our heads and smiled as I zipped her dress up, and she followed suit by zipping the back of mine up, as well.

"Now go in the other room while I finish," she said, shushing me out of my own bedroom.

"Fine, relax," I tried to say as she pushed me out the door and shut it behind me. I smiled and decided that a drink was in order. I pulled a beer out of the fridge and popped the cap. I took a few sips and went to sit on the couch, doing my best not to mess up my dress. I decided to call the restaurant and make a reservation since it was kind of a nice place. I called and spoke with the hostess, and she put down our name for two in about forty-five minutes. Hopefully that would be enough time since Mae might just decide to take her sweet time getting ready. She was usually the one that I waited on. We got lucky that day, since I only waited about five minutes. She came busting out of the bedroom, still putting on one of her earrings.

"This dress is fucking amazing, but kind of hard to move in." She laughed as she took a look in the mirror. She usually preferred that mirror over the bedroom because the light was better. She fixed a bit of her lipstick and fluffed up her hair and blew herself a kiss.

"You blew yourself a kiss and not me?" I said as I walked up to the bathroom door. She turned around and gave me a playful glare.

"You haven't earned it. You forgot about tonight." She over exaggerated her little huff she did at the end of the sentence to show that she was joking around. She took a few more seconds fixing herself in the mirror and turned around to go and grab her purse and shoes. A few minutes later, we were out the door on our way to the restaurant.

The drive there was rather uneventful. We both really loved this place, and it was our go-to whenever there were special occasions. Well, not just any special occasion because this place was rather pricy. We still loved going there and having tons of leftovers for the next day's lunch or dinner. We pulled into the parking lot, and immediately, I thanked myself for getting a renovation, because the place was packed. Mae and I got in and walked through the crowd of people both coming and going and made our way through the front entrance.

"Table two for Chan...Rebecca," I stammered. I had forgotten where I was for a minute. Thankfully, the place was pretty loud, and nobody noticed the blunder, even Mae. The hostess took us to our table, and we sat and waited for someone to take our order.

"What are you going to get?" Mae asked, knowing full well that I was going to get steak and shrimp. She also knew full well that she was going to get the sesame chicken. Like I said before, I was a creature of habit. I just might have rubbed some of that off on my wife.

"The usual of course!" I said, pointing at the menu. "Did you want to get a drink? I'll drive home so you can get a few in. It is our anniversary, by the way." She grinned as she looked over the drink menu. She loved that the drink would come in a little novelty glass, and we must have had a dozen or so at home. She was still missing one of the monkeys, I couldn't remember which one.

After a while, the waitress came and took our orders and Mae's drink order. The drink came out fast, and it was nearly gone before the waitress had a chance to give the rest of us our drinks.

"Just get her a small pitcher, and we should be good." The waitress laughed and nodded her head in agreement. A few minutes later, a small pitcher was brought over, and Mae poured some of its contents into her little novelty glass.

The chef came and did the usual tricks and funny gags that he normally did. If you have ever been to a Hibachi place, you know what I am talking about. The cool stuff with the cutlery and the flaming onion volcano. I loved watching people in the restaurant who had children with them. When the flames hit high in the air, the look of wonder was something that really was an added bonus to this place. On the other hand, Mae still gave those kinds of looks when they did all the tricks, and I usually spent half my time watching other people and half my time watching my adult wife marvel at the spectacle. She would make an amazing mother one day, if that was the path we chose. She saw so much wonder in the world, especially in places that I didn't anymore. It was one of the things I loved most about her and hated all at the same time.

Dinner came and went like it usually does when you're wanting to savor every bit of it. By the time I got the last of my food, a pile was forming on my plate, and I was already separating the food for our doggy bag. Mae, on the other hand, drank that entire pitcher, and apparently it made her grow an extra stomach. Her plate was nearly empty. She looked up from the plate and burped...it sounded as if she was going to throw up. Thankfully, she held it down and gave a cute little laugh when she realized she was safe.

"I think I ate too much," she said, pointing down at her belly. "Omg, I barely fit in this dress anymore." Obviously, she was kidding, because she still looked amazing. I gave her a few jabs to make sure I got back at her for the past few days.

"Oh, shut it!" I laughed as I patted down my stomach as well. "I am full to the top!"

She looked at me with lustful eyes that also had a hint of drunk in them. "Well, you better not be too full for dessert." She put her hand on my bare leg and reached under my dress. I pulled back, both because it both tickled and we were in a public place.

"Mae, stop it. You're so terrible," I said, smacking her hand out of the way. She withdrew and went back to packing up her to-go box. I followed suit, and before we knew it, I was loading her drunk butt in the car and driving home.

Mae kept reaching over toward me on the drive home provocatively, and I struggled to both drive the car and keep her advances at bay. I hadn't realized that she had drunk that much. She wasn't belligerent, but she definitely had something on her mind. I parked the car, and we made our way into the apartment. The second the door closed, she pushed me against the wall and had her hands all over me. Within seconds, my dress was unzipped, and she was trying to pull it down around my torso. Her hands were a flurry as she desperately did her best to remove my dress.

"You going to give me a hand!" she said as she struggled to get the dress around my hips. I was pressed against the wall, so the task was rather poorly planned.

"Let's take this into the bedroom," I said as she pulled away and took my hand. Like a flash of lightning, I was back in the park with Sarah. Her hands firmly in mine, pulling me along the path. A second later, I was back in my apartment. Mae pulled me along into the bedroom and looked back at me. Lightning again, Sarah looking back at me, her eyes filled with hope and wonder.

"Get that dress off and get in the bed!" Mae said as she quickly undressed and stood there. The light from the nightlight in the hallway illuminated her, so I could barely see her features. I sat down in the bed, and she came crawling toward me.

"Chance, I need you to promise me," Sarah's voice echoed in my mind. "Pinky Promise me. I take these fucking things seriously." Her hand was coming toward me, pinky extended. I took it and made the promise to her. Promised that I would not hurt her again. I promised that what happened between Mae and I would not happen again...there I was, breaking that promise. Like lightning again, I was back in the bed with Mae on top of me. Her mouth against my skin, making every cell in my body come to life all at once. Where her hands touched me, it was nearly electric. It was the power that sustained me while on the other side of the poles. It was what kept me alive during the times when I thought I might not make it through the night without her. It was what I needed in order to continue living my other life without her in it.

"Fuck!" I said suddenly. I pushed Mae off me and ran into the bathroom.

"Babe, are you alright?" Mae asked, the concern could be heard in her voice. "What's wrong?"

I knew what was wrong, but how could I tell her that I had made a promise to someone, and it seemed that even though I was on the other side of the poles, my subconscious wanted me to keep it? I turned on the light and went to look in the mirror. My hands were shaking, and I was standing there with only my underwear on and my bra half off. "What the fuck, Rebecca," I said to myself. I pulled a small cup that we used for rinsing our mouth after brushing our teeth. I filled it with tap water and took a drink. "Go fuck your wife," I said to myself over and over. I could hear Mae knocking on the door.

"Becks, are you ok?" she said as she knocked. I had to think on my feet so she didn't get worried. I thought for a second and lifted up the toilet seat and sat down.

"I think I might have eaten too much. My stomach is killing me." I leaned back, not realizing I was sweating. I fixed my bra and took a moment to breathe.

"Fuck, let me in. I'll take care of you," she said, this time only knocking softly.

"I think I might be in here a while, babe." I made noises like I was straining myself. Hoping she would take the hint and go lay down in bed. She'd had a ton to drink, so she might actually fall asleep, and I could take a minute to think about what was actually happening to me.

"Oh, ok," she said sadly. "I'll wait up for you babe. Just let me know if you need anything."

I took a sigh of relief as I sat there, trying my best to calm down. Was I really not going to enjoy this side of the poles because of what I had told Sarah? Was this a one-time thing, or would Sarah's memory still haunt me here? Obviously, I had made the promise not to do anything else as Chance, but I didn't say anything about Rebecca, right? This was like that rule about being in different zip codes, but it was different realities. Did that make it ok? I grappled with this question while calming down for a good fifteen or so minutes. Once I didn't hear anything else coming from the bedroom, I opened the door and poked my head out. Mae was sleeping soundly on the bed. I noticed a glass of water and a bottle of TUMS on the nightstand. I walked up to her and marveled at her while she slept. She had managed to put a shirt on and barely cover herself.

"What am I going to do?" I said as I took the bottle of TUMS and took one out. "Might was well get some calcium," I whispered to myself as I took a tablet and ate it. I forgot how bad they tasted and washed it down with the water. I nuzzled myself next to Mae and tried to get comfortable. My heart was still racing a bit from earlier, and all I wanted to do was sleep with my wife...I guess actually sleeping next to her would have to suffice this evening. I cuddled next to her while she snored like a buffalo. It took a bit longer than usual to fall asleep, thanks to her, but I eventually did. That night, however, I fell asleep thinking of Sarah and the promise that I had made. I fell asleep thinking of her on my couch on the other side, with her hand firmly in mine.

Chapter 17

I woke up and was barely able to move my neck. I opened my eyes to the sight of the underside of my futon. Fuck, it was dirty. I made a mental note to move and at least try to get some of the dust bunnies underneath it. After a few moments of trying, I was able to turn my head to the other side and was greeted by a head of red hair. Sarah had gotten off the futon and had made a small nest next to me. Her head was carefully placed on my chest, and her hand was on my stomach. I could smell the coconut shampoo in her hair. I tried to put my arm around her, but she was laying over it and it was nearly asleep. I was able to slide it out from underneath her without waking her and make myself a bit more comfortable.

I laid with her for about an hour, just wanting to spend time with her while she was sleeping. I feared that when she woke, her wits would return, and she would immediately regret being back with me. I'll be honest with you, I wouldn't even have blamed her. By the time the sun started to shine through the windows, she began to stir.

"Good morning," I said softly as she lifted her head from my chest. A small wet spot was obvious where she had lifted her mouth. She noticed and immediately wiped her face and was embarrassed.

"Sorry," she said, half laughing. "I was just so comfortable." She pushed herself up and stretched a bit. Apparently, she must not have been that comfortable, since she looked just as stiff as I was. She stretched enough where her shirt rode up, and I could see her midriff. She smiled when she caught me staring.

"Why are you smiling?" I said as I tried myself to sit up. She didn't let me and straddled her let over my torso and pinned me down.

"Whoa, who said you can get up?" she said as she reached down and kissed me softly on my lips. She pulled away and bit my lower lip... just like Mae did on the other side of the poles. She smiled again, since she must have noticed I was getting turned on. She came back in and kissed me again, and this time she didn't pull away. We made out like we were teenagers, and that had been a bit longer for me than it had for her. We tangled ourselves on the floor in the blankets for about thirty or so minutes, just enjoying our bodies being next to each other's. She pressed her body closer and closer to mine, so close that I swear to God, if she pushed any harder, we would have merged together. I reached my hand underneath her shirt, and she withdrew slightly.

"I'm sorry," I said, noticing the sudden change in demeanor. She took a deep breath and spoke.

"Don't be...I really want to, but...I think we should take it slow... you know..." She didn't want to say why, but I knew why. I interrupted immediately.

"Sarah, its ok. We don't have to do anything. I just got a bit carried away. Obviously, I am turned on as hell." She smiled a bit and sighed.

"Well then, we need to find something else to do, because I can tell I am going to give you blue balls at this rate." She reached her leg back over my torso and laid down next to me. "What should we do, then?"

"We could go and grab some breakfast?" The words left before I had a chance to think. Where the hell would we go for breakfast? There was only one place in town that actually had a good breakfast, and that would be the diner. Her face lit up at the sound of food.

"Yeah, I guess I could eat," she said, rubbing her belly. "I could really use a big mug full of coffee as well." She stood up and reached down to give me her hand. I took it, and she helped pull me up. Well, she didn't really help, but I pretended that she did.

"You're heavy," she joked as she went into the bathroom and shut the door. "Give me a minute, I need to make sure I don't look like a loser."

"It's just a diner, don't worry about it," I said as I tried to make my pants fit correctly again. They were a bit tighter than they were when I had woken up...Sarah had something to do with that. I went and opened the door to have a cigarette. After a few minutes, Sarah came outside and made the gesture with her hand that she wanted one as well.

"Smoking is bad for you," she said as she lit up the cigarette and inhaled a lung full of smoke. "You should really quit." I smiled at the thought of trying to quit both talking to Mae and smoking all in the same run. I might as well have stopped drinking and taking sleep medication while I was at it. I was mad at myself for thinking the thought angrily. Addicts always confront people who oppose their habits with anger. I tried to calm down before I spoke, but I had to do it quickly.

"Yeah, they haven't killed me yet." I tried to sound sarcastic, but I was thinking she thought I was more annoyed at her comment.

"I was just kidding," she said, looking like I had just yelled at her.

"I know, so was I," I responded immediately, this time softening my tone as much as I could in order to ensure she didn't get too self-conscious.

"Ok good." She smiled, took a few more drags of her cigarette, and placed the butt in yet another empty beer bottle on my windowsill. "Come on, let's get some food, I am starving." I put my cigarette out as well and did as I was told. I grabbed my things from inside the apartment, and we were on our way. It was a bit too cold to take the bike, and I didn't fit inside the Fiero, so we took my stick shift.

We drove downtown and parked a few blocks down from the diner. The walk to the diner was, again, uneventful, and the second I walked in, Al was already there to say hi.

"Hey there, Chance! You look well rested." He paused for a second and then saw Sarah walk in behind me. "Oh, and who is this lovely lady?" he asked while grabbing a second menu.

"Hey," Sarah said awkwardly, not expecting the owner to know me by name. She looked back at me, and I gave her a look that said "just go with it." She turned back to Al. "My name is Sarah, and yours?"

"My name is Al, but you're pretty enough to call me whatever you want to." He reached out his hand and shook hers. "Chance never brings pretty girls into my diner. Well, other than Mae, of course." If Sarah had an issue with that name, she didn't let me notice. Al knew me, and he knew that I was always around with Mae. This, however, was one of the first times I had brought someone other than Mae in with me to his diner. Even then, he was definitely playing wingman for me.

"Well, this one is special," I said as he looked up at me. "Usual booth please, that's if it is open." He motioned with his hand.

"Right this way, young lady," he said to Sarah, and he led us back to my usual booth. "Can I get you guys any coffee or tea to start with?" He turned to me and gave me a look. I knew that look meant he was asking what kind of coffee I needed. Regular, or his special coffee that I'd had the other day. I shook my head, and Sarah ordered her drink as well. "Two black coffees, coming right up."

"Wow, he is so nice. You must come here often." She looked around at the diner and smiled at some of the photos on the walls. It kind of had that fifties diner feel to it, with a touch of modern.

"Yeah, I come here quite a bit, enough for Al to know Mae and I by name." I had forgotten again, and it seemed that Sarah just let it slide. She understood my history and wanted to continue seeing me, so she would have to understand that Mae would come up in conversation. I just wondered how it really made her feel when that name was uttered. It couldn't feel good.

I, myself, had never been cheated on. That being said, I didn't think I had really ever dated someone long enough for them to actually cheat on me. The thought gave me an odd feeling of discomfort, not knowing, myself, how much Sarah was hurting. I guess my karmic payback for all those hurt feelings and broken hearts was obvious.

"What do you usually get here?" she asked as she looked over the menu. "The Denver omelet looks really good. I usually get those when getting breakfast. That or French toast. Have you had that here?"

I shook my head no. "I usually just get the corned beef skillet, but maybe today I will try something new. How about I get the French toast and you can try some of mine." I hated French toast but felt like an olive branch needed to be given in order for this breakfast to continue without me getting punched in the face.

"Ooooh, I like the sound of that," she said while taking another look at the menu. "Yeah, let's do that for sure." Al took that moment to bring us each our coffees and take our order.

"I'll have the French toast," I said as he took the menu. Al laughed and then paused.

"Wait, you're serious. I was just thinking you were going to have your usual. I don't think you have ordered anything else in years." He smiled and looked over at Sarah. "It seems that you're helping teach this old dog new tricks." He paused again and nodded his head looking at Sarah. "I like this girl, Chance." He patted me on the back as he walked back toward the kitchen.

"Wow, you really come here often. I like going out with you. It's like going everywhere with a VIP." She reached over and squeezed my hand. "My boyfriend is a VIP."

"Very Idiotic Person?" I joked as she continued to hold my hand over the table. She reached over with her other one and took a sip of coffee.

"Oh, shush. Oooh, this coffee is really good also." She blew on her mug a bit and kind of bounced in the seat.

We didn't wait long for our food and had a pretty good conversation while waiting. She and I really had not had a real chance to have a conversation since we had first met. Unfortunately, our entire relationship had really only spanned a week, and in that time frame, I had cheated and nearly died. Overall, I thought I was an all-time loser boyfriend and couldn't understand for a second why this girl wanted anything to do with me. I started to feel sorry for myself just as the food arrived.

"This looks good," Sarah said as Al handed her the omelet she had ordered and handed me the plate of French toast.

"Enjoy, you two," Al said as he jabbed me in the shoulder. "This one seems nice," he said softly so Sarah couldn't hear. I nodded in agreement, and he went back behind the counter. A few moments later, another waitress came and refilled our coffee.

We ate and talked a bit more until, obviously, the conversation was as cold as the remnants of food on the plates. Sarah leaned back and patted her stomach. Like lightning, I was back at the Japanese restaurant with Mae, watching her slap her belly.

"You good?" Sarah said. She must have noticed the look on my face changing slightly with the minor reality shift.

"Yeah, I am just stuffed." I patted my stomach just as she did...there was a bit more movement with my stomach than hers. I looked up at her, and she must have been privy to my revelation about my not-so-dad bod. With impeccable timing as usual, Al came by with the check right as we were finishing up and had completely run out of things to talk about.

"Here you go, Chance, I hope you guys had a good visit." He looked over at Sarah. "Make sure you bring this one again." I took out some cash and put it down on the table.

"Keep the change, Al," I said while scooting toward the end of the booth.

"You know I will," he said, and with that, he was gone.

"Well, what should we do the rest of the day?" Sarah said while standing up and straightening out her clothes. "We can do anything we want, right?" I had thought about her coming back to my place, but I had a ton of work to do and also wanted to relax a bit on my own. Being a fucking coward that was afraid to be in the room with himself alone, I gladly agreed to hanging out further into the afternoon.

"Yeah, we can head back to my place and watch a movie or something. Or did you have something else in mind?"

She pondered the question for a few moments and shrugged. "Actually, no. I have nothing else in mind. We can do anything!" she joked. "When was the last time you did something you wanted to do...for you?" Her question caught me off guard...simply because the only thing I really did for myself was drink and abuse my body with either drugs or medications. I hadn't had anyone, including Mae, ask me what I really wanted to do. The thought actually kind of made me depressed since I had no real hobbies to speak of or any real interests other than...well, you know.

"I actually don't know," I responded. "I can't remember the last time that anyone has asked me that. Usually I just do what..." I caught myself. "Other people want me to do." She saw the almost slip but seemed to appreciate the correction.

"Really?" She seemed surprised. "Well, what do you do on your days off?" Again, her question was lost on me.

"Days off?" I laughed. "I am technically self-employed so...every day is a day off for me." She scowled, knowing full well that I knew what she was talking about.

"Don't be difficult, Chance. You haven't always been self-employed. What did you like doing on our days off when you were younger and not your own boss?" She didn't like my response of shrugging.

"I really don't have any idea. I used to hang out with a group of friends I worked with, but that changed when they all graduated and I dropped out." Again, the thought was rather depressing. Did I really not have any fucking hobbies? I tried for a moment to think of what I had done in my spare time recently. Other than the obvious and feeding my vices, there was nothing. Movies and Television shows, maybe, but even that was just random, and there was not really any pattern to it. Whatever was on, I just watched.

"Wow, we definitely need to get you some hobbies." She laughed as she took a look at the bill. "Also, whatever we are doing next, I will pay for. I didn't realize we at so much, I feel bad."

I shrugged it off. "We were hungry, and I think you have earned a few meals free of charge after dealing with all my shit." The callback to the previous days was a mistake, but it was too late to take it back.

She shrugged it off and continued unintentionally making me feel like shit. "Well, let's figure something out." As we left the diner, we walked up and down the strip, looking into shops. She continued her line of questioning to find out things that I may or may not enjoy doing. She asked everything she could think of from A to Z, but there was just nothing that I was that interested in doing. She was also surprised by how much I hated my art, as well. I only really did it as a way to pay the bills. Every time I had to put pencil to paper for anything, I literally hated every moment of it. Yeah, I was talented enough, but it was purely for work and not pleasure. That made her sad.

"So, you don't like painting or anything anymore? Did you like doing it when you were younger?" The thought of doing something every day that you hated had obviously escaped her. That's what work is, right? Doing something purely for money. Nobody is actually happy with what they do, right? I wasn't alone in that; or that was how I felt, at least.

"Well, what about you, Sarah?" I said, finally getting frustrated at the line of questioning. I felt like I was being interviewed. "What do you do for fun?" Her answer was not something I was ready for. With a smile on her face and a skip in her step, she began going through everything that she enjoyed doing. These things ranged from spending time with her family and friends to what she did in her free time. She apparently used to ride horses and wanted to do that again someday. She also wanted to pursue a career in writing, that I knew from our conversation the other day. She still had no clue what she really wanted to do with her degree but knew that she didn't want the reality that I had laid down in front of her. The boring dystopian feeling of working at a job you hated just to pay for the things you needed. You could see the look of fear in her face when she spoke about that situation being completely out of the question.

"Wow," I responded when I felt that she was finally complete with her list of things she loved. If I had thought I felt bad before, I was mistaken. Here was someone that loved doing things, and she was here with someone who had no clue what he loved other than his addictions.

"Wow, what? Maybe we can try some of those things together, and you can see if you like them. Then we can do those things together!" She smiled a coy smile. "We already know what things we are good at together...but we can't just do that all the time, can we?" I knew the thing she was talking about, and she was correct...not appropriate to do all day long. Also, I wasn't that big of a fan of cardio.

"Maybe," I said, not knowing if I really meant it or not, but not wanting to leave her offer hanging. She got really excited and stopped walking.

"So, what are we trying first?" she said as she took my hands. "We can do anything you want to, just tell me and we can do it." I thought for a moment about what I really wanted to do at that moment. I wanted to go back to my apartment and drink until I was unconscious. If Sarah wanted to join me, we could do that together, but unfortunately, I didn't think that was what she had in mind. She saw me struggling and sighed.

"I'm sorry," I said, mentally exhausted from trying to think of something.

"Don't be sorry, Chance." She put her arms around me and pulled me in for a hug. She reached up and kissed me softly on the cheek. "Take my hand and follow me." She pulled away and held out her hand. I did as I was told and put my hand in hers. She dragged me down the sidewalk toward my car, and when we got there, she reached her hands out one more time. "Keys, please." She smiled as she asked. I didn't really feel like driving anyway, so I again did as I was asked. We both got into the car, and she reached into her purse and grabbed out what looked like a bandana.

"What's that for?" I asked, suddenly concerned for my safety.

"Shut up and put it over your eyes." She handed it to me, and I started tying it around my eyes. One eye was still poking out, and she got real close. "Chance, do you trust me?" She pulled the bandana down over my free eye and kissed me on the lips. She pulled away and bit my bottom lip as she did. The feeling took away my ability to speak for a second.

"Yes," was all I could say.

"Good," she said as I felt the car shift into reverse. I was able to buckle up blindfolded, and I swayed from side to side as she turned left and right. I knew this town pretty well, and from the turns, I felt as if we were going to her apartment. I didn't want to spoil the surprise for her, so I kept my mouth shut. A small price to pay to give her a bit of happiness. She obviously wanted to show me something, and the surprise was part of that allure. After a bit, I felt her putting the car in park and the emergency brake going up.

"Here," she said as I reached for my blindfold. "Whoa, not yet." I felt her hand grab the blindfold and hold it in place. "One second." She exited the car, and I expected that she was running around the vehicle to let me out of the other side. Proving my assumption, I heard the door open, and I felt her hand in mine as she pulled me up and made sure I didn't hit my head on the doorframe.

"Thank you," I joked as I felt what she was doing. Making sure I didn't get a concussion on top of everything else today.

"Just walk and listen to my voice," she said as she led me down the sidewalk. She told me if there was a step up or down, and before I knew it, I didn't feel the sun shining on my skin anymore, and we were inside an air-conditioned building. We waited in an elevator for a few moments, and I heard Sarah say hey to someone she knew that must have lived in the building. We opened a door, and she told me to take off the blindfold. I did as I was told, and was, in fact, in her apartment. It was a small student's apartment that had all the things a college student would need. There was a small kitchenette and a bathroom and a single large room where she had her bed and personal effects.

"Nice place," I said, trying to sound surprised.

"Ah, shut up. I figured you knew where we were going, I just wanted to see how long you would play along. I appreciate you sticking with it until the end." She took my hand and sat me down in her bed. Her sheets were infinitely nicer than mine on either side of the poles. I made a mental note to get nicer sheets. "Wait right there." She went into her closet and pulled out a small decorative box and opened it. Inside the box was what looked like a small notebook that was a beautifully bound with a leather strap and copper buckle on the front. She took it and held it close to her chest and came and sat beside me.

She took the book and handed it to me. "Chance, this is something I have literally never showed anyone." I inspected the book and looked at her.

"You want me to read your diary? That's a bit odd," I joked as she whacked me on the arm and sighed.

"No, this is my book of poems I have been writing since I was young. I finally decided to take all the ones I loved and put them into a single place. Chance, this is the poetry collection I want to publish." I went to open it, and she stopped me. "You have to promise me that you won't laugh or make fun. That would kill me." She slowly took her hand off mine and gave me a nod to open it. Before doing that, I looked over at her and put my hand on her shoulder.

"I know what it is like to put yourself out there more than you know. Letting someone see something like this is a huge step for you. Are you sure you want that someone to be me?" She smiled with every part of her being. The well-lit room felt instantly brighter.

"Chance. Yes, I have only known you for about a week. Also, yes, in that week you haven't really shown that you're the most reliable person on this planet. There is something about you that's almost addictive, and no matter how much I might want to pull myself away...I can't. The reason that I am trying to forgive you about Mae is that I feel that way about you. That party wasn't the first time that I have seen you around campus." She paused for a few seconds as if deciding whether she should say what she was about to say. She worked up the courage and continued.

"A few weeks ago, you were at a party with Mae. I saw you sitting on the steps with her, smoking a cigarette, and for some reason, I needed to know you. You two walked into the party, and I didn't have a chance to introduce myself that day." She had a weird look of guilt on her face. I couldn't understand why.

"That makes sense why you were so chatty the night we officially met," I said, smiling at the thought of someone actually wanting to approach me, for a change.

"You don't think its creepy?" she asked awkwardly.

"Nah, I think it is rather sweet," I said, making a face like I was intentionally lying to her. I pulled at my collar a bit like Rodney Dangerfield used to do...she was not pleased.

"Oh, stop it!" She whacked me a few times and eventually ended in a side hug. We sat there for a minute, and I eventually went to open her book of poetry. You could tell that she was a bit nervous, and she went to the refrigerator to grab a wine cooler. She was nice enough to bring me one as well. She sat back in her bed and patted the bed for me to do the same. I took off my shoes and put them by the door and then joined her on what looked like the most girlish bed I had ever laid in...and that was saying something.

I sat in her bed, drinking my wine cooler with her head on my chest. Her hands drew circles on my body as I read each one of her poems out loud. You could feel her cringe every time I started a new one, but after nearly an hour of reading, she fell asleep on top of me. I continued to read and literally could not put the book down. She was talented in a way that Rebecca could never be. Every word was carefully chosen to convey meaning and her message for each verse. They were relatable on multiple levels, and I was in complete and utter awe at how this young girl could have achieved what I was unable to in nearly fifteen years of trying. I wasn't jealous, and I wasn't upset, I was simply happy. By the time that I finished the final poem in the book, it was starting to get dark. Sarah was beginning to stir, so I started to rub her head to see if she would wake up.

"Holy crap," she said as she looked out the window. "It's starting to get dark out." She looked up at me with sleepy eyes and a face that had marks on it from where she had been lying. There also might have been some drool.

"Yeah, you were tired, I guess." I put my hand on her face, and she nuzzled it with her cheek.

"Did you fall asleep, too?" She could tell that I had not really changed positions in the bed from earlier.

"No," I said as I held up her book of poems. "I read all of your poems." Her face went from sleepy to blushing almost instantly.

"You read them all?" She said, getting up and looking a bit self-conscious. "Well...what did you think of them?" To be honest, what came over me next was something that I really couldn't describe. Her poems had touched me in a way that I was really not ok with...emotionally. I sat up and took her face in my hands and kissed her passionately. I then spun her down until she was laying down with me beside her. Like the other day, we just sat in her bed making out for about ten minutes. By the time we both needed to come up for air, we were both completely unkempt and both very turned on.

"Hold on, hold on," she said as she took a minute. A devilish grin and wink later, she was removing her top and asking me to do the same. I followed suit and removed my shirt, and we were back at it. Her hands all over my body until the point I thought I was going to have friction burns from where her fingers trailed down my body.

"Sarah..." I said, trying to gather my breath and actually speak. "You didn't want to take things too fast. We should..." I was shoved down in the bed, and she put her legs over mine and straddled me.

"Shut up," she managed to say as she unclipped her bra and threw it on the ground. She came in to kiss me, and I could feel her unzipping my pants.

"Sarah," I said again, trying to stop her from taking them off. "Sarah, stop it." I said again, the word "stop" apparently got her attention, and she just kind of laid limp on top of me.

"Chance, I want you so bad. Can't we just...this once and then go back to the whole taking it slow thing?" I could feel her heart pounding against mine. She took my lack of a response as my answer. "Fuck," she said, rolling over to the side and cuddling up against me. She started giggling a few moments later and looked over at me, her hair stuck to the sweat on her face. "So, I guess you liked my poems?"

"Yes Sarah. They were literally the best thing I think I have ever read. As in completely unreal." She smiled from ear to ear and placed her head back down on the pillow.

"Well then. There is only one thing to do if we aren't going to have sex," she said, her bluntness and honesty a bit surprising. She didn't seem mad, just aggravated.

"That would be?" I asked, zipping my pants back up and looking for my shirt. Sarah had thrown it on the ground, and I couldn't see it from where I was sitting.

"Uh, dinner..." She looked at me with a playful look, pretending that I was stupid. "I am feeling Chinese." She got up and put her bra back on.

The way she did it was so seamless, and I was impressed. She went over to the refrigerator and grabbed a menu out from one of the magnets and came back to me.

"Let's eat!" she said, pulling out her phone and sitting down next to me. It was from a place that I ordered from once in a while, so I didn't even need to look at the menu. She ordered, and we just sat in bed watching television until it arrived. We spent the rest of the evening just hanging out and eating Chinese. She asked a ton of questions about her poems, and I obliged her with as many answers as I could give her. She continuously shit on herself about her writing, and as someone who felt they know a decent amount about it, it really upset me. I wondered whether this was how I talked about myself when people asked me to stop being so self-deprecating. I had honestly been moved by her writing, and she really just thought I was trying to be nice. We talked at great length about how she should without a doubt try and publish the poems as is. She obviously thought they were shit and was terrified of showing them to anyone else. It was really unfortunate, and I made a promise to myself that night. I wanted to make sure that no matter what happened between myself and Sarah, she would go through with publishing this collection. Once we were completely stuffed from dinner and it had been cleared away, I laid down on her bed and pulled open the book and flipped to one that I had already read several times. By far, it was my favorite piece in her collection. She came over to me with another wine cooler in her hand, she offered it to me, and I declined.

"I appreciate it, but I'm good." She took a sip and put the bottle down on the nightstand.

"So, do you want to spend the night?" she asked. It had gotten rather late, and I must have looked tired. I had only drunk the one wine cooler, so for once, I was actually ok to drive. The fact of the matter was, I didn't want to leave. I wanted to lay with her all night and feel her body against mine. I wanted to spend as much time with this girl as possible before she realized I was a piece of shit and dumped me. Maybe, for all the shit she was dealing with, I could at least give her something back. I could help her with this, and maybe that would be the best thing I ever did for this girl. Hopefully, it wouldn't be the last thing, and maybe, just maybe, I could keep my promise and become a better person for her. I looked up at her

239

and she was expecting an answer to the question. I had gotten in my own head and forgotten to answer.

"Oh, yeah. Definitely," I said, the smile returning to her face. She pointed down at my clothes.

"Are you going to sleep with your pants on?" She laughed at her comment. "Don't worry, I don't bite." I laughed as I wiggled out of my pants and got under the covers. "I have a new toothbrush also, if you want to have one for over here." Obviously not happy about my decision to go to bed without brushing my teeth.

"Yeah, that would be great," I said, jumping out of bed in my boxers.

We both brushed our teeth side by side in her little bathroom. I had memories of Mae and myself on the other side of the poles doing this in our first apartment together. We had only lived there a year, and it was small. It gave me a weird sense of comfort, standing next to her doing this seemingly mundane thing.

When we were done, we both got into the bed and cuddled up next to each other. Her body close to mine and her arms wrapped around me.

"I could get used to this on this side of the poles," I thought to myself as I closed my eyes and tried to get some sleep. The bed was comfortable, but I couldn't get her poems out of my mind. They haunted me; well... one haunted me. The last Haiku in the book ended with a simple sentence that she had probably written about someone else. It echoed in my mind as I laid there in the dark, waiting for sleep to take me.

~ *With you I'm Happy*

Chapter 18

"Ugh," was all I heard when I woke up the following morning. I could hear someone rifling around in the bathroom...turned out, that someone was my wife.

"Hey, there," I said as I sat up and got out of bed. I walked over to the bathroom, and Mae was sitting on our step stool in front of the toilet.

"This is why I don't usually drink that much," she said while taking a piece of toilet paper off the roll and wiping her mouth with it. "I guess it was about time for me to be the one that's hungover." She smiled and burped. A concerned look came across her face as she looked like she would vomit again, only to realize she wasn't going to. She was obviously relieved.

"Yeah, babe. I'm sorry. Can I get you anything?" I asked, pointing toward the kitchen.

"Water and a gun, in no particular order," she said as she nudged the stool back toward the wall. When she couldn't move it anymore, she just leaned back and rested herself on the wall itself.

"Well, water I can do. The gun on the other hand, not so much." I went and got some water and a couple Tylenols from the kitchen and came back to help my wife recover. She took them from me gladly and tossed them in her mouth. She then took the water and swallowed the pills, followed by another burp and another moment of panic. That quickly subsided, and I went to sit next to her on the floor.

"How are you feeling? Last night must have been rough if you didn't want to celebrate our anniversary together." She nudged me and raised an eyebrow, just in case I had forgotten that I was too sick to sleep with her the previous night.

CURTIS MILLER

"Well, I am feeling a whole lot better than you are now," I joked as she just looked at me and stared.

"Don't make me barf on you," she said, from the looks of it, only half kidding. "I think this is what happens when a girl gets...what is it called when you don't get off for a guy?"

"Blue balls?" I said, pretending I hadn't used the term before. "Yeah, I think it's called blue balls."

She laughed at the word. "Yeah, that's it. I got...blue body or something."

"Honey, I think you just have a plain old, run of the mill hangover... and maybe a bit of blue body or whatever." She put her head down in between her knees and sighed. I rubbed her back for a few, and she nearly fell asleep.

"I smell," were the last words she said before getting up. "I am going to take a bath. You should join me." She looked up and winked.

"Yeah, the bathtub really isn't big enough for the two of us, but I think you taking a nice hot bath is a good idea. I have to go and get Albert his stuff anyway. She went to give me a kiss but decided against it. I didn't know if it was because she didn't want to gross me out or because she thought she was going to vomit again.

"Yeah, just leave me here with a bucket. I am totally good with that. I just need a bath and my pajamas." She tried getting up and gave up quickly. I decided to not leave her until she was safely in bed. I started running the bath and went to make a small pot of coffee since I would be the only one drinking it that day. Once I felt that there was enough water in the tub, I went and turned it off. Mae was sleeping on the side of the tub on her arm. How she was comfortable enough to fall asleep in such a manner will confuse me till I die. I was able to get her up and undressed, and thankfully she was able to help with it and I didn't have to do it alone. She was coherent enough to get into the bath, and once her body hit the water, it was like an adrenaline shot.

"Oh wow, that feels so nice," she said as I grabbed a loofah and got some body wash on it.

"Just clean yourself up and try not to drown." She pretended to slink down in the tub. Her head went under, and she laid there staring up at me

242

through the water. After a few moments, she ran out of air and came back up. "You done?" I asked as I handed her the loofah.

"Yeah, sorry," she said, taking it from me and beginning to clean herself. She slopped it around and did her best to get to all the normal spaces. She was hanging, and I decided that, rather than leave her, I would just give her a hand. So, there I was in my mid-thirties, bathing my hungover wife the day after our anniversary, and I hadn't even gotten any the night before. She was so adorable in the bath that I may have poured a few too many cups of water over her head. She was not pleased.

Once her bath was done, I helped her get into some pajamas, got her some water and a bucket, and got her in bed. By the time I had the covers tucked around her chest, she was fast asleep.

"Sleep good, Mae," I said as I kissed her forehead and prepared myself for the day. My plan was simple. I was going to visit Albert and give him the evidence back, this time without giving him a heart attack. After that, I really had to get a bit more work done and see if I had any articles assigned to me. I got ready quickly and left the apartment in the hopes that I would return prior to Mae waking up and maybe we could do something…that was, if she felt well enough. Hopefully, a few extra hours of sleep would do her good, and she would be feeling better when I returned.

When I arrived at the hospital, it felt totally different than it had the day before. The gloom of the place seemed to lift, and knowing that Albert was ok and all the cloak-and-dagger shit was over helped. It could have also had a bit to do with Sarah on the other side. I was lying next to her right now in her apartment, and I felt as if things were changing. I felt as if there was a future…not just for Sarah and I, but just for me. I don't know how to explain it, but I felt like the world was pregnant with possibility, and that if I, of all people, could find happiness, maybe that would be enough.

I met with the receptionist and got my name sticker and signed in. I walked through the same doors I had the other day, this time with a bit more confidence, and quickly reached Albert's room. I took a few deep breaths before opening the door and knocked a few times. I heard someone on the other side say to come inside and I listened. As I walked in, I could see Albert sitting up in a chair having something to drink out of a large tan cup.

"Hey, Rebecca. I wasn't expecting you." He went to stand up to greet

243

me, but I motioned for him to sit down. I went over to him only to find John in the room as well. Albert looked pretty decent; John, on the other hand, didn't.

"Look who it is," he said as I turned to greet him. He completely ignored my extended hand and sat even farther back in his seat. "Albert told me everything." The news took me by surprise, and I turned to look at Albert. He wouldn't let his eyes meet my gaze.

"It's true. I told him what we did, and that there is nothing we can do about it." He put his head to his forehead and just sat there, regretting all the decisions that he made.

"Well…" I tried to say before I was interrupted by John,

"Yeah, so I just want both of you to know how extremely disappointed I am in both of you. You didn't have the decency to come to me and ask what was going on. Now it is all fucking ruined." He sat back with his usual angry expression on his face. "All that hard work, just wasted."

"Wait a second," I interjected. "What do you mean hard work?" This time Albert interrupted.

"He was working with some Federal Agency." His words seemed almost fake. "He was trying to uncover information to hold some of these people accountable."

"Yeah, and now you two idiots sent all that information to wherever, and the investigation is going to be ruined before we had a chance to do anything." I could tell by his aggravation that he might very well have been telling me the truth. "Unbelievable."

I reached into my bag and pulled out the three envelopes that I had recovered the day before. I held them out and handed them to Albert. "Well, maybe I have some good news for you then." He looked confused as he took them and opened one of them. When he pulled the contents out of the first one his face lit up.

"John, the evidence." He said, holding it out to show him. "She got it back."

"No way," he said, reaching over to take the papers from Albert. "How did you get these back?" He paused for a second, trying to figure out how I had retrieved them once they'd been mailed.

"I asked nicely," I responded. Obviously, my response was the last thing the two of them were expecting to hear.

"Fuck off," John said, reaching over to me for me to hand him the other two packages. "Asked nicely." He scoffed as if I was lying.

"No, seriously. That's it." I didn't feel like going too far into my explanation since he was kind of being an asshole. Part of me wished I would have just kept the shit a secret, but if he really was working with someone...he was doing a good thing. He was doing his job.

Albert stood up slowly and walked over to me, his arms stretched out for a hug. "Thanks, Rebecca," was all he said as he squeezed me.

"Any time," I said with little to no air in my lungs. Albert was actually kind of strong. He let go, and he went back to sitting down. Apparently, he was looking good, but was still rather sore form the accident. I looked over at John, and he was looking at the pictures and my notes attached to them.

"You were really going to fucking turn me in, weren't you?" There was more of a wonder to his voice than anger. "Just like that, not even give me the chance to say anything." He handed the papers over to me and put his hands down on his lap. "Really, though, I should be fucking furious...as in really fucking mad, but you two did the right thing." You could tell he was grappling with himself with what to say next. He walked up to me and said something I had never heard him say or ever expected to hear him say to anyone...especially me. "I'm proud of you two. I really think I misjudged you." When the words left his mouth, it was as if he had bees in his mouth. The words sounded unnatural and painful to say, but he said them, nonetheless.

"Well," I said, not even knowing how to respond. "I appreciate that, John. I really do." It was all I could think of without layering on an "I told you so." I decided to take the high road and not gloat...at least not in front of him. He did an odd little head nod thing in our general direction and took one last look at the documents.

"Albert, can I take these to give to...you know." I believed he was being intentionally vague so he didn't have to bring us into the entire thing. He was trusting that we wouldn't say anything to anyone, and too be honest, I had zero reason to trust him. Albert must have had the same reservations, since he responded with what I wanted to.

"Actually, you can have your friends come and pick them up. That way I can know where they are going." The words were one last "fuck you" to John. He knew that there was still a piece of Albert that didn't trust what John had said as the whole truth. Part of him still thought that John was trying to pull one over on him. I admired that he did what he did, especially after all the worrying he did about exposing his uncle.

"Of course," he said, obviously taking the hint. "They might have some questions for you regarding this source of yours. Making sure he doesn't interfere with the investigation again."

"We shall see," Albert said, as John came over and shook his hand. With that, John decided to take his leave and left the room. Before he left, he looked back at me and gave me a slight nod of approval. It was the most respectful thing he had ever done to me. I appreciated it. With that, he was gone.

"Phew!" Albert said, obviously glad that the tension in the room had finally broken.

"Yeah, tell me about it," I said as I walked over and sat down on the edge of his hospital bed. "I was not expecting any of that."

"I guess we shall see if any suits come and pick up that stuff...until then, just put them away and put them by my nightstand." He pointed over toward the table and I did as he asked.

We sat there for a bit, talking about the events that had just transpired, and when I could tell that he was beginning to get a bit tired, I said goodbye.

"Go take care of Mae," he said as I tucked him into his bed, similar to what I had done for my wife earlier that morning.

"I will. You take care of yourself," I said as I grabbed my things and headed for the door. "Get some rest, and I will see you at work when you return." He waved and closed his eyes. I took that moment to exit the room. I left the hospital quickly, since they still kind of give me the creeps, and headed home to take care of my hungover wife. When I returned home, she was just where I had left her. I took a look in the bucket, and it was dry, so that was a good sign, at least.

With her out of commission and considering my extreme urge to procrastinate, I decided to try and clean up the apartment as much as possible. I went through and checked all the expiration dates on the food in the pantry and threw out the items that were a bit too old for my liking. Going through the cupboards, I also noticed that the cupboards themselves were rather dusty. I decided that the best option was to turn on some music, put in my headphones, and just clean the shit out of the place. I couldn't even remember the last time I had done that. Mae usually did it, but this might be a nice surprise for her when she woke up. Maybe then, she could really relax. This would also hold true to my promise of being a better person for her. So triple win, is what I thought.

I cleaned for a few hours and was surprised by how quick it felt. I just jammed out to my favorite running playlist and just kept hitting item after item on my list. I loved crossing items off a checklist, and it felt as if I was being productive, even though I was actually procrastinating from doing what I should have been doing. Once I was done…well, once I felt better about the way things in the apartment looked, I decided to eat my half of the leftovers from the prior evening. It was one of my favorite things about that restaurant. Coming home the next day and frying up the leftovers together in a skillet or something. For some reason the food always tasted better the next day, and it was the perfect snack. Considering that Mae was still comatose, I decided to let her sleep a bit more and just have lunch by myself.

For some reason, while the food cooked, I went into my closet and pulled out some of my writing projects that had been halted over the years. Usually, I printed them up and bound them when I knew that I was either ready for editing or I felt like I couldn't take a project any further. Something about feeling them in your hand made them more real to me than they did sitting on a computer somewhere. I mean, they were also still on my computer or in this box on a CD, but when they were in your hand, it just felt real. I couldn't really describe it. Mae gave me shit for it as well, but it was just how I felt.

Looking through the projects that I had either nearly finished or just had on the editing table made me sick. There were some of the things I had worked so hard on, and I had just never had the guts to do anything with them. Sarah, on the other hand, was able to show me, a guy she barely knew, something that she had never shown anyone. I just felt so lazy and unaccomplished. I needed to finish one of those things and try my hand out at publishing. I sat there with nine manuscripts in front of me and perused through each one. They were definitely rough drafts that required a decent amount of editing, but which one would I start with?

"Ugh," I said in aggravation as I threw down one of my more recent attempts. Writing was the easy part, but editing was something completely different. I could edit something for the magazine relatively easily. Not to mention, there was someone whose entire job was to fine-polish each and every article to make sure they weren't putting out garbage. So even if I screwed something up, someone else usually would catch it and fix it prior to final publication. I suddenly smelled something starting to burn, and I got up quickly to turn off the burner for my lunch. Thankfully I caught it in time, so I stirred it a bit on the skillet and grabbed a plate from the dishwasher that had just finished. As I opened the door, the steam caught me off guard as I pulled the hot plate from one of the racks. I did the same with a spoon and closed the door so that the entire apartment wouldn't be steamy.

I sat down with my plate of leftovers as I continued to look at each stack of papers that lay scattered in front of me. "Just pick one," I said to myself, chewing on a burned piece of steak. "Just pick one and fucking finish it."

"Finish what?" a sleepy Mae said from the other room. I heard her get up and make her way toward the bedroom door. Once out, she shrouded her eyes from the light and looked around. "What time is it?"

"It's a little past three," I said, looking at my phone. "You alive?"

"Unfortunately," she joked as she came and sat down next to me. The small blanket from our bed was still wrapped around her like a shroud. She opened her mouth, expecting me to feed her. I laughed and put my plate down on the table.

"I'll make you yours," I said as I went to the fridge to grab her to-go container. "Leave mine alone!" I heard the spoon hit the plate, and when I looked back, she had a mouth full of food and was trying her best to smile.

"Ok," she managed to say, her words distorted. I placed the contents of her container in the skillet and turned it on, this time a bit lower than I had turned mine on. Mae didn't like burned food. I guess neither did I, but I would eat it all the same.

"Thanks," she said as she reached over and took a sip of the cold coffee I had been drinking that morning.

"Would you like a hot cup?" I asked as she grimaced at the taste of the cold cup.

"Just microwave it," she said, sticking her tongue out. She hated it when I did that, but she was obviously just looking for some caffeine quickly. I did as she asked and grabbed some of the cold coffee from my cup and mixed it with the remnants of the pot still on the counter. I tossed it in for a minute or so. Before you knew it, she had a cup of coffee in her hands. She sipped it slowly and smiled. "Thanks, babe," she said happily.

"No problem. One more minute and you will have something to eat, as well. You think you can handle it?" I looked back and she had another mouthful of my plate.

"Yes," she said. Again, her voice was muffled. She smiled again and finished her chewing.

The rest of the meal had a bit of back and forth like that, and as Mae finished up the last of her plate...and the last of my plate, she started looking at my mess on the table.

"Which one are you going to finish first?" She was holding one of the first things I had ever written and printed. The edges were torn, and the pages were tarnished. There were still a ton of notes in there that I had never even corrected in my master file. If I remembered correctly, I never made it past chapter three in my editing.

"I don't know." Looking at the pile of manuscripts, I just got aggravated. "I can't decide. Here I am talking about being a writer and publishing something, and I can't even choose which piece of mine is good enough to finish." I went and grabbed one from the pile. "I started this when we were still in high school, can you believe it?" I threw it back down on the table and Mae picked it up.

"Oh my god, I remember this. This was the book about you coming out, wasn't it?" She looked up at me and smiled. "This one was good." She herself had never read it, but she must remember me telling her the premise when I was still actively writing it.

"Yeah, but its premise is wasted now, since I obviously am as out as I can be...you know. Married to a woman and all." She picked up another manuscript and looked over at me and smiled, pointing at her ring.

"Yes, you are!" She laughed as she went through the pages of the next pile of papers. "This one is about zombies, or vampires, right?" I sighed.

"Yes, that one is about zombies, but again I missed my mark since zombies aren't as cool as they used to be in pop culture. I just didn't get it done in time, and now why would I even finish it?"

Mae looked at me, confused. "You finish it because you want to finish it. We do things, not because they are easy, but because they are hard." She looked up at me to see if I would get the reference.

"Ok, Kennedy, relax." I went over and slapped her playfully on the side of the head.

"Seriously, though. You want to be a writer...you wrote all this stuff. Why not finish one and then try to publish it?" She looked down at the pile of books and flipped to the end of some of them. "These are, like, almost completely done. Just finish them and start putting them out there."

She didn't understand why I was so afraid. I didn't blame her. She hadn't done anything like that before. I felt more akin to Sarah at that moment than to my own wife. It was an odd feeling.

"What if they are bad and nobody likes them?" I said, trying to get her to understand why I had stopped. Why I had procrastinated so long to finish these books.

"Well, then, just throw them away if you aren't going to finish them." Her candor was starting to piss me off a bit, but I tried to be calm.

"I will finish them, I just...ugh, I don't know." I sat down next to her and looked at the pile. "You tell me which one to finish, and I will do it... but, you will have to read whichever one you pick."

"Wait, like...read a book? Yeah, I really don't want to do that." She gave me a look like I had just asked her to cut off an appendage. "I don't really read, you know that." I glared at her; her words and her actions were kind of unsupportive. She was going to school to help me with this endeavor, and she wouldn't read one book...or at least try. I guess she understood my glare and the words that I said next might have been a bit overkill, but I was actually upset.

"So, you just don't think they are worth reading? That makes the decision easy." I picked up a few of them and went to go and throw them away...like I said, it was a bit overdramatic, but I was pissed off.

"Hey!" she said as she stood up and stopped me from throwing away the stack. "Don't do that. Don't put words in my mouth. I just..." She paused as I could see her get a bit upset. "I just don't think I am smart enough to add anything to your stories. Who am I to give you advice? I haven't even finished college, myself..." She was beginning to cry.

"Mae, don't..." She interrupted immediately.

"Don't what? Think of nobody's feelings but your own...don't worry. That's your fucking job." She stormed off into the bedroom and locked the door behind her. "Seriously, Rebecca." I could hear her from the other side of the door. "You can be a real selfish bitch sometimes." I heard her jump onto the bed, and that was the end of it. I thought about going in and trying to apologize, but what would that do? She was right. I did only think about myself, even after promising that I would be better...I just didn't do it. She had put up with my shit for years, and it was only a matter of time before she got fed up with it. Apparently, today was that day, and there was nobody to blame for her behavior but myself.

I went to the cupboard and pulled out the gift bottle of whiskey that still had a bit left in it. I poured myself a glass and sat down to start reading one of the pieces myself. It was the first one I had ever written and started while in high school. It was about growing up different. Mae saw it as my struggle to come out to my family, but that wasn't the real reason behind the story. I knew immediately that I was different from other people, but not in the way she thought. As long as I had been conscious of it, I had lived these two lives, completely unaware of which one was real... unaware if either of them were, or both. I didn't really know. I knew which I wanted to be real and which one I wished was just over. I don't think I need to tell you which was which. The first glass of whiskey was wasted, giving me the courage to open the book itself. I just stood there, looking at the working title, *Duality*. It was such a shitty title for a book, but what would you expect from a sixteen-year-old girl trying to carve out her first literary piece? She had been so hopeful, back then. She had thought the entire world was at her fingertips, and in those fingertips was a pen she would use to map out her success and career. I laughed at how naïve that little girl had been and how naïve the adult she had grown up to be was. I refilled my glass and finally had the courage to open the book up, and when I read that first sentence, I was back in study hall, scribbling down notes in my journal.

Duality...Oxford's Dictionary defines this as "an instance of opposition or contrast between two concepts or two aspects of something". Simple enough, right? Unfortunately, not for everyone...unfortunately, not for me. I have lived two lives for as long as I can remember, and those lives are exactly what was just described...opposition or contrast between two concepts. Only one of these realities is apparent to everyone around me and the other lives deep inside of me, in the darkness of my soul...if you can even call it that. That other me lives ever-present in my mind and eats away at my sanity, giving me zero respite.

I sit here in my solitude surrounded by a crowd of people that only know half of me. They only know the part of me that I want them to see, which means, depending on how you look at it, all they know is lies. Part of me is sitting here, stone-faced, the other side of me that's hidden is drowning in their fear. Their fear of being discovered for the liar that they are, for the very definition of their existence is exactly that...Duality.

"Wow," I sat back in my chair and took a drink. I hadn't read this in nearly a decade, and I had forgotten how dramatic I used to be. I sighed as I read and reread those first two paragraphs and was saddened that I felt nothing. I didn't feel an ounce of emotion compared to what I had felt reading Sarah's poetry. Cringing at the thought of reading more, I took another swig of liquid courage and skipped forward a couple of chapters and picked another spot to read. In the margins were the last bits of comments that I had made when my first round of editing was slowly beginning to lose steam. I started to read.

There she sits, two rows up and one row to the left. If any person in the world would accept me for who I truly was, it would be her. The fear still lingers inside of me that even her love would not be strong enough. Not strong enough to accept both sides of me, not strong enough to want to love two separate people. Her curly hair shines in the fluorescent light of our third period English class. The teacher is speaking, but I can't hear her. My mother calls it selective hearing. She may be right, but it doesn't matter. She sits and twirls her hair around her finger and looks back at me. She snaps her gum, smiles, and blows me a kiss.

Our love is still new but feels older than the sun. I am starting to realize what I am...my very being seems to be half of a whole. I found the other half in my best friend, my partner. What would she think of me if I told her the truth, the real truth, about me and myself? I say those words carefully because that's how it feels. I am standing beside myself always. One person is at the wheel while the other is just a passenger and with the passing of time they take turns at the wheel. They take turns controlling the very existence of this one mind that shares two selves. They take turns with the assumption that they have the same destination. What happens when the status quo changes? That thought keeps me up at night more times than not.

Hearing the words that this poor girl was saying and knowing the true meaning broke my heart. Almost twenty years later, these words still rang true to what I felt almost daily. Yes, I had found ways to cope with the despair of living these two existences without having the courage to tell anybody about them. The same reason I had kept my mouth shut all these years. Let's be honest, people would think I was fucking nuts and want to medicate me. Even if I was, and they were to put me on medication, what then? Would one of these existences just cease to be? What would happen to the people in that world, the people that I had grown to love my entire life? My decision would end their very existence. They would be gone, just like the life I had been living. That was the thought that truly kept me awake at night when I was young. What if the world that I truly felt at home in…wasn't real? What if half of myself, half of my being, was a fucking lie, and what if it just ended like the snap of a finger…just gone.

I stood up with chills all over my body. I went and poured the last bit of whiskey into the glass and drank it. This was the reason I had never finished this book, I remembered then. This book might mean a lot of things to a lot of people, but it didn't to me. All it meant to me was the truth of what it actually was. It was a cry for help. It was an adolescent's attempt to get someone else to ask if they are actually ok. That's exactly what would have happened if it had been shown to anyone when I was a kid…they would have seen something in me that was wrong and fixed it… with or without my permission. I would have had no choice in the matter.

I went into the fridge and grabbed a beer and sat down on the couch with one simple thought on my mind. How would my life be different if this would have been shown to somebody else? Tears were forming in my eyes, and I could feel the pressure build up inside of me, from somewhere deep. Somewhere long forgotten. I wanted to go and call to Mae, I needed her there with me. I needed her to affirm my whole life. The reason that I was too afraid of asking for help was her…on this side as well as the other side. I started to cry, and not in a pretty way, either. It was uncontrollable. I grasped the document close to my chest and just sat there on the couch alone…well, not alone. My other side was there with me also, just like he had always been. His depression and despair were giving me strength. He had been able to get through this life without her and was doing it even now. The only difference was, for the first time in what felt like my entire life, I was alone, and he wasn't. He had Sarah and I had...it felt like I didn't have anyone. I had started to push the people I cared about away and distanced myself, for some reason. I didn't know the reason yet, but I figured I would find out soon. I figured that the sixteen-year-old girl in the book in my hands knew more than I did. I had become distant from the truth, the real truth. There was something terribly wrong with me, and sooner or later, push would come to shove, and it would need to be fixed. I sat there on the couch, clutching my life in my hands, until it all became too much and I began to fade off to sleep. I was alone on the couch, and Mae was alone in her bed...I was too much of a coward to confront her, full well knowing that she had every right to be mad at me. I feel asleep alone.

Chapter 19

I woke up to a pitch-dark room. It took me a moment to realize where I was based on the sheets and who I could hear snoring besides me. I fumbled around quietly for my phone, which I had put on the nightstand the night before. The light was blinding as I put my thumb on the power button, and I quickly lowered down the brightness so as not to wake up Sarah. It was only a little after five in the morning, and the sun wasn't even up yet. I tried to go back to sleep for a bit and was unable to. For the first time in a while, I felt well rested and was completely awake.

I sat up and looked around a bit, not knowing what to do. By that time, the sun was starting to come up and provided a bit of light in the room. As if by some cosmic force, the light shone directly on Sarah's poetry book on the nightstand. I picked it up and sat on a chair by the window and reread some of my favorite poems. While reading them, I was struck with what some people call inspiration. For me, inspiration was just a dire need to get something that was in my head on paper. Back in high school, that was how my artistic side had starting coming out...I had something, a vision inside my head, that needed to come out. This was the first time that I had felt this in more than a decade, and it hit like a hammer. I looked around in the darkness with the light on my phone acting as a flashlight for something to draw with. Finally, finding a pencil, I took one of the last pages in the book that was blank and started putting pencil to paper and drawing what was inside my head.

After about thirty or so minutes, I had a rough idea of what I wanted it to be and pulled my cell phone out to take a photo. The light wasn't good enough to get the entire image in frame, so I just took the page and tore it out of the notebook. I took the picture and folded it neatly and placed it in my wallet.

"Why are you awake, Chance?" I heard Sarah say. She was half asleep, and the flash from the attempted photo must have woken her up.

"Sorry, couldn't sleep," I said, not telling a complete lie, only omitting certain details. "Go back to bed." I saw her hand reach out from the darkness, beckoning me to come join her. I did as she asked and went to lay down beside her in the bed. She snuggled up against me, and her hand rubbed up and down my leg from beneath the covers. She reached up with her other hand and pulled my face toward hers. Her mouth kissed mine, softly at first and then more forcefully when she got into it. Before I knew it, she was on top of me, and she was rubbing her body up against mine. We kissed again, and I could feel her fingernails caressing what felt like every inch of me. I don't know what came over me, and I don't know why I said what I said. I am sure in the moment I meant it, but it is not something that I usually say to anyone...well, almost anyone. I pulled her away from me and looked at her in the dim morning light.

"Sarah," I said. She looked at me softly, with a look I can only describe as admiration. "I think I am falling in love with you." The mix of adrenaline and testosterone might have been clouding my judgement, but at that moment in time...she was everything to me. This girl was the drug I needed to help me with my withdrawal. She was my methadone.

"Chance?" she said, putting her hand on my face, one of her fingers grazing my mouth gently. "I have already fallen in love with you." We looked at each other in the morning light for a few moments and...well, I guess you get the picture. It was one of the most passionate and intense experiences of my life, and even I was surprised when it was over. We laid there, our bodies entwined and covered in sweat. Every inch of me was on fire, and every square inch of our bodies that were touching felt like they were on fire. I had never felt anything like this on either side of the poles before...not even with Mae. I was barely able to speak and tried to formulate a few words. Sarah laughed.

"I guess that means you had a good time, huh? Way better than that first drunken night." She leaned over and sat over me in a supine pose, her elbows on the bed and her chin resting gracefully on her hands. Her body had a beautiful glow to it in the morning light, and I couldn't help but admire it. "So, I am not a label fan, but…this isn't some fling, right? I mean…" She was trying to get me to say something, and it was obvious what it was.

"Sarah, this isn't some fling. I…I am not a fan of labels or words that begin with L. I just know that I have never in my life felt like this before, and I would be stupid to not hold on to it with all of my might." I knew the next question that she was going to ask, or at least what question she wanted to ask. I could see it all over her face. It was a mix of wonder as well as panic. From the looks of it, she was just as surprised by this morning as I was, but she still had reservations. She still had doubts, and to be honest, I didn't blame her one bit. She eventually worked up the nerve to ask the question.

"What about with Mae?" she said quietly.

"Sarah, what happened between Mae and I was just wrong and will never happen again. I haven't spoken with her in days, and I really don't want to. I want to be better for me, and I want to be better for you. The last few days have been eye opening, and…you're the cause of it. You're the catalyst for the change that's happening inside of me, and I can't be more thankful for it…for you."

The words were what she wanted to hear, and probably more. They were all the truth, too. Usually, I was good at getting out of shitty situations using lies and deception…just like Mae had said. This might have been the most honest thing I had ever said to anyone in my life on either side of the poles.

"I trust you," was all she said before putting her head on my chest and closing her eyes. Her hand played with the hairs on my chest, and I nearly fell back asleep. We lounged around the entire morning, just talking and hanging out. I learned a bit more about her past, and she learned a bit more about mine. For as different as we were, and even with the age difference we were remarkably similar…well, she and Rebecca were. She struggled with similar issues that most adolescent girls did. She hated her body and did what she could to make herself happy with it. She hated her writing and hid it from the world. Hell, if I hadn't met her and read her poems, she might have been in the same situation that Mae and I were in on the other side.

She talked about dreams and a future like someone who actually believed it would happen, not just something that would be cool if it did. She spoke about friends and family in the present tense since she had not alienated everyone in her life over a toxic relationship. I told her about my childhood and growing up without a father. How my mother used to be everything in the world to me and why we were estranged. I could see her putting the pieces together, the pieces of my broken life. With each thread she would pull, the more she would learn that the reason was always the same…Mae.

Every time I saw her face get to the end of one of those threads, I slowly started to realize that Mae and I were really better off apart. Our relationship had always been strained, but with each retelling of an event or fight or whatever, it became more apparent. I don't really know if it was the distance that made things clearer, but to me, they were crystal. Sarah was understanding and cool as a cucumber when her name was mentioned. She listened and added in her two cents when I asked for it, but she never got angry or upset. We laid there in bed, and I learned what seemed to be everything about her…and all I wanted to do was learn more.

Eventually, we had to put clothes on, and Sarah had to get to class, but that morning was nothing less than perfect.

"So, you don't mind that I have school? I will totally skip class if you want. I just don't want you to leave." She had me pressed up against my beater Chevy. She was standing on the curb, so she was a bit taller than normal, and she was almost able to see me eye to eye.

"Sarah, go to school. You know where to find me," I said, pulling out my car keys. I also had no real desire to leave her. Part of me felt that the second she left, I would regress into my normal self. I didn't want that. I really liked who I was with her and how she made me feel. She made me feel happy. I smiled, remembering the last line of my favorite poem in her book.

"Well, I have a few classes today, and I think a study group into the evening. I'll give you a call after?" She pulled my face down so she could kiss me one last time before heading off.

"You better," I said after returning the kiss. With that, she walked toward her car and gave me a wave. She got in, started the two-seater up, and was gone. I pulled out my pack of cigarettes, and there was one more in the pack. I lit it and breathed in the moment as best as I could. The sun shone down on my face, and the wind blew cool. It really was a perfect morning. I reached down into my wallet and grabbed the picture I had drawn earlier while Sarah was still asleep.

"Time to go shopping," I said, putting the picture back in my pocket. I got in my car and went somewhere that I hadn't been in nearly ten years... the hobby store that I used to work at with Mae. There was no real reason why I hadn't gone there other than it was a bit out of the way and most of my work was digital by then, but I needed to get something from the store, something to finish what I had started that morning. I wanted to paint a cover for Sarah's art book. I wanted to paint something, not something for work or for money, but for someone I cared about. I hadn't done something like that since high school. I hadn't actually enjoyed myself painting or doing anything artistic in nearly fifteen years.

I got in my car and headed down the road to the store itself, singing along to the radio as I drove. I reached the parking lot and remembered that I really liked the coffee from the place that shared the parking lot. I went and grabbed a large black coffee and decided to get in quickly and get what I needed.

Walking through the doors was actually a bit unsettling. The place looked identical to what it looked like when we all worked there years ago. The same lights, the same floors, the same paint, it was odd. I walked down the main drive aisle to where the painting supplies were held and took a look at them for a bit.

"These are more expensive than I remember," I said to myself quietly while browsing the shelves.

"That's because inflation is a bitch, Chance," a voice said from down the aisle. I looked over to my right only to find our old store manager, Adam. Other than a few more gray hairs and a different style to his hair, he looked the same as he did back in the day.

"Hey, Adam. How are you?" I went up to him to shake his hand. He returned the gesture and smiled at me.

"Still painting, I see. We haven't seen you in here in a while. Digital media, am I right?" I laughed since he had hit the nail on the head.

"Yeah, I still do commissioned art for a living, but haven't done anything like this in forever. I am wondering if I still remember how."

He scoffed. "Yeah, I think you will be fine, Chance. People still come in here asking if you still teach the painting classes. I don't think that we have had such luck with it since you left." I would have liked to believe what he said, but I did remember a ton of people coming to those classes when I worked there. The money hadn't been bad also, since I had gotten an amount of the money the store earned from sales as well as a per person fee.

"Those were always fun times." I took a set of paints down from the shelf. The colors were new.

"Yeah, those are a newer brand, a bit more expensive than our old house brand, but what can you do?" He looked like he wanted to say something but was too afraid to ask.

"I might have to try them out. I actually am in here for a very specific reason." I reached into my pocket and pulled out the piece of paper from earlier. "I am looking to paint this for a...for a friend. She is publishing a book of poems, and I wanted to paint something she could use as the cover."

"Do you mind?" he asked, taking the paper once I nodded that I didn't mind. He looked at it for a few moments and then held it up to the giant display of colors that hung in the center of the aisle. He took a few minutes holding it up to some of the palette colors until he felt happy.

"What you thinking?" I asked, hating the quiet between us.

"I am thinking pastels for sure, something light but not too Eastery, if you catch my drift. Also, no fine lines, maybe something like a Van Gogh...you know, one of his streaky self-portraits." He handed me back the piece of paper, and I took a look at what he was talking about.

"I hadn't thought of that. Hard lines are always an issue with me, and having it kind of smeared or streaked would solve that. Thanks, Adam!" I said, reaching out and giving him another handshake.

"I was something of an artist myself back in the day. I actually started teaching the classes when you stopped working here. Obviously, they are not as good now, but I still think I have something to teach." He smiled politely.

"You're not wrong," I said, taking the paper and putting it back in my pocket. Adam called for one of his associates to bring a cart, and in a minute or so, they came to the aisle we were in with a small black shopping cart.

"Thank you, Alicia," he said as she brought it. She smiled quickly and left. "Employee of the year, right there." He laughed once she had turned the corner. He helped me get the last few items in my cart and even found me a coupon that was in his apron for fifty percent off one item. I grabbed a large paint set that came complete with brushes and a small wooden palette as well. He walked me up to the counter and rang me out himself.

"Thanks again for all the help," I said as the last item was rung up. I paid my bill, and he continued following me to the door.

"Hey, Chance," he said just as I was walking out. "If you ever want to, give me a call. I would love for you to start teaching those painting classes again. You were simply the best that has ever done it. I know that if you did, you wouldn't only have fun, but it could be pretty profitable as well." He reached into his apron and picked out a small business card. He took a pen, also from his apron, and wrote down his personal number.

"Think about it," he said one final time when handing me the card. He shook my hand, and we said our goodbyes. I left the store with the card in hand.

"Maybe that could be fun," I told myself as I put the bags in the backseat of my car and the card in my wallet. "Who knows?" I got in my car and drove back to my apartment; well, to the liquor store first and then my apartment. I picked up the usual and a twelve pack of something girly for Sarah. I figured she would be over at the apartment more often than not. I returned to my apartment, and when I was done putting things away, I went on a search for some of my old art supplies.

I had still held on to some things from years back. I didn't know if it was because of sentimental reasons or because the stuff actually cost a bit of money. After a bit of scrounging around in my closet, I pulled out my old easel and a dusty box of brushes, some dried old paints, and my old apron. I pulled it out of the box and held it up. It had tons of dried paint on it from years of abuse, and it said in big block letters, *Starving Artist*. Mae had really thought she was funny when she had bought me this as a present in high school. I held it up to myself and laughed because it was about a foot too short. I hadn't hit my growth spurt until after high school, so it made sense. I loved this apron for multiple reasons. It had a ton of small pockets on it that I could use to hold my paintbrushes while they dried, so it really helped with clutter while painting. It also was a gift from Mae,

261

and even though we weren't talking, it seemed like a real waste to throw it away…maybe not quite yet.

I pulled out the last contents of the box, including a thin but effective painting drop cloth. I had learned quickly that I needed one in order to not lose out on my security deposit…but that's another story. After a bit of set up and a quick YouTube session to remind myself how to put my easel together, I was ready to start working.

You could tell by my brush strokes that I was rusty with actual paint. I had prepared for this and bought an extra canvas to practice on. It was definitely worth the investment since I would have definitely been making another trip to get another one after my first thirty or so minutes practicing. It all started coming back to me, the muscle memory, the way I held the brush, and the amount of paint to use for each stroke. Once I felt comfortable that I wouldn't ruin the second canvas, I replaced it and started what I hoped would be a nice surprise for Sarah.

I taped the picture with my notes to the upper right-hand corner of the canvas and turned on some music. I started as I always started: with a quick prayer and a pump-up song. I found the specific song I needed and got to painting. I put paint on the brush and the brush on the canvas and my inspiration from the day before took over. I made quick decisions and changes based on how I felt and the canvas that lay in front of me. I was excited for each stroke rather than dreading every moment of it like I had over the past decade or so. Every time I took the brush away from the canvas, I couldn't wait to put it back on, to create something new. I even caught myself dancing a bit to the song on my iPod as my ideas flowed from my head through my hand and spilled onto the canvas. I kept at it until I was nearly done, and the only thing left to do was put my signature on it…but that felt almost wrong since I felt as if the art was not mine, it was hers. I decided to leave it blank and not to sully the image itself with claiming ownership. It was one of those pretentious things I would have done in art class back in high school. One of those things my teachers would have hated.

I went to the kitchen to take out a glass of whiskey and sit in front of the canvas. I looked at every square inch of it to make sure the brush strokes were just right, to make sure the colors didn't merge together too sloppily and to ensure that it was not just a painting…that it did her poetry justice. I made a few alterations while sitting there and sipped my whiskey as I did. When I felt finally happy with it, I sat back and smiled.

"You've still got it, Chance," I said to myself, physically patting myself on the back. I felt a muscle strain as I did, and I laughed to myself. "Well," I said, looking down at my phone. It was around two in the afternoon, and I had nothing else to do…these were the moments that I hated. "Might as well celebrate," I told myself, needing to hear the confirmation that what I was about to do wasn't a bad thing. I went and poured a slightly larger glass of whiskey from the new bottle and grabbed a cigarette from the freezer. I went onto the porch to relax.

I kicked my feet up on the railing and sipped my drink. I lit the cigarette and tried to pretend I wasn't about to start panicking. I pulled out my phone, and there were no texts or emails from anyone. I was alone. As amazing as I had felt that morning was as terrible as I felt at that moment. The problem with addicts is they need their fix to be happy or to be able to survive. I had traded in one drug for another. I had traded Mae for Sarah, and the problem was simple. Sarah had her own life and wasn't a codependent narcissist like me and Mae. She was able to be away and not completely unravel like I was right now. I sipped the whiskey a bit faster in the hopes that the buzz would begin to calm me down…I was wrong. In trying to recover myself from my downward spiral, I was only delaying the inevitable by drinking, and it might have been slowing the spiral now, but a few more of those and I would be like a lead weight…no spiral, just falling.

I lit my second cigarette and pulled out my phone a second time. This time not to check for messages but to consume my mind in a game or something else. I ended up scrolling social media for a bit and checking in on some of the people I had lost communication with over the years. Zane, another friend of mine from high school, was probably my closest thing to an actual friend other than Mae. Like I normally did, I had pushed him away when he confronted me about getting over Mae. I remembered the conversation like it was yesterday.

"Dude, are you even listening to me?" The look of aggravation was apparent on his face. "Or are you just fucking high again?" Disappointment was written all over his face.

"I'm just a bit buzzed, man. What's your problem?" I wasn't angry at

him, and that was why he was so frustrated. He had been talking to me, and I completely spaced out and must have missed the entire conversation.

"All you do is drink or do drugs. Can't you see what is happening? It's fucking obvious to everyone but you." He sat down on a lawn chair that was adjacent to me and pulled it close so I would understand his sincerity. "I know Mae is your friend, but...dude, she will never want to be with you. She already came out, something you knew long before anyone else. Why do you keep torturing yourself, man?"

"Fuck you, she's my friend and I can't just stop hanging out with her because she's gay. That's fucked up, dude." I was deflecting and I knew that wasn't what he meant. He was a great guy, but he just didn't understand.

"Yeah, man. That's why I'm upset, because I'm homophobic. Do you really think that? If you do, then you're not just a lost cause, you're a fucking idiot." He put his face in his palms and screamed. The act itself probably did more to sober me up than anything that night. I sat back and tried to not let him know it bothered me. He sat there defeated as he took one last sip out of his beer. The night had begun as him wanting to catch up and ended with him leaving...for the last time. He took the empty bottle and threw it into the bonfire.

"I have known you for years. We have been friends since god knows how long. I just can't sit back and watch you fucking kill yourself over some girl... even one as great as Mae. She will never be able to give you what you need, and until you figure that out...just take care, man." He walked off into the darkness and out of my life.

I hadn't spoken to him since that day out by the fire. What was I supposed to do in that situation? He was asking me to pick sides, and that was fucked up. I sat there scrolling through his pictures on social media and seeing everything he had done with his life. I shrugged, knowing that him not talking to me was probably one of the reasons he was able to do anything with his life. Anyone that had any relationship to me would eventually get sucked into my lifestyle and ruin their lives. I went back and refilled my glass again, this time with a little more, and grabbed the rest of the pack out of the freezer. I lit one of the stale Marlboros and sat there on the deck, just reminiscing about all the relationships that Mae had cost me...no, that I had cost me. I could sit back and blame her all I wanted for my life being shit...but only I was to blame.

I sat there for a good long while, scrolling through old friends, lost flames, and people that I really didn't even care for. Looking at how amazing their lives turned out made me fucking sick. Here, these people were just so happy and so content they had the audacity to post all this shit about their lives like anyone actually fucking cared. How self-centered these people must have been to think that their lives were better or they were more important than anyone else. I shoved the phone back in my pocket when I was fed up with the fucking façade...the "grass is always greener" bullshit that just layered on top of itself with each and every scroll or like. I sat there, probably angrier than I needed to be, and continued my downward spiral. My phone vibrated, and I quickly pulled it out, hoping for it to be Sarah. It wasn't...it was actually Zane. He had liked a photo that I was tagged in, a photo that Sarah had tagged me in. A few moments later, I received a text from him.

Hey man, how've you been?

I was surprised to see him message me. I must have accidentally liked one of his photos, or he was being nostalgic just like I was. It was irrelevant either way. We texted back and forth for about an hour, pleasantries mostly, but eventually the question I knew he would ask was in fact asked.

So how is Mae?

I sat there for a few minutes, not wanting to answer...not wanting to give him the satisfaction. He was right all along, they all were. Now what? Did I get a big "I told you so" or a lecture from everyone in my life? I had neither the time nor the patience for all that shit. He messaged again, throwing me off my guard.

Anyway, it doesn't matter. I just hope you're doing well.

I finished the remnants of my glass and went for a refill. I stumbled as I got up and ran into the door jamb into my apartment. I filled up the glass again and went back outside. Getting fed up with the texting, I just decided to call him. I mean, what was the worst thing that could happen? The phone rang a few times and he finally answered.

"Hey, man," his voice said on the other side of the line. He sounded happy to hear from me.

"Hey, long time no talk, eh?" I said, trying my best to not sound drunk...which I was at the time. I lit a cigarette, hoping that its effects would mask my inebriation.

"Yeah, man. My phone's notifications told me you liked a photo of mine, and I saw a picture of you with a redhead. New girlfriend?" He was fishing for information, so I figured I would just give it to him for everything I had put him through.

"Yeah, her name is Sarah. She's really great. We have only been dating about a week, but it's been interesting."

"That's good, man. She getting along with Mae?" Again, I knew it would come down to this. His tone was much more calming than the emptiness of a text message.

"Yeah, they met…" I paused for a moment. "I actually don't really talk to Mae much anymore." He paused on the other end, and I could imagine him doing fist bumps and high fiving people. Obviously, that was just my imagination.

"Oh, I'm sorry to hear that. I know you two were close. Sometimes we have to let old relationships go to start new ones." His tone was less condescending than it had been years ago, and now his words spoke with a hidden wisdom. Maybe it was the fact I had learned these lessons on my own after being lectured for nearly fifteen years. I didn't feel like making the only two conversations we'd had in fifteen years into arguments, so I just went with it.

"Yeah, you're not wrong there." He paused for a moment.

"So, I have to get going. The wife and kids are sitting down for dinner." He paused as if he was fighting a bad idea. "Do you want to, maybe, grab a drink or something this week? You still living out by the college?"

"Yeah, that sounds good. Just let me know when you want to get together, my schedule is pretty open nowadays." I tried to convey sarcasm, but I felt it came across a little aggressive. "Well, take care man." He said goodbye, and the call was over. I put the phone down and was surprised by how it had gone.

"Step eight, my ass," I said, lighting another cigarette and taking another drink. I looked down at my phone and noticed that it was getting to be about the time Sarah would be out of class. I began to get excited, thinking that she would want to hang out. I sat there in anticipation for a bit when I realized I was in fact very hungry. I searched through my cupboards for something that was still in date to eat…there were a few cans of vegetables and some crackers.

"Crackers it is!" I said, taking the half empty box out with me on the front stoop. I sat there eating the somewhat stale box of saltine crackers until I finally received the message I had been waiting for all day. It was Sarah, and she wanted to know if she could come over for dinner. I sent her a picture of me holding up the crackers with the caption, *I am already having dinner without you!*

I hoped that she would find that humorous and laugh. She responded with a smiling emoji and said she was on her way. I sat back, smiling, and took another drag from my cigarette.

"Cute," a familiar voice said. I looked around, and my downward spiral hit hard. It was Mae. I instinctively brushed the crumbs off my shirt and sat up straight.

"What are you doing here?" I asked, the words coming out almost perfectly.

"I needed to see you, Chance. I still do care about you." She crept a bit further. The cigarette hanging from her lips and her low-cut top were intoxicating.

"Yeah, if you care, you should just go." I tried to sound angry, but it came out as sad and drunk. "You're better off without me. Go be with Rebecca." I stood up and started to walk inside the door.

"She broke up with me, Chance. I told her what happened between us, and she just left. She told me she was done and...and I haven't seen her since." I turned to look at her again, this time really focusing on her features. Her eyes were bloodshot, and her makeup was running.

"I'm sorry, Mae, I really am." She came running up to me and wrapped her arms around me. She was sobbing uncontrollably, and I didn't know what to do. I put my arms around her and held her like I had done hundreds of times...hell, thousands of times over the time I had known her. This had been my purpose for more than half my life...Mae. To comfort her when she was sad and to give her encouragement when she needed it. She finally began collecting herself and pulled herself back. She must not have been expecting the outburst either.

"I...I don't know what to do, Chance. I don't know if I can go through this without you." She reached down and held my hand. She caressed it in a manner that she had never done before. I looked into her eyes, and I knew what she wanted. The look on her face said it all.

"Mae, I...Sarah...she's coming over, and I think you should go." The rejection hit her like a jackhammer. She had come over for comfort, and she was obviously either drinking or high…I was, unfortunately, too drunk to tell which one.

"Are you serious?" she said, beginning to get angry. "You're going to tell me to go for her? Some girl you just fucking met?" She lit another cigarette and stood her ground. She was ready to have this argument, more prepared than I was.

"Mae, it's not that," I tried to say calmly, but it came out as an outburst. Her look went from angry to showing signs of concern. "I have loved you for my whole life. All of it. Not a moment of my life has not been about you. Can't you see how fucked up that is? You of all people should be able to see that. Hasn't anyone ever confronted you about how fucking toxic our relationship has become?" She just stood there for a moment with a stunned expression on her face. Slowly, the expression turned into understanding.

"Of course I have, Chance! Of course, people have told me that you were in love with me. Fuck, do you think I am stupid? I just never would have thought you would hide it from me, so I pushed it aside…for our entire life, I pushed it aside. You were my friend, Chance, you were my best fucking friend. The one person in my life who has always been there for me and never let me down…until now." She was right. I was letting her down…but what was I supposed to do? I finally had someone that accepted me for all my faults, someone that I could start building a life with. It was early on, but hell, it had been the closest thing I had to a happily ever after in my life.

"I'm sorry I let you down, Mae. You have no clue how sorry I am. What happened the other night was something I wanted my entire life, but it wasn't right. It was just pretend, Mae. You could never be happy with me, and I could never be happy knowing that you were giving up your happiness for me…" Mae interrupted.

"What if I could be happy with you, Chance!" Her words caught me completely off guard. "What if we tried?"

I couldn't believe it. I don't know if what she said saddened me or angered me more. "You're fucking joking, right? Mae, you're gay, and the last time I checked, I wasn't a woman. Or are you telling me that you might be able to grin and bear it for the sake of not upsetting the way things are?

You would settle for something or someone that would never make you one hundred percent happy?" She looked down at the ground, knowing she had struck a chord. "You don't deserve a half-life and neither do I."

"I...Chance..." She couldn't even say anything in response. She knew I was right. We would never be happy together. She would give up a part of herself to be with me, and I would have to live with that guilt for the rest of my life. She would grow to resent me, and I would resent myself even more. "Chance..." She finally was able to collect herself. "I love you, Chance. I can't not have you in my life. What can I do to fix this? What can we do?"

I went and sat down in my chair, and she came over to me to lean against the railing. She lit another cigarette and gave it to me. She lit one more for herself. She saw the half-empty glass of whiskey and grabbed it, finishing its contents quickly. She cringed as she realized it was a different brand than I was used to, and it was actually a decent bottle.

"We stop talking for a few days, and you start drinking good whiskey?" The olive branch was noted, and I took it. I didn't want to argue as much as she did.

"Yeah, I was celebrating." I took a long drag and exhaled.

"Celebrating what?" she asked. I could smell her perfume and I stuttered for a second. I collected myself and answered the question that I knew would hurt her. I didn't say it to hurt her, I told it to her because it was the truth.

"I told Sarah that I think I love her this morning." The look on her face said it all. "Mae, there is something about this girl that's different than anyone I have ever met, even different than you."

"Different than me? What the hell do you mean by that?" She took the words as an accusation, but that wasn't how I meant them.

"Mae, her and I can be really happy together. She knew that you and I slept together, Mae...and she gave me another chance. She understands...I don't know...she understands me and accepts me." She just looked down at the ground while she smoked. "Mae, I don't want you out of my life either, but I think we need to learn how to live apart before we ever can be together again. I literally can't imagine you not in my life either, but...I have to give Sarah one hundred percent of myself, and I can't do that while

I am giving you that. Because you deserve that, Mae. You deserve that and more...I just can't give it to you anymore."

She took a bit to respond, and at that moment, I realized that Sarah's car was sitting in the parking lot. I couldn't really tell, but it looked like there wasn't anyone inside.

"Then what do we do now?" Her demeanor had changed to that of defeat. "You have Sarah, who exactly do I have?" She was right. I had been speaking from my high horse the entire time...how would I be if Sarah had turned tail and ran? My entire argument felt like it lost all its steam, and I began feeling the same way that Mae looked.

"Mae, you will always have me." I walked up to her and put my arms around her. She reluctantly returned the hug, and I slowly could feel the pressure gain as she held on.

"It doesn't feel like it, Chance. It feels like you're gone, and I am alone."

"Maybe I can help," I heard another familiar voice say. It was Sarah, and she was coming up the steps to the landing where Mae and I were standing.

Mae suddenly stiffened up and pulled away from me. "Hey, Sarah," she said, doing her best to clean up her makeup and look a bit more presentable. "How long have you been standing there?"

The look of kindness on Sarah's face was something out of a storybook. There was no anger, there was only understanding. "I have been standing here long enough, Mae." Sarah came over and stood next to me. I could feel her hand wrap into mine. "Come have dinner with us." The invitation took both Mae and I by surprise.

"What?" was the only thing that could be said. Mae was barely able to get the word out in between her attempts at stifling another crying episode. "Why would you want to hang out with me?"

Sarah took this time to do something she hadn't done before. Assert dominance, but in a way that was so subtle I almost didn't catch it. It was done with such class that I was speechless. "Mae, I don't want to hang out with you...for obvious reasons. I want to be with Chance. Chance, on the other hand, loves you. You're his best friend. That's why I want you to have dinner with us. Because I want to be a part of Chance's life...and you... you're part of his life." She put her hand on Mae's shoulder, and Mae looked up at me. She finally understood what I was talking about. This girl was something special, and for the first time that day, perhaps ever, Mae did something truly for me...no ulterior motive.

"You know what. Maybe another time," she said as she regained her smile. She looked at Sarah and reached in for a hug. "Thank you for understanding. You deserve better than what happened." Sarah nodded, and then Mae came and looked at me. "You treat her right, Chance. I think you're right. We should take a bit of time to learn who we are alone. I think you're right about us both deserving better." Her words were a bit cryptic, but I seemed to understand the gist of it. She grabbed her cigarettes off the ledge and walked down the street toward the bus stop. She turned the corner and was gone.

Sarah looked up at me and smiled. "Let's go lay down." She took my hand and led me into the apartment.

"But what about dinner?" I said, grabbing my box of crackers off the table. We walked into the apartment, and she saw the half empty bottle of whiskey on the counter. She walked over and grabbed it and brought it over to the futon. She sat down and patted the seat beside her, signaling me to come and sit next to her.

"Come here, babe," she said. She scooched over a bit, and I laid down on the couch. "No, here," she said, pointing toward her lap. I turned around and laid my head down on her lap, and she started rubbing my head. She took the bottle, and with one hand, unscrewed the cap and took a large pull. She grimaced and looked down at me and smiled. "Close your eyes, Chance. Today has been a long day, for the both of us." She reached down and kissed me with lips that tasted of liquor. She took another drink, and put the cap back down, propping it up on the pillow. She turned on the television and continued to rub my head. I fell asleep on her lap, her fingers running through my hair.

Chapter 20

I woke up on the couch, cold and alone. I grasped my head as the hangover struck, and my mouth was so dry I couldn't even swallow. I reached for the nearest thing I could find...it was whatever I had been drinking last night. Anything was better than nothing as I swirled the contents around in my mouth. The burning sensation woke me up more and more with every swish. I looked around the room with eyes that had not attuned to the darkness. Slowly, I began to see shapes appear out of the darkness. First the table, then the television, and eventually the remnants of the room. I sat up and took a moment to collect myself. The hangover was pounding, and the fact that I had cried myself to sleep didn't help.

Once I felt as if I wouldn't trip and die in the dark, I went to the bedroom to see if Mae had unlocked the door. I turned on the bathroom light in order to see the hall better, and, in fact, she had unlocked the door, and it was cracked open a few inches. I peered inside to see if I could see her. I looked over toward the bed, and it was empty. I turned on the light for further inspection, and I was right...the room was completely empty. I went back out to the living room and looked for her purse. Both her shoes and her things were gone...she was not home.

"Fuck," I thought to myself as I looked around for my phone. It had fallen into the cushions of the couch, so I ended up looking for a bit longer than I had planned. Once I finally found it, I noticed that there was a single text message from Mae.

I'm going out.

"Out?" I said to myself. I looked at the time, and it was nearly six in the morning. I pulled out my phone to call her, and it immediately went to voicemail. "Her fucking phone is dead." I took a few deep breaths to calm down, and once that didn't work, I went outside to have a cigarette. I sent her a single text message back asking her to call me when she could and that I loved her. I didn't want to flood her inbox with a thousand messages. I, in fact, had done a similar thing just the other day, and she had been amazing about it. We already were having one fight, I didn't need to pile a second one on top of it. My mind started racing with thoughts of where she could be...and with who? My car was still in the parking lot, and she didn't know how to ride my bike...so someone must have picked her up. I sat and finished my cigarette in the morning light. There was a mist coming in from the wood line, and it felt like one of those scenes right out of a movie. I usually didn't wake up this early, but the chill and uncomfortable state I had been sleeping in pulled me from my sleep.

It was rather beautiful and almost calmed me down for a moment as I lit another cigarette and stared off into the distance.

"What the fuck am I supposed to do?" I said out loud to myself. I just sat there, staring off into the distance, watching the sun come up from beyond the tree line. I pulled out my phone, and there were no new messages. I was feeling a million different emotions at that moment. I was angry, worried, and remorseful. This, again, was a moment that I had thought only about myself and hadn't thought of anyone else. I just sat there defeated until I heard a set of footsteps coming up the stairs. I looked up, and it was Mae. I jumped up and hugged her, and she half hugged me back.

"What's your problem?" she said, her voice sounding more sarcastic than serious.

"I'm sorry about last night. I woke up and you were gone, and I was scared." Her arms kind of hung limp as if I were bothering her. I pulled away and took a step back, not wanting to anger her further.

"You were asleep, and I went out with some friends from school. I didn't think you would care." She looked down at the ground and then at me, side-eyed. She then just walked right by me and into the apartment.

"You really didn't think I would care?" I said, following her into the apartment and closing the door.

"Well, you were sleeping...like I said, and I texted you so you would know where I was." She took off her jacket and shoes and threw her things on the couch nonchalantly.

"You said out…just out. What does that mean?" I could tell my questioning was making her angry, but I didn't care.

"Well, we didn't know where we were going. Jason picked me up with his girlfriend and we went downtown. By the time we knew where we were going, my phone was dead. I tried to charge it, but nobody with me had an iPhone." She walked into the bedroom and started taking off her clothes. She was obviously tired from staying out all night and wanted to go to bed.

"So you just didn't even try? Use someone else's phone? I was worried about you, Mae…after last night…I didn't know…" She interrupted.

"Didn't know what? If I was going to go out and do something you didn't approve of? You're my fucking wife, not my mother…even though you're acting like her." The blow hit harder than I think she had intended, but she stuck to her guns and stared me down while saying it. "I'm going to bed, we can talk about it later."

"That's it? You're going to bed?" She closed the door in my face. I just stood there like an idiot, too afraid to do anything else. Just like Chance…Rebecca was a fucking coward as well. Mae and I never argued, which was one of the reasons that I had no clue what to do. She was also uncharacteristically cold about the entire situation, as well…which was not like her at all. I stood there for a few minutes and decided to go sit down and clean up the mess from the night before. The kitchen was pretty much clean other than all my documents and the dishes from dinner. I quickly got everything straightened up, and by that time, it was well past eight or so.

"Well, I am not just going to sit here and fucking mope all day," I finally said to myself, trying my best to pick myself up by my bootstraps. "I am not like Chance," I said quietly. "I can exist without you, Mae. I can have my own life." I don't even think the words were mine…they were his but were still true. Yeah, we were arguing, but did that mean I just had to sit in there and cry all fucking day?

I got up and went into the bedroom quietly. Mae was sound asleep as I could hear her snoring. Her phone was sitting next to her…unplugged. I plugged it in so it would at least charge. I grabbed a set of comfortable clothes from the closet and grabbed my backpack. I pulled out a notepad from the bag and wrote a quick note for Mae and tucked it under her phone.

Mae,

I am sorry about last night, and this morning. I am going to go to the library and try to get some work done. When you wake up, feel free to join me. I will leave the car at home.

XOXOX Your Wife – Rebecca

We were already fighting, so I wanted to at least extend the olive branch. In her mind, the fight was entirely my fault...and she was probably right. I had gotten really heated over what she had done the previous night and that morning...but let's be honest. I had done all those things and more the past few days. I had gotten drunk after work and completely forgot to tell her where I was. I had been selfish and self-centered with little to no regard to her feelings. Hell, I had almost gotten us murdered by some secret agents...well, not really, but we hadn't known that at the time. I put a small bit of lipstick on and kissed the bottom of the note so it left an impression of my lips. I closed the door quietly and packed up some of my manuscripts into my backpack. I left the apartment and headed for the bus stop.

Usually, I don't take the bus since I had a car or my bike, but I needed a bit of time with zero stress. The bus came every thirty or so minutes during the day for the students, and I still had a transit card, so I waited patiently for the bus to come chugging along and hopped on. The bus ride was short since I was one of the last stops before the campus. Basically, it was just a straight shot to the side street that the library was on.

I exited the bus at the stop and quickly made my way to my destination. I passed by dozens of students running to get to class on time. In true college fashion, I also ran into a few that were obviously hungover from a night of drinking who didn't care if they were late or not. I laughed quietly at the contrast between the two, and before I knew it, I was climbing the library steps.

"Good morning," the librarian said, the same one from the other day.

"Is your...friend joining you today?" Her recognition of me meant I had made a bit of an impact the other day.

"No," I said politely, "she has other things to do today. Just me." She scanned my card, and I made my way through the turnstile into the main auditorium. It was a large domed area that had hallways that led to different areas of the building. It reminded me more of a museum than anything else. I shook off the familiar feeling of being unsettled from the large open space and made my way toward the free reading area. I decided to get a spot by the coffee shop and grab my usual black coffee and blueberry scone. The lines were short, so before I knew it, I was unpacking my bag in one of my favorite reading nooks the library had. There was an exterior window that led out into the quad area and a comfy circular bench that surrounded a moderately sized table. It was bolted into the floor so it wouldn't move...and that was my favorite thing about it. A wiggly table was not a table for me.

I pulled out the piece I had been reading the day before and pulled out a new fine-tipped red pen and went to work. I reread the beginning again since I had found several errors in the intro paragraph that I had missed during my first go around. I didn't blame myself too much since I had written it in high school.

Other than the night before, I had not read these words in such a long time, and it was sad to see how much they still resonated with me to that very day. I still struggled with many of the same internal conflicts that I did back then. Yeah, the whole being a lesbian thing didn't really help when I was younger, but that wasn't something that I really hid nowadays. I thought back to my morning coffee disaster with Albert a few days earlier and laughed to myself. I guess I might as well have been that same adolescent girl at heart more than I had thought.

The day went on as I continued to read and edit the rough draft, and I must say, rereading something I had nearly forgotten about gave me a much better view of what the story would be like for someone reading it for the first time. I definitely gave myself a much harsher critique because of that than I would have initially. I thanked myself for procrastinating as long as I had in order to finish the book. I was able to lend more insight on some things that I questioned as a young woman, growing up with a secret...one that she wasn't embarrassed of, but one she was terrified of.

My slight brush with death the other day was another lens through which I could view some of my writing. Lending that experience to the youthful and somewhat hopeful narration would make a nice contrast once I got around to some of the changes I was planning on making.

The book itself wasn't very long and if I remembered correctly, would have been about a six-to-eight-hour total read. That being said, by one thirty, I was nearly halfway completed with a first run-through. I wouldn't have even thought about taking a moment to stop if I hadn't hit a paragraph that really resonated with me...I guess it should all resonate with me since I had written it, but what I meant was it resonated with me now...not as a sixteen-year-old. I didn't quite remember what had been happening in my life at that point, too much time had passed, and my memory wasn't that good.

I have been told that my behavior is sometimes erratic or borderline manic. That I only care about one thing at a time and usually that thing is myself. When you're fighting internal battles daily, is it really selfish to have self-preservation most ever-present in your mind? Why shouldn't I be fearful of what happens to me over someone else when that same person would gladly throw me in front of a bus to save their own skin? It's just exhausting being told one thing by these so-called adults when they constantly prove themselves to be hypocrites. Even people that I once looked at with reverence have become people that...people that no longer have garnered my respect or adoration. What happens when those very same people are the ones keeping you going? What happens when those people are you?

I sat there thinking of what exactly I had been writing about. Obviously, I had been upset at someone...someone that I really looked up to. Most of the occurrences I could equate to some person or event that had taken place, but this one really stood out as a mystery to me. I put a giant circle around the entire passage with a large question mark next to it. I noted it to try and remember what had happened to me to write that passage. It wasn't really necessary for the purpose of editing the book, but...it would bother me until I did.

I was just getting ready to start reading the next section of the book when I heard a familiar voice in the library. I peeked out from behind the nook and my suspicions were confirmed...it was Sarah.

"What the fuck?" I thought as I panicked slightly. "What is she doing here?" I took a minute to remember where I actually was...at a school. What was Sarah, exactly...a student. I peeked around the corner of the nook again and couldn't stop staring. Her hair was a bit different, but it was definitely her. She sat down with another group of girls around her age and pulled out some books and began studying.

I don't know why it was so odd to see her there, maybe because I had been sleeping on her lap last time I checked on the other side of the poles. Or maybe it was because I couldn't just go over there and say hi. She was a woman that I had confessed my love to just the other day, and I couldn't do anything but sit there and stare. I laughed quietly as I thought about how fucking crazy I was being. I sat back in my chair, and then there was another familiar voice...I knew that voice anywhere. It was Mae.

"Hey, Sarah, how are you feeling after last night?" she said, walking up to the table and giving the young girl a hug.

"Yeah, Jason is passed out at my place and his snoring was too loud. I said screw it and came to study. Come and sit with us?" She pointed toward another empty chair, and I couldn't exactly hear what Mae said, but I could tell she denied Sarah's offer. It appeared they said their goodbyes, and Mae made a beeline for the nook she knew I was sitting in. A few moments later, she was standing there with a somewhat apologetic look on her face and an energy drink in her hand.

"Hey, Becks," she said, putting her drink down on the table. "Do you mind if I sit here?" Every angry bone in my body melted as soon as she appeared.

"Of course not, please." I motioned for her to sit and moved a couple of manuscripts. She sat down and looked at me with somewhat sad eyes.

"You know you're a bitch, right?" Well, I guess apologies were out the window. She wasn't wrong, though. I had gone through all of this in my mind this morning when waiting for her to come home.

"I know. I have been awful lately." We both sat there quietly after the first exchange as if we had no clue what to say to one another. We were married and had known each other for our whole lives...but we couldn't even formulate enough words to form a sentence at the moment. The silence in the library was deafening...it was about to reach a crescendo when Mae finally spoke.

"It was about your first...well, only boyfriend." I had no idea what she was talking about. She nudged her head over toward what I was reading and the big circle.

"Wait, you read this?" I said, completely surprised. Like I said earlier... Mae did not read.

"I may have read it right before I decided to go back to school. It also may have been the reason I decided to go back. So you could write more of this." She pointed toward the book. "It was really good. A little bit whiny, but that was to be expected because you were what fifteen...sixteen when you wrote it?"

I was just still amazed she had read it. I was even more amazed that she had been able to completely hide it from me. I felt awful now for what I said before...I really was a bitch. I sat back and reread a bit of the passage, and she was right.

"What was his name?" I asked Mae, hoping she would remember.

"Chris or something. I guess he wasn't your boyfriend, but he really liked you...and well...you were in the closet, so you went along with it." She sat up and laughed. "You seriously didn't put two and two together about that passage? Wow, your memory is worse than mine." She took a drink from her energy drink and grimaced. "Only had sugar free left at the gas station...this thing is awful." We both laughed awkwardly, and the tension began to loosen.

"I remember now, and I think you're right. He had a crush on me, so we went out a few times. He was so nice to me up until I rejected an advance. He didn't take it well." Mae shook her head.

"Didn't he tell everyone you were a prude or something?" You could tell she was really thinking about it and couldn't remember.

"I don't know. I just came to school the next day, and everyone was talking about it. I think I brought it up to one of our teachers and they brushed me off. That's why I was so pissed off." The second part wasn't true but kind of fit the narrative. I remembered the interaction now like it happened thirty seconds ago. I had a friend from the yearbook committee that I spent a ton of time around. I was completely infatuated with Mae, but neither of us had come out yet. We stayed deep in the closet until our senior year...anyways. He developed a bit of a crush on me, and I could tell that he was. I was afraid that would suspect something if I rejected him outright. I also had never had a boyfriend before, so…you know how people talk.

"Yeah, I don't remember what he said exactly, but I remember it was pretty shitty." Mae took another sip of her energy drink. She looked over at the few pieces of scone that were left over and gave me puppy dog eyes.

"Just finish it. I was thinking about grabbing something for a snack, did you want anything?" She had already consumed the last of the scone. She looked up at me, still chewing.

"Get another one of these. It was really good." A few crumbs fell out as she spoke.

"Sounds good." I walked over to the little coffee counter they had and took a look at the pastries that they had in their little glass display. I ordered the last scone for Mae and decided to get an almond croissant. I decided to get a tea rather than a coffee since I was already pretty decently caffeinated and felt like sleeping sometime today.

"Whoa, maybe I want what you got," Mae said as she smelled the croissant. They warmed it up and it really smelled great.

"Let's just split them," I said, pulling the pastries apart and divvying them up equally. We shared our little luncheon meal, and she gave me a few more thoughts she had on the book. It was really nice to see that she did, in fact, care about what I was doing. She was the one person who could have destroyed me if she really didn't care for it. I was glad that she took an interest in it more than just pushing me to complete it. It made the accomplishment feel like more of an "us" thing than a me thing. It made the entire endeavor sweeter.

The afternoon was going well until Sarah came over to talk to Mae about some schoolwork. I had my back to her, and I wasn't prepared for her to come popping around the corner.

"Hey, Mae!" she said, her usual smile on her face. God, she was just beautiful. Like I mentioned, her hair was a bit shorter than on the other side of the poles, but man…she just lit up the room.

"Hey, Sarah," Mae said, noticing I was just sitting there staring. "This is my wife Rebecca…" She looked over, noticing my facial expression. She coughed a few times to get my attention.

"Oh, hey yeah. I'm Rebecca but you can just call me Becky." She reached out to shake my hand. Her hands were soft against mine. When we touched my hair on my arm stood up. I hoped Mae didn't notice.

"Mae has told me so much about you. I feel like I know you already." She motioned to sit down next to Mae, and she scooted into the booth. Mae scooted a bit closer to me to make room. "So, she tells me you're a writer. I have always wanted to publish something, but I am scared to show anyone my work." She blushed a bit. I think I was doing the same thing.

"Yeah, I write for a local magazine...not very prestigious. Mae finally convinced me to start on one of my books again. It's been ages since I started this one, and it has a long way to go."

"I convinced you to start again? I don't remember that." Mae poked fun at my reasoning, but unfortunately Sarah was my reasoning. Just not this Sarah.

"That's still really cool, though. I have never shown my stuff to anyone." She played with her fingers and looked down at the table.

"Not even your boyfriend? What's his name, Jason?" Mae looked at me awkwardly since she was not the one who had told me his name.

"No...I don't think he is really the poetry type. Not really a thinker, that one." She laughed awkwardly as she said it, not knowing if it was insulting or endearing. Mae's glare was burning holes in the side of my head.

"How did you know his name?" Mae said, the fun taken out of her voice.

"I heard you guys talking when you first got here. She mentioned a Jason, and a girl this pretty has to have a boyfriend." I didn't know why I was complimenting her, it just slipped out. I could see Mae's expression change, and I knew I had probably said too much.

"Well, that makes sense," Mae finally said. "We were talking pretty loud." She brushed it off, and I figured that I would hear about it later.

"Well, if you want to, Mae, we are studying for that last big test. I don't want to take you away from your wife, but we could definitely use one more." She looked at me with the same eyes that she looked at Chance with. She could have asked to do whatever she wanted to at that moment, and I probably would have answered the same way.

"Yeah, sure. Whatever you guys want to do," I stammered. I felt like an idiot for acting this way...I just didn't know what had come over me.

"Well," Mae said, how annoyed she was showing in her voice. "With that, I am going to go study with them. See you back at home?" She came over and kissed me on the cheek. It was a quick peck, but I could tell she was upset.

"Yeah, babe. I'll see you at home." She grabbed her things and her and Sarah went to sit at the other table. Once they were out of sight, I was able to relax a bit.

"Get yourself together," I said a few times. Her presence was intoxicating. I hadn't felt that way about anyone other than Mae on this side of the poles...never, not even once.

I sat there watching them work for a few minutes, obsessing over how I had reacted when she was close. After about ten minutes or so of spying on them, I decided to get back to my work and continue editing the book. Once my mind was occupied with the work, I stopped thinking about everything and was able to focus on the task at hand.

I sat there in my little nook for a few more hours. The group that Mae and Sarah had been sitting with dwindled down until it was just Sarah and Mae. Mae eventually left and Sarah was just sitting by herself, chewing on a pencil and playing with her hair. I could no longer concentrate on my book and decided it was time to get going. I collected my things and threw out my trash and headed for the exit. I tried my best to sneak by her without her noticing, but she looked up at the perfect moment to see me coming around the corner.

"Hey, Rebecca!" she shouted. Then realizing that she was in a library, she said again a bit quieter, "Hey, Rebecca," this time adhering to the libraries noise policy.

"Oh, hey," I said as I walked up to her. "Burning the midnight oil?" It wasn't even five, and that comment was stupid, why was I being an idiot right now?

"Well, not really," she said, looking a bit confused. "Burning the late afternoon oil?" she said, smiling at her quick response.

"Yeah, sorry. I guess it's not that late." I tried to wave and leave quickly.

"Actually, do you have a moment?" Her voice sounded a bit concerned and a bit apprehensive.

"Yeah, what's up?" I said as she pulled out something from underneath her notebook. It was a smaller spiral notebook that was covered in stickers.

She opened it to a specific page that she had a small piece of paper in, kind of like a bookmark. "I...Mae said you're really amazing at writing. I wanted to know if you could...I don't know, maybe take a look at something of mine."

"Well, I don't know if I would have anything to add. I am not very good at poetry, myself." I tried to be modest, but to be honest, I just didn't want to help her out over on this side. I was afraid of the way I acted around her, and Rebecca had literally just met her. I wanted to turn and run out the door to the bus stop and not look back. Her eyes just peered into mine with...I don't know. I couldn't explain it. I wanted to kiss her right then and there...obviously, I am not stupid. I understood who I was right then and where I was. I just...the feeling was difficult to control.

She noticed that I looked uncomfortable and immediately withdrew her request. "I am so sorry. I must just seem like an idiot. I barely know you, but...I don't know. Something about you makes me feel like you could help. Like I can trust you." She put her notebook back under her things and sighed.

"No, it's totally fine. I just don't think I would be of any help, is all. I can read it if you still want. It's no bother." The damage had been done, however. She shook her head and smiled.

"No, it was a weird request. They aren't really good, and I think they need a bit more work." Her face had the look of embarrassment, and she went back to chewing her pencil. "You should be getting home. I could hang out with Mae all day, she is definitely something special." I took the hint and nodded.

"Yeah, she really is. Sorry I couldn't help, and just let Mae know if you change your mind. I am sure you have her number." I waved, and she smiled, and I was gone. My heart was racing, and I was clearly sweating a bit more than usual for such a cool room. I walked out into the evening air, and it hit me like a hammer. I don't know if you have ever experienced a panic attack. If not, I hope you never do. I sat down on one of the park benches that lined the path leading into the library and pulled out a pretty old pack of cigarettes from my purse. I lit one up and took it in deep. I don't know if it was the anxiety or the cigarette, but I nearly vomited right there on the sidewalk. I took about ten minutes and a cigarette and a half to calm down and regain my composure.

I started walking toward the bus stop and pulled out my phone. I had a few missed texts from Albert regarding his progress. Apparently, he had been released from the hospital that day, so that was good news. I had a missed one from Mae asking when I was going to be home. I quickly responded that I was on my way and put the phone back in my purse. I saw the bus and started running so I didn't miss it. I didn't feel like sitting idle for thirty minutes while I waited for the next one.

I barely made the bus and quickly walked to the back to sit down. I was a bit more out of breath than I would have liked to admit and leaned back into the seat and rested my head on the window.

"What a day," I said to myself, excited that it was almost over. It was a rare occurrence that I was excited to jump to the other side of the poles... well, as Rebecca, at least. Usually, I looked forward to seeing Mae above all else, but that night I really missed Sarah...my Sarah. I closed my eyes and relaxed for the remainder of the ride. Once the bus reached my stop, I quickly got off and headed back toward the apartment. When I hit the steps, Mae was outside with a beer and what looked like another one of my manuscripts.

"There she is," Mae said, standing up to greet me. "Thought maybe you ditched me to hang out with Sarah." Her tone was half joking and half serious.

"Yeah, funny," I said quickly. "What do you want to do for dinner?" I was trying to get the subject off Sarah.

"Well, I don't know. We have a couple of TV Dinners in the freezer we could just heat up quick." She went into the apartment and pulled them out of the freezer. They hit the counter hard like a piece of ice. We both laughed at the sound.

"Yeah, that's fine with me. Any beer left in there?" I checked the refrigerator and pulled one out. "You want another one?"

"No, I am good for now." She took a moment and read and reread the directions as to not ruin our only chance at an easy meal. "Am I supposed to poke the top or remove the corner? I don't have my glasses." She handed me the package, and I rubbed off some of the frost.

"These are corner pull ones," I said, handing it back to her. She tossed them in the microwave and came to sit down by me. I had taken my beer and gone outside to where she was sitting to see which thing she was reading.

"It's the fantasy fiction one, you know, with the bard or whatever who's family was killed. It looked interesting." She showed me that she was only about ten or so pages into it.

"What do you think?" I took a sip from my beer and sat on the railing. I was excited to hear what she thought. She paused for a moment as if she didn't want to say what was on her mind. "That bad, eh?" I was trying to give her an opening for some harsher criticism.

"I'm sorry, Becks, but...I need to know something." She put the book down and sat back in her seat. "You thought Sarah was hot, didn't you?" I was expecting a few different things, but that was definitely not one of them. I must have confirmed all her suspicions as I took too long to answer the question.

"Well, I mean...she's not ugly." I didn't want to lie to my wife; well I did, but she would know I was lying.

"Yeah, I could tell. You literally stared at her the entire time. I could swear you were drooling at one point." I couldn't tell whether she was just giving me shit or if this really bothered her. I couldn't explain why I was looking at her like that, other than the fact she was attractive.

"I'm sorry Mae, you're right. I have nothing to say to defend how I acted." I didn't want to fight anymore. I just wanted to eat dinner and go to bed.

"Well, can you try to not be a creep next time you see her? She lives out here and is in my class. I would like to keep her as a friend without my wife acting like a schoolgirl with a crush around her." The microwave ended up saving the day and ringing right when I thought she was about to go off again. She walked over to the microwave, pulled the two dinners out, and threw them down on the kitchen table. I went to grab some silverware, and we just quietly sat and ate our meal. Mine was still a bit cold, but I figured there was no way I would complain that night. I just wanted us to get along. I didn't know why, but we just weren't getting along anymore.

Once our sad attempt at dinner was completed, Mae never brought up Sarah again. I think that she had said her peace and she also didn't want to fight again. We both took our turns showering and getting ready for bed, and then...we did just that. I came in from my shower and Mae

285

was already laying down in bed, looking at something on her phone, pretending to not see me take off my towel and dress in front of her. I could tell she peaked a few times, but other than that, there wasn't any playful banter or back and forth like usual. I just put on my pajamas and laid down next to her.

She handed me her phone and asked me to plug it in. I did as she asked, and by the time I was done, she was already turned toward the wall with the covers pulled up to her neck. I plugged my phone in as well and turned off the light. I wanted to snuggle up against her, but it seemed wrong in the moment, and I decided to just go to bed. I fell asleep thinking of how strange it was to be excited to see someone on the other side. My last thought was of Sarah running her hands through my hair.

Chapter 21

I woke up with a terrible kink in my neck. It wasn't dark anymore, so I assumed it was morning. What time, though, I wasn't yet aware. I looked around, and Sarah was nowhere to be seen. I looked around the apartment and wondered…then I smelled the coffee. I got up and took a look at the pot. It had about half remaining. I looked around again and noticed a little red ponytail sticking up from the window. I smiled and poured myself a cup of coffee and decided to join her. I opened the door to the apartment and walked outside. She was sitting back in my chair with her bare feet up on the railing. Her pretty pink toes were bathed in sunlight as she looked up at me and smiled.

"Good morning, sleepyhead." She cuffed her hand over her eyes like a visor since it was extremely sunny for this time of day. "I didn't want to wake you. You were snoring so cute…and drooling. Did I mention you were drooling?"

"Funny. I'm sorry I passed out so quickly last night." I reached into the doorway to grab my pack of cigarettes. I was on my last one.

"Yeah, I was a bit surprised, too, last night when I saw Mae and you talking." She gave me a guilty look. "I initially walked up to confront you two when I heard you talking." She put her coffee down on the window ledge and stood up and came over next to me. "You told her you loved me." A smile came across her face as she spoke. "Even when she…well, it seemed like she was…" I interrupted.

"Sarah, I promised you. Nothing is going to happen between us again. What happened already was the single biggest mistake in my life, and trust me…I have made a bunch of really bad mistakes." My answer to her inquiry must have made her feel better since the guilty look turned back into a smile. "I don't care that you listened in. I would have said the same things if you were here."

"Thanks," she said, wrapping me up in a hug. "Can I ask you something, though?"

"Yeah, anything," I responded as she pulled away.

"Why are you covered in paint?" She pointed at a few spots on my shirt. "That shirt didn't have paint on it when I saw you last…also, why are you still wearing that shirt?" She made an exaggerated look of disgust.

"Shit, I completely forgot." I took her hand and pulled her into the apartment.

"Chance, my coffee!" she yelped as I tugged her toward my bedroom.

"After reading your poems yesterday, I was inspired to do something I haven't done in a long time." I opened the door and held my hands over her eyes. "Those poems really were amazing, and I wanted to do something for you to help you get them published." I led her to right in front of the canvas and removed my hands.

She was speechless. She walked up to the canvas slowly, admiring every inch. "Is this what I think it is?" she said, touching her finger to the canvas to feel the texture of the paint. "It looks like you and me?" I took another look at the painting and turned my head. I guess the blonde was a bit darker and looked red. I grinned to myself as I guess it did kind of resemble Sarah. I had painted myself, and…well myself. Rebecca and Chance were who I painted, but Sarah saw herself in the image. I quickly was able to pivot the conversation, and hopefully she didn't notice.

"The poems seemed to me like a collection, a collection that went through an entire relationship. The good, the bad, and the beautiful. So, I painted what I felt." I walked over to her and put my hand on her shoulder.

"It's a cover for my poetry book." She immediately wrapped me in one of the tightest hugs I have ever encountered. I am pretty sure I heard a rib or two pop.

"Do you like it?" I asked rhetorically.

"Are you fucking kidding me?" She pulled away and grabbed my face in her hands. "This is the best gift anyone has ever gotten me." She went back to admiring the painting. "You seriously painted this yesterday? You said you don't paint anymore?"

"That's the funny thing. After I left your place yesterday, I went back to the art store I used to work at. I met with my old manager, and he helped me pick out what I needed. He actually offered me my old instructor job back...and I am thinking about taking it." I took her hand in mine and kissed it softly. "Sarah, I haven't painted anything that I actually wanted to paint in so long, I had forgotten how much I enjoy it. You helped me realize how much I truly loved painting, even after all this time." She buried her face into my chest and hugged me. I put my arms around her and my face against the side of her head and kissed it. We embraced for a few more moments, and I looked down to hear her stifling a whimper. She wiped her face, and I noticed that she was, in fact, crying.

"I'm sorry. I just...this was just so nice. Thank you, Chance." She looked up, her eyes slightly puffy. Thankfully, she must have taken her makeup off because there was no sign of it running.

"Well, now that it's dry, I can get some good digital photos of it and I will send it over. When I am done, did you want to keep the original?" She punched me on the shoulder.

"Of course, of course. I am never getting rid of it." She pulled out her cell phone and took a selfie with it. "Definitely going on social media later."

The rest of the morning was spent chatting about next steps to possibly get Sarah's poetry collection published. I knew of a few ways...well, Rebecca did, but it was the same knowledge. We spitballed the idea of self-publishing, and she mentioned that she had a bit of money that was a graduation gift form her grandparents. She was saving it for a rainy day, and this might just as well be that day. Her excitement was almost palpable, and her enthusiasm reminded me of when I was younger. Both Chance and Rebecca had been so driven and enthusiastic about their lives and what they would accomplish. Obviously, both of us never really achieved the potential that we thought we could, and our careers hit a plateau once we could earn a living. We became complacent with our lives, and our needs and wants had taken a back seat to our obsession...Mae. Now I felt as if I could see, for the first time in my life, something other than my next fix, my next high. I might be able to give this young woman, who had trusted in me, a bit of something I was never given.

"Well, I had better get going. I have class in a bit, and I have to stop by my place and grab my things. I wasn't planning on spending the night." I looked down at my watch, and it was a little before noon. I didn't want her to go and really wanted her to stay. Unfortunately, I didn't feel like being a bad influence on her and just agreed.

"Yeah, I have a few things I need to do as well. I was thinking about going and accepting that job offer. I want to do it in person." I also had something else in mind for me to do, but I didn't want to let Sarah know about it just yet.

"Well…" she said, procrastinating because it felt as if she didn't want to leave either. "I'll see you later?" She reached up for a kiss, and I obliged.

"Yes Ma'am," I said as I went in for another kiss. Her lip balm tasted like cherry, and I could taste it on my lips when we finished.

"Later, tiger," she said as she walked out the door and down the steps. I watched her get into her car and leave. I went to my phone and searched through the random calls I'd had over the past few days. I knew one of them was Rebecca, but I didn't know which one. I thought back to the last few days and tried to remember the day when I…well, when I had my incident with the sleeping pills. I called every unknown number that day until I finally heard her voice on the other end of the line.

"Hello?" I heard her say, her voice was quiet and sad. "Who's there?"

I knew the second I spoke she would know it was me and hang up. I also knew if I didn't speak quickly, she would hang up anyway. "Rebecca… its Chance." She paused for a moment and then sighed.

"What the hell do you want? Make it quick." Her tone changed from sad to more angry and annoyed.

"Can we meet up?" It was the only way I felt I could get her attention for long enough to say what I wanted to say. I knew that she was about to hang up with me anyway, and I didn't want to have to call her ten times to answer again.

"Why? What could you possibly have to say to me?" This time, she was just plain angry, and there was no sense of annoyance.

"I just want to talk, and I don't want to do it over the phone. Can we just please meet up? Please, Rebecca, I am begging you." She paused on the other end of the line, taking a moment to answer.

"Fine…meet me at the diner." The line went dead.

"Fuck," I said as I called again and there was no answer. I grabbed my bike keys and my things and locked the door behind me. I needed to be there when she got there or else she might leave. I hopped on my bike and left without even closing the garage. I quickly made my way to the diner and parked in a spot in front so she would see my bike. I hurried into the diner and saw Al sitting at the counter reading a paper. There was literally nobody save for a few regulars sitting at the counter doing the same as him.

"Hey, Chance. Alone today?" He peered up from his paper slightly.

"No, I have one more coming. I'll just seat myself, is that ok?" I motioned toward my usual booth.

"Yeah, sure. You need a cup of coffee, or do you need the special stuff?" I thought for a moment about the conversation I was about to have.

"Let's start with one of the special stuff, and then regular from then on out." He gave me a thumbs up and headed into his office, I was assuming to get the special stuff. He came back a few minutes later with two menus, a cup of special coffee, and a carafe of what appeared to be regular coffee.

I sat there for only about ten minutes or so. It felt much longer; one, because Al put way too much whiskey in my coffee, and two, because I didn't want to confront Rebecca in any way, shape, or form. Mae wasn't the only one who had hurt her that night, I had as well. Also, to add insult to injury, I had lied right to her face after the fact. I wouldn't be surprised if she walked in, punched me in the face, and then left. I wouldn't blame her one bit. My heart stopped every time I heard the door open, until eventually, I saw her walk in and take a look around. Her gaze caught mine, and she reluctantly walked toward my booth.

"Let's make this quick," she said, sitting down quickly. She put her purse on her lap in an attempt to show me she wasn't staying long.

"Thank you for meeting with me. I know that I am one of the last people on this planet that you want to see right now." She nodded.

"You're not wrong." Malice dripped from her voice. I took another swig of my special coffee, hoping it would last. She took a page from my book and poured herself one from the carafe as well.

"I just want to tell you how sorry I am about what happened. There is nothing I can say to convey how sorry I am for my part in what happened." I took a few moments to pick my next words carefully. "Mae and I have always had a complicated relationship, and the reason for that has and always will be me. What she did wasn't a reflection on her feelings toward you, in which she has very deep feelings. It has everything to do with how fucked up our relationship has become in the past few years." She stood there stone-faced and nodded for me to continue. "Our relationship has grown toxic and severely codependent. What we both did is inexcusable, but I am not trying to make excuses…again, because there are none." She sat up and took a deep breath.

"Chance, I don't know what you want from me or what Mae wants from me. Why on earth would you think that I wanted to hear this fucking apology from you? In case you want a recap, let me give it to you. Mae… my girlfriend, who is, in fact…gay, was told by her best friend…you, who is not a woman that he was in love with her. You then proceeded to get into an argument regarding said confession and went home. She then came to your apartment and you both fucked. Then, to add insult to injury, I came over the next day because I was worried about her. You looked at me straight in the eyes and told me you hadn't seen her, but she was inside your fucking apartment hiding. Now, you're asking me to what? Do you want me to forgive you, to forgive her? Are you serious? Are you stupid or just drunk…actually, knowing you, you're just drunk." She took a few deep breaths and tried to calm herself down. Once she felt like she could continue, she did. "Does that about sum it all up?" She took a drink of her coffee and sighed. "Fuck, I wish this wasn't coffee." Al had heard her getting heated and had come to check to see what the issue was. I motioned for him to get another special cup of coffee for her, and he did just that. A few moments later, he came back with another cup for her. She looked at him like he was an idiot.

"Just drink the coffee," I said as she picked up the mug and smelled.

"Of course you think this is the answer," she said, smelling the coffee again. She shrugged and took a sip, and then a bit more than a sip…and then the rest of the mug. "Might as well match your level if we are going to do this," she said as she cracked her neck and sat up straight again. It looked like she was going to go for another round of the argument, but she eventually just sighed and sat back in the booth.

"What can I do? What can Mae do to make you trust her or at least give her another Chance?" Moments like this made me hate my name for fear of people thinking I like puns too much. "Pardon the pun," I said, for good measure.

She sat up again and looked at me straight in the eyes. "Did you tell

Sarah what happened, or did you fucking lie to her too? Apparently, you two are back together. Mae might have texted me something about that." It was now my turn for explaining.

"No, I didn't tell her. I didn't have the chance to. We went out a few days later, and she confronted me with the fact that she knew about it, or at least had a feeling. When she asked me, I didn't lie. I needed her to know, not only because it was the right thing, but because I either wanted the relationship to be based on truth or not at all." She put her head down in her hands like she was about to cry. Instead, she just started chuckling quietly. "What's so funny?" I said, worried about her reaction.

"Truth...you say your relationship is based on truth, but it's exactly the opposite. You and Sarah were together for what, like a week or so? Mae actually courted me. We hung out and talked into the night. We told each other all about ourselves. Fuck, she told me all about her best friend she couldn't wait for me to meet. Truth after the fact is just something we sell ourselves to feel better about the shitty things we do." She looked over at Al and held up her glass, giving the gesture that she wanted another one of what he had given her...she looked back at me and held up two fingers instead. She looked back at me. "You're buying, by the way."

A few moments later, Al came back with a carafe of special coffee. He smiled as he placed it down and quickly left. He was used to people having serious conversations in his diner, and he read the room well. Rebecca held up the mug in a mock toast. I did the same, and she and I had a drink. She was beginning to soften a bit and was less hostile, which is always a good thing. She was obviously still upset, though. After a few minutes of silence, I picked up the menu and took a look at it.

"You're seriously thinking about food?" I shrugged.

"Well, this is my second one of these, and I probably will finish the carafe, so...yeah. I should probably eat something." She shrugged and picked up the menu as well. We sat there in silence as we looked over the menu. Al eventually came and took our orders and the menus...then it was just us again. I decided to break the silence since it was nearly killing me.

"Rebecca, you have zero reasons in the world to trust me...hell, you probably have as many not to trust Mae. What happened was one of the worst and best things that could have happened in that scenario." She looked up at me, anger returning to her eyes slightly.

"Yeah, how so?" she said sarcastically.

"Our relationship is the most toxic and codependent relationship you could ever imagine. It has been just us for as long as I can remember. We have always been there for each other in the good times and the bad. The thing is, in order for our relationship to continue, it would consume us both. The only reason in the world that she needed me...was because she didn't have you. I needed her simply because I didn't know that I could ever be happy without her. I am not a fan of being wrong, Rebecca, but I am glad that I was. Sarah might be stupid, or the most amazing woman on the planet, but she is giving me a chance because she understands just how fucked up Mae's and my relationship was." I began to get a bit worked up and took a few deep breaths. Rebecca was intrigued by my argument enough to continue to listen. She sipped from her mug every now and then. "I have never seen Mae as happy as she is with you, and trust me...I have seen her happy before. I have never seen her talk about a future with anyone before...literally anyone, including myself. Her and I just needed each other until we found someone to make us truly happy. Mae found that in you, and I am pretty sure I found it in Sarah."

I started to tear up a bit thinking about my last fifteen years...how pathetic it had been, just following Mae around like a fucking dog. Just going with the flow and doing whatever I could do in order to go to the other side of the poles. To be Rebecca and to be with Mae. It just came out of nowhere, and I started to actually cry. Not like sobbing or anything, let's just call it a manly cry.

"Chance, we don't have to do this. There is no reason to..." I interrupted.

"Rebecca, she loves you. I saw her last night, and she was absolutely destroyed." I paused to wipe the tears from my face. "I have never loved anyone in my life the way I love Mae, until now. I have never had anyone in my life accept me for who I am, until now. Please don't let Mae suffer over me...I am not worth it. I promise, I will never talk to her again if that's what you want. I just can't have the best thing that ever happened to her be fucked up because of me..." I tried to collect myself the best I could. Rebecca's features had definitely softened watching a grown ass man lose it in a public setting. She was mad, she wasn't a monster. I looked into her eyes...I looked into my eyes and just couldn't anymore. I had to accept that I no longer was what was best for Mae. We always thought it was us against the world…that couldn't have been further from the truth. "Rebecca…Mae knowing me literally ruined her life. I can't continue doing that to my best friend."

She wasn't prepared for the emotional breakdown I was currently having. In the long run, it probably helped my cause to make what I was saying seem more genuine. It was actually funny because I had done shit like this in the past because I was a manipulative piece of shit. This was the first time I wasn't lying or trying to manipulate someone even though that may have seemed like what my end goal was. I just didn't want Mae to suffer anymore because of me. I put my head in my hand and just sat there for a moment, just regretting being alive. I felt a hand placed gently on top of mine. I looked up, and Rebecca had a half-smile on her face.

"Chance, you haven't ruined her life. She has told me every story in the book about you. Up until the other day, you were an amazing friend. You stood up for her in high school when she came out and basically shunned from her family. You stayed with her through all the bad relationships and helped her leave. You also helped her through the good ones that ended prematurely. You love her, and I really don't think that will ever change. Even now, you're trying to help her with little regard to yourself." She sighed and shook her head. "It must have been hard for you to come here and confront me, and I appreciate that. I just don't know if I can trust her again…and to be quite honest, I am terrified of the fact that I really might find it in my heart to trust her…and then what? What if this happens again?" She pulled her hand back and poured us both another mug of special coffee.

"It won't ever happen again. I can assure you." I wanted to tell her about the day before when Mae had come over and I had asked her to leave. I wanted to tell her about the fact I couldn't even sleep with my wife on the other side of the poles anymore because of Sarah. I wanted to explain how I couldn't even escape Sarah on the other side. That I was unable to even operate around her as Rebecca. In a perfect world, I could have told her all of these things, and she would begin to understand…but I also didn't want to be taken away to a room with padded walls. I could never explain to her that she was an identical copy of me in an alternate reality where I was married to Mae. I was so sick and tired of this double life bullshit… what was the point of living two half-lives and not being able to live just one whole one? If I could have picked one to live forever and forget the other one, I definitely would...but which one? Part of me knew...part of me always knew.

"Chance, are you ok?" Rebecca must have seen me spiraling. Her question pulled me out.

"Yeah, I just...I don't know anymore." At that time, I noticed that Al was rounding the corner with our meals. Of course, I got the skillet I always did, and Rebecca ordered the same. We seriously felt like the same person, even though it appeared that this Rebecca was an infinitely better person than I could ever hope to be.

"Here you go," Al said, placing each plate on the table. "Be careful, the skillets are hot." He winked at me and asked if we needed anything else. We both didn't, so he went back to reading his paper.

We both ate our meals in silence. I guess we had both drunk much more than we had intended and needed something in our stomachs to soak up all the alcohol. For the next ten minutes, the only sound coming from our table was the scratching of the silverware against the skillets and the sound of us either chewing or breathing. To anyone else in the diner, we must have looked like gluttons.

Eventually the food ran out and Al came and took our plates. With nothing left to fill our mouths, we were forced to resume our conversation. It appeared that during the meal, we had both lost a bit of our steam and enthusiasm. Rebecca sat back in her chair and put her hands on her stomach, and I did the same. She eventually sat up and sighed.

"So...after this whole mess, you want me to try and give Mae another chance?" She was much calmer than she had been earlier.

"Obviously only if you still have feelings for her. If not, there is nothing I can say to help. She is my best friend, and I had to try." I took the last sip out of the special coffee and tried to pour myself another round. It was empty, probably for the best.

"Of course I still have feelings for her, Chance...that was never the problem. The problem was trusting her...trusting you..." She sat back and ran her hands through her hair.

"Mae understands how much she hurt you. Trust me." I sat up and waved for Al to bring me the check. He had it all ready and dropped it off. I laughed at how much it was and threw my credit card down on the pate...I didn't carry that much cash on me. Rebecca tried to pay the tip, but I refused to let her. She thanked me and grabbed her things.

"I'll call her," she said suddenly, almost as if it was nothing to think about.

"Really?" I was excited but didn't want to be too over the top.

"Yes. Chance...I am not promising anything, but...she is hurting and at least deserves an opportunity to try and make it right." She picked up her purse and reached out to shake my hand. I returned the gesture.

"Thank you," was all I could say in response. She nodded and turned around and headed toward the door. Right before leaving, she turned around and smiled.

"Take care of yourself, Chance." She got up and walked out of the diner.

"Fuck," I said, not able to contain my excitement. I gave myself a little fist bump and looked over at Al. He laughed and came over to bring me the receipt from the bill.

"That looked like a fun talk," he joked as I signed the receipt and left a tip. "Isn't that Mae's girlfriend?"

I looked up at him and shrugged. "I hope so, we shall see how their conversation goes." I didn't want to get into the conversation that I'd just had too much, but he worried about Mae and me...we were his best customers.

"Well, have a good one, and stay out of trouble, yeah?" He reached out and shook my hand, and with that, I left. I didn't have any cigarettes, so I decided to go to the liquor store to grab a pack, and maybe a bottle. I didn't quite know yet. While I was checking out, I got a text message from Sarah. She was letting me know that she was out of class and extremely bored. I told her to meet me downtown, and we could maybe catch that movie we had wanted to see the other day. It felt like a much better day now, even in the late afternoon when the sun was high in the sky. Rebecca and I had been in there for a few hours, and I thought it had definitely been worth it. Sarah messaged me that she had to go home and change and that she would meet me at my place. She also knew that I still hadn't changed... she was getting to know me better than I had originally thought. I made my way to my bike and threw the bottle in my saddlebags and hopped on, starting it up quickly and making my way toward my apartment.

It was a sunny afternoon, and it really felt great to ride. The bike was clean; all I had to do was get clean, myself, and go and hang out with Sarah. I hadn't gone and seen a movie at the theater in what seemed like forever, and I was pretty sure movie popcorn should be its own food group.

About ten minutes later, I was pulling into my garage and lighting a cigarette for the walk up to my apartment, only there was someone already there…it was Mae. I walked up the steps, and she was already getting up to greet me.

"Hey, there," she said, walking up to me quietly. "I talked to Rebecca, and she said you two had brunch together."

"Yeah, I had some things that I wanted to say, and I needed to apologize." I scratched my head, expecting to get an ass chewing. Instead, she just slowly came up to me and gave me a hug.

"Thank you," she said softly. I put my arms around her and squeezed her tight.

"Mae, don't thank me. You should be telling me to go fuck myself, right now. I just did what you would do for me." I kissed her on her head and held her tight.

"Well, I am going to go over to Rebecca's to talk to her. Wish me luck?" she said, holding out her hands with her fingers crossed.

"You don't need luck. Just be yourself and let her know how you feel and how sorry you are. That's all I did with Sarah." She grabbed her purse from my chair and headed toward the bus stop. She turned around at the bottom of the steps.

"See you around," she said with a smile, and with that, she was gone. I finished my cigarette and went inside to shower and get clean. The clothes I had been wearing for two days were pretty trashed and covered in paint. I decided to try and dress up a bit and wear a polo or something…I just had to find out where they were. I gave up looking and decided to just take a shower and find them when I was done.

Getting into the shower that day felt different. I felt like I was actually getting ready for something, not just another day or another night out. I was getting ready for something that could actually matter, whether that was just the movie or the fact that I was going there with Sarah. I just hadn't felt like this in so long, the feelings were difficult to comprehend.

By the time I was just about to be finished, I heard a knock at the door and then a familiar voice.

"Hey, Chance, you in there?" she said. She must have come in because she was louder the second time she called.

"I'm in the shower. I'll be right out!" I yelled, trying to be louder than the water. Suddenly, the shower curtain was pulled back, and Sarah's smiling face was right there in front of me. Well, I had some soap in my eyes, so I assumed it was Sarah.

"Give me a kiss," she said as I tried to get my face in the general direction. I felt her lips touch mine, and she laughed as she saw I was getting excited. "Just clean that thing. I bet you smell." She laughed as she closed the curtain.

"I'm just about done." I rinsed off the last of the soap and then grabbed my towel, heading into the bedroom quickly after. Sarah was sitting at my desk, looking at my painting.

"I seriously love it. It is just the most beautiful thing ever," she said, smiling. I went to the closet and dropped my towel to get some underwear on. "Well, second-most beautiful thing ever. She got up and smacked me on the ass.

"Ouch, that hurt." I grabbed the spot where she had slapped me. It actually did hurt quite a bit.

"Well, hurry up and let's go. *Casablanca* is playing at the downtown cinema in about thirty minutes. We can still make it if you hurry the hell up!" She went into the kitchen to grab a beer out of the fridge. "Oh, and we might be able to make the bus and sneak a few beers into the theater." She gave me a devilish grin.

"I can get my flask if you want. Beers only last so long. I bought a new bottle, and it's in the cupboard. The flasks are in the bottom drawer by the silverware." I could hear her rummaging around in the drawer. When she stopped, I assumed she had found what she was looking for.

"Ok, I'll fill them up. You hurry," she said again. I was just putting my pants on and grabbed a pair of socks from the closet. I thought they were clean. I ran out into the living room as she was finishing. She held up the two flasks and handed me one. I put it in my back pocket and reached for the bottle.

"One for the road." I laughed as I took a long pull. I handed it to her, and she did the same.

"I don't have class tomorrow, so let's do it!" I agreed, and we headed toward the bus stop for the quick trip into town. Once on the bus, she sat next to me and put her hand in mine and leaned on my shoulder. No conversation was needed, just her presence was enough. The bus let us out a few blocks down from the theater, and we walked the rest of the way through the afternoon crowd.

When we reached the movie theater, we had about five minutes to spare. I had never known they played older movies in the evening, and the fact they were playing *Casablanca* must have been kismet. It was one of Mae's favorite movies on both sides of the poles. We got into the theater just in time to grab a giant bucket of popcorn, and Sarah really wanted some licorice…she could eat that, I'd eat the popcorn.

We found some seats toward the center back and made our little spot. Once we sat down, she pulled out her flask and motioned for me to do the same.

"Cheers," she said quietly, trying to not draw too much attention. The flask's metallic clink did that well enough on its own. Thankfully, we were one of a few people in the actual theater, and I wasn't too worried about getting in trouble. We sat and watched the previews for some newer movies and then the feature film came on. Sarah slapped my arm a few times when it came on in excitement. She wrapped her arm in mine, and we leaned in close to one another. We sat and watched the entire movie. She was mouthing the words the entire movie, and thankfully, she didn't notice that I was doing the same thing.

During the movie, we did the normal couple things…you know what they are. We definitely made out a bit, once the liquor started to take effect. There was some heavy petting as well, but eventually her interest in the movie outperformed her interest in public displays of affection.

About an hour and forty-two minutes later…yes, I know exactly how long the movie is…we exited the theater with an empty bucket of popcorn, an empty bag of licorice, and a bit left in our flasks. We grabbed some tacos from a local food truck that usually showed up in the evenings. I'd had had it a few times slobbering drunk, so I was interested to see how it tasted while still somewhat coherent. They weren't bad.

We ate our tacos while we walked to the bus stop and did our best to finish both the tacos and the flasks prior to getting on the bus. I didn't feel like getting kicked off the bus and then having to walk home. The bus ride was definitely more interesting than the ride there. A bit to drink and a romantic movie really got her in the mood for other things, if you know what I mean. Once we were back at my apartment, it was as if I couldn't get her off me. We were barely in the apartment, and she pushed me through the door and pinned me against the wall. I spun her around and did the same to her. I closed the door with my free hand and picked her up and carried her to the bedroom.

"The liquor!" she said, pointing toward the bottle on the counter. I went over and grabbed the bottle and carried both of them into the bedroom. We spend the rest of the night entangled in each other's arms. Warmed by our touch, a blanket and of course the bottle of whiskey.

When we were finally done, we couldn't catch our breath. She rolled over and looked at me in the dim light.

"I love you, Chance." She kissed me on the lips and then down my chest. Once she got to my stomach, she blew raspberries and it tickled like hell.

I spun around and pinned her down to the bed, doing the same. Once I had my fill and was afraid she would actually piss herself, I returned the gesture.

"I love you too, Sarah." I wrapped my arms around her and pulled the covers over us. She grabbed my hand in hers and put her fingers through mine, holding them close to her chest.

"Sleep good, see you tomorrow," she said and then nuzzled into my pillow.

"See you tomorrow," was the last thing I said before closing my eyes. I fell asleep with the smell...and unfortunately, the taste, of her hair.

Chapter 22

I woke up to the sound of the front door closing. I could hear footsteps on the walkway outside, and then soon after that, the stairs. I turned to my side, and Mae wasn't in the bed with me. I looked around the room, and there was no sight of her. I noticed a note tucked underneath my phone in our normal fashion.

> *Becks,*
>
> *I went to go study with my final project group at the library. Take the day and work on your book. Please don't come to the library as Sarah will also be here and I don't want to make her feel uncomfortable.*
>
> *Your Wife*

Once I was finished reading the note, I crumpled it up and threw it away. It kind of pissed me off, the way that she just...ugh, maybe she was right. The last thing I needed was to be in more hot water with Mae and also make one of her friends uncomfortable as well. I slammed myself back down in my bed and rolled my head into the pillow and screamed. Things just felt so off between us, and I just was filled with so much anxiety and it felt like my world was unraveling around me. In a huff, I threw the blankets off me and got up to start my day...except...there was literally nothing to do other than work on my book.

After making a pot of coffee and tidying up from dinner the night before, I went to sit down on the couch and continue with editing the book. I stared down at the cover page...not knowing what to call it. I felt as if the title was always the hardest part of the book. Obviously, that's ridiculous, but for me it really was. None of the books I had worked on over the years had titles on them, just my name on the cover page. Even the articles that I would write for work were difficult for me. My editor usually would title them for me so I wouldn't struggle. I opened up the book to the last page I had been reading and began to read, not knowing what to expect. It seemed like from the moment that I had pulled this book out of the closet, my life had literally turned upside down. The poles had reversed in some way, and I didn't know which way was which. The writings of a sixteen-year-old girl were throwing everything off balance and making me remember things that I had chosen to forget from long ago.

Depression and anxiety at a young age are difficult to deal with, but eventually, you come to terms with everything that's happening and learn ways to cope with it. Chance chooses to cope with drinking and drugs. With cigarettes and one-night stands...well, he used to. He had found a new drug in Sarah and had begun showing signs of a different addiction... happiness. I, on the other hand, well Rebecca...always threw herself into something, whether it was writing or sports. She always found constructive ways to deal with her problems. Until now, that is. I decided to lean into the skid and see if we had any alcohol in the house. I couldn't focus on anything and needed something to take the edge off. There was an old dusty bottle of vodka in the back of the cupboard, and I poured myself a stiff screwdriver, feeling a bit better because orange juice is a breakfast thing...right?

I went back to the book and continued reading, hoping that the vodka would soon take the edge off this feeling of dread I couldn't shake. I continued reading until I came across another passage that hit home... as if I was speaking to myself from the past. As if this sixteen-year-old girl was trying to tell me something.

I have never been to therapy, I refuse to find out the things that are wrong with me since that will only make things real. Once a problem is real, there is a solution, and I was always one to make my own solutions for my own problems. I started having anxiety attacks once I realized the truth about myself, the truth about this world. Someone once asked me what it felt like to have a panic attack, and my youthful ignorance said it felt like running from a bear...only there was no bear. Unfortunately, they themselves never having anxiety just equated my issues to being afraid of bears. People like that are the reason I keep my secrets exactly that, my secrets.

The problem with keeping secrets is there is nobody to confide in...well, for me it's almost nobody. My secret, itself, is someone I can confide in. Someone who goes through the same things I do, albeit in a bit different way. They have had all the same heartache and same headaches I have, and they handle them differently. Well, their situation is different, as they do not have what I have here. they do not have a reason to live, or if they do, it's not nearly as good as mine. Sometimes I fear what would happen if my reason ceased to be. If my reason for existing on this world would suddenly vanished, where would I stand? Without a reason to exist...why exist at all?

"Fuck," I said, getting goosebumps as I read. She...well, I, was right. I myself knew what my reason was. It had been, and always would be, Mae. Whether it was truly willful ignorance or cognitive dissonance, I didn't know, but I knew she was truly the center of things. She was truly the reason that I existed. Unfortunately, she was pulling away, and with her, I was losing my ability to simply be naïve to the way things were. I continued to read, even though I wanted to stop. I didn't want anything else to be revealed about my past and about my condition...whatever it was, it was better left unsaid.

So I ask myself this. If I were to choose one life, which would it be? Both my existences, however difficult they are, are a beautiful gift, but is it fair to ask myself to live two halves as opposed to a whole? If coincidence would pluck one of these realities out of existence, which should it be? Could one exist without the other? If one existence couldn't exist without the other, then what does that say about that? Was it even real life, or was it just fantasy. Sooner or later, I feel as if I am going to have to choose one, and with that, would lose the other...or both.

I stood up and walked to the counter to grab a bit more vodka for my drink. My mind was racing a million miles an hour, and it was as if I was trying to help myself find the answer. This book that I had written nearly two decades ago was reminding me of something I had long forgotten. Something I couldn't even think about without spiraling downward into the same depression and angst that I'd had back then. I took a few more sips right from the bottle and went back to reading. I was nearing the end of the manuscript, and I felt as if I remembered what the end was about. I read until I reached the last page, where there was just a simple paragraph. The pages themselves had spots on them. It almost looked like there had been teardrops that had fallen on the pages.

This leaves me to the final choice that I will have to make some day. I want to be honest with myself and grow as a person, but all the questions I have can't be answered by me alone. Both lives that I live need to coexist, which I have come to believe is impossible. Their coexistence will kill me, they will drive me to the edge of insanity where I will inevitably break. This leads to the question that I fear to ask aloud. I fear that breathing it into existence will be like trying to put a genie back in the bottle. It will make its outcome more real than I want it to be, but it needs to be asked. Is one of my lives a lie? If so, which one?

I turned the page, and there was nothing. No answer or notes to be seen. Just the last question I had asked myself years ago. One that I had forgotten because I was truly happy. I finished the drink in my hand and had to stand up. The feeling of the anxiety attack rushed over me like a wave, causing every fiber in my being to shake and pump with adrenaline. My vision became blurry, and I wanted to vomit.

I spent a few minutes pacing, trying to rid myself of this feeling. I went and took a few more swigs from the bottle until it was empty and grabbed my last pack of cigarettes from the freezer. I went outside in my underwear and drew the smoke deep into my lungs. Nothing was working, nothing was calming me down. The morning air was cold, and every hair on my body stood at attention. It was cold enough I had to go and put on a sweatshirt from the hall closet. I stood out there for however long it took me to finish the pack of cigarettes. The nicotine was not helping like it usually did, and the alcohol was doing the opposite of what I needed.

"Fuck," I said to myself out loud. "Fuck, fuck, fuck!" Luckily, my neighbors were at work, or else they probably would have come out and thought I was fucking nuts. I tasted filter on the last cigarette I had on me and went inside. I hadn't realized how cold I was because when I returned inside and closed the door, I immediately starting sweating. I took off the sweatshirt and went into the shower, thinking maybe a cold shower would help with the anxiety and my apparent overheating.

I quickly took my clothes off and turned on the shower. I didn't wait for it to even warm up a little before I was in and underneath the faucet. I let the cold water run down my head and down my body. Every time my heart beat, my vision shook like I was in an earthquake. After about fifteen minutes or so, I started to calm down. Something about staring at the water going down the drain was comforting. Watching the water spiral down was keeping my mind off the existential crisis I was going through. Once I was calmer and I didn't feel as if I was going to have a heart attack, I turned the water on a bit warmer and decided that I should probably clean the cigarettes and sweat off me. I felt disgusting, and I was already a bit intoxicated by the time I was done with the shower, so I made my way to the closet to get dressed.

I definitely didn't care what I was wearing that day because I was still having a bit of trouble with my vision. I grabbed the first undergarments, shirt, and pants I could find and put them on. I looked like I had gone shopping at a garage sale but didn't care. I pulled out my phone, wanting to text Mae. I needed her here with me, but…I knew she was busy and already aggravated with me. I didn't want to just show up at the library after she specifically asked me not to.

"What if I just showed up to see her. I don't have to actually say anything to her." The thought was immature and ill planned, but it was the best idea that I had. I grabbed my purse and a baseball cap and headed out the door. I was so preoccupied that I don't even know if I had locked the door behind me. I didn't think about it until I was too far away to turn around.

I walked with a purpose that day, and the chain smoking from earlier didn't make the task any easier. I struggled to keep my breathing steady because I kept coughing and hacking up the morning's mistakes. I was also having terrible heartburn from the screwdrivers that morning and kept burping up fire every few minutes. I had to stop a few times because I thought I was going to vomit, but the feeling went away after a bit of rest.

I eventually made it to the library and started to get a bit self-conscious about my decision to go there. What would happen if Mae saw me? How would she react to me snooping around? Hopefully I would be able to stay hidden and wouldn't alert her to my presence. I walked into the library and checked in quickly. I knew where they had studied the other day, so that was my first stop. I walked into the main hall and pulled my baseball cap down low, hoping it would help hide my face. I peeked around the corner to the table where I thought Mae would be, and low and behold, she was there, only she was alone. She was just sitting there with her books, studying like she said she was. I breathed a big sigh of relief and leaned back up against the wall. Just seeing her calmed me down.

"Get ahold of yourself, Rebecca," I told myself, taking a few deep breaths. "Just go home and finish working on the book." I laughed at how stupid I was being and went to take one last look at Mae. She was adorable, sitting there playing with her curls. Another student came up to her and sat down next to her and they greeted one another...with a kiss.

"What the fuck?" I said, watching my wife kiss another woman. They sat there holding hands and being coy with one another. Once they were side by side, the flirting was as obvious as anything. They sat there giggling and playing grab-ass the entire time I watched them. The girl eventually went to go get something, either a book or a drink, I didn't know. Mae reached up and kissed her quickly on the lips so no one could see; she was aware of the policy in the library. I just stood there like a fucking idiot, watching them.

I wanted to walk right up to her and let her know I saw her. I wanted to confront the both of them, and I wanted to fucking scream, library be damned. I didn't know what to do...my blood was boiling and the anxiety from this morning was returning, this time with vengeance. I was so preoccupied with the events that were playing in front of me I had completely forgotten to hide myself from view. I was just standing there next to the wall, until eventually, Mae looked up...and saw me. She panicked and threw her books in her bag to come toward me. I didn't let her, and I ran out of the building as fast as I could. I even heard the librarian give me a stern warning about running in the building as I passed. I blew past her and went out the front doors and into the afternoon air. I just started running as fast as I could to get away from the library. A few moments later I heard Mae screaming my name from the steps of the library entrance. I never looked back, I just kept running until I reached a row of the college dorms and leaned up against the wall. I was crying and coughing and could barely breath. Every muscle and fiber in my body was burning at the same time, and I couldn't handle it anymore. I vomited the contents of my stomach against the stucco wall that was supporting me and couldn't stop. I continued until my stomach was empty, and my episode was nothing but dry heaves. I could still hear Mae calling my name, only this time it was faint.

I stood there leaning against the wall crying for God knows how long. I didn't know what to do. She was cheating on me in the middle of the fucking library. They both looked pretty comfortable around each other, and who knows what else they had done. I felt my phone start to vibrate in my purse and I looked down to see that it was Mae. I hung up and she called again. After a few rounds of this, I finally answered, and she was crying on the other end.

"Becks, please come back. I can explain." There was no explanation for what she was doing.

"Fuck you, Mae, just fuck you," I responded and immediately hung up. I shut off the phone for good measure and slid down the wall in defeat, making sure to avoid the pile of vomit a foot or so away from me.

"Why, why?" I said over again as I wept. A few people came and walked by and gave me weird looks. Apparently, a girl crying on the side of a building was regular enough of an occurrence for them to just walk past. After a few more onlookers, I decided that out in the open wasn't the right place for me to have a midlife crisis about my marriage and cheating wife. I tried to straighten myself up as best as I could and left; to where, I didn't know at the time. I kept my composure as well as I could walking down the street until I came to a bench that had some shade underneath a small tree. I sat down and pulled out my phone. I powered it on to see if Mae had texted anything, and the second it came online, a flood of texts came though all at once.

They all said basically the same thing. That she wanted me to come home and she could explain, that she wanted to see me. She was sorry and wanted me to come home. Just one after the other, over and over. The phone finally stopped vibrating, and I gave up reading them because they just made me more and more angry with every word. They made me angry until I started thinking about the day before, at the diner with Rebecca. I had been begging for her to give Mae a second chance, for a chance to explain herself. My own words were that she was worth it and deserved at least an explanation.

"Fuck it!" I said loudly as I responded to her last text. I told her that

I would be home soon. I put the phone on silent and started walking toward the bus stop. Of course, when you don't want to reach a destination quickly, you reach it almost instantly, because before I knew it, I was at the bus stop by the apartment, getting off. I walked up to the apartment, and Mae was sitting outside with a cigarette. She looked like a mess but was still stunning. At first glance, I completely forgot that I had just caught her sneaking a kiss with someone other than her wife. The moment was fleeting, but it gave me some comfort. I might as well have been coming home from the library myself and greeting my wife with a hug and a kiss… but not today.

"Rebecca!" she yelled as she noticed me walking up the path. She came down the stairs and stopped a few feet away. "I don't know what to say, Becks, I just…I love you, you know that right?" Her eyes were swollen and puffy, and her hair a mess. Her makeup was running, and she obviously didn't care.

"What the fuck, Mae?" was the only thing I could think to say. "What the actual fuck?" The words I said didn't seem to bother her, but in the manner I said them…yeah, she was a bit unhinged by the screaming.

"Stop yelling, let's go inside and talk." She reached for my hand, and I pulled away. "Please, I can explain…please." She could barely keep herself from crying. Each word seemed like she was struggling to say it and not lose control completely.

"Explain what? Why you were kissing someone else? Why you were sneaking around behind my back? Who the fuck is that, and how long has this been going on?" I was content having this argument on the steps and didn't feel like getting trapped in the apartment. Mae knew me better than I knew myself, and I felt if I went into that apartment, I would instantly forgive her. I didn't want to forgive her, I wanted to be angry. I deserved to be angry.

"She's nobody. Just some girl from my class." She reached again for my hand, and this time I let her take it. She pulled my hand and gestured for us to go inside. I walked with her until we hit the top of the stairs, and I refused to go the rest of the way.

"I don't want to come inside with you, into our home. You're telling me that you were fucking around with someone that was nobody? I'm your wife, and you cheat on me with nobody?" Her dismissal of this person she obviously had feelings for pissed me off to no end.

"She's just a girl in my class. The other night when I went out...she was there. I only knew her from some projects we did together over that past few months. I was upset, and she comforted me...then..." She paused, and I knew why.

"Then you went back to her place? Then you just gave up on our entire relationship for what, a one-night stand?" Mae pulled out a cigarette, put it between her lips and lit it. She handed it to me, knowing I obviously needed one. I reluctantly took it and took a deep breath...the fact that it tasted like her lip balm made me angrier.

"It wasn't like that, Becks. I was drunk and things have been so hard with you lately. You just, it's like you're miserable, and I feel like I am to blame." She took the last drag of her cigarette and threw it over the railing.

"Yeah, I have been having a hard couple of weeks, but I haven't fucked around on you! You're my wife, Mae, not just some girl I just started dating or barely know. You're my wife and my best fucking friend. How could you do this to me? How could you do this us?" Her sad demeanor changed when I put all of the blame on her.

"Don't just fucking blame me, Rebecca. Yeah, you have had a hard couple of weeks, but how do you think I fucking feel. It's like I am useless and all of the pressure is on you. I can't help and I can't work until I am done with school. The only reason I am going to school is to get a job I fucking hate so you can get a job you will fucking love. To think the other night you had the audacity to say that I didn't care enough to help you?" She had started crying again and was taking a pretty defensive posture to the entire ordeal, but she was right. It wasn't just her that had messed up...I was to blame as well. I had been awful to her, and I knew it. It wasn't like I was completely unaware of it. I had even made a promise to myself to be a better wife and friend to her. I had failed on both accounts and pushed her right into the arms of someone else. My stance softened as her words struck home. I leaned against the railing and took another lung full of smoke and put my head down.

"You're right. I have not been a good wife or a good friend to you...I know I am not perfect. You need to know that I am trying, Mae. I just,

I can't do this anymore. This living two lives bullshit." She looked at me, confused.

"What are you talking about, two lives?" I had half a mind to tell her everything, and then they could just take me away and medicate me into oblivion. I wouldn't care, and she would get what she wanted, freedom.

"Nothing, I just can't do this anymore, Mae. I am going to go and get some things and get a hotel for the night. I can't go back in there with you." I tried to push past her, and she stood in my way.

"No! We can fix this, right? This is not something that we can't fix, please stay and we can talk some more." She took my hand and pulled me in close for a hug. I tried to resist, but I couldn't. She started kissing me on my neck and then my face, and slowly she grazed my lips. I couldn't stop myself, she was intoxicating and her smell and taste pushed me over the edge. She grabbed me and pushed me into the apartment, her hands were already beginning to undress me, and mine were doing the same to her. We wrestled with each other's clothes as we made our way into the bedroom, and I pushed her down into the bed and finished removing my bra. She did the same, and she grabbed me by the waist and pulled me in close to her.

"Rebecca..." she said before I stopped her with my finger to her lips. She listened as I pressed my body against hers and kissed her deeply. My hands touching every inch of her body, causing goosebumps where my fingertips touched. The rest of it was just a blur of skin and emotion. We were in each other's arms for what felt like the last time on this earth. Not wanting to let go for fear of what reality would bring us. The night left us laying in each other's arms, panting and sweating. I could feel her next to me, kissing my neck and down to my chest as we both tried to regain our breath. Her hands trailed up and down my chest over and over until she eventually fell asleep. The day's events had taken a heavy toll on her. I looked outside, and it must have been just about to get dark. I got out of bed and left Mae there, wrapping her body in the blanket to keep her warm.

I went to go get dressed and grab my things, but before I did, I went into my box of books that I had taken from the closet a few days earlier. I was looking for something specific, something I had kept there as a memory. Something I needed that night. I pulled out a small key, an old key, and put it in my pocket.

I went and grabbed my book from my bag and grabbed a big red sharpie. I wrote on the title page in big block letters. Mae Poles. I signed my name and put it down on the nightstand besides Mae. I grabbed her pack of cigarettes and decided to go for a walk.

The sun was beginning to go down, and the walk was going to be a long one. While I put one foot in front of the other, all I could think of was the last conversation I would have with Mae. She was right. I had never been as good of a wife as I should have and had always put myself first. I had always just done whatever I wanted with little regard to the people around me, and that was the crux of my issues in life...or should I say "in lives." Eventually, in order to grow, I would have to put someone else before myself. I would have to care about others regardless of myself.

I laughed as I remembered a conversation I'd had with my mother about this years earlier on the other side of the poles. I had always thought I was putting others before myself, but in fact, I was doing the exact opposite.

"Chance, you act like you're so self-righteous and that you do no wrong. Your relationship with Mae doesn't make you selfless, it makes you selfish. Can't you see?" It was late, and she'd had a bit to drink. It was a family reunion that we had every year when my uncle flew in from the west coast.

"What are you talking about? Everything I do, I do for other people. Mae needs help and I'm there. You want me at a family party in the middle of nowhere, and I'm here. What the fuck else do you want?" I flicked the cigarette, and the ash burned my hand. I tried not to let her notice that I was in pain and brushed it off. It was easy since I'd had a few drinks.

"No...you just don't understand. You don't hang around Mae for her. You never have. You do it for you, because you follow her around like a little fucking puppy dog. Why do you do that to yourself? It's not healthy, Chance. Can't you see that?"

"What, being a good friend isn't a good thing?" She shook her head in disgust.

"You just don't understand. One day you will. I really hope that when you do understand, you won't have messed your life up too much for this girl. This girl that will never love you the way you love her." The last words were meant to hurt, and they did.

"Fuck you," I said, *walking away toward my car. She yelled something else at me, but I wasn't paying attention. I was too pissed at her.*

That was the last time I had seen my mother prior to our meeting the other day at the restaurant. She was right, and I finally understood what she had been saying. Everything circled around Mae, and nothing else mattered. I pretended it was because we were good friends and I wanted to be there for her, but that wasn't the truth. It was what I told myself to get by, on both sides of the poles.

I worked my ass off for years to provide for Mae the way she deserved, but what was the real goal? Was it so she was happy, or I was happy forgetting the truth? Forgetting the truth that a sixteen-year-old me had just shown my adult self. I tell myself daily that I don't remember when I started living on both sides of the poles. That's the truth, I promise you. The thing that I haven't mentioned is that there are memories before that first day, before that first morning I woke up as Rebecca. I woke up that first day having memories of a childhood filled with happiness, and turmoil… but they never felt like my memories, because I hadn't lived them.

My younger self knew the truth because she was much closer to those days than I was. It had been years since I opened that book, and it actually was long enough for me to forget the reason why. That book told me the truth. That book was evidence that I really did know which life of mine was real. All that talk about two half-lives instead of a whole one was my secret. I lit a cigarette as I walked and breathed in the smoke, exhaling only when I'd had my fill. I always enjoyed fire on the back of my tongue, but tonight felt different. This felt more like a victory cigar than a cigarette, and this felt more like the ending rather than a beginning…even though it was both.

I turned down the main street, only about halfway to my destination. I was getting excited, that's the only word I could use to describe my emotion. The sun had started to set, and it was a beautiful sunset. I remembered the last time Mae and I had been at the place I was going. It was a good memory, and I wanted to hold on to it.

We fooled around in the pile of boxes for a good amount of time until finally I couldn't stand it any longer.

"We are going to get caught, we should definitely get out of here." Mae *stood up and held out her hand to help me up.*

"Party pooper," she said with a sad voice and puppy dog eyes. "You don't want to fool around anymore?"

I laughed because it was exactly the opposite. "No, if we don't leave now, we are going to be doing way more than fooling around. Then we will get caught and they will take away my key...for good." We both shook the dust off our clothes, and Mae went over to the large window that overlooked the quad and cracked it open slightly.

"I am surprised that this opens this much. Usually, windows like this are shut or barred." She looked at the old wooden windows that had been sealed more recently than they appeared.

"Nobody has a key for up here, so I guess they aren't that worried. We looked out the window at the scene that lay before us. The area it overlooked was a large field with trees, benches, and a beautiful path that connected each side of the quad. The buildings were rustic and old and looked as though they had stood for hundreds of years, but also strong enough that they could stand for hundreds more.

"Well, I am glad that you do. This place is so beautiful I could just die right now and be happy." She looked out the window and smiled, her curly hair blowing in the wind slightly.

"Yeah, well, let's not think about that right now." I pulled her close and kissed her on the lips. I held it for as long as I could before something happened. I sneezed and barely had enough time to pull away.

"You almost did that right in my face!" she said laughing. The sneeze unsettling the dust and making it fill the area, it flew out the window into the afternoon sun.

As soon as the memory was over, it appeared I was at my destination. I looked up at the tower and smiled. It looked a bit more ominous at night than it had that day with Mae. The library was nearly closed, so I snuck through the hall to where the old tower door stood and put in the key. I twisted the lock and opened the door quietly. I locked it again when on the other side. I climbed those stairs in the low light and saw both Mae and me climbing those years ago. Their images were almost ghostly, as if I was being haunted by the memory, or if the memory was trying to keep me grounded there. It had done everything it could to remain real to me, but unfortunately, I had to make a choice.

I reached the door at the top of the tower and unlocked that door as well. Walking into that room, a flood of memories rushed back. Mae and I pushed up against those boxes in the corner. It looks like they must have cleaned this area up because the boxes and moving blankets were not there anymore. They were replaced by a small desk with some papers on it. It appeared as if someone would come up there and work sometimes, to get away from people. To get away from the world. I smiled at the thought as I walked up to the window and opened it. The night air rushed in and blew my hair back. I stood there for a moment and remembered why I was there. I walked up to the window and put my hands on the ledge and peered out. The quad was empty, save for a few people walking home or to a late-night class.

I sat there for a bit, looking out the window and remembering the first and last time I had tried to tell someone about my condition. It was Mae, and we were just into or junior year of high school.

We sat there in the parking lot on my Oldsmobile, not wanting to leave and not wanting to stay. She had just started smoking back then, and I joined in because I wanted her to like me.

"So, what do you want to do?" she asked, taking a puff from her cigarette. The way she held it was cute and showed that she had just started.

"I don't know. I just...I guess I just don't know." She laughed at the absurdity of my comment.

"What do you mean you don't know?" She took another puff, barely taking any smoke into her lungs.

I started crying, and that caught her off guard. She came and took my hand, but not as a lover...as a friend. "I am just having a really hard time lately. School and Chris and everything else. It just feels like so much."

"What do you mean everything else? And fuck Chris, he is a jerkoff and doesn't deserve you. You deserve someone amazing." Her hand was still in mine, and I could feel her thumb grazing the top of my palm. It was the first time I really felt that she felt for me as more than just friendship. I wanted to open up to her and explain.

"What would you do if you lived two lives, but you could only really handle one?" My question caught her off guard...it was an odd one to just ask, but she wanted to know what I was talking about.

"Is this about that book you're writing? Isn't that done yet?" She continued

to rub my hand until she realized what she was doing. She pulled her hand away quickly.

"No, well…yeah. I don't know how to explain it. What would you do if one of those lives wasn't really you, and the other one was?" I paused for a second, hoping she would be thrown off by the question. She smiled and looked into my eyes.

"Becks, I would just simply choose one and give it your all. Don't hold back and don't think you have to be half of yourself…around anyone." She smiled and came and sat next to me on the hood of the car and leaned back. Both of us just hanging out in the sun.

The sad thing about what she had said was that she understood exactly what I was asking, and none of it at the same time. She had thought that my book was my way of coming out to the world. That my dual lives meant the one that was in front of everyone, and my closeted self. The one I hid from everyone. The truth was, I was asking her how to escape from this loop I had been stuck in for nearly my entire life. She told me to choose one, and up until now, I was unable to. I looked out the window one more time, and with a tear and a jump, I finally chose. My last thought was of her lips touching gently against mine.

Chapter 23

"Fuck!" I screamed as I woke up in a sweat. I had fallen out of bed and hit my head on the nightstand.

"Chance, are you ok?" Sarah said, leaning over the bed and trying not to laugh at me. "Did you really just fall out of bed?" It took a moment for me to remember where I was. I looked around the room and then up at Sarah…she still was stifling a laugh.

"Yeah, I guess I did. Don't just sit there and laugh, help an old man up?" I held out my hand and she took it, pulling me back into the bed and back on top of her.

"Quick, cover up. Nobody should have to see you naked." She pulled the covers over me quickly. "Phew, now I can still be attracted to you."

"But the covers are covering eighty percent of my body." I laughed as I said it, totally unprepared for her silliness.

"Yeah, I can only see the good-looking parts of you now." She pressed her body up against mine and rubbed her fingers down my torso.

"You're kind of mean in the morning, aren't you?" I said, trying not to laugh. Her fingers running up and down my body felt amazing, but on the border of ticklish. I was trying to keep it together. She eventually stopped, and her hand was resting on my stomach and her legs were entangled in mine.

I thought about what had just happened. I had finally chosen, and what that meant, I still didn't know. My heart was still racing as if I had jumped minutes earlier, but I was here and safe in my bed. I was with Sarah, the reason I was able to choose. I would never see Mae again… well, my Mae from the other side of the poles…well, I didn't know that for sure, but I felt it in my bones. I had given up living two half-lives to live a whole one. I looked over at Sarah and could barely contain myself from what I knew was about to happen. She looked over at me with that beautiful smile and made a silly face. She noticed that I was tearing up a bit and immediately got concerned.

"Are you ok? It looks like you're about to cry. Shit, did you really hit your head that hard?" She sat up, completely forgetting she was naked, and started touching my head to make sure I wasn't bleeding.

"I'm fine Sarah. I just…" I looked at her and sat up, taking her hand in mine. "I'm happy. I don't think you understand what an accomplishment for me that is." She took my hand and put it up to her mouth and kissed it.

"Good, I want to make you happy." She kissed my hand again and then paused…and then licked it.

"What the hell?" I said, pulling my hand away from her. "You're odd, has anyone ever told you that?"

"As a matter of fact, they have. Guess what?" she said as she stood up, her naked form completely bathed in sunlight. "I'm all yours." She went over to the pile of clothes on the floor and put her bra and underwear on. She pulled a shirt from my closet and put it on. She took a second and smelled it, just to make sure it was, in fact, clean.

"The ones hung up are clean. Don't worry," I said, following suit. Once dressed, we went and made a pot of coffee and drank them from my ugly mugs on the couch. We spent the morning just lounging around and watching television. I didn't have anything planned and neither did she. We just took pleasure in each other's company. We talked about the holidays coming up and if we wanted to be introduced to each other's families. It turned out that her family was largely from out of town, and they all flew in for a get-together every year. At this get-together, they just celebrated all the holidays at once. They didn't really have a name for it, it just kind of started, and they liked it so much they never stopped.

I told her more about my mother and how she was excited that I had met someone finally. I spoke fondly about growing up with her as my mother, and Sarah looked really excited to eventually meet everyone. I had never talked about these things with someone with the actual intention of following through with the plans. In the past, I had used these same conversations to get girls to break up with me rather than to start planning a future with someone.

Yeah, we had only really known each other for less than two weeks, and in that time frame, I had done some terrible things. She had found it in her heart to forgive me and try again. I had made a promise to myself on the other side of the poles about being a better partner...I made the same promise that morning, and I fully intended on keeping it.

She brought up Mae and Rebecca and hoped that they were able to patch things up. I told her about my lunch the day before and how I had told Rebecca that she should give Mae another chance.

"Well, that must have been one hell of an awkward brunch? What did she say at the end?" It looked as if she was really hoping for a happy ending.

"She said she would talk to Mae and try to work things out. I hope that they do." She could see on my face that I was being sincere. If she wanted to make any wisecracks about the situation, I never would have known. She had acted so mature and wise beyond her or anyone's years about this whole thing that I wondered whether her ending up with me was a good thing or not.

"Well, only time will tell I suppose." She reached over to her cold cup of coffee and proposed a toast. "To happy endings?" I held up my coffee and toasted back.

"If you want to get a massage, we can go get one. I am not a big fan of happy endings though." She smacked me on the arm.

"We were having a nice moment, and you ruined it. I better get used to that kind of stuff, eh?" She made a face like she was regretting all her recent relationship decisions. Then looked over at me side-eyed and smiled.

"Funny, you're so funny," I said, pulling her close and holding on. She nearly spilled her coffee.

"So, Sarah, what do you want to do today?" She looked over at me and was grinning from ear to ear.

"Chance, we can do whatever you want. All you have to do is choose."

Epilogue

6 Months Later

We walked down the street toward the movie theater. It was a Saturday, and the streets were fairly packed. Sarah's hand firmly in mine, pulling me to our destination.

"Hurry up, Chance! I want to get a picture before anyone else shows up!" We navigated through the passersby and did our best not to bump into too many people.

"I'm walking as fast as I can...you, on the other hand, are running. You said you wanted to walk here, not run." She turned around and gave me a glare.

"Well, you're too slow." She doubled down and pulled harder. She was stronger than she looked. A few minutes and a nearly dislocated shoulder later, we arrived at the bookstore. "Here we are!" she said, getting ready to walk in. "Wait a second, take a picture!" She posed in front of the door and did a little pose. I took about a hundred pictures just to make sure she couldn't blame me for taking a bad one.

"Ok, let's go inside. It's hot out here." She opened the door, and we walked inside to be greeted by the store owner and a few staff.

"We are so delighted to see you again, Sarah. Can you do me a favor?" She held out a copy of Sarah's book. "Can you please sign this for me?" Sarah looked at me and giggled with glee.

"This is my first time signing a book!" She looked over at me. "So, maybe I would like a picture of it." Hinting again.

"Oh, yeah." I pulled out the camera again and took about fifty photos of her signing the book and smiling. She was hilarious.

"Thank you so much," the owner said. "Let me show you the table we have set up for you." We walked into the back of the store and saw the small setup they had for her signing and some chairs and a reading nook for the reading.

Sarah had obviously published the collection of poetry, and it was already doing amazingly. Things had gone fast since we'd had it all ready to go, and I knew a few local publishers that I had done art for and had gotten her a meeting. The morning went by pretty quickly, and the reading went amazing. By the time she was signing books, she was already exhausted but was doing her best to stay enthusiastic. She asked me to get a cup of coffee for her from the place across the street, so I quickly did and returned so that I wouldn't miss too much of the excitement.

"Thanks, babe!" she said, smelling the cup and then taking a sip. "Perfect!" Just then, we heard a familiar voice. I looked up and it was Mae.

"Hey there, strangers!" she said, with a copy of Sarah's book in her hand. "Looks like I know a local celebrity."

"Oh, wow! We haven't seen you in forever! How are you?" Whether Sarah was being sarcastic or not I will never know. If she was, I was too dumb to see it.

"Yeah, it's been a while." A young woman walked up behind her and smiled at me. They were holding hands.

"Hey, Chance," the young woman said, taking me by surprise. I couldn't recognize her in the slightest but did what anyone else would do in that situation and pretended I remembered her as well.

"Hey, there! Long time no see!" She smiled and we all exchanged pleasantries for a few moments since the lines were a bit slow at the moment. After we exhausted all our small talk, Mae decided it was time to leave.

"Well, this has been fun. You two should call us and maybe we could double date! It will go better this time, I promise." She laughed awkwardly and so did the young woman with her. With that, they both waved, and we said our goodbyes.

Once they left, I knelt down next to Sarah and tapped her on her shoulder as she signed another book.

"Who was that with Mae?" I asked. Sarah signed another book and thanked the woman for coming and then turned to me.

"Is that Al's special coffee?" She laughed. "That was Rebecca. They must have gotten back together." She shook someone's hand and signed another book.

"Really? I didn't even recognize her." Sarah laughed it off and continued signing another book. I stood up and looked at the two of them walking out of the bookstore. Right before she opened the door, Mae turned back, and her eye caught mine and she smiled.

I don't know whether we will ever have that second double date she mentioned, but I like to think we will. I watched her walk out of that bookstore, and possibly my life, for good. Like I said before, she was better off without me.

Printed in the United States
by Baker & Taylor Publisher Services